A DISTANT THUNDER

A DISTANT THUNDER

SCOTTISH WAR STORIES

SELECTED BY TREVOR ROYLE

First published in 1999 in Great Britain by Polygon,
an imprint of Birlinn Ltd. This edition published in 2025 by Polygon.

Birlinn Ltd
West Newington House
10 Newington Road
Edinburgh
EH9 1QS

www.polygonbooks.co.uk

1

ISBN 978 1 84697 722 0

British Library Cataloguing-in-Publication Data
A catalogue record for this book is available on request
from the British Library.

Typeset by 3b Typesetting, Edinburgh

Printed and bound by Clays Ltd, Elcograf, S.p.A.

Contents

Preface

From the earliest times Scots have made good soldiers; indeed, it has often been noted that war is an essential ingredient of Scottish spiritual and cultural life. The nation's history is bloody with battles, some fought against Scotland's nearest neighbour; many more fought amongst the Scots themselves, family against family, clan against clan. Like many other countries on Europe's poorer extremities – Albania, Prussia, Croatia, for example – war became something of a homespun industry and one which could be easily exported.

To meet the needs of that soldier's trade Scots mercenaries fought in the service of France, Spain, Russia and Sweden, gaining names for themselves as skilled and hardy fighters. The tradition continued with the creation of the great Scottish regiments which were raised in the aftermath of the failure of successive doomed Jacobite attempts to return the Stewarts to the throne of Britain. With their panoply of kilts, sporrans and colourful pipe bands they became a distinctive group within the British Army. Certainly, in no other part of the country did the myth of the soldier put down deeper roots than in Scotland and the kilted Jock became a very important person indeed.

Hardly surprisingly, given Scotland's long and distinctive military history, war stories have made a significant contribution to the nation's literature and many writers have served in the armed forces – John Buchan, Eric Linklater, Neil McCallum and James Leslie Mitchell, for example. The best of the genre are intensely evocative, providing a writer's view of ordinary men experiencing unimaginable horrors or of civilians coming to terms with death and loss. None avoid the dehumanising effects of war: the execution of Lewis Grassic Gibbon's Ewan Tavendale or the survivors of the Japanese prisoner of war camps in James Allan Ford's 'The Mourners from 19D'. Others are anti-heroic, or at least anti-war in tone; although Mitchell's 'The Defile of the Beast' provides a chillingly accurate description of trench life in the First World War. And then there is the surreal anarchic humour of the common soldier caught up in the madness of the military machine in Linklater's Private Angelo or Buchan's Peter Galbraith.

Because warfare and the business of fighting is such an intensely personal experience I have also included some non-fictional accounts. The poet Robert Garioch wrote about his wartime experiences later in life, as did Lord Elliott, whose book *Esprit de Corps* provides one of the best descriptions of what it was like to be a young officer experiencing battle for the first time. And from an earlier period another junior subaltern,

G. R. Gleig, provides an equally telling account of the part he played in Wellington's Peninsula Campaign.

Although the stories are war stories in that most of them are concerned with the business of warfare and its consequences for others, none glorifies the suffering that accompanies battle. Indeed, it is a distinctive feature of Scottish writing to make light of heroics and to underscore realism with some subtle irony. The mood is often subversive and gently mocking as if warfare is simply too serious a business to be taken too seriously. From Smollett's unwilling sailors at Cartagena to the Jocks of George Macdonald Fraser's thinly disguised Highland infantry battalion it is possible to hear a voice which is at once highly individual and indelibly Scottish.

Trevor Royle

The Siege of Cartagena (1748)

Tobias Smollett

Our forces being landed and stationed [. . .] set about erecting a fascine battery to cannonade the principal fort of the enemy; and in something more than three weeks, it was ready to open. That we might do the Spaniards as much honour as possible, it was determined, in a council of war, that five of our largest ships should attack the fort on one side, while the battery, strengthened by two mortars and twenty-four cohorns, should ply it on the other.

Accordingly, the signal for our ship to engage, among others, was hoisted, we being advertised, the night before, to make everything clear for that purpose; and, in so doing, a difference happened between Captain Oakhum and his well-beloved cousin and counsellor Mackshane, which had well nigh terminated in an open rupture. The doctor, who had imagined there was no more danger of being hurt by the enemy's shot in the cockpit than in the centre of the earth, was lately informed that a surgeon's mate had been killed in that part of the ship by a cannon-ball from two small redoubts, that were destroyed before the disembarkation of our soldiers; and therefore insisted upon having a platform raised for the convenience of the sick and wounded in the after-hold, where he deemed himself more secure than on the deck above. The captain, offended at this extraordinary proposal, accused him of pusillanimity, and told him there was no room in the hold for such an occasion; or if there was, he could not expect to be indulged more than the rest of the surgeons of the navy, who used the cockpit for that purpose. Fear rendering Mackshane obstinate, he persisted in his demand, and showed his instructions, by which it was authorised; the captain swore these instructions were dictated by a parcel of lazy poltroons who were never at sea; nevertheless he was obliged to comply, and sent for the carpenter to give him orders about it. But before any such measure could be taken, our signal was thrown out, and the doctor compelled to trust his carcass in the cockpit, where Morgan and I were busy in putting our instruments and dressings in order.

Our ship, with others destined for this service, immediately weighed, and in less than half an hour came to an anchor before the castle of Bocca Chica, with a spring upon our cable, and the cannonading (which indeed was dreadful) began. The surgeon, after having crossed himself, fell flat on the deck, and the chaplain and purser, who were stationed with us in quality of assistants, followed his example, while the Welshman and

I sat upon a chest looking at one another with great discomposure, scarce able to refrain from the like prostration. And that the reader may know, it was not a common occasion that alarmed us thus, I must inform him of the particulars of this dreadful din that astonished us. The fire of the Spaniards proceeded from eighty-four great guns, besides a mortar and small arms, in Bocca Chica; thirty-six in Fort St. Joseph; twenty in two fascine batteries, and four men-of-war, mounting sixty-four guns each. – This was answered by our land battery, mounted with twenty-one cannon, two mortars, and twenty-four cohorns, and five great ships of seventy or eighty guns, that fired without intermission.

We had not been many minutes engaged, when one of the sailors brought another on his back to the cockpit, where he tossed him down like a big of oats, and pulling out his pouch, put a large chew of tobacco in his mouth, without speaking a word. Morgan immediately examined the condition of the wounded man, and cried out, 'As I shall answer now, the man is as dead as my great-grandfather.' 'Dead', said his comrade; 'he may be dead now, for ought I know, but I'll be damned if he was not alive when I took him up.' So saying, he was about to return to his quarters, when I bade him carry the body along with him, and throw it over board. – 'Damn the body!' said he, 'I think 'tis fair enough if I take care of my own.' My fellow mate snatching up the amputation knife, pursued him halfway up the cockpit ladder, crying, 'You lousy rascal, is this the churchyard, or the charnel-house, or the sepulchre, or the golgotha of the ship?' – but was stopped in his career by one calling, 'Yo he, avast there – scaldings.' – 'Scaldings!' answered Morgan; 'God knows 'tis hot enough indeed: who are you?' 'Here's one!' replied the voice; and I immediately knew it to be that of my honest friend Jack Rattlin, who coming towards me, told me, with great deliberation, he was come to be docked at last, and discovered the remains of one hand, which had been shattered to pieces with grape shot. I lamented with unfeigned sorrow his misfortune, which he bore with heroic courage, observing, that every shot had its commission; 'It was well it did not take him in the head, or if it had, what then? He should have died bravely, fighting for his king and country. Death was a debt which every man owed, and must pay; and that now was as well as another time.' I was much pleased and edified with the maxims of this sea-philosopher, who endured the amputation of his left hand without shrinking, the operation being performed (at his request) by me, after Mackshane, who was with difficulty prevailed to lift his head from the deck, had declared there was a necessity for his losing the limb.

While I was employed in dressing the stump, I asked Jack's opinion of the battle, who, shaking his head, frankly told me, he believed we should do no good: 'For why? Because, instead of dropping anchor close under shore, where we should have to deal with one corner of Bocca Chica only, we had opened the harbour, and exposed ourselves to the whole fire of the enemy from their shipping and Fort St. Joseph, as well as from the castle we intended to cannonade; that, besides, we lay at too great a distance to damage the walls, and three parts in four of our shot did not take place; for there was scarce anybody on board who understood the pointing of a gun. 'Ah! God help us!' continued he. 'If your kinsman, Lieutenant Bowling, had been here, we should have had other guess work.' By this time, our patients had increased to such a number, that we did not know which to begin with; and the first mate plainly told the surgeon, that if he did not get up immediately and perform his duty, he would complain of his behaviour to the admiral, and make application for his warrant. This remonstrance effectually roused Mackshane, who was never deaf to an argument in which he thought his interest was concerned; he therefore rose up, and in order to strengthen his resolution, had recourse more than once to a case-bottle of rum, which he freely communicated to the chaplain, and purser, who had as much need of such extraordinary inspiration as himself. Being thus supported, he went to work, and arms and legs were hewed down without mercy. The fumes of the liquor mounting into the parson's brain, conspired, with his former agitation of spirits, to make him quite delirious; he stript himself to the skin; and, besmearing his body with blood, could scarce be withheld from running upon deck in that condition. Jack Rattlin, scandalised at this deportment, endeavoured to allay his transports with reason; but finding all he said ineffectual, and great confusion occasioned by his frolics, he knocked him down with his right hand, and by threats kept him quiet in that state of humiliation. But it was not in the power of rum to elevate the purser, who sat on the floor wringing his hands, and cursing the hour in which he left his peaceable profession of a brewer in Rochester, to engage in such a life of terror and disquiet.

While we diverted ourselves at the expense of this poor devil, a shot happened to take us between wind and water, and (its course being through the purser's store room) made a terrible havoc and noise among the jars and bottles in its way, and disconcerted Mackshane so much, that he dropped his scalpel, and falling down on his knees, pronounced his *Paternoster* aloud; the purser fell backward, and lay without sense of motion; and the chaplain grew so outrageous, that Rattlin with one hand could not keep him under; so that we were obliged to confine him in the surgeon's cabbin, where he was no doubt guilty of a thousand extravagancies. Much about this time, my old antagonist, Crampley, came down, with express orders, as he said, to bring me up to the quarter-deck, to dress a slight wound the captain had received by a splinter: his reason for honouring me in particular with this piece of service, being, that in case I should be killed or disabled by the way, my death or mutilation would be of less consequence to the ship's company, than that of the doctor or his first mate. At another time, perhaps, I might have disputed this order, to which I was not bound to pay the least regard; but as I thought my reputation depended upon my compliance, I was resolved to convince my rival that I was no more afraid than he of exposing myself to danger. With this view I provided myself with dressings, and followed him immediately to the quarter-deck, through a most infernal scene of slaughter, fire, smoke, and uproar. Captain Oakhum, who leaned against the mizen-mast, no sooner saw me approach in my shirt, with the sleeves tucked up to my armpits, and my hands dyed with blood, than he signified his displeasure by a frown, and asked why the doctor himself did not come? I told him Crampley had singled me out, as if by express command; at which reply he seemed surprised, and threatened to punish the midshipman for his presumption, after the engagement. In the meantime, I was sent back to my station, and ordered to tell Mackshane, that the captain expected him immediately. I got safe back, and delivered my commission to the doctor, who flatly refused to quit the post assigned to him by his instructions; whereupon Morgan, who, I believe, was jealous of my reputation for courage, undertook the affair, and ascended with great intrepidity. The captain, finding the surgeon obstinate, suffered himself to be dressed, and swore he would confine Mackshane as soon as that service should be over.

[. . .]

Having cannonaded the fort during the space of four hours, we were all ordered to slip our cables, and sheer off; but next day the engagement was renewed, and continued from the morning till the afternoon, when the enemy's fire from Bocca Chica slackened, and towards evening was quite silenced. A breach being made on the other side, by our land battery, large enough to admit a middle-sized baboon, provided he could find means to climb up to it, our general proposed to give the assault that very night, and actually ordered a detachment on that duty. Providence stood our friend upon this occasion, and put it into the hearts of the Spaniards to abandon the fort, which might have been maintained by resolute men, to the day of judgment against all the force we could exert in the attack. And while our soldiers took possession of the enemy's ramparts without resistance, the same good luck attended a body of sailors, who made themselves masters of Fort St. Joseph, the fascine batteries, and one Spanish man-of-war; the other three being burnt or sunk by the foe, that they might not fall into our hands. The taking of these forts, in the strength of which the Spaniards chiefly confided, made us masters of the outward harbour, and occasioned great joy among us, as we laid our accounts at finding little or no opposition from the town: and indeed, if a few great ships had sailed up immediately, before they had recovered from the confusion and despair that our unexpected success had produced among them, it is not impossible that we might have finished the affair to our satisfaction, without any more bloodshed; but this step our heroes disdained as a barbarous insult over the enemy's distress, and gave them all the respite they could desire, in order to recollect themselves. In the meantime, Mackshane, taking the advantage of this general exultation, waited on our captain, and pleaded his own cause so effectually that he was re-established in his good graces; and as for Crampley, there was no more notice taken of his behaviour towards me during the action. But of all the consequences of the victory, none was more grateful than plenty of fresh water, after we had languished five weeks on the allowance of a purser's quart per day for each man, in the Torrid Zone, where the sun was vertical, and the expense of bodily fluid so great, that a gallon of liquor could scarce supply the waste of twenty-four hours; especially as our provision consisted of putrid salt beef, to which the sailors gave the name of Irish horse; salt pork, of New England, which, though neither fish nor flesh, savoured of both; bread from the same country, every biscuit whereof, like a piece of clockwork, moved by its own internal impulse, occasioned by the myriads of insects that dwelt within it; and butter served out by the gill, that tasted like train oil thickened with salt. Instead of small beer, each man was allowed three half-quarterns of brandy or rum, which were distributed every morning, diluted with a certain quantity of his water, without either sugar or fruit to render it palatable, for which reason, this composition was by the sailors not unaptly styled Necessity. Nor was this limitation of simple element owing to a scarcity of it on board, for there was at this time water enough in the ship for a voyage of six months, at the rate of half a gallon per day to each man: but this fast must, I suppose, have been enjoined by way of penance on the ship's company for their sins; or rather with a view to mortify them into a contempt of life, that they might thereby become more resolute and regardless of danger. How simply then do those people argue, who ascribe the great mortality among us, to our bad provision and want of water; and affirm, that a great many valuable lives might have been saved, if the useless transports had been employed in fetching fresh stock, turtle, fruit, and other refreshments, from Jamaica and other adjacent islands, for the use of the army and fleet! seeing, it is to be hoped, that those who died went to a better place, and those who survived were the more easily maintained. After all, a sufficient number remained to fall before the walls of St. Lazar, where they behaved like their own country mastiffs, which shut their eyes, run into the jaws of a bear, and have their heads crushed for their valour.

But to return to my narration. After having put garrisons into the forts we had taken, and re-embarked our soldiers and artillery (a piece of service which detained us more than a week), we ventured up to the mouth of the inner harbour, guarded by a large fortification on one side, and a small redoubt on the other, both of which were deserted before our approach, and the entrance of the harbour blocked up by several old galleons and two men-of-war that the enemy had sunk in the channel. We made shift, however, to open a passage for some ships that favoured a second landing of our troops at a place called La Quinta, not far from the town, where, after a faint resistance from a body of Spaniards, who opposed their disembarkation, they encamped with a design of besieging the castle of St. Lazar, which overlooked and commanded the city. Whether our renowned general had nobody in his army who knew how to approach it in form, or that he trusted entirely to the fame of his arms, I shall not determine; but, certain it is, a resolution was taken in a council of war, to attack the place with musquetry only. This was put in execution, and succeeded accordingly; the enemy giving them such a hearty reception, that the greatest part of their detachment took up their everlasting residence on the spot.

Our chief, not relishing this kind of complaisance in the Spaniards, was wise enough to retreat on board with the remains of his army, which, from eight thousand able men landed on the beach near Bocca Chica, was now reduced to fifteen hundred fit for service. The sick and wounded were squeezed into certain vessels, which thence obtained the name of hospital ships, though methinks they scarce deserved such a creditable title, seeing few of them could boast of either surgeon, nurse, or cook; and the space between decks was so confined that the miserable patients had not room to sit upright in their beds. Their wounds and stumps, being neglected, contracted filth and putrefaction, and millions of maggots were hatched amid the corruption of their sores. This inhuman disregard was imputed to the scarcity of surgeons; though it is well known that every great ship in the fleet could have spared one at least for this duty, an expedient which would have been more than sufficient to remove this shocking inconvenience. But perhaps our general was too much of a gentleman to ask a favour of this kind from his fellow chief, who, on the other hand, would not derogate so much from his own dignity, as to offer such assistance unasked; for, I may venture to affirm, that by this time the Dæmon of discord, with her sooty wings, had breathed her influence upon our counsels; and it might be said of these great men (I hope they will pardon the comparison) as of Cæsar and Pompey, the one could not brook a superior, and the other was impatient of an equal; so that, between the pride of one and insolence of another, the enterprise miscarried, according to the proverb, 'Between two stools the backside falls to the ground.' Not that I would be thought to liken any public concern to that opprobrious part of the human body, though I might with truth assert, if I durst use such a vulgar idiom, that the nation did hang on arse at its disappointment on this occasion; neither would I presume to compare the capacity of our heroic leaders to any such wooden convenience as a joint-stool or a close-stool; but only to signify by this simile, the mistake the people committed in trusting to the union of two instruments that were never joined.

A day or two after the attempt on St. Lazar, the admiral ordered one of the Spanish men-of-war we had taken to be mounted with sixteen guns, and manned with detachments from our great ships, in order to batter the town; accordingly, she was towed into the inner harbour in the night, and moored within half a mile of the walls, against which she began to fire at daybreak; and continued about six hours exposed to the opposition of at least thirty pieces of cannon, which at length obliged our men to set her on fire, and get off as well as they could in their boats. This piece of conduct afforded matter of speculation to all the wits, either in the army or the navy, who were at last fain to acknowledge it a stroke of policy above their comprehension. Some entertained such an irreverent opinion of the admiral's understanding, as to think he expected the town would surrender to his floating battery of sixteen guns: others imagined his sole intention was to try the enemy's strength, by which he should be able to compute the number of great ships that would be necessary to force the town to a capitulation. But this last conjecture soon appeared groundless, in as much as no ships of any kind whatever were afterwards employed on that service. A third sort swore that no other cause could be assigned for this undertaking than that which induced Don Quixote to attack the windmill. A fourth class (and that the most numerous, though, without doubt, composed of the sanguine and malicious) plainly taxed this commander with want of honesty as well as sense; and alleged that he ought to have sacrificed private pique to the interest of his country; that, where the lives of so many brave fellow citizens were concerned, he ought to have concurred with the general without being solicited or even desired, towards their preservation and advantage, that, if his arguments could not dissuade him from a desperate enterprise, it was his duty to have rendered it as practicable as possible, without running extreme hazard; that this could have been done, with a good prospect of success, by ordering five or six large ships to batter the town while the land forces stormed the castle; by these means, a considerable diversion would have been made in favour of those troops, who, in their march to the assault and in the retreat, suffered much more from the town than from the castle! That the inhabitants seeing themselves vigorously attacked on all hands would have been divided, distracted, and confused, and in all probability unable to resist the assailants. But all these suggestions surely proceeded from ignorance or malevolence, or else the admiral would not have found it such an easy matter, at his return to England, to justify his conduct to a ministry at once so upright and discerning. True it is, that those who undertook to vindicate him on the spot, asserted, there was not water enough for our great ships near the town; though this was a little unfortunately urged, because there happened to be pilots in the fleet perfectly well acquainted with the soundings of the harbour, who affirmed there was water enough for five eighty-gun ships to lie abreast almost up to the very walls. The disappointments we suffered occasioned a universal dejection, which was not at all alleviated by the objects that daily and hourly entertained our eyes, nor by the prospect of what must have inevitably happened, had we remained much longer in this place. Such was the economy in some ships that, rather than be at the trouble of interring the dead, their commanders ordered their men to throw the bodies overboard, many without either ballast or winding-sheet; so that numbers of human carcasses floated in the harbour, until they were devoured by sharks and carrion crows, which afforded no agreeable spectacle to those who survived. At the same time the wet season began, during which a deluge of rain falls, from the rising to the setting sun, without intermission, and that no sooner ceases than it begins to thunder and lighten with such continued flashing, that one can see to read a very small print by the illumination.

The Battle of Prestonpans (1814)

Walter Scott

Although the Highlanders marched on very fast, the sun was declining when they arrived upon the brow of those high grounds which command an open and extensive plain stretching northwards to the sea, on which are situated, but at a considerable distance from each other, the small villages of Seaton and Cockenzie, and the larger one of Preston. The low coast-road to Edinburgh passed through this plain, issuing upon it from the inclosures of Seaton-house, and at the town or village of Preston again entering the defiles of an inclosed country. By this way the English general had chosen to approach the metropolis, both as most commodious for his cavalry, and as being probably of opinion that by doing so, he would meet in front with the Highlanders advancing from Edinburgh in the opposite direction. In this he was mistaken, for the sound judgment of the Chevalier, or of those to whose advice he listened, left the direct passage free, but occupied the strong ground by which it was overlooked and commanded.

When the Highlanders reached the heights commanding the plain described, they were immediately formed in array of battle along the brow of the hill. Almost at the same instant, the van of the English appeared issuing from among the trees and inclosures of Seaton, with the purpose of occupying the plain between the high ground and the sea. The space which divided the armies being only about half a mile in breadth, Waverley could plainly see the squadrons of dragoons issue, one after another, from the defiles, with their videttes in front, and form upon the plain, with their front opposed to the line of the Prince's army. They were followed by a train of field-pieces, which, when they reached the flank of the dragoons, were also brought into line, and pointed against the heights. The march was continued by three or four regiments of infantry marching in open column, their fixed bayonets shewing like successive hedges of steel, and their arms glancing like lightning, as, at a signal given, they at once wheeled into line, and were placed in direct opposition to the Highlanders. A second train of artillery, with another regiment of horse, closed the long march, and formed on the left flank of the infantry, the whole line facing southwards.

While the English army went through these evolutions, the Highlanders shewed equal promptitude and zeal for battle. As fast as the clans came upon the ridge which fronted their enemy, they were formed into line, so that both armies got into complete order of battle at the same moment. When this was accomplished, the Highlanders set up a tremendous yell, which was re-echoed by the heights behind them. The regulars, who were in high spirits, returned a loud shout of defiance, and fired one or two of their cannon, upon an advanced post of the Highlanders. The latter displayed great earnestness to proceed instantly to the attack, Evan Dhu urging to Fergus, by way of argument, that 'the *sidier roy* was tottering like an egg upon a staff, and that they had a' the vantage of the onset, for even a haggis (God bless her!) could charge down hill.'

But the ground through which the mountaineers must have descended, although not of great extent, was impracticable in its character, being not only marshy, but intersected with walls of dry stone, and traversed in its whole length by a very broad and deep ditch, circumstances which must have given the musketry of the regulars dreadful advantages. The authority of the commanders was therefore interposed to curb the impetuosity of the Highlanders, and only a few marksmen were sent down the descent to skirmish with the enemy's advanced posts, and to reconnoitre the ground.

Here then was a military spectacle of no ordinary interest, or usual occurrence. The two armies, so different in aspect and discipline, yet each admirably trained to their peculiar mode of war, upon whose conflict the temporary fate at least of Scotland appeared to depend, now faced each other like two gladiators in the arena, each meditating upon the mode of attacking their enemy. The leading officers and the general's staff of each army could be distinguished in front of their lines, busied with their spy-glasses to watch each others' motions, and occupied in dispatching the orders and receiving the intelligence conveyed by the aides-de-camp and orderly-men, who gave life to the scene by galloping along in different directions, as if the fate of the day depended upon the speed of their horses. The space between the armies was at times occupied by the partial and irregular contest of individual sharp-shooters, and a hat or

15

bonnet was occasionally seen to fall, or a wounded man was borne off by his comrades. These, however, were but trifling skirmishes, for it suited the view of neither party to advance in that direction. From the neighbouring hamlets, the peasantry cautiously shewed themselves as if watching the issue of the expected engagement; and at no great distance in the bay were two square-rigged vessels bearing the English flag, whose tops and yards were crowded with less timid spectators.

When this awful pause had lasted for a short time, Fergus, with another Chieftain, received orders to detach their clans towards the village of Preston, in order to threaten the right flank of Cope's army. and compel him to a change of disposition. In order to execute these orders, the Chief of Glennaquoich occupied the church-yard of Tranent, a commanding situation, and a convenient place, as Evan Dhu remarked, for any gentleman who might have the misfortune to be killed, and chanced to be curious about Christian burial. To check or dislodge this party, the English general detached two guns, escorted by a strong party of cavalry. They approached so near that Waverley could plainly recognize the standard of the troop he had formerly commanded, and hear the trumpets and kettle-drums sound the advance, which he had so often obeyed. He could hear, too, the well-known word given in the English dialect, by the equally well-distinguished voice of the commanding officer for whom he had once felt so much respect. It was at that instant, that looking around him, he saw the wild dress and appearance of his Highland associates, heard their whispers in an uncouth and unknown language, looked upon his own dress, so unlike that which he had worn from his infancy, and wished to awake from what seemed at the moment a dream, strange, horrible, and unnatural. 'Good God,' he thought, 'am I then a traitor to my country, a renegade to my standard, and a foe, as that poor dying wretch expressed himself, to my native England!'

Ere he could digest or smother the recollection, the tall military form of his late commander came full in view, for the purpose of reconnoitering. 'I can hit him now,' said Callum, cautiously raising his fusee over the wall under which he lay couched, scarce sixty yards distance.

Edward felt as if he were about to see a parricide committed in his presence; for the venerable grey hair and striking countenance of the veteran, recalled the almost paternal respect with which his officers universally regarded him. But ere he could say 'Hold,' an aged Highlander, who lay beside Callum Beg, stopped his arm. 'Spare your shot,' said the seer, 'his hour is not yet come. But let him beware of to-morrow — I see his winding-sheet high upon his breast.'

Callum, flint to other considerations, was penetrable to superstition. He turned pale at the words of the *Taishatr,* and recovered his piece. Colonel G——, unconscious of the danger he had escaped, turned his horse round, and rode slowly back to the front of his regiment.

By this time the regular army had assumed a new line, with one flank inclined towards the sea, and the other resting upon the village of Preston; and, as similar difficulties occurred in attacking their new position, Fergus and the rest of the detachment were recalled to their former post. This alteration created the necessity of a corresponding change in General Cope's army, which was again brought into a line parallel with that of the Highlanders. In these manœuvres on both sides the day-light was nearly consumed, and both armies prepared to rest upon their arms for the night in the lines which they respectively occupied.

'There will be nothing done to-night,' said Fergus to his friend Waverley; 'ere we wrap ourselves in our plaids, let us go see what the Baron is about in rear of the line.'

When they approached his post, they found the good old careful officer, after having sent out his night patroles and posted his sentinels, engaged in reading the Evening Service of the Episcopal church to the remainder of his troop. His voice was loud and sonorous, and though his spectacles upon his nose, and the appearance of Saunders Saunderson, in military array, performing the functions of clerk, had something ludicrous, yet the circumstances of danger in which they stood, the military costume of the audience, and the appearance of their horses, saddled and picquetted behind them, gave an impressive and solemn effect to the office of devotion.

'I have confessed to-day, ere you were awake,' whispered Fergus to Waverley, 'yet I am not so strict a catholic as to refuse to join in this good man's prayers. Edward assented, and they remained till the Baron had concluded the service.

As he shut the book, 'Now, lads,' said he, 'have at them in the morning with heavy hands and light consciences.' He then kindly greeted Mac-Ivor and Waverley, who requested to know his opinion of their situation. 'Why, you know Tacitus saith, "*In rebus bellicis maxime dominatur Fortuna*," which is equiponderate with our vernacular adage. "Luck can maist in the mellee." But credit me, gentlemen, yon man is not his craft's master. He damps the spirits of the poor lads he commands, by keeping them on the defensive, whilk of itself implies inferiority or fear. Now will they lie on their arms yonder, as anxious and as ill at ease as a toad under a harrow, while our men will be quite fresh and blithe for action in the morning, – Well, good night – One thing troubles me, but if to-morrow goes well off, I will consult you about it, Glennaquoich.'—

'I could almost apply to Mr Bradwardine the character which Henry gives of Fluellen,' said Waverley, as his friend and he walked towards their *bivouac*;

Though it appears a little out of fashion,
There is much care and valour in this 'Scotchman.'

'He has seen much service,' answered Fergus, 'and one is sometimes astonished to find how much nonsense and reason is mingled in his composition. I wonder what can be troubling his mind – probably something about Rose. – Hark! the English are setting their watch.'

The roll of the drums and shrill accompaniment of the fifes swelled up the hill – died away – resumed its thunder – and was at length hushed. The trumpets and kettle-drums of the cavalry were next heard to perform the beautiful and wild point of war appropriated as signal for that piece of nocturnal duty, and then finally sunk upon the wind with a shrill and mournful cadence.

The friends, who had now reached their post, stood and looked round them ere they lay down to rest. The western sky twinkled with stars, but a frost-mist rising from the ocean, covered the eastern horizon, and rolled in white wreaths along the plain where the adverse army lay couched upon their arms. Their advanced posts were pushed as far as the side of the great ditch at the bottom of the descent, and had kindled large fires at different intervals, gleaming with obscure and hazy lustre through the heavy fog which appeared to encircle them with a doubtful halo.

The Highlanders, 'thick as leaves in Valambrosa,' lay stretched upon the ridge of the hill, buried (excepting their sentinels) in the most profound repose. 'How many of these brave fellows will sleep more soundly before to-morrow night, Fergus!'

'You must not think of that. You must only think of your sword, and by whom it was given. All other reflections are now TOO LATE.'

With the opiate contained in this undeniable remark, Edward endeavoured to lull the tumult of his conflicting feelings. The Chieftain and he combining their plaids, made a comfortable and warm couch. Callum, sitting down at their head, (for it was his duty to watch upon the immediate person of the Chief,) began a long mournful song in Gaelic, to a low and uniform tune, which, like the sound of the wind at a distance, soon lulled them to sleep.

When they had slept for a few hours, they were awakened, and summoned to attend the Prince. The distant village clock was heard to toll three as they hastened to the place where he lay. He was already surrounded by his principal officers and the chiefs of clans. A bundle of pease-straw, which had been lately his couch, now served for his seat. Just as Fergus reached the circle, the consultation had broken up. 'Courage, my brave friends!' said the Chevalier, 'and each one put himself instantly at the head of his command; a faithful friend has offered to guide us by a practicable, though narrow and circuitous route, which, sweeping to our right, traverses the morass, and enables us to gain the firm and open plain, upon which the enemy are lying. This difficulty surmounted, Heaven and your good swords must do the rest.'

The proposal spread unanimous joy, and each leader hastened to set his men into order with as little noise as possible. The army, moving by its right from off the ground on which they had rested, soon entered the path through the morass, conducting their march with astonishing silence and great rapidity. The mist had not risen to the higher grounds, so that for some time they had the advantage of star-light. But this was lost as the stars faded before approaching day, and as the head of the marching column, continuing its descent, plunged as it were into the heaving ocean of fog, which rolled its white waves over the whole plain, and over the sea, by which it was bounded. Some difficulties were now to be encountered inseparable from darkness, a narrow, broken, and marshy path, and the necessity of preserving union in the march. These, however, were less inconvenient to Highlanders, from their habits of life, than they would have been to any other troops, and they continued a steady and swift movement.

As the clan of Ivor approached the firm ground, following the track of those who preceded them, the challenge of a patrole was heard through the mist, though they could not see the dragoon by whom it was made – 'Who goes there?'

'Hush,' cried Fergus, 'hush! Let none answer, as he values his life – Press forward,' and they continued their march with silence and rapidity.

The patrole fired his carabine upon the body, and the report was instantly followed by the clang of his horse's feet as he galloped off. '*Hylax in limine latrat,*' said the Baron of Bradwardine, who heard the shot, 'that loon will give the alarm.'

The clan of Fergus had now gained the firm plain, which had lately borne a large crop of corn. But the harvest was gathered in, and the expanse was unbroken by tree, bush, or interruption of any kind. The rest of the army were following fast, when they heard the drums of the enemy beat the general. Surprise, however, had made no part of their plan, so they were not disconcerted by this intimation that the foe was upon his guard, and prepared to receive them. It only hastened their dispositions for the combat, which were very simple.

The Highland army, which now occupied the eastern end of the wide plain, or corn field, so often referred to, was drawn up in two lines, extending from the morass towards the sea. The first was destined to charge the enemy, the second to act as a reserve. The few horse, whom the Prince headed in person, remained between the two lines. The Adventurer had intimated a resolution to charge in person at the head of his first line; but his purpose was deprecated by all around him, and he was though with difficulty induced to abandon it.

Both lines were now moving forward, the first prepared for instant combat. The clans, of which it was composed, formed each a sort of separate phalanx, narrow in front, and in depth ten, twelve, or fifteen files, according to the strength of the following.

The best armed and best born, for the words were synonymous, were placed in front of each of these irregular subdivisions. The others in the rear shouldered forward the front, and by their pressure added both physical impulse, and additional ardour and confidence, to those who were first to encounter the danger.

'Down with your plaid, Waverley,' cried Fergus, throwing off his own; 'we'll win silks for our tartans before the sun is above the sea.'

The clansmen on every side stript their plaids, prepared their arms, and there was an awful pause of about three minutes, during which the men, pulling off their bonnets, raised their faces to heaven, and uttered a short prayer. Waverley felt his heart at that moment throb as it would have burst from his bosom. It was not fear, it was not ardour, – it was a compound of both, a new and deeply energetic impulse, that with its first emotion chilled and astounded, then fevered and maddened his mind. The sounds around him combined to exalt his enthusiasm, the pipes played, and the clans rushed forward, each in its own dark column. As they advanced they mended their pace, and the muttering sounds of the men to each other began to swell into a wild cry.

At this moment the sun, which was now above the horizon, dispelled the mists. The vapours rose like a curtain, and shewed the two armies in the act of closing. The line of the regulars was formed directly fronting the attack of the Highlanders; – it glittered with the appointments of a complete army, and was flanked by cavalry and artillery. But the sight impressed no terror on the assailants. 'Forward, sons of Ivor,' cried their Chief, 'or the Camerons will draw the first blood.' They rushed on with a tremendous yell.

The rest is well known. The horse, who were commanded to charge the advancing Highlanders in the flank, received a fire from their fusees as they ran on, and, seized with a disgraceful panic, wavered, halted, disbanded, and galloped from the field.

The artillery-men, deserted by the cavalry, fled after discharging their pieces, and the Highlanders, who dropped their guns when fired, and drew their broadswords, rushed with headlong fury against the infantry.

It was at this moment of confusion and terror that Waverley remarked an English officer, apparently of high rank, standing alone and unsupported by a field-piece, which, after the flight of the men by whom it was wrought, he had himself levelled and discharged against the clan of Mac-Ivor, the nearest group of Highlanders within his aim. Struck with his tall martial figure, and eager to save him from inevitable destruction, Waverley outstripped for an instant even the speediest of the warriors, and reaching the spot first, called to him to surrender. The officer replied by a thrust with his sword, which Waverley received in his target, and in turning it aside the Englishman's weapon broke. At the same time the battle-axe of Dugald Mahony was in the act of descending upon the officer's head. Waverley intercepted and prevented the blow, and the officer, perceiving further resistance unavailing, and struck with Edward's generous anxiety for his safety, resigned the fragment of his sword, and was committed by Waverley to Dugald, with strict charge to use him well, and not to pillage his person, promising him, at the same time, full indemnification for the spoil.

On Edward's right the battle still raged fierce and thick. The English infantry, trained in the wars of Flanders, stood their ground with great courage. But their extended files were pierced and broken in many places by the close masses of the clans, and in the personal struggle which ensued, the nature of the High-landers arms, and their extraordinary fierceness and activity, gave them a decided superiority over those who had been accustomed to trust much to their array and discipline, and now felt that the one was broken and the other useless. Waverley, as he cast his eyes toward this scene of smoke and slaughter, observed

Colonel G——, deserted by his own soldiers in spite of all his attempts to rally them, yet spurring his horse through the field to take the command of a small body of infantry, who, with their backs arranged against the wall of his own park, (for his house was close by the field of battle,) continued a desperate and unavailing resistance. Waverley could perceive that he had already received many wounds, his clothes and saddle being marked with blood. To save this good and brave man, became the instant object of Edward's anxious exertions. But he only could witness his fall. Ere Edward could make his way among the Highlanders, who, furious and eager for spoil, now thronged upon each other, he saw his former commander brought from his horse by the blow of a scythe, and beheld him receive, while on the ground, more wounds than would have let out twenty lives. When Waverley came up, however, perception had not entirely fled. The dying warrior seemed to recognize Edward, for he fixed his eye upon him with an upbraiding yet sorrowful look, and appeared to struggle for utterance. But he felt that death was dealing closely with him, and resigning his purpose, and folding his hands as if in devotion, he gave up his soul to his Creator. The look with which he regarded Waverley in his dying moments did not stike him so deeply at that crisis of hurry and confusion, as when it recurred to his imagination at the distance of some time.

Loud shouts of triumph now echoed over the whole field. The battle was fought and won, and the whole baggage, artillery, and military stores of the regular army remained in possession of the victors. Never was a victory more complete. Scarce any escaped from the battle, excepting the cavalry who had left it at the very onset, and even these were broken into different parties and scattered all over the country. The loss of the victors was very trifling: So far as our tale is concerned, we have only to relate the fate of Balmawhapple, who, mounted on a horse

as headstrong and stiff-necked as his rider, pursued the flight of
the dragoons above four miles from the field of battle, when
some dozen of the fugitives took heart of grace, turned round,
and cleaving his skull with their broad-swords, satisfied the
world that the unfortunate gentleman had actually brains, the
end of his life thus giving proof of a fact greatly doubted during
its progress. His death was lamented by few. Most who knew
him agreed in the pithy observation of Ensign Maccombich,
that there 'was mair *lint* (lost) at Sheriff-Muir.' His friend,
Lieutenant Jinker, bent his eloquence only to exculpate his
favourite mare from any share in contributing to the catastrophe. 'He had tauld the laird a thousand times,' he said, 'that
it was a burning shame to pit a martingale upon the puir thing,
when he would ride her wi' a curb of half a yard lang; and that
he could na but bring himself (no to say her) to some mischief,
by bringing her down, or otherwise, whereas if he had had a
wee bit rinning ring on the snafle, she wad a rein'd as cannily
as a cadger's ponie.'

Such was the elegy of the Laird of Balmawhapple.

Davy Jones and the Yankee Privateer (1830)

Michael Scott

We had refitted and been four days at sea, on our voyage to Jamaica, when the gun-room officers gave our mess a blowout.

The increased motion and rushing of the vessel through the water, the groaning of the masts, the howling of the rising gale, and the frequent trampling of the watch on deck, were prophetic of wet jackets to some of us. Still, midshipmanlike, we were as happy as a good dinner and some wine could make us, until the old gunner shoved his weatherbeaten phiz and bald pate in at the door.

'Beg pardon, Mr Splinter, but if you will spare Mr Cringle on the forecastle for an hour until the moon rises.'

'Why, Mr Kennedy, why? Here, man, take a glass of grog.'

'I thank you, sir. It is coming on a roughish night, sir. The running ships should be crossing us hereabouts. Indeed more than once I thought there was a strange sail close aboard of us, the scud is flying so low, and in such white flakes; and none of us has an eye like Mr Cringle, unless it be John Crow, and he is all but frozen.'

'Well, Tom, I suppose you *will* go, brush *instanter*.'

Having changed my uniform, for shag-trousers, pea-jacket, and south-west cap, I went forward, and took my station, in no pleasant humour, on the stowed jib, with my arm round the stay. I had been half an hour there, the weather was getting worse, the rain was beating in my face, and the spray from the stem was flashing over me, as it roared through the waste of sparkling and hissing waters. I turned my back to the weather for a moment to press my hand on my strained eyes. When I opened them, I saw the gunner's gaunt high-featured visage thrust anxiously forward. His profile looked as if it had been rubbed over with phosphorus, and his whole person as if we had been playing at snap dragon.

'What has come over you, Mr Kennedy? Who is burning the bluelight now?'

'A wiser man than I am must tell you that. Look forward, Mr Cringle – look there. What do your books say to that?'

I looked forth, and saw, at the extreme end of the jib-boom, what I had read of, certainly, but never expected to see, a pale, greenish, glow-worm coloured flame, of the size and shape of the frosted glass shade over the swinging lamp in the gun-room. It drew out and flattened as the vessel pitched and rose again, and as she sheered about it, wavered round the point that seemed to attract it, like a soapsud bubble blown from a tobacco pipe before it is shaken into the air. At the core it was comparatively bright, but faded into a halo. It shed a baleful and ominous light on the surrounding objects. The group of sailors on the forecastle looked like spectres, and they shrank together, and whispered when it began to roll slowly along the spar towards where the boatswain was sitting at my feet. At this instant something slid down the stay, and a cold clammy hand passed round my neck. I was within an ace of losing my hold, and tumbling overboard.

'Heaven have mercy on me, what's that?'

'It's that skylarking son of a gun, Jem Sparkle's monkey, sir. You, Jem, you'll never rest till that brute is made shark bait of.'

But Jackoo vanished up the stay again, chuckling and grinning in the ghostly radiance, as if he had been the 'Spirit of the Lamp'. The light was still there, but a cloud of mist, like a burst of vapour from a steam boiler, came down upon the gale, flew past, and disappeared. I followed the white mass as it sailed down the wind. It did not, as it appeared to me, vanish in the darkness, but seemed to remain in sight to leeward, as if checked by a sudden flaw; yet none of our sails was taken aback. A thought flashed on me. I peered still more intensely into the night. I was now certain. 'A sail, broad on the lee-bow.' The ship was in a buzz in a moment.

The captain answered from the quarterdeck, 'Thank you, Mr Cringle. How shall we steer?'

'Keep her away a couple of points, sir, steady.'

'Steady,' sang the man at the helm; and a slow melancholy cadence, although a familiar sound to me, now moaned through the rushing of the wind, and smote upon my heart as if it had been the wailing of a spirit.

I turned to the boatswain, who was now standing beside me. 'Is that you or *Davy* steering, Mr Nipper? If you had not been there bodily at my elbow, I could have sworn that was your *voice*.'

When the gunner made the same remark it startled the poor fellow. He tried to take it as a joke, but could not. 'There may be a laced hammock with a shot in it, for some of us ere morning.'

At this moment, to my dismay, the object we were chasing, shortened, gradually fell abeam of us, and finally disappeared.

'The Flying Dutchman.'

I can't see her at all now.'

'She will be a fore-and-aft-rigged vessel that has tacked, sir.' And sure enough, after a few seconds, I saw the white object lengthen, and draw out again abaft our beam. 'The chase has tacked, sir, put the helm down, or she will go to windward of us.'

We tacked also, and time it was we did so, for the rising moon now showed us a large schooner under a crowd of sail. We edged down on her, when finding her manœuvre detected, she brailed up her flat sails, and bore up before the wind. This was our best point of sailing, and we cracked on, the captain rubbing his hands. 'It's my turn to be the big un this time.'

Although blowing a strong north-wester, it was now clear moon-light, and we hammered away from our bow guns, but whenever a shot told amongst the rigging, the injury was repaired as if by magic. It was evident we had repeatedly hulled her, from the glimmering white streaks along her counter and across her stern, occasioned by the splintering of the timber, but it seemed to produce no effect.

At length we drew well up on her quarter. She continued all black hull and white sail, not a soul to be seen on deck, except a dark object, which we took for the man at the helm.

'What schooner's that?' No answer. 'Heave to, or I'll sink you.' Still all silent. 'Sergeant Armstrong, do you think you could pick off that chap at the wheel?'

The marine jumped on the forecastle, and levelled his piece, when a musket shot from the schooner crashed through his skull, and he fell dead. The old skipper's blood was up.

'Forecastle there! Mr Nipper, clap a canister of grape over the round shot, into the boat gun, and give it to him.'

'Aye, aye, sir!' gleefully rejoined the boatswain, forgetting the augury and everything else in the excitement of the moment. In a twinkling, the square foresail – top-gallant – royal – and studding-sail haulyards were let go by the run on board of the schooner, as if they had been shot away, and he put his helm hard aport as if to round to.

'Rake him, sir, or give him the stern. He has *not* surrendered. – I know their game. Give him your broadside, sir, or he is off to windward of you like a shot. No, no, we have him now; heave to, Mr Splinter, heave to!'

We did so, and that so suddenly, that the studding-sail booms snapped like pipe shanks, short off by the irons. Notwithstanding we had shot two hundred yards to the leeward before we could lay our maintopsail to the mast. I ran to windward. The schooner's yards and rigging were now black with men, clustered like bees swarming, her square sails were being close furled, her fore and aft sails set, and away she was dead to windward of us. 'So much for undervaluing our American friends,' grumbled Mr Splinter.

We made all sail in chase, blazing away to little purpose. We had no chance on a bowline, and when our 'Amigo' had satisfied himself of his superiority by one or two short tacks, he deliberately took a reef in his mainsail, hauled down his flying jib and gaff topsail, triced up the bunt of his foresail, and fired his long thirty-two at us. The shot came in at the third aftermost port on the starboard side, and dismounted the carronade, smashing the slide, and wounding three men. The second shot missed, and as it was madness to remain to be peppered, probably winged, whilst every one of ours fell short, we reluctantly kept away on our course, having the gratification of hearing a clear well-blown bugle on board the schooner play up 'Yankee Doodle'. As the brig fell off, our long gun was run out to have a parting crack at her, when the third and last shot from the schooner struck the sill of the midship port, and made the white splinters fly from the solid oak like bright silver sparks in the moonlight. A sharp piercing cry rose into the air – my soul identified that death-shriek with the voice that I had heard, and I saw the man who was standing with the lanyard of the lock in his hand drop heavily across the breech, and discharge the gun in his fall. Thereupon a blood-red glare shot up into the cold blue sky, as if a volcano had burst forth from beneath the mighty deep, followed by a roar, and a shattering crash, and a mingling of unearthly cries and groans, and a concussion of the air, and of the water, as if our whole broadside had been fired at once. Then a solitary splash here, and a dip there, and short sharp yells, and low choking bubbling moans, as the hissing fragments of the noble vessel we had seen fell into the sea, and the last of her gallant crew vanished for ever beneath that pale broad moon.

We were alone, and once more all was dark, and wild, and stormy. Fearfully had that ball sped, fired by a dead man's hand. But what is it that clings black and doubled across that fatal cannon, dripping and heavy, and choking the scuppers with clotting gore, and swaying to and fro with the motion of the vessel, like a bloody fleece?

'Who is it that was hit at the gun there?'

'Mr Nipper, the boatswain, sir. The last shot has cut him in two.'

The Girl I Left Behind Me (1829)

G. R. Gleig

There are not many scenes in human life more striking or more harrowing to the feelings of him who regards it for the first time, than the departure of a regiment upon foreign service. By the customs of the army only six women for each company are allowed to follow their husbands, who are chosen by lot out of perhaps twenty or thirty. The casting of lots is usually deferred till, at least, the evening previous to the marching of the corps, probably with the humane design of leaving to each female, as long as it can be left, the enjoyment of that greatest of all earthly blessings, hope. The consequence then is, that a full sense of her forlorn condition coming all at once upon the wretched creature who is to be abandoned, produces, in many instances, a violence of grief, the display of which it is impossible to witness with any degree of indifference. Many were the agonizing scenes of the kind which it was my fortune this day to witness; but there was one so peculiarly distressing, so much more affecting in all its points than the rest, that I am tempted to give a detail of it, even at the risk of being thought the writer of a romance. I recollect having read in that amusing work, 'The Hermit in the Country,' an anecdote very similar in many respects, to the one which I am now going to relate. The reader is not, however, to suppose, that the two stories bear a common origin, namely the imaginations of those by whom they are told. The worthy Hermit's tale probably rests upon no better foundation; but mine is a true story, and its truth will no doubt be attested by several of my readers: that is, supposing me to have any readers in the – regiment of foot.

About three months previous to the day of embarkation, a batch of recruits had joined the regiment from Scotland. Among them was a remarkably fine young Highlander; a native, if I recollect right, of Balquidder, called Duncan Stewart. Duncan was in all respects a good soldier; he was clean, sober, orderly, and well behaved; but he seemed to be of a singularly melancholy temper; never mixing in the sports and amusements of his comrades, nor even speaking except when he was obliged to speak. It so happened that the pay-serjeant of Duncan's company was likewise a Highlander; and Highlanders being of all description of persons the most national, he very soon began to interest himself about the fate of the young recruit. At first Duncan shrunk back even from his advances, but it is not natural for the human heart, especially during the season of youth, to continue long indifferent to acts of kindness; so Duncan gradually permitted honest M'Intyre to insinuate himself into his good graces; and they became, before long, bosom friends.

When they had continued for some weeks on a footing of intimacy, Duncan did not scruple to make his friend the serjeant acquainted with the cause of his dejection. It was simply this:–

Duncan was the son of a Highland farmer, who, like many of his countrymen in that situation, cultivated barley for the purpose of making whisky; in plain language, was a determined smuggler. Not far from the abode of Stewart, dwelt an excise-man of the name of Young, who, being extremely active in the discharge of his duty, had on various occasions made seizure of his neighbours' kegs as they were on their march towards the low-countries. This was an offence which the Highlander, of course, could not forgive; and there accordingly subsisted between the smuggler and the gauger, a degree of antipathy far surpassing anything of which it is easy for us to form a concep-tion. It must, however, be confessed, that the feeling of hatred was all on one side. Stewart hated Young for presuming to inter-fere with his honest calling; and despised him, because he had the misfortune to be born in the shire of Renfrew; whereas Young was disposed to behave civilly to his neighbour, on every occasion except when his whisky casks happened to come in the way.

Gauger Young had an only and a very pretty daughter, a girl of eighteen years of age, with whom Duncan, as a matter of course, fell in love. The maiden returned his love, at which I am by no means surprised, for a handsomer or more manly-looking youth one would not desire to see; but alas! old Stewart would not hear of their union; absolutely commanding his son, under penalty of his heaviest malediction, not to think of her again. The authority of parents over their children, even after they have grown up to the age of manhood, is in Scotland very great; so Duncan would not dispute his father's will, and finding all entreaty to alter it useless, he determined to sacrifice inclination to duty, and to meet his pretty Mary no more.

To this resolution he adhered for several days, but, to use his own words, 'Gang where I would, and do what I liket, I aye saw her before me. I saw her once, to tell her what my father had said; indeed, we were baith gay sure how it would be, before I spak to him ava; and oh! the look she gae me, M'Intyre, I ne'er forgot it, and I never can forget it. It haunted me like a ghaist baith night and day.'

The consequence of constantly beholding such a vision may easily be imagined. Duncan forgot his determination and his duty, and found himself one evening, he scarce knew how, once more walking with Mary by the loch side. This occurred again and again. The meetings were the more sweet because they were secret, and they ended – as such stolen meetings generally end among persons of their station in life. Duncan was assured of becoming a father, before he was a husband.

This, however, was not to be permitted; Duncan was too tenderly attached to Mary, to suffer disgrace to fall upon her, even though he should incur the threatened penalty of a father's curse by marrying, so he resolved, at all hazards, to make her his wife. The reader is no doubt aware, that marriages are much more easily contracted in Scotland, than on the south side of the Tweed. An exchange of lines, as it is called, that is to say, a mutual agreement to live as man and wife, drawn up and signed by a young man and a young woman, constitutes as indisputable a union in North Britain, as if the marriage ceremony had been read or uttered by a clergyman; and to this method of uniting their destinies Duncan and Mary had recourse. They addressed a letter, the one to the other, in which he acknowledged her to be his wife, and she acknowledged him to be her husband; and, having made an exchange of them, they became to all intents and purposes a married couple.

Having thus gone in direct opposition to the will of his father, Duncan was by no means easy in his own mind. He well knew the unforgiving temper of the man with whom he had to deal; he knew likewise that his disobedience could not be long kept a secret, and the nearer the period approached which would compel a disclosure, the more anxious and uncomfortable he became. At length the time arrived when he must either acknowledge his marriage, or leave Mary to infamy. It was the season of Doun Fair, and Duncan was intrusted with the care of a drove of sheep which were to be disposed of at that market. Having bid farewell to his wife, he set out, still carrying his secret with him, but determined to disclose it by letter, as soon as he should reach Doun. His object in acting thus was, partly, to escape the first burst of his father's anger, and partly with the hope, that, having escaped it, he might be received at his return with forgiveness; but alas! the poor fellow had no opportunity of ascertaining the success of his scheme.

When he reached Doun, Duncan felt himself far too unhappy to attend to business. He accordingly intrusted the sale of his sheep to a neighbour; and sitting down in one of the public houses, wrote that letter which had been the subject of his meditations ever since he left Balquidder. Having completed this, Duncan bravely determined to forget his sorrows for a while, for which purpose he swallowed a dose of whisky, and entered into conversation with the company about him, among whom were several soldiers, fine, merry, hearty fellows, who, with their corporal, were on the look-out for recruits. The leader of the party was a skilful man in his vocation; he admired the fine proportions of the youth before him, and determined to inlist him if he could. For this purpose more whisky was ordered, – funny histories were told by him and his companions, – Duncan was plied with dram after dram, till at length he became completely inebriated, and the shilling was put into his hand. No time was given him to recover from his surprise; for, long ere the effects of intoxication had evaporated, Duncan was on his way to Edinburgh. Here he was instantly embarked with a number of young men similarly situated; and he actually reached head-quarters without having had an opportunity so much as to inform his relations of his fate.

The sequel of Duncan's story is soon told. Having obtained permission from the commanding officer, he wrote to Scotland for his wife, who joyfully hastened to join him. Her father did what he could, indeed, to prevent this step; not from any hatred towards his daughter, to whom he had behaved with great kindness in her distress, but because he knew how uncomfortable was the sort of life which she must lead as the wife of a private soldier; but Mary resisted every entreaty to remain apart from Duncan, she had been in a state of utter misery during the many weeks in which she was left in ignorance of his situation; and, now that she knew where he was to be found, nothing should hinder her from following him. Though far gone in a state of pregnancy, she set out instantly for the south of England; and having endured with patience all inconveniences attendant upon her want of experience as a traveller, she succeeded in reaching Hythe, just one week previous to the embarkation of the regiment.

This ill-fated couple were hardly brought together when they were once more doomed to part. Poor Mary's name came up among the names of those who should remain behind the regiment, and no language of mine can do justice to the scene which took place. I was not present when the women drew their tickets; but I was told by M'Intyre, that when Mary unrolled the slip of paper, and read upon it the fatal words, 'To be left,' she looked as if Heaven itself were incapable of adding one additional pang to her misery. Holding it with both hands, at the full stretch of her arms from her face, she gazed upon it for some minutes without speaking a word, though the rapid succession of colour and deadly paleness upon her cheeks, told how severe was the struggle which was going on within; till at length, completely overpowered by her own sensations, she crushed it between her palms, and fell senseless into the arms of a female who stood near.

That night was spent by Duncan and his wife exactly as it was to be supposed that it would be spent. They did not so much as lie down; but the moments sped on in spite of their watchfulness, – and at last the bugle sounded. When I came upon the ground, I saw Duncan standing in his place, but Mary was not near him. The wives of the few soldiers who were left behind to form a depot, having kindly detained her in the barrack-room. But, just before the column began to move, she rushed forth; and the scream which she uttered, as she flew towards Duncan, was heard throughout the whole of the ranks. – 'Duncan, Duncan!' the poor thing cried, as she clung wildly round his neck: 'Oh, Duncan, Duncan Stewart, ye're no gawn to leave me again, and me sae near being a mother! O, Serjeant M'Intyre, dinna tak' him awa'! if ye hae ony pity, dinna, dinna tak' him! – O, sir, ye'll let me gang wi' him?' she added, turning to one of the officers who stood by; 'for the love of Heaven, if ye hae ony pity in ye, dinna separate us!'

Poor Duncan stood all this while in silence, leaning his forehead upon the muzzle of his firelock, and supporting his wretched wife upon his arm. He shed no tears – which is more than I can say for myself, or indeed for almost any private or officer upon the parade – his grief was evidently beyond them. 'Ye may come as far as Dover, at least,' he at length said, in a sort of murmur; and the poor creature absolutely shrieked with delight at the reprieve.

The band now struck up, and the column began to move, the men shouting, partly to drown the cries of the women, and partly to express their own willingness to meet the enemy. Mary walked by the side of her husband; but she looked more like a moving corpse than a living creature. – She was evidently suffering acutely, not only in mind but in body; indeed, we had not proceeded above three miles on our journey, before she was seized with the pains of labour. It would have been the height of barbarity to have hindered her unfortunate husband, under these circumstances, from halting to take care of her; so having received his promise to join the regiment again before dark, we permitted him to fall out of the ranks. Fortunately, a cottage stood at no great distance from the road side, into which he and his friend M'Intyre removed her; and while there, I have reason to believe, she was received with great humanity, and treated with kindness; indeed, the inhabitants of the cottage must have been devoid of everything human except the form, had they treated a young woman so situated, otherwise than kindly.

A four hours' march brought the regiment in high spirits, and in good order, into Dover. As a matter of course, the inhabitants filled their windows, and thronged the streets, to witness the embarkation of a body of their countrymen, of whom it was more than probable that few would return; nor have I any cause to doubt the sincerity of the good wishes which they expressed, for our success and safety. It is only during the dull times of peace, or, which amounts to the same thing, when troops are lying idly in a garrison town, that feelings of mutual jealousy arise between the inhabitants and the soldiers.

As the men came in fresh, and, which by no means invariably follows, sober, little more than half an hour was spent in embarking. The transports, fortunately, lay along-side the pier; consequently, there was no need to employ boats for the removal of the troops and baggage; but boards being placed as bridges from the pier to the deck, the companies filed easily and regularly into their respective ships. We were not, however, to sail till the following morning, the remainder of that day being allowed for laying in sea-stock; and hence, as soon as they had seen the men comfortably housed, the officers adjourned to the various inns in the place.

Like my companions, I returned again to shore as soon as I had attended to the comforts of my division; but my mind was too full of the image of poor Mary, to permit my entering with gusto into the various amusements of my friends. I preferred walking back in the direction of Hythe, with the hope of meeting M'Intyre, and ascertaining how the poor creature did. I walked, however, for some time, before any traveller made his appearance. At length, when the interest which I had felt in the fate of the young couple was beginning in some degree to moderate, and I was meditating a return to the inn, I saw two soldiers moving towards me. As they approached, I readily discovered that they were Duncan and his friend; so I waited for them. 'Duncan Stewart,' said I, 'how is your wife?' – The poor fellow did not answer, but, touching his cap, passed on. 'How is his wife, M'Intyre?' said I to the serjeant, who stood still. The honest Scotchman burst into tears, and as soon as he could command himself, he laconically answered, 'She is at rest, sir.' From this I guessed that she was dead; and on more minute inquiry, I learned that it was even so; – she died a few minutes after they removed her into the cottage, without having brought the child into the world. An attempt was made to save the infant, by performing the Cæsarean operation, but without effect; it hardly breathed at all.

Though the officer who commanded the depot was sent for, and offered to take the responsibility upon himself, if Duncan wished to remain behind for the purpose of burying his wife, the poor fellow would not avail himself of the offer. All that he desired was a solemn assurance from the officer that he would see his dear Mary decently interred; and as soon as the promise was given, the young widower hastened to join his regiment. He scarcely spoke after; and he was one of the first who fell after the regiment landed in Spain.

The Story of Farquhar Shaw (1859)

James Grant

This soldier, whose name, from the circumstances connected with his remarkable story, daring courage, and terrible fate, is still remembered in the regiment, in the early history of which he bears so prominent a part, was one of the first who enlisted in Captain Campbell of Finab's independent band of the *Reicudan Dhu*, or Black Watch, when the six separate companies composing this Highland force were established along the Highland Border in 1729, to repress the predatory spirit of certain tribes, and to prevent the levy of black mail. The company were independent, and at that time wore the clan tartan of their captains, who were Simon Frazer, the celebrated Lord Lovat; Sir Duncan Campbell of Lochnell; Grant of Ballindalloch; Alister Campbell of Finab, whose father fought at Darien; Ian Campbell of Carrick, and Deors Monro of Culcairn.

The privates of these companies were all men of a superior station, being mostly cadets of good families – gentlemen of the old Celtic and patriarchal lines, and of baronial proprietors. In the Highlands, the only genuine mark of aristocracy was descent from the founder of the tribe; all who claimed this were styled *uislain*, or gentlemen, and, as such, when off duty, were deemed the equal of the highest chief in the land. Great care was taken by the six captains to secure men of undoubted courage, of good stature, stately deportment, and handsome figure. Thus, in all the old Highland regiments, but more especially the *Reicudan Dhu*, equality of blood and similarity of descent, secured familiarity and regard between the officers and their men – for the latter deemed themselves inferior to no man who breathed the air of heaven. Hence, according to an English engineer officer, who frequently saw these independent companies, 'many of those private gentlemen-soldiers have gillies or servants to attend upon them in their quarters, and upon a march, to carry their provisions, baggage, and firelocks.'

Such was the composition of the corps, now first embodied among that remarkable people, the Scottish Highlanders – 'a people,' says the Historian of Great Britain, 'untouched by the Roman or Saxon invasions on the south, and by those of the Danes on the east and west skirts of their country – the *unmixed remains* of that vast Celtic empire, which once stretched from the Pillars of Hercules to Archangel.'

The *Reicudan Dhu* were armed with the usual weapons and accoutrements of the line; but, in addition to these, had the arms of their native country – the broadsword, target, pistol, and long dagger, while the sergeants carried the old Celtic *tuagh*, or

Lochaber axe. It was distinctly understood by all who enlisted in this new force, that their military duties were to be confined *within* the Highland Border, where, from the wild, predatory spirit of those clans which dwelt next the Lowlands, it was known that they would find more than enough of military service of the most harassing kind. In the conflicts which daily ensued among the mountains – in the sudden marches by night; the desperate brawls among Caterans, who were armed to the teeth, fierce as nature and outlawry could make them, and who dwelt in wild and pathless fastnesses secluded amid rocks, woods, and morasses, there were few who in courage, energy, daring, and activity equalled Farquhar Shaw, a gentleman from the Braes of Lochaber, who was esteemed the *premier* private in the company of Campbell of Finab, which was then quartered in that district, for each company had its permanent cantonment and scene of operations during the eleven years which succeeded the first formation of the *Reicudan Dhu.*

Farquhar was a perfect swordsman, and deadly shot alike with the musket and pistol, and his strength was such, that he had been known to twist a horse-shoe, and drive his *skene dhu* to the hilt in a pine log; while his activity and power of enduring hunger, thirst, heat, cold and fatigue, became a proverb among the companies of the Watch: for thus he had been reared and trained by his father, a genuine old Celtic gentleman and warrior, whose memory went back to the days when Dundee led the valiant and true to the field of Rinrory, and in whose arms the viscount fell from his horse in the moment of victory, and was borne to the house of Urrard to die. He was a true Highlander of the old school; for an *old school* has existed in all ages and everywhere, even among the Arabs, the children of Ishmael, in the desert; for they, too, have an olden time to which they look back with regret, as being nobler, better, braver, and purer than the present. Thus, the father of Farquhar Shaw was a grim *duinewassal*, who never broke bread or saw the sun rise without uncovering his head and invoking the names of 'God, the Blessed Mary, and St. Colme of the Isle'; who never sat down to a meal without opening wide his gates, that the poor and needy might enter freely, who never refused the use of his purse and sword to a friend or kinsman, and was never seen unarmed, even in his own dining-room; who never wronged any man; but who *never* suffered a wrong or affront to pass, without sharp and speedy vengeance; and who, rather than acknowledge the supremacy of the House of Hanover, died sword in hand at the rising in Glenshiel. For this act, his estates were seized by the House of Breadalbane, and his only son, Farquhar, became a private soldier in the ranks of the Black Watch.

It may easily be supposed, that the son of such a father was imbued with all his cavalier spirit, his loyalty and enthusiasm, and that his mind was filled by all the military, legendary, and romantic memories of his native mountains, the land of the Celts, which, as a fine Irish ballad says, was THEIRS

> *Ere the Roman or the Saxon, the Norman or the Dane,*
> *Had first set foot in Britain, or trampled heaps of slain,*
> *Whose manhood saw the Druid rite, at forest tree and rock –*
> *And savage tribes of Britain round the shrines of Zernebok,*
> *Which for generations witnessed all the glories of the Gael,*
> *Since their Celtic sires sang war-songs round the sacred fires of Baal.*

When it was resolved by Government to form the six independent Highland companies into one regiment, Farquhar Shaw was left on the sick list at the cottage of a widow, named Mhona Cameron, near Inverlochy, having been wounded in a skirmish with Caterans in Glennevis, and he writhed on his sickbed when his comrades, under Finab, marched for the Birks of Aberfeldy, the muster-place of the whole, where the companies were to be united into one battalion, under the celebrated John, Earl of Crawford and Lindesay, the last of his ancient race, a hero covered with wounds and honours won in the services of Britain and Russia.

Weak, wan, and wasted though he was (for his wound, a slash from a pole-axe, had been a severe one), Farquhar almost sprang from bed when he heard the notes of their retiring pipes dying away, as they marched through Maryburgh, and round by the margin of Lochiel. His spirit of honour was ruffled, moreover, by a rumour, spread by his enemies the Caterans, against whom he had fought repeatedly, that he was growing faint-hearted at the prospect of the services of the Black Watch being extended beyond the Highland Border. As rumours to this effect were already finding credence in the glens, the fierce, proud heart of Farquhar burned within him with indignation and unmerited shame.

At last, one night, an old crone, who came stealthily to the cottage in which he was residing, informed him that, by the same outlaws who were seeking to deprive him of his honour, a subtle plan had been laid to surround his temporary dwelling, and put him to death, in revenge for certain wounds inflicted by his sword upon their comrades.

The energy and activity of the Black Watch had long since driven the Caterans to despair, and nothing but the anticipation of killing Farquhar comfortably, and chopping him into ounce pieces at leisure, enabled them to survive their troubles with anything like Christian fortitude and resignation.

'And this is their plan, mother?' said Farquhar to the crone.

'To burn the cottage, and you with it.'

'Dioul! say you so, Mother Mhona,' he exclaimed; 'then 'tis time I were betaking me to the hills. Better have a cool bed for a few nights on the sweet-scented heather, than be roasted in a burning cottage, like a fox in its hole.'

In vain the cotters besought him to seek concealment elsewhere; or to tarry until he had gained his full strength.

'Were I in the prime of strength, I would stay here,' said Farquhar; 'and when sleeping on my sword and target, would fear nothing. If these dogs of Caterans came, they should be welcome to my life, if I could not redeem it by the three best lives in their band; but I am weak as a growing boy, and so shall be off to the free mountain side, and seek the path that leads to the Birks of Aberfeldy.'

'But the Birks are far from here, Farquhar,' urged old Mhona.

'*Attempt*, and *Did-not*, were the worst of Fingal's hounds,' replied the soldier. 'Farquhar will owe you a day in harvest for all your kindness; but his comrades wait, and go he must! Would it not be a strange thing and a shameful, too, if all the *Reicudan Dhu* should march down into the flat, bare land of the Lowland clowns, and Farquhar not be with them? What would Finab, his captain, think? and what would all in Brae Lochaber say?'

'Yet pause,' continued the crones.

'Pause! Dhia! my father's bones will soon be clattering in their grave, far away in green Glensheil, where he died for King James, Mhona.'

'Beware,' continued the old woman, 'lest you go for ever, Farquhar.'

'It is longer to *for ever* than to Beltane, and by that day I must be at the Birks of Aberfeldy.'

Then, seeing that he was determined, the crones muttered among themselves that the *tarvecoill* would fall upon him; but Farquhar Shaw, though far from being free of his native superstitions, laughed aloud, for the *tarvecoill* is a black cloud, which, if seen on a new-year's eve, is said to portend stormy weather; hence it is a proverb for a misfortune about to happen.

'You were unwise to become a soldier, Farquhar,' was their last argument.

'Why?'

'The tongue may tie a knot which the teeth cannot untie.'

'As your husbands' tongues did, when they married you all, poor men!' was the good-natured retort of Farquhar. 'But fear not for me; ere the snow begins to melt on Ben Nevis, and the sweet wallflower to bloom on the black Castle of Inverlochy, I will be with you all again,' he added, while belting his tartan-plaid about him, slinging his target on his shoulder, and whistling upon Bran, his favourite stag-hound; he then set out to join the regiment, by the nearest route, on the skirts of Ben Nevis, resolving to pass the head of Lochlevin, through Larochmohr, and the deep glens that lead towards the Braes of Rannoch, a long, desolate, and perilous journey, but with his sword, his pistols, and gigantic hound to guard him, his plaid for a covering, and the purple heather for a bed wherever he halted, Farquhar feared nothing.

His faithful dog Bran, which had shared his couch and plaid since the time when it was a puppy, was a noble specimen of the Scottish hound, which was used of old in the chase of the white bull, the wolf, and the deer, and which is in reality the progenitor of the common greyhound; for the breed has degenerated in warmer climates than the stern north. Bran (so named from Bran of old) was of such size, strength, and courage, that he was able to drag down the strongest deer; and, in the last encounter with the Caterans of Glen Nevis, he had saved the life of Farquhar, by tearing almost to pieces one who would have slain him, as he lay wounded on the field. His hair was rough and grey; his limbs were muscular and wiry; his chest was broad and deep; his keen eyes were bright as those of an eagle. Such dogs as Bran bear a prominent place in Highland song and story. They were remarkable for their sagacity and love of their master, and their solemn and dirgelike howl was ever deemed ominous and predictive of death and woe.

Bran and his master were inseparable. The noble dog had long been invaluable to him when on hunting expeditions, and now since he had become a soldier in the *Reicudan Dhu*, Bran was always on guard with him, and the sharer of all his duties; thus Farquhar was wont to assert, 'that for watchfulness on sentry, Bran's two ears were worth all the rest in the Black Watch put together.'

The sun had set before Farquhar left the green thatched clachan, and already the bases of the purple mountains were dark, though a red glow lingered on their heath-clad summits. Lest some of the Cateran band, of whose malevolence he was now the object, might already have knowledge or suspicion of his departure and be watching him with lynx-like eyes from behind some rock or bracken bush, he pursued for a time a path which led to the westward, until the darkness closed completely in; and then, after casting round him a rapid and searching glance, he struck at once into the old secluded drove-way or Fingalian road, which descended through the deep gorge of Corriehoilzie towards the mouth of Glencoe.

On his left towered Ben Nevis – or 'the Mountain of Heaven' – sublime and vast, four thousand three hundred feet and more in height, with its pale summits gleaming in the starlight, under a coating of eternal snow. On his right lay deep glens yawning between pathless mountains that arose in piles above each other, their sides torn and rent by a thousand watercourses, exhibiting rugged banks of rock and gravel, fringed by green waving bracken leaves and black whin bushes, or jagged by masses of stone, lying in piles and heaps, like the black, dreary, and Cyclopean ruins 'of an earlier world'. Before him lay the wilderness of Larochmohr, a scene of solitary and solemn grandeur, where, under the starlight, every feature of the landscape, every waving bush, or silver birch; every bare scalp of porphyry, and every granite block, torn by storms from the cliffs above; every rugged watercourse, tearing in foam through its deep marl bed between the tufted heather, seemed shadowy, unearthly, and weird – dark and mysterious; and all combined, were more than enough to impress with solemnity the thoughts of any man, but more especially those of a Highlander; for the savage grandeur and solitude of that district at such an hour the gloaming – were alike, to use a paradox, soothing and terrific.

There was no moon. Large masses of crape-like vapour sailed across the blue sky, and by gradually veiling the stars, made yet darker the gloomy path which Farquhar had to traverse. Even the dog Bran seemed impressed by the unbroken stillness, and trotted close as a shadow by the bare legs of his master.

For a time Farquhar Shaw had thought only of the blood-thirsty Caterans, who in their mood of vengeance at the Black Watch in general, and at him in particular, would have hewn him to pieces without mercy; but now as the distance increased between himself and their haunts by the shores of the Lochy and Eil, other thoughts arose in his mind, which gradually became a prey to the superstition incident alike to his age and country, as all the wild tales he had heard of that sequestered district, and indeed of that identical glen which he was then traversing, crowded upon his memory, until he, Farquhar Shaw, who would have faced any six men sword in hand, or would have charged a grape-shotted battery without fear, actually sighed with apprehension at the waving of a hazel bush on the lone hill side.

Of many wild and terrible things this *locale* was alleged to be the scene, and with some of these the Highland reader may be as familiar as Farquhar.

A party of the Black Watch in the summer of 1738, had marched up the glen, under the command of Corporal Malcolm

MacPherson (of whom more anon), with orders to seize a flock of sheep and arrest the proprietor, who was alleged to have 'lifted' (*i.e.*, stolen) them from the Camerons of Lochiel. The soldiers found the flock to the number of three hundred, grazing on a hill side, all fat black-faced sheep with fine long wool, and seated near them, crook in hand, upon a fragment of rock, they found the person (one of the Caterans already referred to) who was alleged to have stolen them. He was a strange-looking old fellow, with a long white beard that flowed below his girdle; he was attended by two huge black dogs of fierce and repulsive aspect. He laughed scornfully when arrested by the corporal, and hollowly the echoes of his laughter rang among the rocks, while his giant hounds bayed and erected their bristles, and their eyes flashed as if emitting sparks of fire.

The soldiers now surrounded the sheep and drove them down the hill side into the glen, from whence they proceeded towards Maryburgh, with a piper playing in front of the flock, for it is known that sheep will readily follow the music of the pipe. The Black Watch were merry with their easy capture, but none in MacPherson's party were so merry as the captured shepherd, whom, for security, the corporal had fettered to the left hand of his brother Samuel; and in this order they proceeded for three miles, until they reached a running stream; when, lo! the whole of the three hundred fat sheep and the black dogs turned into clods of brown earth; and, with a wild mocking laugh that seemed to pass away on the wind which swept the mountain waste, their shepherd vanished, and no trace of his presence remained but the empty ring of the fetters which dangled from the left wrist of Samuel MacPherson, who felt every hair on his head bristle under his bonnet with terror and affright.

This sombre glen was also the abode of the *Daoine Shie*, or Good Neighbours, as they are named in the Lowlands; and of this fact the wife of the pay-sergeant of Farquhar's own company could bear terrible evidence. These imps are alleged to have a strange love for abstracting young girls and women great with child, and leaving in their places bundles of dry branches or withered reeds in the resemblance of the person thus abstracted, but to all appearance dead or in a trance; they are also exceeding partial to having their own bantlings nursed by human mothers.

The wife of the sergeant (who was Duncan Campbell of the family of Duncaves) was without children, but was ever longing to possess one, and had drunk of all the holy wells in the neighbourhood without finding herself much benefited thereby. On a summer evening when the twilight was lingering on the hills, she was seated at her cottage door gazing listlessly on the waters of the Eil, which were reddened by the last flush of the west, when suddenly a little man and woman of strange aspect appeared before her – so suddenly that they seemed to have sprung from the ground – and offered her a child to nurse. Her husband, the sergeant, was absent on duty at Dumbarton; the poor lonely woman had no one to consult, or from whom to seek permission, and she at once accepted the charge as one long coveted.

'Take this pot of ointment,' said the man, impressively, giving Moina Campbell a box made of shells, 'and be careful from time to time to touch the eyelids of our child therewith.'

'Accept this purse of money,' said the woman, giving her a small bag of green silk; ''tis our payment in advance, and anon we will come again.'

The quaint little father and mother then each blew a breath upon the face of the child and disappeared, or as the sergeant's wife said, seemed to melt away into the twilight haze. The money given by the woman was gold and silver; but Moina knew not its value, for the coins were ancient, and bore the head of King Constantine IV. The child was a strange, pale and wan little creature, with keen, bright, and melancholy eyes; its lean freakish hands were almost transparent, and it was ever sad and moaning. Yet in the care of the sergeant's wife it throve bravely, and always after its eyes were touched with the ointment it laughed, crowed, screamed, and exhibited such wild joy that it became almost convulsed.

This occurred so often that Moina felt tempted to apply the ointment to her own eyes, when lo! she perceived a group of the dwarfish *Daoine Shie* – little men in trunk hose and sugar-loaf hats, and little women in hoop petticoats and all of a green colour – dancing round her, and making grimaces and antic gestures to amuse the child, which to her horror she was now convinced was a bantling of the spirits who dwelt in Larochmohr!

What was she to do? To offend or seem to fear them was dangerous, and though she was now daily tormented by seeing these green imps about her, she affected unconsciousness and seemed to observe them not; but prayed in her heart for her husband's speedy return, and to be relieved of her fairy charge, to whom she faithfully performed her trust, for in time the child grew strong and beautiful; and when, again on a twilight eve, the parents came to claim it, the woman wept as it was taken from her, for she had learned to love the little creature, though it belonged neither to heaven nor earth.

Some months after, Moina Campbell, more lonely now than ever, was passing through Larochmohr, when suddenly within the circle of a large green fairy ring, she saw thousands, yea myriads of little imps in green trunk hose and with sugar-loaf hats, dancing and making merry, and amid them were the child she had nursed and its parents also, and in terror and distress she addressed herself to them.

The tiny voices within the charmed circle were hushed in an instant, and all the little men and women became filled with anger. Their little faces grew red, and their little eyes flashed fire.

'How do *you* see us?' demanded the father of the fairy child, thrusting his little conical hat fiercely over his right eye.

'Did I not nurse your child, my friend!' said Moina, trembling.

'But how do you *see us?*' screamed a thousand little voices.

Moina trembled, and was silent.

'Oho!' exclaimed all the tiny voices, like a breeze of wind, 'she has been using our ointment, the insolent mortal!'

'I can alter that,' said one fairy man (who being three feet high was a giant among his fellows), as he blew upward in her face, and in an instant all the green multitude vanished from her sight; she saw only the fairy ring and the green bare sides of the silent glen. Of all the myriads she had seen, not one was visible now.

'Fear not, Moina,' cried a little voice from the hill side, 'for your husband will prosper.' It was the fairy child who spoke.

'But his fate will follow him,' added another voice, angrily.

Full of fear the poor woman returned to her cottage, from which, to her astonishment, she had been absent ten days and nights; but she saw her husband no more: in the meantime he had embarked for a foreign land, being gazetted to an ensigncy; thus so far the fairy promise of his prospering proved true.

Another story flitted through Farquhar's mind, and troubled him quite as much as its predecessors. In a shieling here a friend of his, when hunting, one night sought shelter. Finding a fire already lighted therein he became alarmed, and clambering into the roof sat upon the cross rafters to wait the event, and ere long there entered a little old man two feet in height. His head, hands, and feet were enormously large for the size of his person; his nose was long, crooked, and of a scarlet hue; his eyes brilliant as diamonds, and they glared in the light of the fire. He took from his back a bundle of reeds, and tying them together, proceeded to blow upon them from his huge mouth and distended cheeks, and as he blew, a skin crept over the dry bundle, which gradually began to assume the appearance of a human face and form.

These proceedings were more than the huntsman on his perch above could endure, and filled by dread that the process below might end in a troublesome likeness of himself, he dropped a six pence into his pistol (for everything evil is proof to *lead*) and fired straight at the huge head of the spirit or gnome, which vanished with a shriek, tearing away in his wrath and flight the whole of the turf wall on one side of the shieling, which was thus in a moment reduced to ruin.

These memories, and a thousand others of spectral Druids and tall ghastly warriors, through whose thin forms the twinkling stars would shine (but these orbs were hidden now) as they hovered by grey cairns and the grassy graves of old, crowded on the mind of Farquhar; for there were then, and even now *are*, more ghosts, devils, and hobgoblins in the Scottish Highlands than ever were laid of yore in the Red Sea. Nor need we be surprised at this superstition in the early days of the Black Watch, when Dr. Henry tells us, in 1831, that within the last twenty years, when a couple agreed to marry in Orkney, they went to the Temple of the Moon, which was semi-circular, and then, on her knees, the woman solemnly invoked the spirit of Woden!

Farquhar, as he strode on, comforted himself with the reflection that those who are born at night – as his mother had a hundred times told him he had been – *never saw spirits*; so he took a good dram from his hunting-flask, and belted his plaid tighter about him, after making a sign of the cross three times, as a protection against all the diablerie of the district, but chiefly against a certain malignant fiend or spirit, who was wont to howl at night among the rocks of Larochmohr, to hurl storms of snow into the deep vale of Corriehoilzie, and toss huge blocks of granite into the deep blue waters of Loch Leven. He shouted on Bran, whistled the march of the Black Watch, 'to keep his spirits cheery,' and pushed on his way up the mountains, while the broad rain drops of a coming tempest plashed heavily in his face.

He looked up to the 'Hill of Heaven.' The night clouds were gathering round its awful summit, wheeling, eddying, and floating in whirlwinds from the dark chasms of rock that yawn in its sides. The growling of the thunder among the riven peaks of granite overhead announced that a tempest was at hand; but though Farquhar Shaw had come of a brave and adventurous race, and feared nothing *earthly*, he could not repress a shudder lest the mournful gusts of the rising wind might bear with them the cry of the *Tar Uisc*, the terrible Water Bull, or the shrieks of the spirit of the storm!

The lonely man continued to toil up that wilderness till he reached the shoulder of the mountain, where, on his right, opened the black narrow gorge, in the deep bosom of which lay Loch Leven, and, on his left, opened the glens that led towards Loch Treig, the haunt of *Damh mohr a Vonalia*, or Enchanted Stag, which was alleged to live for ever, and be proof to mortal weapons; and now, like a tornado of the tropics, the storm burst forth in all its fury!

The wind seemed to shriek around the mountain summits and to bellow in the gorges below, while the thunder hurtled across the sky, and the lightning, green and ghastly, flashed about the rocks of Loch Leven, shedding, ever and anon, for an instant, a sudden gleam upon its narrow stripe of water, and on the brawling torrents that roared down the mountain sides, and were swelling fast to floods, as the rain, which had long been falling on the frozen summit of Ben Nevis, now descended in a broad and blinding torrent that was swept by the stormy wind over hill and over valley. As Farquhar staggered on, a gleam of lightning revealed to him a little turf shieling under the brow of a pine-covered rock, and making a vigorous effort to withstand the roaring wind, which tore over the bare waste with all the force and might of a solid and palpable body, he reached it on his hands and knees. After securing the rude door, which was composed of three cross bars, he flung himself on the earthen floor of the hut, breathless and exhausted, while Bran, his dog, as if awed by the elemental war without, crept close beside him.

As Farquhar's thoughts reverted to all that he had heard of the district, he felt all a Highlander's native horror of remaining in the *dark* in a place so weird and wild; and on finding near him a quantity of dry wood – bog-pine and oak, stored up, doubtless, by some thrifty and provident shepherd – he produced his flint and tinder-box, struck a light, and, with all the readiness of a soldier and huntsman, kindled a fire in a corner of the shieling, being determined that if it was the place where, about 'the hour when churchyards yawn and graves give up their dead,' the brownies were alleged to assemble, they should not come upon him unseen or unawares.

Having a venison steak in his haversack, he placed it on the embers to broil, heaped fresh fuel on his fire, and drawing his plaid round Bran and himself, wearied by the toil of his journey on foot in such a night, and over such a country, he gradually dropped asleep, heedless alike of the storm which raved and bellowed in the dark glens below, and round the bare scalps of the vast mountain whose mighty shadows, when falling eastward at eve, darken even the Great Glen of Albyn.

In his sleep, the thoughts of Farquhar Shaw wandered to his comrades, then at the Birks of Aberfeldy. He dreamt that a long time – how long he knew not – had elapsed since he had been in their ranks; but he saw the Laird of Finab, his captain, surveying him with a gloomy brow, while the faces of friends and comrades were averted from him.

'Why is this – how is this?' he demanded.

Then he was told that the *Reicudan Dhu* were disgraced by the desertion of three of its soldiers, who, on that day, were to die, and the regiment was paraded to witness their fate. The scene with all its solemnity and all its terrors grew vividly before him; he heard the lamenting wail of the pipe as the three doomed men marched slowly past, each behind his black coffin, and the scene of this catastrophe was far, far away, he knew not where; but it seemed to be in a strange country, and then the scene, the sights, and the voices of the people, were foreign to him. In the background, above the glittering bayonets and blue bonnets of the Black Watch, rose a lofty castle of foreign aspect, having a square keep or tower, with four turrets, the vanes of which were shining in the early morning sun. In his ears floated the drowsy hum of a vast and increasing multitude.

Farquhar trembled in every limb as the doomed men passed so near him that he could see their breasts heave as they breathed; but their faces were concealed from him, for each had his head muffled in his plaid, according to the old Highland fashion, when imploring mercy or quarter.

Lots were cast with great solemnity for the firing party or executioners, and, to his horror, Farquhar found himself one of the twelve men chosen for this, to every soldier, most obnoxious duty!

When the time came for firing, and the three unfortunates were kneeling opposite, each within his coffin, and each with his head muffled in a plaid, Farquhar mentally resolved to close his eyes and fire at random against the wall of the castle opposite; but some mysterious and irresistible impulse compelled him to look for a moment, and lo! the plaid had fallen from the face of one of the doomed men, and, to his horror, the dreamer beheld *himself!*

His own face was before him, but ghastly and pale, and his own eyes seemed to be glaring back upon him with affright, while their aspect was wild, sad, and haggard. The musket dropped from his hand, a weakness seemed to overspread his limbs, and writhing in agony at the terrible sight, while a cold perspiration rolled in bead-drops over his clammy brow, the dreamer started, and awoke, when a terrible voice, low but distinct, muttered in his ear –

'*Farquhar Shaw, bithidh duil ri fear feachd, ach cha bhi duil ri fear lic!*'*

He leaped to his feet with a cry of terror, and found that he was *not* alone, as a little old woman was crouching near the embers of his fire, while Bran, his eyes glaring, his bristles erect, was growling at her with a fierce angry sound, that rivalled the bellowing of the storm, which still continued to rave without.

The aspect of this hag was strange. In the light of the fire which brightened occasionally as the wind swept through the crannies of the shieling, her eyes glittered, or rather glared like fiery sparks; her nose was hooked and sharp; her mouth like an ugly gash; her hue was livid and pale. Her outward attire was a species of yellow mantle, which enveloped her whole form; and her hands, which played or twisted nervously in the generous warmth of the glowing embers, resembled a bundle of freakish knots, or the talons of an aged bird. She muttered to herself at times, and after turning her terrible red eyes twice or thrice covertly and wickedly towards Farquhar, she suddenly snatched the venison steak from amid the flames, and, with a chuckle of satisfaction, devoured it steaming hot, and covered

---

* A man may return from an expedition; but there is no hope that he may return from the grave. – *Gaelic Proverb.*

as it was with burning cinders.

On Farquhar secretly making a sign of the cross, when beholding this strange proceeding, she turned sharply with a savage expression towards him, and rose to her full stature, which was not more than three feet; and he felt, he knew not why, his heart tremble; for his spirit was already perturbed by the effect of his terrible dream, and clutching the steel collar of Bran (who was preparing to spring at this strange visitor, and seemed to like her aspect as little as his master) he said –

'Woman, who are you?'

'A traveller like yourself, perhaps. But who are *you*?' she asked in a croaking voice.

'Do you know our proverb in Lochaber –

What sent the messengers to hell,
But asking what they knew full well?'

was the reply of Farquhar, as he made a vigorous effort to restrain Bran, whose growls and fury were fast becoming quite appalling; and at this proverb the eyes of the hag seemed to blaze with fresh anger, while her figure became more than ever erect.

'Oich! oich!' grumbled Farquhar, 'I would as readily have had the devil as this ugly hag. I have got a shelter, certainly; but with her 'tis out of the cauldron and into the fire. Had she been a brown-eyed lass, to a share of my plaid she had been welcome; but this wrinkled *cailloch* – down, Bran, down!' he added aloud, as the strong hound strained in his collar, and tasked his master's hand and arm to keep him from springing at the intruder.

'Is this kind or manly of you,' she asked, 'to keep a wild brute that behaves thus, and to a woman too? Turn him out into the storm; the wind and rain will soon cool his wicked blood.'

'Thank you; but in that you must excuse me. Bran and I are as brothers.'

'Turn him out, I say,' screamed the hag, 'or worse may befall him!'

'I shall not turn him out woman,' said Farquhar, firmly, while surveying the stranger with some uneasiness; for, to his startled gaze, she seemed to have grown *taller* within the last five minutes. 'You have a share of our shelter, and you have had all our supper; but to turn out poor Bran – no, no, that would never do.'

To this Bran added a roar of rage, and the fear or fury which blazed in the eyes of the woman fully responded to those of the now infuriated staghound. The glances of each made those of the other more and more fierce.

'Down, Bran; down, I say,' said Farquhar. 'What the devil hath possessed the dog? I never saw him behave thus before. He must be savage, mother, that you left him none of the savoury venison steak; for all the supper we had was that road-collop from one of MacGillony's brown cattle.'

'MacGillony,' muttered the hag, spreading her talon-like hands over the embers; 'I knew him well.'

'You!' exclaimed Farquhar.

'I have said so,' she replied with a grin.

'He was a mighty hunter five hundred years ago, who lived and died on the Grampians!'

'And what are five hundred years to me, who saw the waters of the deluge pour through Corriehoilzie, and subside from the slope of Ben Nevis?'

'This is a very good joke, mother,' said poor Farquhar, attempting to laugh, while the hideous old woman, who was so small when he first saw her as to be almost a dwarf, was now, palpably, veritably, and without doubt, nearly a head taller than himself; and watchfully he continued to gaze on her, keeping one hand on his dirk and the other on the collar of Bran, whose growls were louder now than the storm that careered through the rocky glen below.

'Woman!' said Farquhar, boldly, 'my mind misgives me – there is something about you that I little like; I have just had a dreadful dream.'

'A morning dream, too!' chuckled the hag with an elfish grin.

'So I connect your presence here with it.'

'Be it so.'

'What may that terrible dream foretell?' pondered Farquhar; 'for morning dreams are but warnings and presages unsolved. The blessings of God and all his saints be about me!'

At these words the beldame uttered a loud laugh.

'You are, I presume, a Protestant?' said Farquhar, uneasily.

At this suggestion she laughed louder still, but seemed to grow more and more in stature, till Farquhar became well-nigh sick at heart with astonishment and fear, and began to revolve in his mind the possibility of reaching the door of the shieling and rushing out into the storm, there to commit himself to Providence and the elements. Besides, as her stature grew, her eyes waxed redder and brighter, and her malevolent hilarity increased.

It was a fiend, a demon of the wild, by whom he was now visited and tormented in that sequestered hut.

His heart sank, and as her terrible eyes seemed to glare upon him, and pierce his very soul, a cold perspiration burst over all his person.

'Why do you grasp your dirk, Farquhar – ha! ha!' she asked.

'For the same reason that I hold Bran – to be ready. Am I not one of the King's *Reicudan Dhu*? But how you know my name?'

''Tis a trifle to me, who knew MacGillony.'

'From whence came you to-night?'

'From the Isle of Wolves,' she replied, with a shout of laughter.

'A story as likely as the rest,' said Farquhar, 'for that isle is in the Western sea, near unto Coll, the country of the Clan Gillian. You must travel fast.'

'Those usually do who travel on the skirts of the wind.'

'Woman!' exclaimed Farquhar, leaping up with an emotion of terror which he could no longer control, for her stature now overtopped his own, and ere long her hideous head would touch the rafters of the hut; 'thou art either a liar or a fiend! which shall I deem thee?'

'Whichever pleases you most,' she replied, starting to her feet.

'Bran, to the proof!' cried Farquhar, drawing his dirk, and preparing to let slip the now maddened hound; 'at her, Bran, and hold her down. Good, dog – brave dog! oich, he has a slippery handful that grasps an eel by the tail! at her, Bran, for thou art strong as Cuchullin.'

Uttering a roar of rage, the savage dog made a wild bound at the hag, who, with a yell of spite and defiance, and with a wondrous activity, by one spring, left the shieling, and dashing the frail door to fragments in her passage, rushed out into the dark and tempestuous night, pursued by the infuriated but baffled Bran – baffled now, though the fleetest hound on the Braes of Lochaber.

They vanished together in the obscurity, while Farquhar gazed from the door breathless and terrified. The storm still howled in the valley, where the darkness was opaque and dense, save when a solitary gleam of lightning flashed on the ghastly rocks and narrow defile of Loch Leven; and the roar of the bellowing wind as it tore through the rocky gorges and deep granite chasms, had in its sound something more than usually terrific. But, hark! other sounds came upon the skirts of that hurrying storm.

The shrieks of a fiend, if they could be termed so; – for they were shrill and high, like cries of pain and laughter mingled. Then came the loud deep baying, with the yells of a dog, as if in rage and pain, while a thousand sparks, like those of a rocket, glittered for a moment in the blackness of the glen, below. The heart of Farquhar Shaw seemed to stand still for a time, while, dirk in hand, he continued to peer into the dense obscurity. Again came the cries of Bran, but nearer and nearer now; and in an instant more, the noble hound sprang, with a loud whine, to his master's side, and sank at his feet. It was Bran, the fleet, the strong, the faithful and the brave; but in what a condition. Torn, lacerated, covered with blood and frightful wounds – disembowelled and dying; for the poor animal had only strength to loll out his hot tongue in an attempt to lick his master's hand before he expired.

'Mother Mary,' said Farquhar, taking off his bonnet, inspired with horror and religious awe, 'keep thy blessed hand over me, for my dog has fought with a demon!'

It may be imagined how Farquhar passed the remainder of that morning – sleepless and full of terrible thoughts, for the palpable memory of his dream, and the episode which followed it, were food enough for reflection.

With dawn, the storm subsided. The sun arose in a cloudless sky, the blue mists were wreathed round the brows of Ben Nevis, and a beautiful rainbow seemed to spring from the side of the mountain far beyond the waters of Loch Leven; the dun deer were cropping the wet glistening herbage among the grey rocks; the little birds sang early, and the proud eagle and ferocious gled were soaring towards the rising sun; thus all nature gave promise of a serene summer day.

With his dirk, Farquhar dug a grave for Bran, and lined it with soft and fragrant heather, and there he covered him up and piled a cairn, at which he gave many a sad and backward glance (for it marked where a faithful friend and companion lay) as he ascended the huge mountains of rock, which, on one hand, led to the *Uisc Dhu*, or Vale of the Black Water, and on the other, by the tremendous steep named the Devil's Staircase, to the mouth of Glencoe.

In due time he reached the regiment at its cantonments on the Birks of Aberfeldy, where the independent companies, for the first time were exercised as a battalion by their Lieutenant-Colonel, Sir Robert Munro of Culcairn, who, six years afterwards, was slain at the battle of Falkirk.

Farquhar's terrible dream and adventure in that Highland wilderness were ever before him, and the events subsequent to the formation of the Black Watch into a battalion, with the excitement produced among its soldiers by an unexpected order *to march into England*, served to confirm the gloom that preyed upon his spirits.

The story of how the Black Watch were deceived is well known in the Highlands, though it is only one of the many acts of treachery performed in those days by the British Government in their transactions with the people of that country, when seeking to lessen the adherents of the Stuart cause, and ensnare them into regiments for service in distant lands; hence the many dangerous mutinies which occurred after the enrolment of all the *old* Highland corps.

This unexpected order to march into England caused such a dangerous ferment in the Black Watch, as being a violation of the principles and promise under which it was enrolled, and on which so many Highland gentlemen of good family enlisted in its ranks, that the Lord President, Duncan Forbes of Culloden, warned General Clayton, the Scottish Commander-in-Chief, of the evil effects likely to occur if this breach of faith was persisted in, and to prevent the corps from revolting *en masse*, that officer informed the soldiers that they were to enter England 'solely to be seen by King George, who had never seen a highland soldier, and had been graciously pleased to express, or feel great curiosity on the subject'.

Cajoled and flattered by this falsehood, the soldiers of the *Reicudan Dhu,* all unaware that shipping was ordered to convey them to Flanders, began their march for England, in the end of March, 1743; and if other proof be wanting that they were deluded, the following announcement in the *Caledonian Mercury* of that year affords it:–

'On Wednesday last, the Lord Sempills Regiment of Highlanders began their march for England, *in order to be reviewed by his Majesty.*'

Everywhere on the march throughout the north of England, they were received with cordiality and hospitality by the people, to whom their garb, aspect, and equipment were a source of interest, and in return, the gentlemen and soldiers of the *Reicudan Dhu* behaved to the admiration of their officers and of all magistrates; but as they drew nearer to London, according to Major Grose, they were exposed to the malevolent mockery and the national 'taunts of the true-bred English clowns, and became gloomy and sullen. Animated even to the humblest private with the feelings of gentlemen,' continues this English officer, 'they could ill brook the rudeness of boors, nor could they patiently submit to affronts in a country to which they had been called by the *invitation* of their sovereign.'

On the 30th April, the regiment reached London, and on the 14th May was reviewed on Finchley Common, by Marshal Wade, before a vast concourse of spectators; but the King, whom they expected to be present, had sailed from Greenwich for Hanover on the same night they entered the English metropolis. Herein they found themselves deceived; for 'the King had told them a lie,' and the spark thus kindled was soon fanned into a flame.

After the review at Finchley Common, Farquhar Shaw and Corporal Malcolm MacPherson were drinking in a tavern, when three English gentlemen entered, and seating themselves at the same table, entered into conversation, by praising the regiment, their garb, their country, and saying those compliments which are so apt to win the heart of a Scotchman when far from home; and the glens of the Gael seemed then indeed, far, far away, to the imagination of the simple souls who manned the Black Watch in 1743.

Both Farquhar and the corporal being gentlemen, wore the wing of the eagle in their bonnets, and were well educated, and spoke English with tolerable fluency.

'I would that his Majesty had seen us, however,' said the corporal; 'we have had a long march south from our own country on a bootless errand.'

'Can you possibly be so simple as to believe that the King cared a rush on the subject?' asked a gentleman, with an incredulous smile; for he and his companions, like many others who hovered about these new soldiers, were Jacobites and political incendiaries.

'What mean you, sir?' demanded MacPherson, with surprise.

'Why, you simpleton, that story of the King wishing to see you was all a table of a tub – a snare.'

'A snare!'

'Yes – a pretext of the ministry to lure you to this distance from your own country, and then transport you bodily for life.'

'To where?'

'Oh, that matters little – perhaps to the American plantations.'

'Or, to Botany Bay,' suggested another, maliciously; 'but take another jorum of brandy, and fear nothing; wherever you go, it can't well be a worse place than your own country.'

'Thanks, gentlemen,' replied Farquhar, loftily, while his hands played nervously with his dirk; 'we want no more of your brandy.'

'Believe me, sirs,' resumed their informant and tormentor,

'the real object of the ministry is to get as many fighting men, Jacobites and so forth, out of the Highlands as possible. This is merely part of a new system of government.'

'Sirs,' exclaimed Farquhar, drawing his dirk with an air of gravity and determination which caused his new friends at once to put the table between him and them, 'will you swear this upon the dirk?'

'How – why?'

'Upon the Holy Iron – we know no oath more binding,' continued the Highlander, with an expression of quiet entreaty.

'I'll swear it by the Holy Poker, or anything you please,' replied the Englishman, reassured on finding the Celt had no hostile intentions.

''Tis all a fact,' he continued, winking to his companions, 'for so my good friend Phil Yorke, the Lord Chancellor, who expects soon to be Earl of Hardwick, informed me.'

The eyes of the corporal flashed with indignation; and Farquhar struck his forehead as the memory of his terrible dream in the haunted glen rushed upon his memory.

'Oh! yes,' said a third gentleman, anxious to add his mite to the growing mischief; 'it is all a Whig plot of which you are the victims, as our kind ministry hope that you will all die off like sheep with the rot; or like the Marine Corps; or the Invalids, the old 41st, in Jamaica.'

'They dare not deceive us!' exclaimed MacPherson, striking the basket-hilt of his claymore.

'Dare not!'

'No.'

'Indeed – why?'

'For in the country of the clans fifty thousand claymores would be on the grindstone to avenge us!'

A laugh followed this outburst.

'King George made you rods to scourge your own

countrymen, and now, as useless rods, you are to be flung into the fire,' said the first speaker, tauntingly.

'By God and Mary!' began MacPherson, again laying a hand on his sword with sombre fury.

'Peace, Malcolm,' interposed Farquhar; 'the Saxon is right, and we have been fooled. *Bithidh gach ni mar is aill Dhiu.* (All things must be as God will have them.) Let us seek the *Reicudan Dhu*, and woe to the Saxon clowns and to that German churl, their King, if they have deceived us!'

On the march back to London, MacPherson and Farquhar Shaw brooded over what they had heard at Finchley; while to other members of the regiment similar communications had been made, and thus, ere nightfall, every soldier of the Black Watch felt assured that he had been entrapped by a royal falsehood, which the sudden, and to them unaccountable, departure of George II to Hanover seemed beyond all doubt to confirm.

'In those whom he knows,' according to General Stewart, 'a Highlander will repose perfect confidence, and if they are his superiors will be obedient and respectful; but ere a stranger can obtain this *confidence*, he must show that he *merits* it. When once it is given, it is constant and unreserved; but if confidence be lost, no man is more suspicious. Every officer of a Highland regiment, on his first joining the corps, must have observed in his little transactions with the men how minute and strict they are in every item; but when once confidence is established, scrutiny ceases, and his word or nod of assent is as good as his bond. In the case in question (the Black Watch), notwithstanding the arts which were practised to mislead the men, they proceeded to no violence, but believing themselves deceived and betrayed, the only remedy that occurred to them was to get back to their own country.'

The memory of the commercial ruin at Darien, and of the massacre at Glencoe (the Cawnpore of King William), were too

fresh in every Scottish breast not to make the flame of discontent and mistrust spread like wildfire; and thus, long before
the bell of St. Paul's had tolled the hour of midnight, the con-
viction that he had been betrayed was firmly rooted in the
mind of every soldier of the Black Watch, and measures to baffle
those who had deluded and lured them so far from their native
mountains were at once proposed, and as quickly acted upon.

At this crisis, the dream of Farquhar was constantly before
him, as a foreboding of the terrors to come, and he strove to
thrust it from him; but the words of that terrible warning – a
man may return from an expedition, but never from the
grave – seemed ever in his ears!

On the night after the review, the whole regiment, except
its officers, most of whom knew what was on the *tapis*, assembled at twelve o'clock on a waste common near Highgate. The
whole were in heavy marching order; and by direction of
Corporal Malcolm MacPherson, after carefully priming and
loading with ball-cartridge, they commenced their march in
silence and secrecy and with all speed for Scotland – a wild,
daring, and romantic attempt, for they were heedless and
ignorant of the vast extent of hostile country that lay between
them and their homes, and scarcely knew the route to pursue.
They had now but three common ideas, – to keep together, to
resist to the last, and to march *north*.

With some skill and penetration they avoided the two great
highways, and marched by night from wood to wood,
concealing themselves by day so well, that for some time no
one knew how or where they had gone, though, by the Lords
Justices orders had been issued to all officers commanding
troops between London and the Scottish Borders to overtake
or intercept them; but the 19th May arrived before tidings
reached the metropolis that the Black Watch, one thousand
strong, had passed Northampton, and a body of Marshal Wade's

Horse (now better known as the 3rd or Prince of Wales's Dragoon Guards) overtook them, when faint by forced and rapid marches, by want of food, of sleep and shelter, the unfortunate regiment had entered Ladywood, about four miles from the market town of Oundle-on-the-Nen, and had, as usual, concealed themselves in a spacious thicket, which, by nine o'clock in the evening, was completely environed by strong columns of English cavalry under General Blakeney.

Captain Ball, of Wade's Horse, approached their bivouac in the dusk, bearer of a flag of truce, and was received by the poor fellows with every respect, and Farquhar Shaw, as interpreter for his comrades, heard his demands, which were, 'that the whole battalion should lay down its arms, and surrender at discretion as mutineers.'

'Hitherto we have conducted ourselves quietly and peacefully in the land of those who have deluded and wronged us, even as they wronged and deluded our forefathers,' replied Farquhar; 'but it may not be so for one day more. Look upon us, sir; we are famished, worn, and desperate. It would move the heart of a stone to know all we have suffered by hunger and thirst, even in this land of plenty.'

'The remedy is easy,' said the captain.

'Name it, sir.'

'Submit.'

'We have no such word in our mother-tongue, then how shall I translate it to my comrades, so many of whom are gentlemen?'

'That is your affair, not mine. I give you but the terms dictated by General Blakeney.'

'Let the general send us a written promise.'

'Written?' reiterated the captain, haughtily.

'By his own hand,' continued the Highlander, emphatically; 'for here in this land of strangers we know not whom to trust when our King has deceived us.'

'And to what must the general pledge himself?'

'That our arms shall not be taken away, and that a free pardon be given to all.'

'Otherwise –'

'We will rather be cut to pieces.'

'This is your decision?'

'It is,' replied Farquhar, sternly.

'Be assured it is a rash one.'

'I weigh my words, Saxon, ere I speak them. No man among us will betray his comrade; we are all for one and one for all in the ranks of the *Reicudan Dhu!*'

The captain reported the result of his mission to the general, who, being well aware that the Highlanders had been entrapped by the Government on one hand, and inflamed to revolt by Jacobite emissaries on the other, was humanely willing to temporize with them, and sent the captain to them once more.

'Surrender yourselves prisoners,' said Ball; 'lay down your arms, and the general will use all his influence in your favour with the Lords Justices.'

'We know of no Lords Justices,' they replied. 'We acknowledge no authority but the officers who speak our mother-tongue, and our native chiefs who share our blood. To be without arms, in our country, is in itself to be dishonoured.'

'Is this still the resolution of your comrades?' asked Captain Ball.

'It is, on my honour as a gentleman and soldier,' replied Farquhar.

The English captain smiled at these words, for he knew not the men with whom he had to deal.

'Hitherto, my comrade,' said he, 'I have been your friend, and the friend of the regiment, and am still anxious to do all I can to save you; but, if you continue in open revolt one hour longer, surrounded as you all are by the King's troops, not a man of you can survive the attack, and be assured that even I, for one, will give quarter to none! Consider well my words – you may survive banishment for a time, but from the grave there is no return.'

'The words of my dream!' exclaimed Farquhar, in an agitated tone of voice; '*Bithidh duil ri fear feachd, ach cha bhi duil ri fear lic*. God and Mary, how come they from the lips of this Saxon captain?'

The excitement of the regiment was now so great that Captain Ball requested of Farquhar that two Highlanders should conduct him safely from the wood. Two *duinewassals* of the Clan Chattan, both corporals, named MacPherson, stepped forward, blew the priming from their pans, and accompanied him to the outposts of his own men – the Saxon *Seidar Dearg*, or Red English soldiers, as the Celts named them.

Here, on parting from them, the good captain renewed his entreaties and promises, which so far won the confidence of the corporals, that, after returning to the regiment, the whole body, in consequence of their statements, agreed to lay down their arms and submit the event to Providence and a court-martial of officers, believing implicitly in the justice of their cause and the ultimate adherence of the Government to the letters of *local* service under which they had enlisted.

Farquhar Shaw and the two corporals of the Clan Chattan nobly offered their own lives as a ransom for the honour and liberties of the regiment, but their offer was declined; for so overwhelming was the force against them, that all in the battalion were alike at the mercy of the ministry. On capitulating, they were at once surrounded by strong bodies of horse, foot, and artillery, with their field-pieces grape-shotted; and the most severe measures were faithlessly and cruelly resorted to by those in authority and those in whom they trusted. While, in defiance of all stipulation and treaty with the Highlanders, the main body of the regiment was marched under escort towards Kent, to embark for Flanders, two hundred privates, chiefly gentlemen or cadets of good family, were selected from its ranks and sentenced to banishment, or service for life in Minorca, Georgia, and the Leeward Isles. The two corporals, Samuel and Malcolm MacPherson, with Farquhar Shaw, were marched back to London, to meet a more speedy, and to men of such spirit as theirs, a more welcome fate.

The examinations of some of these poor fellows prove how they had been deluded into service for the Line.

'I did not desert, sirs,' said John Stuart, a gentleman of the House of Urrard, and private in Campbell of Carrick's company. 'I repel the insinuation,' he continued, with pride; 'I wished only to go back to my father's roof and to my own glen, because the inhospitable Saxon churls abused my country and ridiculed my dress. We had no leader; we placed no man over the rest.'

'I am neither a Catholic nor a false Lowland Whig,' said another private – Gregor Grant, of the family of Rothiemurcus; 'but I am a true man, and ready to serve the King, though his actions have proved him a liar! You have said, sirs, that I am afraid to go to Flanders. I am a Highlander, and never yet saw the man I was afraid of. The Saxons told me I was to be transported to the American plantations to work with black slaves. Such was not our bargain with King George. We were but a Watch to serve along the Highland Border, and to keep broken clans from the Braes of Lochaber.'

'We were resolved not to be tricked,' added Farquhar Shaw. 'We will meet the French or Spaniards in any land you please; but we will die, sirs, rather than go, like Saxon rogues, to hoe sugar in the plantations.'

'What is your faith?' asked the president of the court-martial.

'The faith of my fathers a thousand years before the hateful sound of the Saxon drum was heard upon the Highland Border!'

'You mean that you have lived —'

'As, please God and the Blessed Mary, I shall die — a Catholic and a Highland gentleman; stooping to none and fearing none —'

'*None*, say you?'

'Save Him who sits upon the right hand of His Father in Heaven.'

As Farquhar said this with solemn energy, all the prisoners took off their bonnets and bowed their heads with a religious reverence which deeply impressed the court, but failed to save them.

On the march to the Tower of London, Farquhar was the most resolute and composed of his companions in fetters and misfortune; but on coming in sight of that ancient fortress, his firmness forsook him, the blood rushed back upon his heart, and he became deadly pale; for in a moment he recognised the castle of his strange dream — the castle having a square tower, with four vanes and turrets — and then the whole scene of his foreboding vision, when far away in lone Lochaber, came again upon his memory, while the voice of the warning spirit hovered again in his ear, and he knew that the hour of his end was pursuing him!

And now, amid crowds of country clowns and a rabble from the lowest purlieus of London, who mocked and reviled them, the poor Highlanders were marched through the streets of that mighty metropolis (to them, who had been reared in the mountain solitudes of the Gael, a place of countless wonders!) and were thrust into the Tower as prisoners under sentence.

Early on the morning of the 12th July, 1743, when the sun was yet below the dim horizon, and a frowsy fog that lingered on the river was mingling with the city's smoke to spread a gloom over the midsummer morning, all London seemed to be pouring from her many avenues towards Tower Hill, where an episode of no ordinary interest was promised to the sight-loving Cockneys – a veritable military execution, with all its stern terrors and grim solemnity.

All the troops in London were under arms, and long before daybreak had taken possession of an ample space enclosing Tower Hill, and there, conspicuous above all by their high and absurd sugar-loaf caps, were the brilliantly accoutred English and Scots Horse Grenadier Guards, the former under Viscount Cobham, the latter under Lieutenant-General John Earl of Rothes, K.T., and Governor of Duncannon; the Coldstream Guards, the Scots Fusiliers; and a sombre mass in the Highland garb of dark-green tartan, whom they surrounded with fixed bayonets.

These last were the two hundred men of the *Reicudan Dhu* selected for banishment, previous to which they were compelled to behold the death, or – as they justly deemed it – the deliberate murder under trust, of three brave gentlemen, their comrades.

The gates of the Tower revolved, and then the craped and muffled drums of the Scots Fusilier Guards were heard beating a dead march before those who were 'to return to Lochaber no more.' Between two lines of Yeomen of the Guard, who faced inwards, the three prisoners came slowly forth, surrounded by an escort with fixed bayonets, each doomed man marching behind his coffin, which was borne on the shoulders of four soldiers. On approaching the parade, each politely raised his bonnet and bowed to the assembled multitude.

'Courage, gentlemen,' said Farquhar Shaw; 'I see no gallows here. I thank God we shall not die a dog's death!'

''Tis well,' replied MacPherson, 'for honour is more precious than refined gold.'

The murmur of the multitude gradually subsided and

died away, like a breeze that passes through a forest, leaving it silent and still, and then not a sound was heard but the baleful rolling of the muffled drums and the shrill but sweet cadence of the fifes. Then came the word, *Halt!* breaking sharply the silence of the crowded arena, and the hollow sound of the three empty coffins, as they were laid on the ground, at the distance of thirty paces from the firing party.

Now the elder brother patted the shoulder of the other, as he smiled and said –

'Courage – a little time and all will be over – our spirits shall be with those of our brave forefathers.'

'No coronach will be cried over us here, and no cairn will mark in other times where we sleep in the land of the stranger.'

'Brother,' replied the other, in the same forcible language, 'we can well spare alike the coronach and the cairn, when to our kinsmen we can bequeath the death task of avenging us!'

'If that bequest be valued, then we shall not die in vain.'

Once again they all raised their bonnets and uttered a pious invocation; for now the sun was up, and in the Highland fashion – a fashion old as the days of Baal – they greeted him.

'Are you ready?' asked the provost-marshal.

'All ready,' replied Farquhar; '*moch-eirigh 'luain, a ni'n t-suain 'mhairt.*'*

This, to them, fatal 12th day of July was a *Monday*, so the proverb was solemnly applicable.

Wan, pale, and careworn they looked, but their eyes were bright, their steps steady, their bearing erect and dignified. They felt themselves victims and martyrs, whose fate would find a terrible echo in the Scottish Highlands; and need I add, that echo *was heard*, when two years afterwards Prince Charles

---

* Early rising on *Monday* gives a sound sleep on *Tuesday*. – See Macintosh's *Gaelic Proverbs*.

unfurled his standard in Glenfinnan? Thus inspired by pride of birth, of character, and of country – by inborn bravery and conscious innocence, at this awful crisis, they gazed around them without quailing, and exhibited a self-possession which excited the pity and admiration of all who beheld them.

The clock struck the fatal hour at last!

'It is my doom,' exclaimed Farquhar; 'the hour of my end hath followed me.'

They all embraced each other, and declined having their eyes bound up, but stood boldly, each at the foot of his coffin, confronting the levelled muskets of thirty privates of the Grenadier Guards, and they died like the brave men they had lived. One brief paragraph in *St. James's Chronicle* thus records their fate.

'On Monday, the 12th, at six o'clock in the morning, Samuel and Malcolm MacPherson, corporals, and Farquhar Shaw, a private-man, three of the Highland deserters, were shot upon the parade of the Tower pursuant to the sentence of the court-martial. The rest of the Highland prisoners were drawn out to see the execution, and joined in their prayers with great earnestness. They behaved with perfect resolution and propriety. Their bodies were put into three coffins by three of the prisoners, *their clansmen and namesakes*, and buried in one grave, near the place of execution.'

Such is the matter-of-fact record of a terrible fate!

To the slaughter of these soldiers, and the wicked breach of faith perpetrated by the Government, may be traced much of that distrust which characterized the Seaforth Highlanders and other clan regiments in their mutinies and revolts in later years, and nothing inspired greater hatred in the hearts of those who 'rose' for Prince Charles in 1745, than the story of the deception and *murder* (for so they named it) of the three soldiers of the *Reicudan Dhu* by King George at London. 'There must have been something more than common in the case and character of these unfortunate men,' to quote the good and gallant old General Stewart of Garth, 'as Lord John Murray, who was afterwards colonel of the regiment, had portraits of them hung in his dining-room.'

This was the first episode in the history of the Black Watch, which soon after covered itself with glory by the fury of its charge at Fontenoy, and on the field of Dettingen exulted that among the dead who lay there was General Clayton, 'the Sassenach' whose specious story first lured them from the Birks of Aberfeldy.

The Medal of Brigadier Gerard (1896)

Arthur Conan Doyle

The Duke of Tarentum, or Macdonald, as his old comrades prefer to call him, was, as I could perceive, in the vilest of tempers. His grim, Scotch face was like one of those grotesque door-knockers which one sees in the Faubourg St Germain. We heard afterwards that the Emperor had said in jest that he would have sent him against Wellington in the South, but that he was afraid to trust him within the sound of the pipes. Major Charpentier and I could plainly see that he was smouldering with anger.

'Brigadier Gerard of the Hussars,' said he, with the air of

the corporal with the recruit.

I saluted.

'Major Charpentier of the Horse Grenadiers.'

My companion answered to his name.

'The Emperor has a mission for you.'

Without more ado he flung open the door and announced us.

I have seen Napoleon ten times on horseback to once on foot, and I think that he does wisely to show himself to the troops in this fashion, for he cuts a very good figure in the saddle. As we saw him now he was the shortest man out of six by a good hand's breadth, and yet I am no very big man myself, though I ride quite heavy enough for a hussar. It is evident, too, that his body is too long for his legs. With his big, round head, his curved shoulders, and his clean-shaven face, he is more like a Professor at the Sorbonne than the first soldier in France. Every man to his taste, but it seems to me that, if I could clap a pair of fine light cavalry whiskers, like my own, on to him, it would do him, it would do him no harm. He has a firm mouth, however, and his eyes are remarkable. I have seen them once turned on me in anger, and I had rather ride at a square on a spent horse than face them again. I am not a man who is easily daunted, either.

He was standing at the side of the room, away from the window, looking up at a great map of the country which was hung upon the wall. Berthier stood beside him, trying to look wise, and just as we entered, Napoleon snatched his sword impatiently from him and pointed with it on the map. He was talking fast and low, but I heard him say, 'The valley of the Meuse,' and twice he repeated 'Berlin.' As we entered, his aide-de-camp advanced to us, but the emperor stopped him and beckoned us to his side.

'You have not yet received the cross of honour, Brigadier Gerard?' he asked.

I replied that I had not, and was about to add that it was not for want of having deserved it, when he cut me short in his decided fashion.

'And you, Major?' he asked.

'No, sire.'

'Then you shall both have your opportunity now.'

He led us to the great map upon the wall and placed the tip of Berthier's sword on Rheims.

'I will be frank with you, gentlemen, as with two comrades. You have both been with me since Marengo, I believe?' He had a strangely pleasant smile, which used to light up his pale face with a kind of cold sunshine. 'Here at Rheims are our present headquarters on this the 14th of March. Very good. Here is Paris, distant by road a good twenty-five leagues. Blücher lies to the north, Schwarzenberg to the south.' He prodded at the map with the sword as he spoke.

'Now,' said he, 'the further into the country these people march, the more completely I shall crush them. They are about to advance upon Paris. Very good. Let them do so. My brother, the King of Spain, will be there with a hundred thousand men. It is to him that I send you. You will hand him this letter, a copy of which I confide to each of you. It is to tell him that I am coming at once, in two days' time, with every man and horse and gun to his relief. I must give them forty-eight hours to recover. Then straight to Paris! You understand me, gentlemen?'

Ah, if I could tell you the glow of pride which it gave me to be taken into the great man's confidence in this way. As he handed our letters to us I clicked my spurs and threw out my chest, smiling and nodding to let him know that I saw what he would be after. He smiled also, and rested his hand for a moment upon the cape of my dolman. I would have given half my arrears of pay if my mother could have seen me at that instant.

'I will show you your route,' said he, turning back to the map. 'Your orders are to ride together as far as Bazoches. You will then separate, the one making for Paris by Oulchy and Neuilly, and the other to the north by Braine, Soissons, and Senlis. Have you anything to say, Brigadier Gerard?'

I am a rough soldier, but I have words and ideas. I had begun to speak about glory and the peril of France when he cut me short.

'And you, Major Charpentier?'

'If we find our route unsafe, are we at liberty to choose another?' said he.

'Soldiers do not choose, they obey.' He inclined his head to show that we were dismissed, and turned round to Berthier. I do not know what he said, but I heard them both laughing.

Well, as you may think, we lost little time in getting upon our way. In half an hour we were riding down the High Street of Rheims, and it struck twelve o'clock as we passed the Cathedral. I had my little grey mare, Violette, the one which Sebastiani had wished to buy after Dresden. It is the fastest horse in the six brigades of light cavalry, and was only beaten by the Duke of Rovigo's racer from England. As to Charpentier, he had the kind of horse which a horse grenadier or a cuirassier would be likely to ride: a back like a bedstead, you understand, and legs like the posts. He is a hulking fellow himself, so that they looked a singular pair. And yet in his insane conceit he ogled the girls as they waved their handkerchiefs to me from the windows, and he twirled his ugly red moustache up into his eyes, just as if it were to him that their attention was addressed.

When we came out of the town we passed through the French camp, and then across the battle-field of yesterday, which was still covered both by our own poor fellows and by the Russians. But of the two the camp was the sadder sight. Our army was thawing away. The Guards were all right, though the young guard was full of conscripts. The artillery and the heavy cavalry were also good if there were more of them, but the infantry privates with their under officers looked like school-boys with their masters. And we had no reserves. When one considered that there were 80,000 Prussians to the north and 150,000 Russians and Austrians to the south, it might make even the bravest man grave.

For my own part, I confess that I shed a tear until the thought came that the Emperor was still with us, and that on that very morning he had placed his hand upon my dolman and had promised me a medal of honour. This set me singing, and I spurred Violette on, until Charpentier had to beg me to have mercy on his great, snorting, panting camel. The road was beaten into paste and rutted two feet deep by the artillery, so that he was right in saying that it was not the place for a gallop.

I have never been very friendly with this Charpentier; and now for twenty miles of the way I could not draw a word from him. He rode with his brows puckered and his chin upon his breast, like a man who is heavy with thought. More than once I asked him what was on his mind, thinking that, perhaps, with my quicker intelligence I might set the matter straight. His answer always was that it was his mission of which he was thinking, which surprised me, because, although I had never thought much of his intelligence, still it seemed to me to be impossible that anyone could be puzzled by so simple and soldierly a task.

Well, we came at last to Bazoches, where he was to take the southern road and I the northern. He half turned in his saddle before he left me, and he looked at me with a singular expression of inquiry in his face.

'What do you make of it, Brigadier?' he asked.

'Of what?'

'Of our mission.'

'Surely it is plain enough.'

'You think so? Why should the Emperor tell us his plans?'

'Because he recognized our intelligence.'

My companion laughed in a manner which I found annoying.

'May I ask what you intend to do if you find these villages full of Prussians?' he asked.

'I shall obey my orders.'

'But you will be killed.'

'Very possibly.'

He laughed again, and so offensively that I clapped my hand to my sword. But before I could tell him what I thought of his stupidity and rudeness he had wheeled his horse, and was lumbering away down the other road. I saw his big fur cap vanish over the brow of the hill, and then I rode upon my way, wondering at his conduct. From time to time I put my hand to the breast of my tunic and felt the paper crackle beneath my fingers. Ah, my precious paper, which should be turned into the little silver medal for which I had yearned so long. All the way from Braine to Sermoise I was thinking of what my mother would say when she saw it.

I stopped to give Violette a meal at a wayside auberge on the side of a hill not far from Soissons – a place surrounded by old oaks, and with so many crows that one could scarce hear one's own voice. It was from the innkeeper that I learned that Marmont had fallen back two days before, and that the Prussians were over the Aisne. An hour later, in the fading light, I saw two of their vedettes upon the hill to the right, and then, as darkness gathered, the heavens to the north were all glimmering from the lights of a bivouac.

When I heard that Blücher had been there for two days, I was much surprised that the Emperor should not have known that the country through which he had ordered me to carry my precious letter was already occupied by the enemy. Still, I thought of the tone of his voice when he said to Charpentier that a soldier must not choose, but must obey. I should follow the route he had laid down for me as long as Violette could move a hoof or I a finger upon her bridle. All the way from Sermoise to Soissons, where the road dips up and down, curving among fir woods, I kept my pistol ready and my sword-belt braced, pushing on swiftly where the path was straight, and then coming slowly round the corners in the way we learned in Spain.

When I came to the farmhouse which lies to the right of the road just after you cross the wooden bridge over the Crise, near where the great statue of the Virgin stands, a woman cried to me from the field, saying that the Prussians were in Soissons. A small party of their lancers, she said, had come in that very afternoon, and a whole division was expected before midnight. I did not wait to hear the end of her tale, but clapped spurs into Violette, and in five minutes was galloping her into the town.

Three Uhlans were at the mouth of the main street, their horses tethered, and they gossiping together, each with a pipe as long as my sabre. I saw them well in the light of an open door, but of me they could have seen only the flash of Violette's grey side and the black flutter of my cloak. A moment later I flew through a stream of them rushing from an open gateway. Violette's shoulder sent one of them reeling, and I stabbed at another but missed him. Pang, pang, went two carbines, but I had flown round the curve of the street, and never so much as heard the hiss of the balls. Ah, we were great, both Violette and I. She lay down to it like a coursed hare, the fire flying from her hoofs. I stood in my stirrups and brandished my sword. Some-one sprang for my bridle. I sliced him through the arm, and I heard him howling behind me. Two horsemen closed upon me. I cut one down and outpaced the other. A minute later I was clear of the town, and flying down a broad white road with the black poplars on either side. For a time I heard the rattle of hoofs behind me, but they died and died until I could not tell them from the throbbing of my own heart. Soon I pulled up and listened, but all was silent. They had given up the chase.

Well, the first thing that I did was to dismount and to lead my mare into a small wood through which a stream ran. There I watered her and rubbed her down, giving her two pieces of sugar soaked in cognac from my flask. She was spent from the sharp chase, but it was wonderful to see how she came round with a half-hour's rest. When my thighs closed upon her again, I could tell by the spring and the swing of her that it would not be her fault if I did not win my way safe to Paris.

I must have been well within the enemy's lines now, for I heard a number of them shouting one of their rough drinking songs out of a house by the roadside, and I went round by the fields to avoid it. At another time two men came out into the moonlight (for by this time it was a cloudless night) and shouted something in German, but I galloped on without heeding them, and they were afraid to fire, for their own hussars are dressed exactly as I was. It is best to take no notice at these times, and then they put you down as a deaf man.

It was a lovely moon, and every tree threw a black bar across the road. I could see the countryside just as if it were daytime, and very peaceful it looked, save that there was a great fire raging somewhere in the north. In the silence of the nighttime, and with the knowledge that danger was in front and behind me, the sight of that great distant fire was very striking and awesome. But I am not easily clouded, for I have seen too many singular things, so I hummed a tune between my teeth and thought of little Lisette, whom I might see in Paris. My mind was full of her when, trotting round a corner, I came straight upon half-a-dozen German dragoons, who were sitting round a brushwood fire by the roadside.

I am an excellent soldier. I do not say this because I am prejudiced in my own favour, but because I really am so. I can weigh every chance in a moment, and decide with as much certainty as though I had brooded for a week. Now I saw like a flash that, come what might, I should be chased, and on a horse which had already done a long twelve leagues. But it was better to be chased onwards than to be chased back. On this moonlit night, with fresh horses behind me, I must take my risk in either case; but if I were to shake them off, I preferred that it should be near Senlis than near Soissons.

All this flashed on me as if by instinct, you understand. My eyes had hardly rested on the bearded faces under the brass helmets before my rowels had touched Violette, and she was off with a rattle like a pas-de-charge. Oh, the shouting and rushing and stamping from behind us! Three of them fired and three swung themselves on to their horses. A bullet rapped on the crupper of my saddle with a noise like a stick on a door. Violette sprang madly forward, and I thought she had been wounded, but it was only a graze above the near fore-fetlock. Ah, the dear little mare, how I loved her when I felt her settle down into that long, easy gallop of hers, her hoofs going like a Spanish girl's castanets. I could not hold myself. I turned on my saddle and shouted and raved, 'Vive l'Empereur!' I screamed and laughed at the gust of oaths that came back to me.

But it was not over yet. If she had been fresh she might have gained a mile in five. Now she could only hold her own with a very little over. There was one of them, a young boy of an officer, who was better mounted than the others. He drew ahead with every stride. Two hundred yards behind him were two troopers, but I saw every time that I glanced round that the distance between them was increasing. The other three who had waited to shoot were a long way in the rear.

The officer's mount was a bay – a fine horse, though not to be spoken of with Violette; yet it was a powerful brute, and it seemed to me that in a few miles its freshness might tell. I waited until the lad was a long way in front of his comrades, and then I eased my mare down a little – a very, very little, so that he might think he was really catching me. When he came within pistol-shot of me I drew and cocked my own pistol, and laid my chin upon my shoulder to see what he would do. He did not offer to fire, and I soon discerned the cause. The silly boy had taken his pistols from his holsters when he had camped for the night. He wagged his sword at me now and roared some threat or other. He did not seem to understand that he was at my mercy. I eased Violette down until there was not the length of a long lance between the grey tail and the bay muzzle.

'Rendez-vous!' he yelled.

'I must compliment monsieur upon his French,' said I, resting the barrel of my pistol upon my bridle-arm, which I have always found best when shooting from the saddle. I aimed at his face, and could see, even in the moonlight, how white he grew when he understood that it was all up with him. But even as my finger pressed the trigger I thought of his mother, and I put my ball through his horse's shoulder. I fear he hurt himself in the fall, for it was a fearful crash, but I had my letter to think of, so I stretched the mare into a gallop once more.

But they were not so easily shaken off, these brigands. The two troopers thought no more of their young officer than if he had been a recruit thrown in the riding-school. They left him to the others and thundered on after me. I had pulled up on the brow of a hill, thinking that I had heard the last of them; but, my faith, I soon saw there was no time for loitering, so away we went, the mare tossing her head and I my shako, to show what we thought of two dragoons who tried to catch a hussar. But at this moment, even while I laughed at the thought, my heart stood still within me, for there at the end of the long white road was a black patch of cavalry waiting to receive me. To a young soldier it might have seemed the shadow of the trees, but to me it was a troop of hussars, and, turn where I could, death seemed to be waiting for me.

Well, I had the dragoons behind me and the hussars in front. Never since Moscow have I seemed to be in such peril. But for the honour of the brigade I had rather be cut down by a light cavalryman than by a heavy. I never drew bridle, therefore, or hesitated for an instant, but I let Violette have her head. I remember that I tried to pray as I rode, but I am a little out of practice at such things, and the only words I could remember were the prayer for fine weather which we used at the school on the evening before holidays. Even this seemed better than nothing, and I was pattering it out, when suddenly I heard French voices in front of me. Ah, mon Dieu, but the joy went through my heart like a musket-ball. They were ours – our own dear little rascals from the corps of Marmont. Round whisked my two dragoons and galloped for their lives, with the moon gleaming on their brass helmets, while I trotted up to my friends with no undue haste, for I would have them understand that though a hussar may fly, it is not in his nature to fly very fast. Yet I fear that Violette's heaving flanks and foam-spattered muzzle gave the lie to my careless bearing.

Who should be at the head of the troop but old Bouvet, whom I saved at Leipzig! When he saw me his little pink eyes filled with tears, and, indeed, I could not but shed a few myself at the sight of his joy. I told him of my mission, but he laughed when I said that I must pass through Senlis.

'The enemy is there,' said he. 'You cannot go.'

'I prefer to go where the enemy is,' I answered.

'But why not go straight to Paris with your despatch? Why should you choose to pass through the one place where you are almost sure to be taken or killed?'

'A soldier does not choose – he obeys,' said I, just as I had heard Napoleon say it.

Old Bouvet laughed in his wheezy way, until I had to give my moustachios a twirl and look him up and down in a manner which brought him to reason.

'Well', said he, 'you had best come along with us, for we are all bound for Senlis. Our orders are to reconnoitre the place. A squadron of Poniatowski's Polish Lancers are in front of us. If you must ride through it, it is possible that we may be able to go with you.'

So away we went, jingling and clanking through the quiet night until we came up with the Poles – fine old soldiers all of them, though a trifle heavy for their horses. It was a treat to see them, for they could not have carried themselves better if they had belonged to my own brigade. We rode together, until in the early morning we saw the lights of Senlis. A peasant was coming along with a cart, and from him we learned how things were going there.

His information was certain, for his brother was the Mayor's coachman, and he had spoken with him late the night before. There was a single squadron of Cossacks – or a polk, as they call it in their frightful language – quartered upon the Mayor's house, which stands at the corner of the market-place, and is the largest building in the town. A whole division of Prussian infantry was encamped in the woods to the north, but only the Cossacks were in Senlis. Ah, what a chance to avenge ourselves upon these barbarians, whose cruelty to our poor countryfolk was the talk at every camp fire.

We were into the town like a torrent, hacked down the vedettes, rode over the guard, and were smashing in the doors of the Mayor's house before they understood that there was a Frenchman within twenty miles of them. We saw horrid heads at the windows – heads bearded to the temples, with tangled hair and sheepskin caps, and silly, gaping mouths. 'Hourra! Hourra!' they shrieked, and fired with their carbines, but our fellows were into the house and at their throats before they had wiped the sleep out of their eyes. It was dreadful to see how the Poles flung themselves upon them, like starving wolves upon a herd of fat bucks – for, as you know, the Poles have a blood feud against the Cossacks. The most were killed in the upper rooms, whither they had fled for shelter, and the blood was pouring down into the hall like rain from a roof. They are terrible soldiers, these Poles, though I think they are a trifle heavy for their horses. Man for man, they are as big as Kellerman's cuirassiers. Their equipment is, of course, much lighter, since they are without the cuirass, back-plate, and helmet.

Well, it was at this point that I made an error – a very serious error it must be admitted. Up to this moment I had carried out my mission in a manner which only my modesty prevents me from describing as remarkable. But now I did that which an official would condemn and a soldier excuse.

There is no doubt that the mare was spent, but still it is true that I might have galloped on through Senlis and reached the country, where I should have had no enemy between me and Paris. But what hussar can ride past a fight and never draw rein? It is to ask too much of him. Besides, I thought that if Violette had an hour of rest I might have three hours the better at the other end. Then on the top of it came those heads at the windows, with their sheepskin hats and their barbarous cries. I sprang from my saddle, threw Violette's bridle over a rail-post, and ran into the house with the rest. It is true that I was too late to be of service, and that I was nearly wounded by a lance-thrust from one of these dying savages. Still, it is a pity to miss even the smallest affair, for one never knows what opportunity for advancement may present itself. I have seen more soldierly work in outpost skirmishes and little gallop-and-hack affairs of the kind than in any of the Emperor's big battles.

When the house was cleared I took a bucket of water out for Violette, and our peasant guide showed me where the good Mayor kept his fodder. My faith, but the little sweetheart was ready for it. Then I sponged down her legs, and leaving her still tethered I went back into the house to find a mouthful for myself, so that I should not need to halt again until I was in Paris.

And now I come to the part of my story which may seem singular to you, although I could tell you at least ten things every bit as queer which have happened to me in my life time. You can understand that, to a man who spends his life in scouting and vedette duties on the bloody ground which lies between two great armies, there are many chances of strange experiences. I'll tell you, however, exactly what occurred.

Old Bouvet was waiting in the passage when I entered, and he asked me whether we might not crack a bottle of wine together. 'My faith, we must not be long,' said he. 'There are ten thousand of Theilmann's Prussians in the woods up yonder.'

'Where is the wine?' I asked.

'Ah, you may trust two hussars to find where the wine is,' said he, and taking a candle in his hand, he led the way down the stone stairs into the kitchen.

When we got there we found another door, which opened on to a winding stair with the cellar at the bottom. The Cossacks had been there before us, as was easily seen by the broken bottles littered all over it. However, the Mayor was a *bon-vivant*, and I do not wish to have a better set of bins to pick from. Chambertin, Graves, Alicant, white wine and red, sparkling and still, they lay in pyramids peeping coyly out of sawdust. Old Bouvet stood with his candle looking here and peeping there, purring in his throat like a cat before a milk-pail. He had picked upon a Burgundy at last, and had his hand out-stretched to the bottle when there came a roar of musketry from above us, a rush of feet, and such a yelping and screaming as I have never listened to. The Prussians were upon us!

Bouvet is a brave man: I will say that for him. He flashed out his sword and away he clattered up the stone steps, his spurs clinking as he ran. I followed him, but just as we came out into the kitchen passage a tremendous shout told us that the house had been recaptured.

'It is all over,' I cried, grasping at Bouvet's sleeve.

'There is one more to die,' he shouted, and away he went like a madman up the second stair. In effect, I should have gone to my death also had I been in his place, for he had done very wrong in not throwing out his scouts to warn him if the Germans advanced upon him. For an instant I was about to rush up with him, and then I bethought myself that, after all, I had my own mission to think of, and that if I were taken the important letter of the Emperor would be sacrificed. I let Bouvet die alone, therefore, and I went down into the cellar again, closing the door behind me.

Well, it was not a very rosy prospect down there either. Bouvet had dropped the candle when the alarm came, and I, pawing about in the darkness, could find nothing but broken bottles. At last I came upon the candle, which had rolled under the curve of a cask, but, try as I would with my tinderbox, I could not light it. The reason was that the wick had been wet in a puddle of wine, so suspecting that this might be the case, I cut the end off with my sword. Then I found that it lighted easily enough. But what to do I could not imagine. The scoundrels upstairs were shouting themselves hoarse, several hundred of them from the sound, and it was clear that some of them would soon want to moisten their throats. There would be an end to a dashing soldier, and of the mission and of the medal. I thought of my mother and I thought of the Emperor. It made me weep to think that the one would lose so excellent a son and the other the best light cavalry officer he ever had since Lasalle's time. But presently I dashed the tears from my eyes. 'Courage!' I cried, striking myself upon the chest. 'Courage, my brave boy. Is it possible that one who has come safely from Moscow without so much as a frost-bite will die in a French wine-cellar?'

At the thought I was up on my feet and clutching at the letter in my tunic, for the crackle of it gave me courage.

My first plan was to set fire to the house, in the hope of escaping in the confusion. My second to get into an empty wine-cask. I was looking round to see if I could find one, when suddenly, in the corner, I espied a little low door, painted of the same grey colour as the wall, so that it was only a man with quick sight who would have noticed it. I pushed against it, and at first I imagined that it was locked. Presently, however, it gave a little, and then I understood that it was held by the pressure of something on the other side. I put my feet against a hogshead of wine, and I gave such a push that the door flew open and I came down with a crash upon my back, the candle flying out of my hands, so that I found myself in darkness once more. I picked myself up and stared through the black archway into the gloom beyond.

There was a slight ray of light coming from some slit or grating. The dawn had broken outside, and I could dimly see the long, curving sides of several huge casks, which made me think that perhaps this was where the Mayor kept his reserves of wine while they were maturing. At any rate, it seemed to be a safer hiding-place than the outer cellar, so gathering up my candle, I was just closing the door behind me, when I suddenly saw something which filled me with amazement, and even, I confess, with the smallest little touch of fear.

I have said that at the further end of the cellar there was a dim grey fan of light striking downwards from somewhere near the roof. Well, as I peered through the darkness, I suddenly saw a great, tall man skip into this belt of daylight, and then out again into the darkness at the further end. My word, I gave such a start that my shako nearly broke its chin-strap! It was only a glance, but, none the less, I had time to see that the fellow had a hairy Cossack cap on his head, and that he was a great, long-legged, broad-shouldered brigand, with a sabre at his waist. My faith, even Etienne Gerard was a little staggered at being left alone with such a creature in the dark.

But only for a moment. 'Courage!' I thought. 'Am I not a hussar, a brigadier, too, at the age of thirty-one, and the chosen messenger of the Emperor?' After all, this skulker had more cause to be afraid of me than I of him. And then suddenly I understood that he was afraid – horribly afraid. I could read it from his quick step and his bent shoulders as he ran among the barrels, like a rat making for its hole. And, of course, it must have been he who had held the door against me, and not some packing-case or wine-cask as I had imagined. He was the pursued then, and I the pursuer. Aha, I felt my whiskers bristle as I advanced upon him through the darkness! He would find that he had no chicken to deal with, this robber from the North. For the moment I was magnificent.

At first I had feared to light my candle lest I should make a mark of myself, but now, after cracking my shin over a box, and catching my spurs in some canvas, I thought the bolder course the wiser. I lit it, therefore, and then I advanced with long strides, my sword in my hand. 'Come out, you rascal!' I cried. 'Nothing can save you. You will at last meet with your deserts.'

I held my candle high, and presently I caught a glimpse of the man's head staring at me over a barrel. He had a gold chevron on his black cap, and the expression of his face told me in an instant that he was an officer and a man of refinement.

'Monsieur,' he cried, in excellent French, 'I surrender myself on a promise of quarter. But if I do not have your promise, I will then sell my life as dearly as I can.'

'Sir,' said I, 'a Frenchman knows how to treat an unfortunate enemy. Your life is safe.' With that he handed his sword over the top of the barrel, and I bowed with the candle on my heart. 'Whom have I the honour of capturing?' I asked.

'I am the Count Boutkine, of the Emperor's own Don Cossacks,' said he. 'I came out with my troop to reconnoitre Senlis, and as we found no sign of your people we determined to spend the night here.'

'And would it be an indiscretion,' I asked, 'if I were to inquire how you came into the back cellar?'

'Nothing more simple,' said he. 'It was our intention to start at early dawn. Feeling chilled after dressing, I thought that a cup of wine would do me no harm, so I came down to see what I could find. As I was rummaging about, the house was suddenly carried by assault so rapidly that by the time I had climbed the stairs it was all over. It only remained for me to save myself, so I came down here and hid myself in the back cellar, where you have found me.'

I thought of how old Bouvet had behaved under the same conditions, and the tears sprang to my eyes as I contemplated the glory of France. Then I had to consider what I should do next. It was clear that this Russian Count, being in the back cellar while we were in the front one, had not heard the sounds which would have told him that the house was once again in the hands of his own allies. If he should once understand this the tables would be turned, and I should be his prisoner instead of he being mine. What was I to do? I was at my wits' end, when suddenly there came to me an idea so brilliant that I could not but be amazed at my own invention.

'Count Boutkine,' said I, 'I find myself in a most difficult position.'

'And why?' he asked.

'Because I have promised you your life.'

His jaw dropped a little.

'You would not withdraw your promise?' he cried.

'If the worst comes to the worst I can die in your defence,' said I; 'but the difficulties are great.'

'What is it, then?' he asked.

'I will be frank with you,' said I. 'You must know that our fellows, and especially the Poles, are so incensed against the Cossacks that the mere sight of the uniform drives them mad. They precipitate themselves instantly upon the wearer and tear him limb from limb. Even their officers cannot restrain them.'

The Russian grew pale at my words and the way in which I said them.

'But this is terrible,' said he.

'Horrible!' said I. 'If we were to go up together at this moment I cannot promise how far I could protect you.'

'I am in your hands,' he cried. 'What would you suggest that we should do? Would it not be best that I should remain here?'

'That worst of all.'

'And why?'

'Because our fellows will ransack the house presently, and then you would be cut to pieces. No, no, I must go and break it to them. But even then, when once they see that accursed uniform, I do not know what may happen.'

'Should I then take the uniform off?'

'Excellent!' I cried. 'Hold, we have it! You will take your uniform off and put on mine. That will make you sacred to every French soldier.'

'It is not the French I fear so much as the Poles.'

'But my uniform will be a safeguard against either.'

'How can I thank you?' he cried. 'But you — what are you to wear?'

'I will wear yours.'

'And perhaps fall a victim to your generosity?'

'It is my duty to take the risk,' I answered; 'but I have no fears. I will ascend in your uniform. A hundred swords will be turned upon me. "Hold!" I will shout, "I am the Brigadier Gerard!" Then they will see my face. They will know me.

And I will tell them about you. Under the shield of these clothes you will be sacred.'

His fingers trembled with eagerness as he tore off his tunic. His boots and breeches were much like my own, so there was no need to change them, but I gave him my hussar jacket, my dolman, my shako, my sword-belt, and my sabre-tasche, while I took in exchange his high sheepskin cap with the gold chevron, his fur-trimmed coat, and his crooked sword. Be it well understood that in changing the tunics I did not forget to change my thrice-precious letter also from my old one to my new.

'With your leave,' said I, 'I shall now bind you to a barrel.'

He made a great fuss over this, but I have learned in my soldiering never to throw away chances, and how could I tell that he might not, when my back was turned, see how the matter really stood, and break in upon my plans? He was leaning against a barrel at the time, so I ran six times round it with a rope, and then tied it with a big knot behind. If he wished to come upstairs he would, at least, have to carry a thousand litres of good French wine for a knapsack. I then shut the door of the back cellar behind me, so that he might not hear what was going forward, and tossing the candle away I ascended the kitchen stair.

There were only about twenty steps, and yet, while I came up them, I seemed to have time to think of everything that I had ever hoped to do. It was the same feeling that I had at Eylau when I lay with my broken leg and saw the horse artillery galloping down upon me. Of course, I knew that if I were taken I should be shot instantly as being disguised within the enemy's lines. Still, it was a glorious death – in the direct service of the Emperor – and I reflected that there could not be less than five lines, and perhaps seven, in the *Moniteur* about me. Palaret had eight lines, and I am sure that he had not so fine a career.

When I made my way out into the hall, with all the

nonchalance in my face and manner that I could assume, the very first thing that I saw was Bouvet's dead body, with his legs drawn up and a broken sword in his hand. I could see by the black smudge that he had been shot at close quarters. I should have wished to salute as I went by, for he was a gallant man, but I feared lest I should be seen, and so I passed on.

The front of the hall was full of Prussian infantry, who were knocking loopholes in the wall, as though they expected that there might be yet another attack. Their officer, a little man, was running about giving directions. They were all too busy to take much notice of me, but another officer, who was standing by the door with a long pipe in his mouth, strode across and clapped me on the shoulder, pointing to the dead bodies of our poor hussars, and saying something which was meant for a jest, for his long beard opened and showed every fang in his head. I laughed heartily also, and said the only Russian words that I knew. I learned them from little Sophie, at Wilna, and they meant: 'If the night is fine we shall meet under the oak tree, but if it rains we shall meet in the byre.' It was all the same to this German, however, and I have no doubt that he gave me credit for saying something very witty indeed, for he roared laughing, and slapped me on my shoulder again. I nodded to him and marched out of the hall-door as coolly as if I were the commandant of the garrison.

There were a hundred horses tethered about outside, most of them belonging to the Poles and hussars. Good little Violette was waiting with the others, and she whinnied when she saw me coming towards her. But I would not mount her. No. I was much too cunning for that. On the contrary, I chose the most shaggy little Cossack horse that I could see, and I sprang upon it with as much assurance as though it had belonged to my father before me. It had a great bag of plunder slung over its neck, and this I laid upon Violette's back, and led her along beside me. Never have you seen such a picture of the Cossack returning from the foray. It was superb.

Well, the town was full of Prussians by this time. They lined the side-walks and pointed me out to each other, saying, as I could judge from their gestures, 'There goes one of those devils of Cossacks. They are the boys for foraging and plunder.'

One or two officers spoke to me with an air of authority, but I shook my head and smiled, and said, 'If the night is fine we shall meet under the oak tree, but if it rains we shall meet in the byre,' at which they shrugged their shoulders and gave the matter up. In this way I worked along until I was beyond the northern outskirt of the town. I could see in the roadway two lancer vedettes with their black and white pennons, and I knew that when I was once past these I should be a free man once more. I made my pony trot, therefore, Violette rubbing her nose against my knee all the time, and looking up at me to ask how she had deserved that this hairy doormat of a creature should be preferred to her. I was not more than a hundred yards from the Uhlans when, suddenly, you can imagine my feelings when I saw a real Cossack coming galloping along the road towards me.

Ah, my friend, you who read this, if you have any heart, you will feel for a man like me, who had gone through so many dangers and trials, only at this very last moment to be confronted with one which appeared to put an end to everything. I will confess that for a moment I lost heart, and was inclined to throw myself down in my despair, and to cry out that I had been betrayed. But, no; I was not beaten even now. I opened two buttons of my tunic so that I might get easily at the Emperor's message, for it was my fixed determination when all hope was gone to swallow the letter and then die sword in hand. Then I felt that my little, crooked sword was loose in its sheath, and I trotted on to where the vedettes were waiting.

They seemed inclined to stop me, but I pointed to the other Cossack, who was still a couple of hundred yards off, and they, understanding that I merely wished to meet him, let me pass with a salute.

I dug my spurs into my pony then, for if I were only far enough from the lancers I thought I might manage the Cossack without much difficulty. He was an officer, a large, bearded man, with a gold chevron in his cap, just the same as mine. As I advanced he unconsciously aided me by pulling up his horse, so that I had a fine start of the vedettes. On I came for him, and I could see wonder changing to suspicion in his brown eyes as he looked at me and at my pony, and at my equipment. I do not know what it was that was wrong, but he saw something which was as it should not be. He shouted out a question, and then when I gave no answer he pulled out his sword. I was glad in my heart to see him do so, for I had always rather fight than cut down an unsuspecting enemy. Now I made at him full tilt, and, parrying his cut, I got my point in just under the fourth button of his tunic. Down he went, and the weight of him nearly took me off my horse before I could disengage. I never glanced at him to see if he were living or dead, for I sprang off my pony and on to Violette, with a shake of my bridle and a kiss of my hand to the two Uhlans behind me. They galloped after me, shouting, but Violette had had her rest, and was just as fresh as when she started. I took the first side road to the west and then the first to the south, which would take me away from the enemy's country. On we went and on, every stride taking me further from my foes and nearer to my friends. At last, when I reached the end of a long stretch of road, and looking back from it could see no sign of any pursuers, I understood that my troubles were over.

And it gave me a glow of happiness, as I rode, to think that I had done to the letter what the Emperor had ordered. What would he say when he saw me? What could he say which would do justice to the incredible way in which I had risen above every danger? He had ordered me to go through Sermoise, Soissons, and Senlis, little dreaming that they were all three occupied by the enemy. And yet I had done it. I had borne his letter in safety through each of these towns. Hussars, dragoons, lancers, Cossacks, and infantry – I had run the gauntlet of all of them, and had come out unharmed.

When I had got as far as Dammartin I caught a first glimpse of our own outposts. There was a troop of dragoons in a field, and of course I could see from the horsehair crests that they were French. I galloped towards them in order to ask them if all was safe between there and Paris, and as I rode I felt such a pride at having won my way back to my friends again, that I could not refrain from waving my sword in the air.

At this a young officer galloped out from among the dragoons, also brandishing his sword, and it warmed my heart to think that he should come riding with such ardour and enthusiasm to greet me. I made Violette caracole, and as we came together I brandished my sword more gallantly than ever, but you can imagine my feelings when he suddenly made a cut at me which would certainly have taken my head off if I had not fallen forward with my nose in Violette's mane. My faith, it whistled just over my cap like an east wind. Of course, it came from this accursed Cossack uniform which, in my excitement, I had forgotten all about, and this young dragoon had imagined that I was some Russian champion who was challenging the French cavalry. My word, he was a frightened man when he understood how near he had been to killing the celebrated Brigadier Gerard.

Well, the road was clear, and about three o'clock in the afternoon I was at St Denis, though it took me a long two hours to get from there to Paris, for the road was blocked with commissariat waggons and guns of the artillery reserve, which was going north to Marmont and Mortier. You cannot conceive the excitement which my appearance in such a costume made in Paris, and when I came to the Rue de Rivoli I should think I had a quarter of a mile of folk riding or running behind me. Word had got about from the dragoons (two of whom had come with me), and everybody knew about my adventures and how I had come by my uniform. It was a triumph – men shouting and women waving their handkerchiefs and blowing kisses from the windows.

Although I am a man singularly free from conceit, still I must confess that, on this one occasion, I could not restrain myself from showing that this reception gratified me. The Russian's coat had hung very loose upon me, but now I threw out my chest until it was as tight as a sausage-skin. And my little sweetheart of a mare tossed her mane and pawed with her front hoofs, frisking her tail about as though she said, 'We've done it together this time. It is to us that commissions should be entrusted.' When I kissed her between the nostrils as I dismounted at the gate of the Tuileries, there was as much shouting as if a bulletin had been read from the Grand Army.

I was hardly in costume to visit a King, but, after all, if one has a soldierly figure one can do without all that. I was shown up straight away to Joseph, whom I had often seen in Spain. He seemed as stout, as quiet, and as amiable as ever. Talleyrand was in the room with him, or I suppose I should call him the Duke of Benevento, but I confess that I like old names best. He read my letter when Joseph Buonaparte handed it to him, and then he looked at me with the strangest expression in those funny little, twinkling eyes of his.

'Were you the only messenger?' he asked.

'There was one other, sir,' said I. 'Major Charpentier, of the Horse Grenadiers.'

'He has not yet arrived,' said the King of Spain.

'If you had seen the legs of his horse, sire, you would not wonder at it,' I remarked.

'There may be other reasons,' said Talleyrand, and he gave that singular smile of his.

Well, they paid me a compliment or two, though they might have said a good deal more and yet have said too little. I bowed myself out, and very glad I was to get away, for I hate a Court as much as I love a camp. Away I went to my old friend Chaubert, in the Rue Miromesnil, and there I got his hussar uniform, which fitted me very well. He and Lisette and I supped together in his rooms, and all my dangers were forgotten. In the morning I found Violette ready for another twenty-league stretch. It was my intention to return instantly to the Emperor's headquarters, for I was, as you may well imagine, impatient to hear his words of praise, and to receive my reward.

I need not say that I rode back by a safe route, for I had seen quite enough of Uhlans and Cossacks. I passed through Meaux and Château Thierry, and so in the evening I arrived at Rheims, where Napoleon was still lying. The bodies of our fellows and of St Prest's Russians had all been buried, and I could see changes in the camp also. The soldiers looked better cared for; some of the cavalry had received remounts, and everything was in excellent order. It was wonderful what a good general can effect in a couple of days.

When I came to the headquarters I was shown straight into the Emperor's room. He was drinking coffee at a writing-table, with a big plan drawn out on paper in front of him. Berthier and Macdonald were leaning, one over each shoulder, and he was talking so quickly that I don't believe that either of them could catch a half of what he was saying. But when his eyes fell upon me he dropped the pen on to the chart, and he sprang up with a look in his pale face which struck me cold.

'What the deuce are you doing here?' he shouted. When he was angry he had a voice like a peacock.

'I have the honour to report to you, sire,' said I, 'that I have delivered your despatch safely to the King of Spain.'

'What!' he yelled, and his two eyes transfixed me like bayonets. Oh, those dreadful eyes, shifting from grey to blue, like steel in the sunshine. I can see them now when I have a bad dream.

'What has become of Charpentier?' he asked.

'He is captured,' said Macdonald.

'By whom?'

'The Russians.'

'The Cossacks?'

'No, a single Cossack.'

'He gave himself up?'

'Without resistance.'

'He is an intelligent officer. You will see that the medal of honour is awarded to him.'

When I heard those words I had to rub my eyes to make sure that I was awake.

'As to you,' cried the Emperor, taking a step forward as if he would have struck me, 'you brain of a hare, what do you think that you were sent upon this mission for? Do you conceive that I would send a really important message by such a hand as yours, and through every village which the enemy holds? How you came through them passes my comprehension; but if your fellow-messenger had had but as little sense as you, my whole plan of campaign would have been ruined. Can you not see, coglione, that this message contained false news, and that it was intended to deceive the enemy whilst I put a very different scheme into execution?'

When I heard those cruel words and saw the angry, white face which glared at me, I had to hold the back of a chair, for my mind was failing me and my knees would hardly bear me up.

But then I took courage as I reflected that I was an honourable gentleman, and that my whole life had been spent in toiling for this man, and for my beloved country.

'Sire,' said I, and the tears would trickle down my cheeks whilst I spoke, 'when you are dealing with a man like me you would find it wiser to deal openly. Had I known that you had wished the despatch to fall into the hands of the enemy, I would have seen that it came there. As I believed that I was to guard it, I was prepared to sacrifice my life for it. I do not believe, sire, that any man in the world ever met with more toils and perils than I have done in trying to carry out what I thought was your will.'

I dashed the tears from my eyes as I spoke, and with such fire and spirit as I could command I gave him an account of it all, of my dash through Soissons, my brush with the dragoons, my adventure in Senlis, my rencontre with Count Boutkine in the cellar, my disguise, my meeting with the Cossack officer, my flight, and how at the last moment I was nearly cut down by a French dragoon. The Emperor, Berthier, and Macdonald listened with astonishment on their faces. When I had finished Napoleon stepped forward and he pinched me by the ear.

'There, there!' said he. 'Forget anything which I may have said. I would have done better to trust you. You may go.'

I turned to the door, and my hand was upon the handle, when the Emperor called upon me to stop.

'You will see,' said he, turning to the Duke of Tarentum, 'that Brigadier Gerard has the special medal of honour, for I believe that if he has the thickest head he has also the stoutest heart in my army.'

The Oldest Air
in the World
(1920)

Neil Munro

Col Maclean, on two sticks, and with tartan trousers on, came
down between the whins to the poles where the nets were
drying, and joined the Trosdale folk in the nets' shade. 'Twas
the Saturday afternoon; they were frankly idling, the township
people – except that the women knitted, which is a way of
being indolent in the Islands – and had been listening for an
hour to an heroic tale of the old sea-robber days from Patrick
Macneill, the most gifted liar in the parish. A little fire of green
wood burned to keep the midges off, and it was hissing like
a gander.

'Take your share of the smoke and let down your weariness,

darling,' said one of the elder women, pushing towards the piper a herring firken. Nobody looked at his sticks nor his dragging limb – not even the children; had he not been a Gael himself Maclean might have fancied his lameness was unperceived. He bitterly knew better, but pushed his sticks behind the nets as he seated himself, and seated, with his crutches absent, he was a fellow to charm the eye of maid or sergeant-major.

'Your pipes might be a widow, she's so seldom seen or heard since you came home,' said one of the fishermen.

'And that's the true word,' answered Col Maclean. 'A widow indeed, without her man! Never in all my life played I *piob mhor* but on my feet and they jaunty! I'll never put a breath again in sheepskin. If they had only blinded me!'

There was in the company, Margaret, daughter of the bailie; she had been a toddling white-haired child when Col went to France, and had to be lifted to his knees; now she got up on them herself at a jump, and put her arms round his neck, tickling him with her fingers till he laughed.

'Oh bold one! Let Col be!' her mother commanded; 'thou wilt spoil his beautiful tartan trews.'

'It is Col must tell a story now,' said the little one, thinking of the many he used to tell her before he became a soldier.

'It is not the time for wee folks stories,' said the mother; 'but maybe he will tell us something not too bloody for Sunday's eve about the Wars.'

Col Maclean, for the first time, there and then, gave his tale of The Oldest Air in the World.

'I was thinking to myself,' said he, 'as I was coming through the whins there, that even now, in creeks of the sea like this, beside their nets adrying, there must be crofter folk in France, and they at *ceilidh* like yourselves, telling of tales and putting to each other riddles.'

'*Ubh! ubh!* It is certain there are no crofters in France, whatever,' said William-the-Elder. 'It is wine they drink in France, as I heard tell from the time I was the height of a Lorne shoe, and who ever heard of crofters drinking wine?'

'Wherever are country people and the sea beside them to snatch a meal from, you will find the croft,' insisted Col the piper. 'They have the croft in France, though they have a different name for it from ours, and I'll wager the bulk of the land they labour is as bare as a bore's snout, for that is what sheep and deer have left in Europe for the small spade-farmer.'

'Did'st see the crofting lands out yonder?' asked Margaret's mother.

'No,' said the piper; 'but plenty I saw of the men they breed there; I ate with them, and marched with them, and battled at their side, for we were not always playing the pipes, we music-fellows.

'And that puts me in mind of a thing – there is a people yonder, over in France, that play the bagpipe – they call them Brettanach – the Bretons. They are the same folk as ourselves though kind of Frenchmen too, wine drinking, dark and Papist. Race, as the old-word says, goes down to the rock, and you could tell at the first glance of a Brettanach that he was kin to us though a kilt was never on his loins, and not one word in his head of the Gaelic language. 'Tis history! Someway – some time – far back – they were sundered from us, the Brettanach, and now have their habitation far enough from Albyn of the mountains, glens and heroes. Followers of the sea, fishermen or farmers; God-fearing, good hard drinkers, in their fashion – many a time I looked at one and said to myself, "There goes a man of Skye or Lewis!"'

'And the girls of them?' said Ranald Gorm, with a twinkle of the eyes.

'You have me there!' said Col. 'I never saw woman-kind

of the Brettanach; the war never went into their country, and the Bretons I saw were in regiments of the army, far enough from home like myself, in the champagne shires where they make the wine.

'We came on them first in a town called Corbie, with a church so grand and spacious a priest might bellow his head off and never be heard by the poor in the seats behind. 'Twas on a week-day, a Mass was making; that was the first and last time ever I played pipes in the House of God, and faith! that not by my own desiring. 'Twas some fancy of the priests, connived between them and the Cornal. Fifteen of us marched the flag-stones of yon kirk of Corbie playing "Fingal's Weeping."'

'A good brave tune!' remarked the bailie.

'A brave tune, and a bonny! I'll warrant yon one made the rafters shiver! The kirk was filled with a corps of the tribe I mention – the Brettanach – and they at their Papist worshipping; like ourselves, just country folk that would sooner be at the fishing or the croft than making warfare.

'My eye fell, in particular, on a fellow that was a sergeant, most desperate like my uncle Sandy – so like I could have cried across the kirk to him "Oh uncle! what do ye do so far from Salen?" The French, for ordinary, are black as sloes, but he was red, red, a noble head on him like a bullock, an eagle nose, and a beard cut square and gallant.

'When the kirk spilled out its folk, they hung awhile about the burial-yard as we do ourselves in Trosdale, spelling the names on the headstones, gossiping, and by-and-bye slipped out, I doubt not, to a change-house for a dram, and all the pipers with them except myself.'

'God bless me!' cried Ronald Gorm.

'Believe it or not, but I hung back and sought my friend the red one. He was sitting all his lone on a slab in the strangers' portion of the grave-yard, under yews, eating bread and onion and sipping wine from his flask of war. Now the droll thing is that though I knew he had not one word of Christian Gaelic in his cheek, 'twas the Gaelic I must speak to him.

"'Just man," says I to him. "Health to you and a hunter's hunger! I was looking at you yonder in the kirk, and a gentleman more like my clansman Sandy Ruadh of Salen is surely not within the four brown borders of the world nor on the deeps of ocean. Your father must have come from the Western Isles, or the mother of you been wandering."

'Of all I said to him he knew but the one word that means the same thing, as they tell me, in all Celtdom – *eaglais*. To his feet got the Frenchman, stretched out to me his bread and wine, with a half-laugh on him most desperate like Uncle Sandy, and said *eaglais* too, with a flourish of the heel of his loaf at the kirk behind him to show he understood that, anyway. We sat on the slab, the pair of us, my pipes stretched out between us, and there I assure, folk, was the hour of conversation!'

'But if you could not speak each other's tongue?' said a girl.

'*Tach!* two men of the breed with a set of pipes between them can always follow one another. 'Tis my belief if I stood his words on end and could follow them backwards they would be good Gaelic of Erin. The better half of our speech was with our hands; he had not even got the English; and most of the time we talked pipe-music, as any man can do that's fit to pucker his lips and whistle. The Breton people *canntarach* tunes too, like ourselves – soft-warbling them to fix them in the memory, and blyth that morning was our warbling; he could charm, my man, the very thrush from trees! But Herself – the *piob mhor* – was an instrument beyond his fingering; the pipes he used at home he called *biornieu*, fashioned differently from ours. Yet the same wind blows through reeds in France or Scotland, and everywhere they sing of old and simple things; you are deaf indeed if you cannot understand.

'He was from the seashore – John his name – a mariner to his trade – with a wife and seven children; himself the son of a cooper.

'I am a good hand at the talking myself, as little Margaret here will tell you, but his talk was like a stream in spate, and the arms of him went flourishing like drum-sticks. Keep mind of this – that the two of us, by now, were all alone in the kirk-yard, on a little hillock with the great big cliff of a kirk above us, and the town below all humming with the soldiers, like a byke of bees.

'He bade me play on the pipes at last and I put them in my oxter and gave him "Lochiel's awa' to France." A fine tune! but someway I felt I never reached him. I tried him then with bits of "The Bugle Horn," "Take your gun to the Hill," "Bonnie Ann" and "The Persevering Lover," he beat time with a foot to them, and clapped my shoulder, but for all that they said to him I might as well be playing on a fiddle.

'It was only when I tried an old *port-mor* – "The Spoil of the Lowlands now graze in the Glen" that his whiskers bristled, and at that said I to myself "I have you Uncle Sandy!"

'Before the light that flickered was gone from him I blew it up to a height again with "Come to me Kinsman!"

'He was like a fellow that would be under spells!

'"The Good Being be about me!" cried he, and his eyes like flambeaux, "what tune is that?"

'You never, never, never saw a man so much uplifted!

'"They call it," said I, "Come to me Kinsman," (*Thigibh a so a charaid!*), and it has the name, in the small Isles of the West, of the Oldest Air of the World. The very ravens know it; what is it but the cry of men in trouble? It's older than the cairns of Icolmkill, and cried the clans from out of the Isles to Harlaw. Listen you well!' and I played it to him again – not all the MacCrimmons that ever came from Skye could play it better!

for grand was the day and white with sun, and to-morrow we were marching. And many a lad of ours was dead behind us.

'When I was done, he did a droll thing then, the red fellow – put his arms about my shoulders and kissed me on the face! And the beard of him like a flaming whin!

'What must he do but learn it? Over and over again I had to whistle it to him till he had it to the very finish, and all the time the guns were going in the east.

'"If ever you were in trouble," I said to him – though of course he could no understand me, "and you whistled but one blast of the air, it is Col Maclean would be at your side though the world were staving in below your feet like one of your father's barrels!"'

The day was done in Trosdale. Beyond the rim of the sea the sun had slid to make a Sabbath morning further round the world, and all the sky in the west was streaming fire. Over the flats of Heisker the light began to wink on the Monach islets. Ebbed tide left bare sand round Kirkibost, and the sea-birds settled on them, rising at times in flocks and eddying in the air as if they were leaves and a wind had blown them. Curlews were piping bitterly.

Behind the creek where the folk were gathered on the sea-pinks, talking, Trosdale clachan sent up the reek of evening fires, and the bairns were being cried in from the fields.

The Catechist, sombre fellow, already into his Sabbath, though 'twas only Saturday nine o' the clock, came through the whins and cast about him a glance for bagpipes. He had seen Maclean's arrival with misgiving. A worthy man, and a face on him like the underside of a two-year skate-fish.

Col Maclean turned on him a visage tanned as if it had been in the cauldron with the catechu of the barking nets.

'Take you a firken too, and rest you, Catechist,' said he.

'You see I have not my pipes to-night, but I'm at *sgeulachd*.'

But the Catechist sat not; and leaning against a net-pole sighed.

''Twas two years after that,' said Col, again into the rapture of his story, 'when my regiment went to the land of wine, where we battled beside the French. I assure you we did nobly! nobly! Nor, on the soul of me! were the Frenchmen slack!'

'The French,' ventured Patrick Macneill, 'are renowned in story for all manly parts. Oh King! 'tis they have suffered!'

''Tis myself, just man, that is not denying it! We were yonder in a land like Keppoch desolate after the red cock's crowing. The stars themselves, that are acquaint with grief, and have seen great tribulation in the dark of Time would sicken at the sight of it! Nothing left of the towns but *larochs* – heaps of lime and rubble where the rat made habitation, and not one chimney reeking in a hundred miles. Little we ken of trees here in the Islands, but they were yonder planted thick as bracken and cut down to the stump the way you would be cutting winter kail. And the fields that the country folk had laboured! – were the Minch drained dry, the floor of it would seem no likelier place for cropping barley or for pasturing goats.

'There was a day of days, out yonder, that we mixed up with the French and cleared the breadth of a parish of *am boche*, who was ill to shift. But the mouth of the night brought him back on us most desperate altogether, and half we had gained by noon was lost by gloaming.

'Five score and ten of our men were missing at the roll-call. The Cornal grunted. "Every man of them out of Lewis!" says he; "they're either dead or wandered. Go you out Col Maclean with your beautiful, lovely, splendid pipes, and gather at least the living."

'Not one morsel of meat had I eaten for twenty hours, and the inside of me just one hole full of hunger, but out went Col and his pipes to herding!

'Oh King of the Elements! but that was the night most foul, with the kingdom of France a rag for wetness, and mire to the hose-tops. Rain lashed; a scouring wind whipped over the country, and it was stinking like a brock from tatters that had been men. The German guns were pelting it, the sound of them a bellow no more broken than the roar on skerries at Martinmas, the flash of them in the sky like Merry Dancers.

'I got in a while to the length of a steading with a gable standing; tuned up *piob mhor* and played the gathering. They heard me, the lads – the living of them; two-over-twenty of them came up to me by the gable, with no more kenning of what airt they were in than if a fog had found them midway on the Long Ford of Uist. I led them back to King George's furrows where our folk were, and then, *mo chreach!* when we counted them, one was missing!

'"It is not a good herd you are, Maclean," said the Cornal, "you will just go back and find Duncan Ban; he's the only man in the regiment I can trust to clean my boots."

'So back went Col in search of Duncan.'

'Oh lad! weren't you the gallant fellow!' cried Margaret's mother, adoring.

'I was that, I assure you! If it were not the pipes were in my arm-pit like a girl, my feet would not keep up on me the way I would be pelting any other road than the way I had to go. But my grief! I never got my man, nor no man after ever found him. I went to the very ditches where *am boche* was lying, and 'twas there that a light went up that made the country round about as white-bright as the day, and I in the midst of it with my pipes in hand. They threw at me grey lead as if it had been gravel, and I fell.'

'*Och, a mheudail bhochd!* – Oh Treasure!' said the women of Trosdale all together.

'I got to my knees in a bit and crawled, as it might be for a lifetime, one ache from head to heel, till I came to a hole as deep's a quarry where had been the crossing of roads, and there my soul went out of me. When I came to myself I was playing pipes and the day was on the land. The Good Being knows what I played, but who should come out across the plain to me but a Frenchman!'

> *He moved as spindrift from spindrift,*
> *As a furious winter wind –*
> *So swiftly, sprucely, cheerily,*
> *Oh! proudly,*
> *Through glens and high-tops,*
> *And no stop made he*
> *Until he came*
> *To the city and court of Maclean,*
> *Maclean of the torments,*
> *Playing his pipes.*

The Catechist writhed; the people of Trosdale shivered; Patrick Macneill wept softly, for Col Maclean, the cunning one, by the rhyming trick of the ancient sennachies, had flung them, unexpected, into the giddiness of his own swoound, and all of them, wounded, dazed, saw the Frenchman come like a shadow into the world of shades.

'He flung himself in the hole beside me, did the Frenchman, gave me a sup of spirits and put soft linen to my sores, and all the time grey lead was snarling over us.

'"Make use of thy good male feet, lad," said I to him, "and get out of this dirty weather! Heed not the remnants of Col Maclean. What fetched thee hither?"

'He put his hand on my pipes and whistled a stave of the old tune.

'"How learned ye that?" I asked him.

'Although he was Brettanach he had a little of the English. "Red John our sergeant, peace be with him! heard you playing it all last night," said he, "took a craze at the tune of you and went out to find you, but never came back. Then another man, peace be with him! a cousin of John, heard your playing and went seeking you, but he came back not either. I heard you first, myself, no more than an hour ago, and had no sooner got your tune into my head than it quickened me like drink, and here am I, kinsman!"

'"Good lad!" I cried, "all the waters in the world will not wash out kinship, nor the Gael be forsaken while there is love and song."'

'Vain tales! Vain tales!' groaned the Catechist, and hid face like a skate.

The King of Ypres
(1918)

John Buchan

Private Peter Galbraith, of the 3rd Lennox Highlanders, awoke
with a splitting headache and the consciousness of an intolerable
din. At first he thought it was the whistle from the forge,
which a year ago had pulled him from his bed when he was a
puddler in Motherwell. He scrambled to his feet, and nearly
cracked his skull against a low roof. That, and a sound which
suggested that the heavens were made of canvas which a giant
hand was rending, cleared his wits and recalled him to the
disagreeable present. He lit the dottle in his pipe, and began to
piece out his whereabouts.

Late the night before, the remnants of his battalion had been brought in from the Gheluvelt trenches to billets in Ypres. That last week he had gone clean off his sleep. He had not been dry for a fortnight, his puttees had rotted away, his greatcoat had disappeared in a mud-hole, and he had had no stomach for what food could be got. He had seen half his battalion die before his eyes, and day and night the shells had burst round him till the place looked like the ironworks at Motherwell on a foggy night. The worst of it was that he had never come to grips with the Boches, which he had long decided was the one pleasure left to him in life. He had got far beyond cursing, though he had once had a talent that way. His mind was as sodden as his body, and his thoughts had been focussed on the penetrating power of a bayonet when directed against a plump Teutonic chest. There had been a German barber in Motherwell called Schultz, and he imagined the enemy as a million Schultzes – large, round men who talked with the back of their throat.

In billets he had scraped off the worst part of the mud, and drunk half a bottle of wine which a woman had given him. It tasted like red ink, but anything liquid was better than food. Sleep was what he longed for, but he could not get it. The Boches were shelling the town, and the room he shared with six others seemed as noisy as the Gallowgate on a Saturday night. He wanted to get deep down into the earth where there was no sound; so, while the others snored, he started out to look for a cellar. In the black darkness, while the house rocked to the shell reverberations, he had groped his way down the stairs, found a door which led to another flight, and, slipping and stumbling, had come to a narrow, stuffy chamber which smelt of potatoes. There he had lain down on some sacks and fallen into a frowsty slumber.

His head was spinning, but the hours of sleep had done him good. He felt a slight appetite for breakfast, as well as an intolerable thirst. He groped his way up the stairs, and came out in a dilapidated hall lit by a dim November morning.

There was no sign of the packs which had been stacked there the night before. He looked for a Boche's helmet which he had brought in as a souvenir, but that was gone. Then he found the room where he had been billeted. It was empty, and only the stale smell of tobacco told of its occupants.

Lonely, disconsolate, and oppressed with thoughts of future punishment, he moved towards the street door. Suddenly the door of a side room opened and a man came out, a furtive figure, with a large, pasty face. His pockets bulged, and in one hand was a silver candle-stick. At the sight of Galbraith he jumped back and held up a pistol.

'Pit it down, man, and tell's what's come ower this place?' said the soldier. For answer, a bullet sang past his ear and shivered a plaster Venus.

Galbraith gave his enemy the butt of his rifle and laid him out. From his pockets he shook out a mixed collection of loot. He took possession of his pistol, and kicked him with some vehemence into a cupboard.

'That yin's a thief,' was his spoken reflection. 'There's something michty wrong wi' Wipers the day.'

His head was clearing, and he was getting very wroth. His battalion had gone off and left him in a cellar, and miscreants were abroad. It was time for a respectable man to be up and doing. Besides, he wanted his breakfast. He fixed his bayonet, put the pistol in his pocket, and emerged into the November drizzle.

The streets suddenly were curiously still. The occasional shell-fire came to his ears as if through layers of cotton-wool. He put this down to dizziness from lack of food, and made his way to what looked like an *estaminet*. The place was full of riotous people who were helping themselves to drinks, while a distracted landlord wrung his hands. He flew to Galbraith, the tears running down his cheeks, and implored him in broken words.

'Vere ze Engleesh?' he cried. 'Ze méchants rob me. Zere is une émeute. Vere ze officers?'

'That's what I'm wantin' to ken mysel',' said Galbraith.

'Zey are gone,' wailed the innkeeper. 'Zere is no gendarme or anyzing, and I am rob.'

'Where's the polis? Get the Provost, man. D'ye tell me there's no polis left?'

'I am rob,' the wail continued. 'Ze méchants rob ze magasins and ve vill be assassinés.'

Light was dawning upon Private Galbraith. The British troops had left Ypres for some reason which he could not fathom, and there was no law or order in the little city. At other times he had hated the law as much as any man, and his relations with the police had often been strained. Now he realised that he had done them an injustice. Disorder suddenly seemed to him the one thing intolerable. Here had he been undergoing a stiff discipline for weeks, and if that was his fate no civilian should be allowed on the loose. He was a British soldier – marooned here by no fault of his own – and it was his business to keep up the end of the British Army and impose the King's peace upon the unruly. His temper was getting hot, but he was curiously happy. He marched into the *estaminet*. 'Oot o' here, ye scum!' he bellowed. 'Sortez, ye cochons!'

The revellers were silent before the apparition. Then one, drunker than the rest, flung a bottle which grazed his right ear. That put the finishing touch to his temper. Roaring like a bull, he was among them, prodding their hinder parts with his bayonet, and now and then reversing his rifle to crack a head. He had not played centre-forward in the old days at Celtic Park for nothing. The place emptied in a twinkling – all but one man whose legs could not support him. Him Private

Galbraith seized by the scruff and the slack of his trousers, and tossed into the street.

'Now I'll hae my breakfast,' he said to the trembling landlord.

Private Galbraith, much the better for his exercise, made a hearty meal of bread and cold ham, and quenched his thirst with two bottles of Hazebrouck beer. He had also a little brandy, and pocketed the flask, for which the landlord refused all payment. Then, feeling a giant refreshed, he sallied into the street.

'I'm off to look for your Provost,' he said. 'If ye have ony mair trouble, ye'll find me at the Toun Hall.'

A shell had plumped into the middle of the causeway, and the place was empty. Private Galbraith, despising shells, swaggered up the open, his disreputable kilt swinging about his putteeless legs, the remnant of a bonnet set well on the side of his shaggy red head, and the light of battle in his eyes. For once he was arrayed on the side of the angels, and the thought encouraged him mightily. The brandy had fired his imagination.

Adventure faced him at the next corner. A woman was struggling with two men – a slim pale girl with dark hair. No sound came from her lips, but her eyes were bright with terror. Galbraith started to run, shouting sound British oaths. The men let the woman go, and turned to face him. One had a pistol, and for the second time that day a bullet just missed its mark. An instant later a clean bayonet thrust had ended the mortal career of the marksman, and the other had taken to his heels.

'I'll learn thae lads to be sae free wi' their popguns,' said the irate soldier. 'Haud up, Mem. It's a' by wi' noo. Losh! The wumman's fentit!'

Private Galbraith was as shy of women as of his Commanding Officer, and he had not bargained for this duty. She was clearly a lady from her dress and appearance, and this did not make it easier. He supported her manfully, addressing to her the kind of encouragements which a groom gives to a horse. 'Canny now, Mem. Haud up! Ye've no cause to be feared.'

Then he remembered the brandy in his pocket, and with much awkwardness managed to force some drops between her lips. To his vast relief she began to come to. Her eyes opened and stared uncomprehendingly at her preserver. Then she found her voice.

'Thank God, the British have come back!' she said in excellent English.

'No, Mem; not yet. It's just me, Private Galbraith, "C" Company, 3rd Battalion, Lennox Highlanders. Ye keep some bad lots in this toun.'

'Alas! what can we do? The place is full of spies, and they will stir up the dregs of the people and make Ypres a hell. Oh, why did the British go? Our good men are all with the army, and there are only old folk and wastrels left.'

'Rely upon me, Mem,' said Galbraith stoutly. 'I was just settin' off to find your Provost.'

She puzzled at the word, and then understood.

'He has gone!' she cried. 'The Maire went to Dunkirk a week ago, and there is no authority in Ypres.'

'Then we'll make yin. Here's the minister. We'll speir at him.'

An old priest, with a lean, grave face, had come up.

'Ah, Mam'selle Omèrine,' he cried, 'the devil in our city is unchained. Who is this soldier?'

The two talked in French, while Galbraith whistled and looked at the sky. A shrapnel shell was bursting behind the cathedral, making a splash of colour in the November fog. Then the priest spoke in careful and constrained English.

'There is yet a chance for a strong man. But he must be very strong. Mam'selle will summon her father, Monsieur le Procureur, and we will meet at the Mairie. I will guide you there, *mon brave.*'

The Grande Place was deserted, and in the middle there was a new gaping shell-hole. At the door of a great building, which Galbraith assumed to be the Town Hall, a feeble old porter was struggling with a man. Galbraith scragged the latter and pitched him into the shell-hole. There was a riot going on in a café on the far side which he itched to have a hand in, but he postponed that pleasure to a more convenient season.

Twenty minutes later, in a noble room with frescoed and tapestried walls, there was a strange conference. The priest was there, and Galbraith, and Mam'selle Omèrine, and her father, M. St Marais. There was a doctor too, and three elderly citizens, and an old warrior who had left an arm on the Yser. Galbraith took charge, with Mam'selle as his interpreter, and in half an hour had constituted a Committee of Public Safety. He had nervous folk to deal with.

'The Germans may enter at any moment, and then we will all be hanged,' said one.

'Nae doot,' said Galbraith; 'but ye needna get your throats cut afore they come.'

'The city is full of the ill-disposed,' said another. 'The Boches have their spies in every alley. We who are so few cannot control them.'

'If it's spies,' said Galbraith firmly, 'I'll take on the job my lone. D'ye think a terrier dowg's feared of a wheen rottens?'

In the end he had his way, with Mam'selle's help, and had put some confidence into civic breasts. It took him the best part of the afternoon to collect his posse. He got every wounded Belgian that had the use of his legs, some well-grown boys, one or two ancients, and several dozen robust women. There was no lack of weapons, and he armed the lot with a strange collection of French and English rifles, giving pistols to the section leaders. With the help of the Procureur, he divided the city into beats and gave his followers instructions. They were drastic orders, for the situation craved for violence.

He spent the evening of his life. So far as he remembered afterwards, he was in seventeen different scraps. Strayed revellers were leniently dealt with – the canal was a cooling experience. Looters were rounded up, and, if they showed fight, summarily disposed of. One band of bullies made a stout resistance, killed two of his guards, and lost half-a-dozen dead. He got a black eye, a pistol-bullet through his sleeve, a wipe on the cheek from a carving-knife, and he lost the remnants of his bonnet. Fifty-two prisoners spent the night in the cellars of the Mairie.

About midnight he found himself in the tapestried chamber. 'We'll hae to get a Proclamation,' he had announced; 'a gude strong yin, for we maun conduct this job according to the rules.' So the Procureur had a document drawn up bidding all inhabitants of Ypres keep indoors except between the hours of 10 A.M. and noon, and 3 and 5 P.M.; forbidding the sale of alcohol in all forms; and making theft and violence and the carrying of arms punishable by death. There was a host of other provisions which Galbraith imperfectly understood, but when the thing was translated to him he approved its spirit. He signed the document in his large sprawling hand – 'Peter Galbraith, 1473, Pte., 3rd Lennox Highlanders, Acting Provost of Wipers.'

'Get that prentit,' he said, 'and pit up copies at every street corner and on a' the public-hooses. And see that the doors o' the publics are boardit up. That'll do for the day. I'm feelin' verra like my bed.'

Mam'selle Omèrine watched him with a smile. She caught his eye and dropped him a curtsey.

'Monsieur le Roi d'Ypres,' she said.

He blushed hotly.

For the next few days Private Galbraith worked harder

125

than ever before in his existence. For the first time he knew responsibility, and that toil which brings honour with it. He tasted the sweets of office; and he, whose aim in life had been to scrape through with the minimum of exertion, now found himself the inspirer of the maximum in others.

At first he scorned advice, being shy and nervous. Gradually, as he felt his feet, he became glad of other people's wisdom. Especially he leaned on two, Mam'selle Omèrine and her father. Likewise the priest, whom he called the minister.

By the second day the order in Ypres was remarkable. By the third day it was phenomenal; and by the fourth a tyranny. The little city for the first time for seven hundred years fell under the sway of a despot. A citizen had to be on his best behaviour, for the Acting Provost's eye was on him. Never was seen so sober a place. Three permits for alcohol and no more were issued, and then only on the plea of medical necessity. Peter handed over to the doctor the flask of brandy he had carried off from the *estaminet* – Provosts must set an example.

The Draconian code promulgated the first night was not adhered to. Looters and violent fellows went to gaol instead of the gallows. But three spies were taken and shot after a full trial. That trial was the master effort of Private Galbraith – based on his own regimental experience and memories of a Sheriff Court in Lanarkshire, where he had twice appeared for poaching. He was extraordinarily punctilious about forms, and the three criminals – their guilt was clear, and they were the scum of creation – had something more than justice. The Acting Provost pronounced sentence, which the priest translated, and a file of *mutilés* in the yard did the rest.

'If the Boches get in here we'll pay for this day's work,' said the judge cheerfully; 'but I'll gang easier to the grave for havin' got rid o' thae swine.'

On the fourth day he had a sudden sense of dignity. He

examined his apparel, and found it very bad. He needed a new bonnet, a new kilt, and puttees, and he would be the better of a new shirt. Being aware that commandeering for personal use ill suited with his office, he put the case before the Procureur, and a *Commission de Ravitaillement* was appointed. Shirts and puttees were easily got, but the kilt and bonnet were difficulties. But next morning Mam'selle Omèrine brought a gift. It was a bonnet with such a dicing round the rim as no Jock ever wore, and a skirt – it is the truest word – of that pattern which graces the persons of small girls in France. It was not the Lennox tartan, it was not any kind of tartan, but Private Galbraith did not laugh. He accepted the garments with a stammer of thanks – 'They're awfu' braw, and I'm much obliged, Mem' – and, what is more, he put them on. The Ypriotes saw his splendour with approval. It was a proof of his new frame of mind that he did not even trouble to reflect what his comrades would think of his costume, and that he kissed the bonnet affectionately before he went to bed.

That night he had evil dreams. He suddenly saw the upshot of it all – himself degraded and shot as a deserter, and his brief glory pricked like a bubble. Grim forebodings of court-martials assailed him. What would Mam'selle think of him when he was led away in disgrace – he who for a little had been a king? He walked about the floor in a frenzy of disquiet, and stood long at the window peering over the Place, lit by a sudden blink of moonlight. It could never be, he decided. Something desperate would happen first. The crash of a shell a quarter of a mile off reminded him that he was in the midst of war – war with all its chances of cutting knots.

Next morning no Procureur appeared. Then came the priest with a sad face and a sadder tale. Mam'selle had been out late the night before on an errand of mercy, and a shell, crashing through a gable, had sent an avalanche of masonry into the street.

She was dead, without pain, said the priest, and in the sure hope of Heaven.

The others wept, but Private Galbraith strode from the room, and in a very little time was at the house of the Procureur. He saw his little colleague laid out for death after the fashion of her Church, and his head suddenly grew very clear and his heart hotter than fire.

'I maun resign this job,' he told the Committee of Public Safety. 'I've been forgettin' that I'm a sodger and no a Provost. It's my duty to get a nick at thae Boches.'

They tried to dissuade him, but he was adamant. His rule was over, and he was going back to serve.

But he was not allowed to resign. For that afternoon, after a week's absence, the British troops came again into Ypres.

They found a decorous little city, and many people who spoke of 'le Roi' – which they assumed to signify the good King Albert. Also, in a corner of the cathedral yard, sitting disconsolately on the edge of a fallen monument, Company Sergeant-Major Macvittie of the 3rd Lennox Highlanders found Private Peter Galbraith.

'Ma God, Galbraith, ye've done it this time! *You'll* catch it in the neck! Absent for a week wi'out leave, and gettin' yoursel' up to look like Harry Lauder! You come along wi' me!'

'I'll come quiet,' said Galbraith with strange meekness. He was wondering how to spell Omèrine St Marais in case he wanted to write it in his Bible.

The events of the next week were confusing to a plain man. Galbraith was very silent, and made no reply to the chaff with which at first he was greeted. Soon his fellows forbore to chaff him, regarding him as a doomed man who had come well within the pale of the ultimate penalties.

He was examined by his Commanding Officer, and inter-viewed by still more exalted personages. The story he told was so bare as to be unintelligible. He asked for no mercy, and gave no explanations. But there were other witnesses besides him – the priest, for example, and Monsieur St Marais, in a sober suit of black and very dark under the eyes.

By and by the Court gave its verdict. Private Peter Galbraith was found guilty of riding roughshod over the King's Regulations; he had absented himself from his battalion without permission; he had neglected his own duties and usurped without authority a number of superior functions; he had been the cause of the death or maltreatment of various persons who, whatever their moral deficiencies, must be regarded for the purposes of the case as civilian Allies. The Court, however, taking into consideration the exceptional circumstances in which Private Galbraith had been placed, inflicted no penalty and summarily discharged the prisoner.

Privately, his Commanding Officer and the still more exalted personages shook hands with him, and told him that he was a devilish good fellow and a credit to the British Army.

But Peter Galbraith cared for none of these things. As he sat again in the trenches at St Eloi in six inches of water and a foot of mud, he asked his neighbour how many Germans were opposite them.

'I was hearin' that there was maybe fifty thoosand,' was the answer.

Private Galbraith was content. He thought that the whole fifty thousand would scarcely atone for the death of one slim, dark-eyed girl.

...And Some Fell
by the Wayside
(1915)

Ian Hay

'Firing parrty, revairse arrms!'

Thus the platoon sergeant – a little anxiously; for we are new to this feat, and only rehearsed it for a few minutes this morning.

It is a sunny afternoon in late February. The winter of our discontent is past. (At least, we hope so.) Comfortless months of training are safely behind us, and lo, we have grown from a fortuitous concourse of atoms to a cohesive unit of fighting men. Spring is coming; spring is coming; our blood runs quicker; active service is within measurable distance; and the future beckons to us with both hands to step down at last into the arena, and try our fortune amid the uncertain but illimitable chances of the greatest game in the world.

To all of us, that is, save one.

The road running up the hill from the little mortuary is lined on either side by members of our company, specklessly turned out and standing to attention. At the foot of the slope a gun-carriage is waiting, drawn by two great dray-horses and controlled by a private of the Army Service Corps, who looks incongruously perky and cockney amid that silent, kilted assemblage. The firing party form a short lane from the gun-carriage to the door of the mortuary. In response to the sergeant's command, each man turns over his rifle, and setting the muzzle carefully upon his right boot – after all, it argues no extra respect to the dead to get your barrel filled with mud – rests his hands upon the buttplate and bows his head, as laid down in the King's Regulations.

The bearers move slowly down the path from the mortuary, and place the coffin upon the gun-carriage. Upon the lid lie a very dingy glengarry, a stained leather belt, and a bayonet. They are humble trophies, but we pay them as much reverence as we would to the baton and cocked hat of a field-marshal, for they are the insignia of a man who has given his life for his country.

On the hill-top above us, where the great military hospital rears its clock-tower four-square to the sky, a line of convalescents, in natty blue uniforms with white facings and red ties, lean over the railings deeply interested. Some of them are bandaged, others are in slings, and all are more or less maimed. They follow the obsequies below with critical approval. They have been present at enough hurried and promiscuous interments of late – more than one of them has only just escaped being the central figure at one of these functions – that they are capable of appreciating a properly conducted funeral at its true value.

'They're puttin' away a bloomin' Jock,' remarks a gentleman with an empty sleeve.

'And very nice, too,' responds another on crutches, as the firing party present arms with creditable precision.

'Not 'arf a bad bit of eye-wash at all for a bandy-legged lot of coal-shovellers.'

That lot's out of K(i),' explains a well-informed invalid with his head in bandages. 'Pretty 'ot stuff they're gettin'. *Très moutarde!* Now we're off.'

The signal is passed up the road to the band, who are waiting at the head of the procession, and the pipes break into a lament. Corporals step forward and lay four wreaths upon the coffin – one from each company. Not a man in the battalion has failed to contribute his penny to those wreaths; and pennies are not too common with us, especially on a Thursday, which comes just before pay-day. The British private is commonly reputed to spend all, or most of, his pocket-money upon beer. But I can tell you this, that if you give him his choice between buying himself a pint of beer and subscribing to a wreath, he will most decidedly go thirsty.

The serio-comic charioteer gives his reins a twitch, the horses wake up, and the gun-carriage begins to move slowly along the lane of mourners. As the dead private passes on his way the walls of the lane melt, and his comrades fall into their usual fours behind the gun-carriage.

So we pass up the hill towards the military cemetery, with the pipes wailing their hearts out, and the muffled drums marking the time of our regulation slow step. Each foot seems to hang in the air before the drums bid us put it down.

In the very rear of the procession you may see the company commander and three subalterns. They give no orders, and exact no attention. To employ a colloquialism, this is not their funeral.

Just behind the gun-carriage stalks a solitary figure in civilian clothes – the unmistakable 'blacks' of an Elder of the Kirk. At first sight, you have a feeling that someone has strayed into the procession who has no right there. But no one has a better. The sturdy old man behind the coffin is named Adam Carmichael, and he is here, having travelled south from Dumbarton by the night train, to attend the funeral of his only son.

Peter Carmichael was one of the first to enlist in the regiment. There was another Carmichael in the same company, so Peter at roll-call was usually addressed by the sergeant as 'Twenty-seeven fufty-fower Carmichael,' 2754 being his regimental number. The army does not encourage Christian names. When his attestation paper was filled up, he gave his age as nineteen; his address, vaguely, as Renfrewshire; and his trade, not without an air, as a 'holder-on'. To the mystified Bobby Little he entered upon a lengthy explanation of the term in a language composed almost entirely of vowels, from which that officer gathered, dimly, that holding-on had something to do with shipbuilding.

Upon the barrack-square his platoon commander's attention was again drawn to Peter, owing to the passionate enthusiasm with which he performed the simplest evolutions, such as forming fours and sloping arms – military exercises which do not intrigue the average private to any great extent. Unfortunately, desire frequently outran performance. Peter was undersized, unmuscular, and extraordinarily clumsy. For a long time Bobby Little thought that Peter, like one or two of his comrades, was left-handed, so made allowances. Ultimately he discovered that his indulgence was misplaced: Peter was equally incompetent with either hand. He took longer in learning to fix bayonets or present arms than any other man in the platoon. To be fair, Nature had done little to help him. He was thirty-three inches round the chest, five feet four in height, and weighed possibly nine stone. His complexion was pasty, and, as Captain Wagstaffe remarked, you could hang your hat on any bone in his body. His eyesight was not all that the Regulations require, and on the musketry-range he was 'put back', to his deep distress, 'for further instruction'. Altogether, if you had not known the doctor who passed him, you would have said it was a mystery how he passed the doctor.

But he possessed the one essential attribute of the soldier. He had a big heart. He was keen. He allowed nothing to come between him and his beloved duties. ('He was aye daft for to go sogerin',' his father explained to Captain Blaikie, 'but his mother would never let him away. He was ower wee, and ower young.') His rifle, buttons, and boots were always without blemish. Further, he was of the opinion that a merry heart goes all the way. He never sulked when the platoon were kept on parade five minutes after the breakfast bugle had sounded. He made no bones about obeying orders and saluting officers – acts of abasement which grated sorely at times upon his colleagues, who reverenced no one except themselves and their Union. He appeared to revel in muddy route-marches, and invariably provoked and led the choruses. The men called him 'Wee Pe'er', and ultimately adopted him as a sort of company mascot. Whereat Pe'er's heart glowed; for when your associates attach a diminutive to your Christian name, you possess something which millionaires would gladly give half their fortune to purchase.

And certainly he required all the social success he could win, for professionally Peter found life a rigorous affair. Sometimes, as he staggered into barracks after a long day, carrying a rifle made of lead and wearing a pair of boots weighing a hundred-weight apiece, he dropped dead asleep on his bedding before he could eat his dinner. But he always hotly denied the imputation that he was 'sick'.

Time passed. The regiment was shaking down. Seven of Peter's particular cronies were raised to the rank of lance-corporal – but not Peter. He was 'off the square' now – that is to say, he was done with recruit drill for ever. He possessed a sound knowledge of advance-guard and outpost work; his conduct-sheet was a blank page. But he was not promoted. He was 'ower wee for a stripe,' he told himself. For the present he must expect to be passed over. His chance would come later, when he had filled out a little and got rid of his cough.

The winter dragged on: the weather was appalling: the grousers gave tongue with no uncertain voice, each streaming field-day. But Wee Pe'er enjoyed it all. He did not care if it snowed ink. He was a 'sojer'.

One day, to his great delight, he was 'warned for guard' – a particularly unpopular branch of a soldier's duties, for it means sitting in the guardroom for twenty-four hours at a stretch, fully dressed and accoutred, with intervals of sentry-go, usually in heavy rain, by way of exercise. When Peter's turn for sentry-go came on he splashed up and down his muddy beat – the battalion was in billets now, and the usual sentry's veranda was lacking – as proud as a peacock, saluting officers according to their rank, challenging stray civilians with great severity, and turning out the guard on the slightest provocation. He was at his post, soaked right through his greatcoat, when the orderly officer made his night round. Peter summoned his colleagues; the usual inspection of the guard took place; and the sleepy men were then dismissed to their fireside. Peter remained; the officer hesitated. He was supposed to examine the sentry in his knowledge of his duties. It was a profitless task as a rule. The tongue-tied youth merely gaped like a stranded fish, until the sergeant mercifully intervened, in some such words as these, 'This man, sirr, is liable to get over-excited when addressed by an officer.'

Then soothingly, 'Now, Jimmy, tell the officer what would ye dae in case of fire?'

'Present airrms!' announces the desperate James. Or else, almost tearfully, 'I canna mind. I had it all fine just noo, but it's awa' oot o' ma heid!'

Therefore it was with no great sense of anticipation that the orderly officer said to Private Carmichael, 'Now, sentry, can you repeat any of your duties?'

Peter saluted, took a full breath, closed both eyes, and replied rapidly, 'For tae tak' chairge of all Government property within sicht of this guairdhoose tae turrn oot the guaird for all arrmed pairties approaching also the commanding officer once a day tae salute all officers tae challenge all pairsons approaching this post tae . . .'

His recital was interrupted by a fit of coughing.

'Thank you,' said the officer hastily, 'that will do. Good night!'

Peter, not sure whether it would be correct to say 'good night' too, saluted again, and returned to his cough.

'I say,' said the officer, turning back, 'you have a shocking cold.'

'Och, never heed it, sirr,' gasped Peter politely.

'Call the sergeant,' said the officer.

The fat sergeant came out of the guardhouse again buttoning his tunic.

'Sirr?'

'Take this man off sentry-duty and roast him at the guardroom fire.'

'I will, sirr,' replied the sergeant; and added, paternally, 'This man has no right for to be here at all. He should have reported sick when warned for guard; but he would not. He is very attentive to his duties, sirr.'

'Good boy!' said the officer to Peter. 'I wish we had more like you.'

Wee Pe'er blushed, his teeth momentarily ceased chattering, his heart swelled. Appearances to the contrary, he felt warm all through. The sergeant laid a fatherly hand upon his shoulder.

'Go you your ways intil the guardroom, boy,' he commanded, 'and send oot Dunshie. He'll no hurt. Get close in ahint the stove, or you'll be for Cambridge!'

(The last phrase carries no academic significance. It simply means that you are likely to become an inmate of the great Cambridge Hospital at Aldershot.)

Peter, feeling thoroughly disgraced, cast an appealing look at the officer.

'In you go!' said that martinet.

Peter silently obeyed. It was the only time in his life that he ever felt mutinous.

A month later Brigade Training set in with customary severity. The life of company officers became a burden. They spent hours in thick woods with their followers, taking cover, ostensibly from the enemy, in reality from brigade-majors and staff officers. A subaltern never tied his platoon in a knot but a general came trotting round the corner. The wet weather had ceased, and a biting east wind reigned in its stead.

On one occasion an elaborate night operation was arranged. Four battalions were to assemble at a given point five miles from camp, and then advance in column across country by the light of the stars to a position indicated on the map, where they were to deploy and dig themselves in. It sounded simple enough in operation orders; but when you try to move four thousand troops – even well-trained troops – across three miles of broken country on a pitch-dark night, there is always a possibility that someone will get mislaid. On this particular occasion a whole battalion lost itself without any delay or difficulty whatsoever. The other three were compelled to wait for two hours and a half, stamping their feet and blowing on their fingers, while overheated staff officers scoured the country for the truants. They were discovered at last waiting virtuously at the wrong rendezvous, three-quarters of a mile away. The brazen-hatted strategist who drew up the operation orders had given the point of assembly for the brigade as: . . . the field s.w. of WELLINGTON WOOD and due E. of HANGMAN'S COPSE, immediately below the first O in GHOSTLY BOTTOM, but omitted to underline the O indicated. The result was that three battalion commanders assembled at the O in 'ghostly' while the fourth, ignoring the adjective in favour of the noun, took up his station at the first O in 'bottom'.

The operations had been somewhat optimistically timed to end at eleven p.m., but by the time that the four battalions had effected a most unloverly tryst, it was close on ten, and beginning to rain. The consequence was that the men got home to bed, soaked to the skin, and asking the Powers Above rhetorical questions, at three o'clock in the morning.

Next day Brigade Orders announced that the movement would be continued at nightfall, by the occupation of the hastily-dug trenches, followed by a night attack upon the hill in front. The captured position would then be re-trenched.

When the tidings went round, fourteen of the more quick-witted spirits of 'A' Company hurriedly paraded before the Medical Officer and announced that they were 'sick in the stomach'. Seven more discovered abrasions upon their feet, and proffered their sores for inspection, after the manner of Oriental mendicants. One skrim-shanker, despairing of producing any bodily ailment, rather ingeniously assaulted a comrade-in-arms, and was led away, deeply grateful, to the guardroom. Wee Peter, who in the course of last night's operations had stumbled into an old trench half-filled with ice-cold water, and whose temperature today, had he known it, was a hundred and two, paraded with his company at the appointed time. The company, he reflected, would get a bad name if too many men reported sick at once.

Next day he was absent from parade. He was 'for Cambridge' at last.

Before he died, he sent for the officer who had befriended him, and supplemented, or rather corrected, some of the information contained in his attestation paper.

He lived in Dumbarton, not Renfrewshire. He was just sixteen. He was not – this confession cost him a great effort – a full-blown 'holder-on' at all; only an apprentice. His father was 'weel kent' in the town of Dumbarton, being a chief engineer, employed by a great firm of ship-builders to extend new machinery on trial trips.

Needless to say, he made a great fight. But though his heart was big enough, his body was too frail. As they say on the sea, he was over-engined for his beam.

And so, three days later, the simple soul of Twenty-seven fifty-four Carmichael, 'A' Company, was transferred, on promotion, to another company – the great Company of Happy Warriors who walk the Elysian Fields.

'Firing parrty, one round blank – load!'

There is a rattle of bolts, and a dozen barrels are pointed heavenwards. The company stands rigid, except the buglers, who are beginning to finger their instruments.

'Fire!'

There is a crackling volley, and the pipes break into a brief, sobbing wail. Wayfarers upon the road below look up curiously. One or two young females with perambulators come hurrying across the grass, exhorting apathetic babies to sit up and admire the pretty funeral.

Twice more the rifles ring out. The pipes cease their wailing, and there is an expectant silence.

The drum-major crooks his little finger, and eight bugles come to the 'ready'. Then 'Last Post', the requiem of every soldier of the King, swells out, sweet and true.

The echoes lose themselves among the dripping pines. The chaplain closes his book, takes off his spectacles, and departs.

Old Carmichael permits himself one brief look into his son's grave, resumes his crape-bound tall hat, and turns heavily away. He finds Captain Blaikie's hand waiting for him. He grips it, and says, 'Weel, the laddie has had a grand sojer's funeral. His mother will be pleased to hear that.'

He passes on, and shakes hands with the platoon sergeant and one or two of Peter's cronies. He declines an invitation to the Sergeants' Mess.

'I hae a trial-trup the morn,' he explains. 'I must be steppin'. God keep ye all, brave lads!'

The old gentleman sets off down the station road. The company falls in, and we march back to barracks, leaving Wee Pe'er – the first name on our Roll of Honour – alone in his glory beneath the Hampshire pines.

Sunk
(1916)

A. F. Whyte

She was an old battleship whose day of power was long past. At the great naval review held to celebrate the sixtieth year of Queen Victoria's reign, you might have seen her in one of the proudest stations of the Fleet, but when the Great War broke out hers was the least of the Battle Squadrons, and she herself a neglected unit at the very tail of British Sea Power, almost ready for the ship-breaker's yard. War brought her to life again and to a glorious end. Being one of the ships concerned in the much-discussed Test Mobilisation of the Third Fleet which took the place of Naval Manœuvres in 1914, she was unusually ready when war broke out: full complement on board, guns' crews less rusty than usual, and showing a remarkable turn of speed for a lady of her years, though slow as a dray compared with her younger sisters. In company with others of her age and kind she made part of that strange squadron, a motley of ancient and modern, headed by the greatest ship in the world, which won renown at the Dardanelles. Written off by the callous Lords Commissioners of the Admiralty as 'of no military significance', she yet told her tale of shelling sound and fury to the Turkish enemy in such a fashion as to make it signify some considerable damage to him, and to show that even the tail of our Sea Power had a good deal of nasty sting left in it.

One morning in May 1915 she entered the Straits, the last of five battleships in line ahead told off to support an advance of the troops on shore. With their guns trained on the European side they turned their backs, as it were, upon the Turkish batteries on the Asiatic shore, and when the latter began to bother them our ship was ordered to take station somewhere off Kum Kale and enfilade the Turkish position with her 12-inch guns. Steadily all day the booming of the guns sounded across the water and went echoing up the Hellespont: and, as if to prove that this was something more than Battle Practice at last, a spout of water would rise now and then not a cable's-length ahead and others of the same round about. Rarely, and even then without great effect, did enemy shells fall aboard; but they came near enough to keep the ship's company awake and lively all day. In the soft evening light the guns of this enfilading ship looked like long grey pencils, but where the lead should have been there came ever and anon a red tongue that flashed and vanished; and after the red tongue a great cloud; and after the cloud a voice of thunder; and far up the Asiatic shore the shell found its mark. Then sunset came and put an end to the noisy day's work; and the ship took her night station under the lee of the European shore, put out her torpedo-netting anew like a great steel skirt, and lay awaiting the return of day. Darkness gathered about her with that sudden descent that surprises men from the north used to the long twilight of summer, and long before midnight land and sea were lost to view under the heavy cloak of a black starless sky.

The officer of the watch, a Royal Naval Reserve lieutenant from the Orkneys, peered into the night and listened to the low gurgle and murmur of the tide running strongly through the torpedo-netting and making the ship swing slowly to her anchor. And as he listened an old Orcadian rhyme came into his head –

Eynhallow frank, Eynhallow free,
Eynhallow stands in the middle of the sea,
With a roarin' roost on every side,
Eynhallow stands in the middle of the tide.

So he stood: in the middle of another tide with a roarin' roost on every side, and a ship under his feet which seemed as firm as the Eynhallow rock itself. Little did he think that before dawn she would prove but a frail refuge. As little did he realise that the campaign on which he was engaged was but the latest link in a long chain of stirring events that had made the Hellespont famous from the most distant times. Had he been of a reflective turn of mind he might have conjured up before him the whole matchless pageant of history that lies folded in those narrow waters: the Trojan scene; the oft-repeated passage of that great sea-river by conquerors from East and West; the glory of Byzantium and its decay; the prowess and cruelty of the Ottoman Turks; and all the lore of those waters of ancient memory. But he was a simple seaman from the merchant service, drawn into the service of the King at war, and no such high historic thoughts came to distract him from the duties of his watch.

Presently he was joined by another officer who came up from below for a breath of fresh air. They talked together for a while, recalling the incidents of the day's work, speculating upon the old theme of Ships v Forts, pitying the 'poor devils ashore' who were never out of fire, and wondering when Achi Baba would fall. They talked 'shop' because there was nothing else to talk about; and though the subjects never varied, they never seemed to lose their zest. In every ward-room of the motley fleet assembled round the snout of the Gallipoli Peninsula, the same kind of talk might be heard, varied a little in each ship, and always flavoured with the expressive service slang so beloved and so little understood by the Gentlemen of the Press who accompanied them. The officer of the watch and his companion continued their conversation in low tones for a while, and then stood for a moment silent. With a 'Good night; I'm going to turn in', the latter had set his foot on the topmost rail of the steel ladder and was about to descend when a sudden exclamation arrested him. He turned.

'What's that?' said the officer of the watch in a sharp whisper.

'Where?'

'Over there,' he pointed to the shore on the port side.

'I can't see a thing.'

They strained their eyes, peering out into the night. They listened intently, but heard nothing except the murmuring tide now sounding its eerie accompaniment to the inaudible movement out of sight. They strained their ears; but neither sight nor hearing but some other uncanny sense was awake in them hinting of something about to happen.

The officer of the watch spoke again.

'I can't see a thing, and I can't hear anything; but I swear there's something moving out there.' He pointed again to the European shore.

'Troops, perhaps?'

'Can't be; we'd have been warned.'

They waited again in silence. How long they stood tense, neither could afterwards say: each second was a long agony of suspense. The eddying tide whispered and bubbled beneath them. A faint stirring of the night air caressed their faces. But to their anxious questions no answer came. In the deep shadow under the land there was a secret, holding life or death perhaps, a moving threat hidden in the night. But what it was? or whence? or why? they could not tell.

Suddenly the officer of the watch clutched his companion's arm.

'A destroyer. Look!'

Just where a gully dipped to the sea there was a patch where land and water met that was faintly luminous. It was not light, merely less black than the rest, but the contrast was enough to give the eye an impression of light. With bursting pulses the watchkeeper saw a long, low, black shape pass stealthily across the patch.

'Shall I challenge? It may be one of our "Beagles" coming back from the Narrows. They went up towards Chanak, two of them, after dinner. I saw them.'

'No; it can't be. They'd never come like that. You've had no signal from the Flagship?'

'No.'

'Then it's *der Tag* for us, old man! Keep your eye on him, and I'll tell the skipper. You'd better pass the word for "Action Stations" to the port battery. We must be quick about it, and quiet; otherwise our number's up.'

He went to rouse the captain. The officer of the watch made his preparations, watched his orders being swiftly and almost noiselessly carried out, and turned again to peer through the darkness. Two minutes passed. He inflated his 'Gieve', and as he tucked away the tube, a faint splash was heard in the darkness away on the port-beam.

'God! A torpedo,' he exclaimed.

He waited for the torpedo to strike – another long suspense: but within thirty seconds the splash was answered by a roar from the 4-in. port battery of his own ship. Tongues of flame leapt from the muzzles, lighting up the night, and the shells whistled to their all but invisible mark. But before they could fire another round, the torpedo struck. The ship quivered, a tremor running through every plate and rivet: her stern shivered like the hindquarters of a dog coming out of water. Then she was heaved upwards by some monstrous power beneath. A great spout of water rose, and a great flame leapt out of the ship's belly with a deafening roar, sending its licking tongues high in the midnight sky. And all this was simultaneous: the quiver, the heave, the spout, and the flame were all blended in one vast, hot, terrifying chaos. A second explosion followed, rending the ship to her very vitals. Guns, boats, men, all were flung into the air like leaves in a whirlwind: one of the steamboats was seen spinning like a blazing top a hundred feet up in the air. The great ship herself rolled over to port, hung awhile with her decks steep aslant, and then plunged with a terrible hiss and roar to the bottom. The spot where she had been was thick with men and debris, the awful flotsam of a torpedoed battleship now lit up by a searchlight's occasional gleam. The risk to other ships was too great at first to permit anything more than a momentary and fitful use of their welcome beams by the destroyers and auxiliary craft hastening to the rescue. Death might still lurk in the dark corners of the land on either side. And so, until the screening patrols had swept the strait, a wholesome caution shrouded the life-saving operations in gloom. Even without the pall of darkness the night was eerie enough. The cries of the injured men suffering agonies in the ice-cold water rang hideously through the still air; and though the work of rescue was well and quickly done as the picket-boats and trawlers nosed their way about, death was too often too quick for them; and of those that lived, even with all the despatch and skill of the rescuers, many a survivor suffered the tortures of the damned in a desperate struggle with the freezing cold and the still more freezing fear that in the confusion and darkness he would not be picked up.

Two hours later the last searchlight had swept the eddying surface, the last picket-boat had returned. The sudden danger had passed, leaving a wreck on its track: and the

> *Waters of Asia, westward-beating waves*
> *Of estuaries, and mountain-warded straits,*
> *Whose solitary beaches long had lost*
> *The ashen glimmer of the dying day,*
> *Listened in darkness to their own lone sound*
> *Moving about the shores of sleep . . .*

The following evening four officers sat at a bridge table in the deck smoking-room of an auxiliary lying in Mudros harbour. A burly merchant captain, wearing the woven stripes of a lieutenant-commander in the R.N.R. – the 'tea-cosy' decoration, as a facetious merchant skipper once called it, his chief engineer, a good Scot, in great demand all over the harbour for his inexhaustible stock of yarns, a lieutenant-commander, R.N., rescued ten days before from a torpedoed battleship, and now awaiting 'disposal'; and a King's messenger in the uniform of the Volunteer Reserve – as well-mixed a foursome as ever played a hand. The call of war had brought them together from their vocations of peace and had dumped them temporarily in the good ship *Fauvette*, which was wont in happier times to ply a busy trade between London and Bordeaux. They had hardly dealt the cards for a second game when a movement on deck disturbed them, and before they could rise to ascertain the cause a troupe of strangely clad youngsters appeared at the door.

'May we come in, sir?' said one of them, who was, in sober truth, a 'thing of shreds and patches'.

'Make yourselves at home, boys,' said the skipper, waving a chubby hand round the room.

A signalman entered with his pad, and handed it to the skipper.

'Gad! Of course,' he cried, 'you're the stowaways we've been expecting all day. Well, what's it like being torpedoed?'

There was silence. None of these midshipmen was adept at public speech in the presence of unknown superiors. So for the moment the skipper's questions remained unanswered. As they settled in a group in the corner of the smoking-room they presented a fine study in motley. Every stitch on their backs had been borrowed from willing lenders. One waddled in the blue overalls of a benevolent but too burly friend; another looked like an example of record promotion, for there were three gold stripes half-concealed under the folded cuff of a sleeve that was a hand's-length too long for the wearer; a third wore the tweeds of a war correspondent, who had doubtless exacted 'copy' as interest on the loan of his clothes; and the rest of them, in various ways, completed the picture of incongruity. But for all that they had passed through one of the greatest ordeals of war, they showed but little sign of strain or fatigue, and only asked whether they might have something to smoke and whether they could write home. Their needs were supplied; and the skipper repeated his question –

'Come on and tell us what it's like being torpedoed.'

'It's always the same,' broke in the lieutenant-commander at the card table. 'A frightful din; and a bit of a shake an' a heave, and then you're in the water. Your "Gieve" does the rest. That's all there is to it.'

'I wish to God it was,' said a new hollow voice at the door. 'I was on watch when the damned thing struck us, and I was in the water among the bodies for a hell of a time; and if that's all you knew when your packet sank, you're lucky. Damned lucky!' he repeated slowly in a dull voice.

The figure in the doorway was at once familiar and strange, like that of a strong man grown suddenly wizened. He was visibly shrunken, and as he walked unsteadily across the room and sat down on a swivel-seat, he talked continuously but almost incoherently, half to himself and half to the watching group. The contrast between him and the unscathed midshipmen was very strong and unexpected. He and they had come from the same ship, passed through the same night of alarm, and been hauled out of the same cold water by the same rescuing hands. The experience had set no mark upon the boys: yet in the grown man it had wrought such a sea-change as made one almost fear to look at him. His tanned cheeks were still brown, but it was a bloodless tint; and the lines that seamed his face gave him a sepulchral look. His eyes alone were bright – too bright. The softer quality that makes the human eye so expressive was gone, and there remained a vivid stare as of eyes straining to see the invisible. There he was, in our company, but certainly not of it; for his brain was working and wandering whither we could not follow, and the words that came from his lips were the half-automatic expression of an absent mind. 'Gimme a cig'ret,' he said with the husky slurred articulation of a drunk man, and he sat puffing and biting the end of it into pulp. Then he would grip the short arms of his seat, start up and look downwards between his knees, and then sit down again with the look of shamed annoyance. He was clearly struggling to get away from something, and we were powerless to help.

We tried to distract him. The steward brought a tray loaded with sandwiches and drinks, which he refused. We were getting a little uneasy about our strange guest; the doctor whom the skipper had sent for was long in coming, and each renewal of our efforts to divert the patient failed. We gave him the *Bystander* and *Punch*, but he was beyond the reach of Bairnsfather and George Morrow: we tried to draw him into a game at the table – poker, bridge, patience, anything – but he remained immovable.

At last the doctor, a thick-set bearded Fleet Surgeon, came and took charge, and reversed our procedure. Where we had been gentle, almost timid, he was rough. Where we had coaxed, he ordered. Where we had fumbled and faltered with the unknown, he acted with the confidence of experience. After a rapid examination and cross-examination, in the course of which he drew more from his victim in five minutes than we had extracted in an hour and more, he hustled him below and packed him into a bunk with various aids to sleep which he did not specify. Then the Fleet Surgeon returned to the smoking-room.

'You're a bright lot,' he said; 'why didn't you put him to bed at once? He's absolutely done, but if he can sleep, he'll be all right soon. Never seen a man quite so worn out.'

'Do you mean to say that he's only tired? He looked like he was going off his chump.'

'So would you if your nerves had been living on shocks without any solid support. What he went through has got such a hold on him that until he's had a good twenty-four hours' sleep as a preliminary and a course of feeding up and regular sleep without any work to do after that, he won't quite know where he is. But I bet he's sitting up and taking nourishment this time tomorrow. He was on the verge of being a bad case, but we've caught him just in time.'

The doctor was right. Our patient slept till midday next day, took a light meal and slept again till sunset. Then he awoke and dined; but in an hour he was asleep again. Clearly he had been put to bed at the psychological moment. By the following afternoon he was taking the air in a deck-chair, and ready – perhaps a little too ready, for his health – to talk about the sinking of his ship.

When the explosion occurred he was thrown clear of the ship on the starboard side. He was half-stunned, but his swimming waistcoat kept him afloat. The rest must be told in his own words:

'I don't know how long it was before I realised where I was, but it was long enough to let me get pretty cold. You know what the water's like. I picked up two men close by me, still swimming, but pretty nearly done. Neither of them had belts on. One, I knew by his voice, was a ward-room steward. They hung on to me for a while, the "Gieve" keeping us all afloat as long as we made a bit of an effort ourselves. We could hear the picket-boats going about, and sometimes a searchlight picked us up; but nothing came near enough to rescue us. And before long one of the fellows hanging on to me began to groan and his teeth chattered. I told him to keep moving, but it was no good. He slipped off, and I never saw him again. That was bad enough, but when the other fellow's teeth began the same game, I got the creeps; but I couldn't save him, and after a few moments he went too. It was a ghastly feeling. The sudden silence, and the cold creeping right into me made me want to give up too, when suddenly I thought I had touched bottom. I tried to walk, but the thing I touched slipped away, and I realised with a shudder what it was. And after that I swear

I must have touched a dozen of them before I was picked up. That's what knocked me out. But, I say, let's chuck it. I must get away from it.'

He passed his hand over his face. The old troubled look came back, and for the moment I could see that, like Orestes pursued by the Furies, his spirit was haunted by the ghosts of men whose bodies his feet had touched in the dark waters of the Hellespont. He had indeed suffered a sea-change, and the war was over for him.

Shot at Dawn
(1932)

Lewis Grassic Gibbon

Chae had lain in a camp near by and had heard of the thing by chance, he'd read Ewan's name in some list of papers that was posted up. And he'd gone the night before Ewan was shot, and they'd let him see Ewan, and he'd heard it all, the story he was telling her now – *better always to know what truth's in a thing, for lies come creeping home to roost on unco rees, Chris quean. You're young yet, you've hardly begun to live, and I swore to myself that I'd tell you it all, that you'd never be vexed with some twisted bit in the years to come. Ewan was shot as a deserter, it was fair enough, he'd deserted from the front line trenches.*

He had deserted in a blink of fine weather between the rains that splashed the glutted rat-runs of the front. He had done it quickly and easily, he told to Chae, he had just turned and walked back. And other soldiers that met him had thought him a messenger, or wounded, or maybe on leave, none had questioned him, he'd set out at ten o'clock in the morning and by afternoon, taking to the fields, was ten miles or more from the front. Then the military policemen came on him and took him, he was marched back and court-martialled and found to be guilty.

And Chae said to him, they sat together in the hut where he waited the coming of the morning, *But why did you do it, Ewan? You might well have known you'd never get free.* And Ewan looked at him and shook his head, *It was that wind that came with the sun, I minded Blawearie, I seemed to waken up smelling that smell. And I couldn't believe it was me that stood in the trench, it was just daft to be there. So I turned and got out of it.*

In a flash it had come on him, he had wakened up, he was daft and a fool to be there; and, like somebody minding things done in a coarse wild dream there had flashed on him memory of Chris at Blawearie and his last days there, mad and mad he had been, he had treated her as a devil might, he had tried to hurt her and maul her, trying in the nightmare to waken, to make her waken him up; and now in the blink of sun he saw her face as last he'd seen it while she quivered away from his taunts. He knew he had lost her, she'd never be his again, he'd known it in that moment he clambered back from the trenches; but he knew that he'd be a coward if he didn't try though all hope was past.

So out he had gone for that, remembering Chris, wanting to reach her, knowing as he tramped mile on mile that he never would. But he'd made her that promise that he'd never fail her, long syne he had made it that night when he'd held her so bonny and sweet and a quean in his arms, young and desirous and kind. So mile on mile on the laired French roads:

she was lost to him, but that didn't help, he'd try to win to her side again, to see her again, to tell her nothing he'd said was his saying, it was the foulness dripping from the dream that devoured him. And young Ewan came into his thoughts, he'd so much to tell her of him, so much he'd to say and do if only he might win to Blawearie . . .

Then the military policemen had taken him and he'd listened to them and others in the days that followed, listening and not listening at all, wearied and quiet. *Oh, wearied and wakened at last, Chae, and I haven't cared, they can take me out fine and shoot me to-morrow, I'll be glad for the rest of it, Chris lost to me through my own coarse daftness. She didn't even come to give me a kiss at good-bye, Chae, we never said good-bye, but I mind the bonny bead of her down-bent there in the close. She'll never know, my dear quean, and that's best — they tell lies about folk they shoot and she'll think I just died like the rest, you're not to tell her.*

Then he'd been silent long, and Chae'd had nothing to say, he knew it was useless to make try for reprieve, he was only a sergeant and had no business even in the hut with the prisoner. And then Ewan said, sudden-like, it clean took Chae by surprise, *Mind the smell of dung in the parks on an April morning, Chae? And the peewits over the rigs? Bonny they're flying this night in Kinraddie, and Chris sleeping there, and all the Howe happed in mist.* Chae said that he mustn't mind about that, he was feared that the dawn was close, and Ewan should be thinking of other things now, had he seen a minister? And Ewan said that an old bit billy had come and blethered, an officer creature, but he'd paid no heed, it had nothing to do with him. Even as he spoke there rose a great clamour of guns far up in the front, it was four miles off, not more; and Chae thought of the hurried watches climbing to their posts and the blash and flare of the Verey lights, the machine-gun crackle from pits in the mud, things he himself mightn't hear for long: Ewan'd never hear it at all beyond this night.

And not feared at all he looked, Chae saw, he sat there in his kilt and shirt-sleeves, and he looked no more than a young lad still, his head between his hands, he didn't seem to be thinking at all of the morning so close. For he started to speak of Blawearie then and the parks that he would have drained, though he thought the land would go fair to hell without the woods to shelter it. And Chae said that he thought the same, there were sore changes waiting them when they went back; and then he minded that Ewan would never go back, and could near have bitten his tongue in half, but Ewan hadn't noticed, he'd been speaking of the horses he'd had, Clyde and old Bess, fine beasts, fine beasts – did Chae mind that night of lightning when they found Chris wandering the fields with those two horses? That was the night he had known she liked him well – *nothing more than that, so quick and fierce she was, Chae man, she guarded herself like a queen in a palace, there was nothing between her and me till the night we married. Mind that – and the singing there was, Chae? What was it that Chris sang then?*

And neither could remember that, it had vexed Ewan a while, and then he forgot it, sitting quiet in that hut on the edge of morning. Then at last he'd stood up and gone to the window and said *There's bare a quarter of an hour now, Chae, you'll need to be getting back.*

And they'd shaken hands, the sentry opened the door for Chae, and he tried to say all he could for comfort, the foreshadowing of the morning in Ewan's young eyes was strange and terrible, he couldn't take out his hand from that grip. And all that Ewan said was *Oh man, mind me when next you hear the peewits over Blawearie – look at my lass for me when you see her again, close and close, for that kiss that I'll never give her.* So he'd turned back into the hut, he wasn't feared or crying, he went quiet and calm; and Chae went down through the hut lines grouped about that place, a farm-place it had been, he'd got to the lorry that waited him, he was cursing and weeping then and the driver thought him daft, he hadn't known himself how he'd been. So they'd driven off, the wet morning had come crawling across the laired fields, and Chae had never seen Ewan again, they killed him that morning.

Grey Boy
(1969)

Eona Macnicol

The piermaster lived in a little cottage that seemed to have fallen from its place in the hamlet of Clachanree down into the midst of the hazel woods. From the opposite side of Loch Ness, its cat-eared shape, with the surrounding pasture and the field, looked utterly cut off, engulfed in trees. Indeed, the end of its road was hard to find as you went up the Clachanree Brae, so overgrown was it; and when you had found it, going along it was like going along a tunnel. It was as if the place wanted to remain hidden.

The piermaster, Uisdean Dubh mac Coinneach, was an impressive personage, patriarchal, like pictures of Moses, with a great square beard – black it must once have been, it was silver when I knew him. He had coal-black eyes that blazed with fury when passengers were slow in getting on or off the steamer, staring about them at the view or looking for their tiresome luggage, thus showing disrespect for him and his important avocations. For in addition to his official duties of attending upon the steamer and maintaining the pier and its approach road, he had his croft to see to – not to speak of his own inner life.

My contacts with him had been mostly in the line of his official duties. But I was once or twice taken to visit him socially, for he married as his second wife one of my grandaunts, and was reckoned to have entered our family. That he was a celebrity I could divine, though whether it was fame or notoriety was hard to determine. There was a story about him, in his widower days, during the Great War.

Uisdean found himself, one afternoon after the steamer had gone back eastwards, in such a downpour of rain as did not fall often even in the Great Glen. The drops bounced like balls on the grey surface of the Loch, the water wagtails were cowering under beam and spar of the pier trying to keep their twitching tails dry. It looked like being a night of it. How was he to get in the hay that was still out in ricks though it was close on October? He drew an old sack over his head to protect his beard, and decided to make for the house.

Time was when a cheerful fire would be there to welcome him, and a hot meal. But Mairread was dead and gone. And what did They have to do but call up Tommag, sending him over to France to do other folks' business, with his own waiting for him here and falling upon his father! There was too much work for one man. They wouldn't give Tommag time, with all the fighting and carry on, to do more than send wee postcards printed in English: 'I am well.' 'I am wounded.'

Uisdean tramped morosely up his short cut through the wet woods and across the melancholy field where bracken was encroaching and rabbits were getting through because there were holes in the wire-netting and the fence was falling down. The wind had got the covers off some of the hayricks, the hay would be soaking. He passed the neglected garden, approaching the byre. The cow would be roaring to be milked.

But Daisag was silent. In a moment he had learned why. No sooner had he opened the door than there was a movement inside which was not Daisag's. Someone left her side and darted on to the pile of bedding bracken. The small milking can, the *skellad*, fell from his hand with a spurt of milk.

Uisdean was beside himself. This tramp, this tink, had not only taken possession of the byre but coolly helped himself to milk! Breaking into a torrent of Gaelic and English he menaced the culprit with uplifted hand. Raindrops coruscated in all directions. His beard wagged terribly. Yet for all his anger he had the prudence to push aside with his foot the pitchfork that lay near by. He need not have troubled to do so, for the stranger cringed from him, raising his arms as if to float up to the roof.

'. . . and who might you think you are?' Uisdean ended his harangue.

Well might he ask, for the stranger's appearance was gruesome. He was dressed all in grey, a most displeasing kind of grey. On his head was a round cap, then came, in evil descent, a short loose coat, baggy trousers and great high boots covered in mud. There was something disgusting and frightful about him, as there is about a snake. His very face was grey. And he made an ugly noise with his mouth.

'Out with you! *Mach sin thu!*' roared Uisdean.

The creature cowered still; he seemed almost disposed to burrow right into the bracken. Uisdean did not fancy the job of laying hands on him.

'*Mach sin!*' he roared again, but the creature ceased his burrowing only to lie utterly inert. He was fast asleep!

There was nothing for it but to milk Daisag as quick as ever he could. He was glad to shut the byre door after him. It seemed hardly decent to leave the poor cow in such uncouth company, but a man's safety comes before a beast's.

As Uisdean lay in bed that night listening to the rain, he tried to think that the creature was only an apparition. Had he not once seen, rising from the Loch, a dreadful head with huge round eyes that stared at him till he all but lost his senses? Folk laughed at him and at his story of a *beoch mor* – great beast – in the Loch, imagining he had a drop taken. Perhaps this grey thing likewise having appeared once would never appear again. Yet, waking in the small hours in a panic, he wondered whether having seen one he would not see more – a grey thing at the well, at the peatstack, in the kitchen, even at the pier.

When he had dressed himself next morning, read a Chapter and had his porridge, Uisdean went to let Daisag out of the byre. The rain was over, but the grey fellow was still there. He sat up, then leapt to his feet. When he saw Uisdean standing silent, staring, he made a grimace and pointed to his mouth. Maybe it was hunger as much as the rain that had brought him. Maybe he was empowered to levy a tax of food and would go only when it was given. Slowly Uisdean went to the house and returned with a hunk of bread. He threw it to the grey creature who seized it and devoured it with inhuman rapidity.

When he had consumed the last crumb he looked up at Uisdean with eyes of a pale blue colour – the only part of him that was not grey. He began to speak, if you could call it speaking which was not even English.

'Speak right!' Uisdean bade him with asperity. 'I canna understand. The rain is now over, so be off with you. And never you come here to trouble me again.'

He went off to the steamer. He did not mind the delays, nor did he find the passengers so aggravating; it was a comfort to see ordinary people. He hoped when he got home he would find nothing.

But the grey fellow was still there, although he was no longer grey. He was standing at the side of the little burn that leaves the Eas and makes its own entry into the Loch below. And he was washing himself. Washing! He stood there in the light of day stark naked, all smooth and white. Uisdean had never seen the adult human body completely naked before, and he was shocked. He could find not a word to say. The fellow went on with what he was doing, pouring bucketfuls of water over himself – and it close on October! – rubbing himself dry with bracken. His hair was now of a pale straw colour. There was no sign of his grey garb, except for his boots which stood near by, upright, like persons in their own right.

'Have you no shame, grey boy?' Uisdean shouted as soon as he had recovered his breath. 'Are you no thinking who'll be seeing you?'

The grey fellow began to jabber as if pleading. Uisdean could not make out one word. But for very decency's sake he went to the kist and turned about in its disordered contents till he found an old shirt of Tommag's and moleskin trousers of his own. These he flung angrily at the shameless fellow who, to do him credit, lost no time in putting them on. When he was dressed he pointed to the midden, from which protruded a grey sleeve. 'Aye, aye. Well, let them bide there,' Uisdean muttered in some relief.

Whether it was that he had lost his fear of the creature now that he was no longer grey, or whether it was natural annoyance at having to provide him with clothes, Uisdean decided to try to get some work out of him. Pointing to the bucket, then to the byre, he hinted that the grey boy could be giving it a clean since he was so fond of cleanness. And the boy understood!

He made Uisdean a bow. You never saw such a carry on, clicking his heels together in the high boots like bairns playing at soldiers, then off he went and got water and began on the byre, walls first then floor. Uisdean stood watching him and making threatening remarks in Gaelic to intimidate him. Then he left him at it and took Daisag to the field where he had to turn over the top of the hay.

When he came back you could have eaten your dinner off the byre floor. 'All right then, my mannie,' Uisdean said, making an effort to conceal his pleasure, 'while I'm making my dinner you could be breaking a few sticks.' He wondered about putting the axe into the creature's hands. But he did no harm with it and set about chopping the wood as if he had been trained to do it.

'Aye, aye, you're a worker!' Uisdean said sardonically.

An idea struck him. 'Come you here, grey boy. Since you're so good at the wood you could be making two-three posts for the fence.' He threw a log or two down and made signs about shaping them. He kept him at it till the pale face was fairly wet with sweat and the boy gasping, and it was time for the afternoon call of the steamer.

By the time he got back the grey boy had four posts shaped and a fifth under his hand. Uisdean felt more benign than he had done for many a day. It was fine having someone under his thumb. By the time the boy had tidied up the shavings and helped Uisdean to put new covers on the hay, night had fallen, a sharp autumn night – too late to send a living body from the door. 'There's nothing for it, my mannie, but stay here itself.' Uisdean put a heel of loaf into the fellow's hand and gave him a shove into the byre again.

Uisdean was not the earliest of risers, there being neither comfort nor company to leave his bed for. The sun was on the window when he rose. When he went out he could not believe his eyes. There was the grey boy hard at it, cleaning out the byre – and it done only yesterday! He had something green in his mouth. Uisdean exclaimed in disgust, for it was a dandelion leaf. There he was, chewing at it and swallowing. When he saw Uisdean he said something in his daft lingo. He was not right in the head, and that was it.

On a more hospitable impulse Uisdean went into the house and scraped out the remainder of the porridge, thus departing from his usual practice of laying the pot out at his door for the hens to pick clean. He poured on a dash of milk and took up a spoon. With no great enthusiasm he held out the plate to the creature who came quickly and grabbed it. Then was heard a sound familiar to Uisdean, the eager scraping of spoon on plate, but there was a wolfishness about the business that was comical.

It was as well Uisdean got a laugh then, for the folk off the morning steamer were slower than usual. He had to flash his eyes and mutter his imprecations at them. They were all having a confab together, something about the war – the war, the war! Uisdean was fair sick of it – something about prisoners. If they would only mind their own business and let the steamer go on its way and not hinder him. His mind was on whether he had shown the grey boy how he wanted holes dug to take the new posts he had made the day before.

When he got free he went up to the house by the short cut, and there at the edge of the field was the grey boy with the five posts in, giving them good dunts with the head of the axe to settle them in the ground. 'Aye, aye, well!' Uisdean merely said, suppressing any show of satisfaction. There was no need for the fellow to be sinfully uplifted.

For his dinner that day Uisdean was having potatoes and salt herring. It seemed hardly nice, since he was getting work out of him, not to offer the grey boy a share. He handed a plate over the doorstep to him, and he polished it off before Uisdean's grace was well begun.

Uisdean always took a sit and a smoke at his pipe after his dinner till he saw the funnel of the steamer coming from the west for the afternoon call. But the grey boy never halted. Without bidding he began to tidy up the peatstack and to brush the hard earth before the door, throwing the rubbish up on top of the midden. You would think it was the inside of a house he was at. Uisdean felt a little nettled at such excessive zeal. But 'Aye, that's you!' was all he said.

Alie the Post came up from the steamer with Uisdean, carrying the bag of mail. He did not observe how the piermaster hummed and hawed at the road end, and he accompanied him to the house for a dram, as he often did on warm days, before climbing the hill. He stared around. 'It's yourself has been busy, Uisdean! My golly, but you're neat, man!' His astonished eyes went from the brushed earth to the ordered byre seen through its half-open door. 'Whatever's come over you? Man, man, you're gey neat.'

Uisdean finished his dram more quickly than was his custom, and set his glass down on the table with an air of finality. When that failed to hasten his visitor, he tilted his magnificent head: 'Am I hearing someone on the Brae bawling on you? See will anyone be after his letters?' At which Alie picked up his bag and went.

The grey boy was nowhere to be seen. But when Uisdean went to the byre there he was, his head and shoulders coming up from the bracken. Uisdean was glad he had made himself scarce when Alie was around. It was a kind of shameful thing for a God-fearing man to have such an oddity about the place. 'Away off down to the field then,' he said gruffly, 'and see are we needing any more posts in the fence.'

And just as well, for not half an hour later who came but

the miller. He added to his proper duties the wartime one of mending the surface of the low road and the Brae.

'I will be having salt herring, if you will sit in with me.' Uisdean thought that by making a mention of supper he might get him to go. 'There's no occasion,' the miller murmured politely. 'No occasion indeed.'

'You will take a drop of the cratur then?' Uisdean felt bound to suggest. To this the miller made no objection, showing only the hesitancy which good manners required. Uisdean talked with untypical affability. But in the midst of his discourse the miller raised his hand, listening with head inclined. 'Am I hearing singing?'

'It'll be the Eas, what else?' Uisdean answered. 'And it in spate after the heavy rain.'

'It isna the Eas. I suppose now you would not be having company?'

'What company would I have?'

'Then I willna stay,' the miller said, with unexpected and sinister tact. 'I thought I'd heard from someone you had help with the croft. But I will be wrong, I'm thinking. It isna Tommag you have home?' When Uisdean shook his head he looked at him slyly. 'I see. Well, it was like a dream on me I heard a young man singing.'

The piermaster was ready, when the miller had gone, to take it out on the grey boy. Indeed he landed a cuff on the side of his head. 'Singing and carrying on! What way is this to behave?' The grey boy cringed from him. It was wonderful to have someone in fear of you!

And there was something wonderfully soothing to the spirit in the state of things. Daisag milked and tethered on the grass, the byre so neat, and the house – the grey boy took it upon himself to enter the house, and now its stone floor was scrubbed and the hearth was all black and white the way Mairread had had it. And that evening there was a meal. What a surprise Uisdean got when the grey boy lifted a pot lid and showed a rabbit stewed with onions in brown gravy. When last did he smell anything so good? 'See and let us not be growing fond of the temporal mercies,' Uisdean remembered to say with becoming sternness as they both sat down to the table. And by returning thanks at length afterwards he strove to keep his jubilation within Christian bounds. There was no doubt he was a knacky one, this grey boy.

He was eerie too. For in the frying-pan what had he done for himself but a puckle of toadstools! Before Uisdean's eyes he ate them as if they were food.

'You'll be dead, my mannie!' Uisdean warned him. 'Eating puddockstools!'

And he was not a good boy. The next day was the Sabbath, and yet early in the morning what did Uisdean rise to hear but the sound of posts being driven in. There he was, the grey fellow, hammering and singing as if it were any other day. Uisdean ran out to him in his nightshirt crying, 'Stop, stop! Mercy on us, do you no' know what day this is?'

The grey boy gaped and said, 'Pliss?' – a great word with him.

Uisdean had to snatch the hammer from his hand. 'Come you and sit inside, wiselike,' he bade him. 'It is too much temptation for you out here.'

You would think, even supposing he did not understand what was said, the creature would jalouse when he saw Uisdean put on his black suit and his good boots that he was going to the church at Lochend, and it was the Lord's Day. But what was he after but tidying the house? Uisdean on his return found the very mattress from his bed flung over the windowsill in the sun. 'Mercy on us!' he cried. 'Are you no feared folk will be seeing us from across the Loch itself?' The grey boy got a fright at that seemingly, for away he ran into the byre and burrowed into the bracken.

Uisdean regretted he had not spoken of his guest to any at the church, seeing it was a kind of hold the fellow was gaining on him, drawing his affections to things below. Only Himself was off in haste to visit a sick woman at Bona. And the folk were full of idle talk, about prisoners-of-war still. Of the two that had escaped one had been caught, the other was at large, so they said. 'Is this a day to be talking of such things?' Uisdean reproved them fiercely, looking very like Moses. 'Vain talk in the very courts of the sanctuary!' He glowered at the miller, and Alie and An Craggoch, glad that since it was the Sabbath they would not come to visit him.

It seemed the grey boy would have no Sabbath at all, but Uisdean got down the Gaelic Bible and sat him down and read a long Chapter to him. 'Are you no a Christian?' he asked, but with more sadness than anger, seeing the pale eyes wide and the mouth agape. Suddenly the poor body seemed to under-stand. He began singing in what you could only call a Godly tune. 'Aye, aye, I see. But I doubt at best you will be a Papist,' Uisdean said. Then squaring his chest he showed what he could do, giving out the line and coming in with the congre-gation's part as well. The fellow looked edified.

But that night, having had less work on hand, Uisdean had more time to speculate. He could no longer evade the know-ledge that what he had on his hands was no wandering tinker, no idiot, no fiend or fairy, but might be . . . My golly, if that was it!

So as soon as he saw him on Monday morning he bore down on the grey boy, who was industriously shaping one more post for the fence. Uisdean seized the axe from his hands and mena-ced him, 'Are you a German, eh? Are you?'

'Pliss?' came the puzzled reply.

Uisdean for further testing threw down a log of wood on the ground and saying, 'If this was the Kaiser I would do *this* to him,' he split it with one blow. He scowled at the boy to see how he would take it. He had a pleased smile on his face, and said in what you might almost call English, 'I – help – you.'

He would seem to have come successfully through the tests. He said he was not a German, and who but himself should know?

'Very well, then. Away off and find yourself a job. If anybody comes, mind you and hide and do not be bringing shame on me. Are you hearing?' The grey boy seemed to get the gist of it. There was no doubt he was a bit sharper in the uptake than he had been.

Alie the Post, and the miller, together with An Craggoch, came up the Brae with Uisdean, and in spite of his attempt to put them off they came along the tunnel through the wood. An Craggoch, a slow man, had difficulty in bringing out his meaning. 'They are telling me, Uisdean, you have your place very neat these days? You would not be having help, now?'

Uisdean let a terrible silence fall by way of rebuke. Then: 'Aye, but the rain has spoilt my bit hay.'

The Post approached the subject from another angle: 'I'm hearing, Uisdean, there's one of the German prisoners not caught yet.'

They walked twenty yards before Uisdean acknowledged the remark. 'Aye, are you telling me?'

'I'm thinking he may be hiding in the woods here.'

'Do you say so? They'd have a job to be looking for him.'

'I'm thinking they're afraid he is getting shelter and his food.'

'Is that so, now?'

The miller became irritated by such calm. 'We're saying, man, it's against the law. It's against the law, Uisdean. They say the guards are out looking for him as far as Fort Augustus. But that's not to say they winna come back here. We don't know what they will do to the man that is sheltering him.'

'That will be their concern,' Uisdean blandly agreed.

'But we're saying, man, it's against the law.'

They were wasting their breath, Uisdean cared little for the law. It did not enter into his calculations at all. His ancestors had made their whisky from their own barley with supreme unconcern for the excise. In like manner he did not see why he should not keep a grey boy who had come so providentially to him. It was his affair. He watched his friends go in a silence more awful than any denunciation could have been, his eyes flashed, his beard wagged as never before.

At first he could not see the grey boy; then he found him crouching among the high weeds in the garden, trying to clear them away from the remnants of cabbage and onions Uisdean had sowed in the spring and then completely forgotten. When he heard Uisdean he lifted a pleased face. By golly, he looked like a human being.

'Aye,' Uisdean said, in perfect understanding, 'we could be giving this place a clear out, and dung it from the byre. Maybe next year, if we're spared, yourself and myself, we could make something of it.' Next year . . . With a burst of sudden unaccountable anger he roared, 'Is yon cow milked yet?' So that the poor fellow jumped up in great fear and made that quick bow of his.

But in the evening, by the glowing peats, he softened to his guest again. And not only because there was a meal ready, a pot of broth with cabbage and onions and potatoes and bits of rabbit, but because the creature was kind of company. After the meal they sat on awhile drinking, Uisdean his whisky, the other a foul concoction from a tin left by Tommag when he was on leave, 'caffyolay' he called it. In the warmth, with the autumn wind whistling outside in the trees and beating upon the small thick window-panes, they spoke without understanding and yet with a fair inkling of each other's meaning. For when

Uisdean began telling of his wife's notion that there were water spirits in the pool of the Eas, acting as if combing long hair, the grey boy began to nod his head and to comb likewise. Never in the four days had he been so cheery. 'Better bed down in the kitchen itself,' Uisdean invited him, taking a couple of musty blankets from the kist. What for no? He was not so different from Mairread or Tommag – except that he was better at taking a telling.

Rain fell again on Tuesday morning. Uisdean woke to the splashing sound of the drops falling through the trees. It was chilly too, as he found when he put his legs out of bed to rise. He had scarcely set foot to the floor when he heard a gentle chinking sound indicative of porridge being stirred with a metal spoon in the dookbag three-legged pot. There was a squeak as of a cupboard door opening. A faint scent of frying entered the damp closeness of the room. It must be the grey boy making breakfast for the two of them – a thought to give a man courage for the day.

'Hallo there, grey boy!' Uisdean called in Gaelic (Gaelic or English, it was all one to the creature). 'Keep my porridge by the fire, see will they grow cold on me. You can take your own and be off out and see to Daisag.'

When the boy had gone out, Uisdean lay thankfully in bed and watched the drops run on the window. Sometimes he dozed and sometimes he thought. The idea passed through his mind that on very rough days he might let the boy not only do the jobs about the croft but also go down to attend the steamer. He had a smile to himself, picturing the passengers asking all their foolish questions, the grey boy saying nothing but 'Pliss? Pliss?' It would be the price of them!

But like a judgement on him for his levity, when he returned from the steamer he saw Alie and the miller coming to his door. Their sudden appearance filled him with gloom.

They had no need to speak; the way they stood, silent, as if evading the duty of telling something to disquiet – his mind went back to the day when Tommag was reported missing feared killed. The minister Himself and an elder then it was that stood there, wordless, waiting for courage to tell.

Alie and the miller did not stay wordless long. 'We're saying, Uisdean, the German prisoner, him we are speaking of . . .' They disregarded Uisdean's front of anger. 'Listen here, man! It seems the searchers are very near. They are coming back up the Glen, searching the houses.'

'And what has this to do with me? Let them that search search. And let them that work work. And let them leave each the other.'

'We're saying, Uisdean, they will search every house, byre and barn in Clachanree. And if they missed yourself the first time it is not to be taken for granted they will miss you a second.'

'It is idle speaking that is on you!' Uisdean roared out at them. 'What has all this to do with me?'

And indeed it would have seemed to have but little, were it not that up from the field, blithely whistling, came the young fellow, the sun on his pale strawy hair, his eyes bright with pleasure at the tune he was making. He called to Uisdean in his lingo and what next! – held up a couple of puddocks – frogs – by their legs as if they were cockerels. He was making signs he was going to eat them when, suddenly spying the other two, he stopped dead, threw the puddocks into the air, and bolted for the byre.

Alie said desperately, 'We know nothing, Uisdean. We could say nothing even upon oath. For all we know it is just some poor *amadan* [idiot] you have that is giving you a bit hand with things. One of the boarded out ones from the south, and what more likely? We do not know anything at all.'

'For all we know,' said the miller, not to be outdone, 'it

might be Tommag himself, that has taken a scunner at the war and come back home.'

'For the last time, Uisdean,' Alie laid a hand on the piermaster's arm, 'what we are saying is this: if any man round here did happen to have such a thing as a German prisoner-of-war about his place, then Uisdean, I'm telling you, and see will you close your ears, it would be that man's wisdom to be putting him back into his uniform and sending him off to fend for himself in the woods. For it's against the law to keep one. It's against the law.'

'I am hearing you,' Uisdean said with grim amusement. 'I am hearing all you say.'

When they were gone, Uisdean took the pitchfork and turned over the top of the midden, prising out with a face of disgust the tunic and trousers that now to their greyness had added filth. With these he went in search of the grey boy who was at his washing again beside the burn. 'Here,' Uisdean bade him, 'put these on you.' But well pleased was he when his slave disobeyed, backing away, then bursting into laughter. Indeed Uisdean himself could not forbear to give a smile which he hid in his beard. He went back to the midden and buried the things. 'Och aye, well,' he said. Then lest he should have shown weakness he bawled out, 'Is yon cow no milked yet? What for no? And see you and carry in the night's peats.'

What happened in the end was to Uisdean like a dream, the normal tenor of life quite overthrown. For here, in his own domain, They questioned him, insolently, expecting direct replies; and They searched his place without reference to him. The grey boy was found deep in the bracken and hauled out. His boots were his undoing; he might have passed muster if it had not been he was wearing his high boots. He was hustled away, looking longingly back at Uisdean. His eerie garb was recovered from the midden and taken away with him.

For Uisdean there was a rough escort to the town, not without a show of handcuffs. It was a position he had never expected to find himself in, short of the Judgement Pay. He could only hope it would not come to Tommag's ears; or if it did he would be too taken up with the war to be heeding it.

He could not understand all that the crowds were saying as he went in and out of the courthouse during his trial, but he guessed enough:

'Such a fine-looking old man to be a pro-German!'

'His son away at the Front too! You would think he would be ashamed.'

'Didn't he give the Boche his son's clothes as a disguise?'

'He should be shot. They should both be shot.'

'You canna shoot a prisoner-of-war, man!'

'A fine-looking man – venerable. He was only trying to be kind.'

'Kind, is it? Taking work out of him all the time? Made a perfect slave of him, so they say, kept him half-starved.'

'And folk might all have been murdered in their beds. He's a pro-German, a spy.'

He was not to know at that point that he would first be put in prison, then be released by popular demand, turn into a hero and have his name and his face (beard and all) in all the newspapers from here to London. All he felt at any time, I suppose, in addition to the loss of dignity, was a certain sadness, a sense of the transience of life, seeing he had lost the poor daft grey boy that had for those few days been his very own.

The Defile of the Beast (1931)

James Leslie Mitchell

Subchapter i

He spent over two years in France, he was not once wounded or gassed or fever-stricken, he became a corporal and then a sergeant; he was twice pressed to accept a commission, declined like Metaxa, and was victimized in consequence, he grew to regard unclean equipment and unpolished buttons with a passionate disfavour; he robbed a German prisoner of three hundred American dollars and then shot that prisoner as the man turned on him threateningly, he sat three days in a shell-hole at Bois Louange, he and two others, marooned in a maelstrom of retreat and advance; he found a rat-eaten woman's corpse in the depths of a staff dug-out in the Hindenburg Line; he commandeered an abandoned Leyland lorry in the Spring retreat of 1918 and drove a score of men for thirty miles, and fell asleep, and awoke still driving them; he lived a life so fantastic that his memory was to refuse to treat it seriously, or, in self-defence, became deliberately treacherous.

He never spent a 'first day in the trenches.' They massed in emplacements and sunken roads in front of the gun-clamour of that July 16th and then went forward into a draggled, copse-strewn waste, a-vomit in sudden volcanic eruptions, drifting long clouds of gas. They jumped the last bank of the sunken road and yelled and went forward at a stumbling run. The air was filled with a whispering rush of bullets – Malcom was to remember that whispering sound first heard, like the sound of exhausted hail. The forward sky flickered and winked with gun-flashes; behind, the sound of the British barrage leapt forward and forward on their backs, like the leaping of pursuing dinosaurs. The upper air was populous and filled with an insane racket, while from copses to left and right arose a whoop-whoop presently merging into the whoo-oo-oor of gun-belts. Malcom found himself plunging forward, an interested automaton, above the rhythmic play of his Army boots. His company commander raced three paces in front of him, sobbing a foolish chant: 'Oh, you bloody bloody bloody – oh, you bloody bloody SWINE!' Suddenly his hat vanished and with it the roof of his skull. He swayed and fell. Malcom tripped over him, stumbled, recovered, with vision below his eyes of a thing like an archaic cranium filled with a seething mess of dun-coloured jelly . . .

He was in 'A' company, 'B' was at its heels. Sergeant-Major Metaxa, grinning, a knobkerrie in his hand, raced past. By then the smoke-mist so patched the ground that they lost direction and found themselves enfiladed from the right. The battalion's attack was north of the Bois de Trones and south of Longueval. From the trees to the right, lines of echeloned machine-guns raved at them. Men beyond Malcom doubled and crumpled and sprawled – he saw one man impale himself on his own bayonet – and suddenly a shell burst brightly against the infernal wood and the gun-flashes. Unharmed, Malcom ran forward through a raining spray of metal, saw Metaxa and a few others, joined them, and was presently fighting and falling and scrambling into the pits of the machine-gunners.

Then something happened which he was never to see recorded. The machine-gunners, as Metaxa's company leapt amongst them, cheered and laughed, as though it was some game. Malcom stabbed one of those laughing gunners through the stomach, and fell on top of him in an attempt to retrieve his bayonet, and was trampled underfoot by the others. When he struggled up again his hands and tunic were soaked with blood and his mouth and throat sick with the smell of excrement . . .

Nine officers and four hundred and eighty other ranks of the battalion failed to answer that night, and were provisionally posted 'missing' until when and if their exact fate could be ascertained. The most of them had died like bogged flies in the spider's web of trenches and cellars which guarded the riven lands of Waterlot Farm.

Malcom spent most of the night in a captured trench, an acting-corporal, and, overcome by his queasy stomach, again and again very sick indeed because of the smell of his own body.

Subchapter ii

Delville Wood, Trones Wood, Longueval, Ginchy – they marched and counter-marched, took and re-took, stormed and fell back amid those immense names for three weeks. Then they were relieved and marched out and gave place to battalions of felt-hatted Australians who were to die in the mud and rains and futility of the Ancre. Thirty miles behind the lines, in rest-camp, the depleted Norsex were joined by drafts from England and set again to marching and training under an idiot colonel who believed in the imminence of open warfare. Malcom changed his tunic and acquired one that was unstained and had stripes sewn on it. He became smart and attentive in the presence of officers and blasphemous and capable in the presence of those who lacked both stripes and commissions. Metaxa organized vigorous football matches and Corporal Maudslay, battalion heavyweight, became a centre-forward of considerable proficiency.

Indeed, the battalion Soccer team acquired a reputation. It would go miles in lorries to play rival division teams. In one away-match Malcom tripped over and sat on a sturdy half-back who was blunt and blasphemous and Scotch.

It was his brother Robert.

He had joined the Seaforth Highlanders, but was then in training as a gunner for the Tanks. Amazed strangers, they sat either side of a packing case in the barn of Robert's company, and looked at each other uncertainly and unconvincedly. Robert tried to break through the veils of unreality.

'Christ – Malcom, little Malcom. A corporal – an d'ye mind when I smacked ye for stealin oat-cakes? . . . Never sent me that six pounds, never wrote. Ginchy? Christ, I was at Longueval. Why'd you never write hame? Auntie Ellen's dead. We heard you'd left Glasgow; Auld Ian was there an looked in to see ye, and you'd gane. . . . What'd you join an English regiment for?'

'What do you think of it all, Robert?'

'It's jist fair hell.' He sighed. 'Though I dinna say onything . . . Hae ye ever seen a German?'

Malcom nodded. Robert smoothed his short, brindled hair. 'Never seen ane o them. The daft B's. Why the hell did they start it? Mebbe they didna. We're as daft as they are.' He sighed again. 'God, I'd like richt weel a plate o new bannocks and warm milk, and then go ower the brae by Tocherty and see the Leekan lichts below. Mind them, Malcom?' He suddenly grew shy. 'I was married afore I cam oot. Ane o the Murray lassies.' He had a flash of the old, whimsical arrogance. 'Jean, the bonniest ane.'

'Jean was the bonniest,' Malcom said, gently. Robert kindled, his kind eyes shining.

'You mind her? I wantit you there for my best man. She's kept a piece o the cake for you. I'll write an tell her to send it . . . She's lonely there, up in the cotter hoose at Pittaulds. A weet summer, she says, but the corn comin fine. The clover'll stand thick and bonny below the Stane Muir at Chapel – mind the lang field?' He glanced out below the barn eaves and muttered to himself. 'They'll be bringin hame the kye the noo.'

And suddenly all that was peasant in Malcom wept for his brother, this strayed, lost peasant. He sat and gripped his hands in his pockets and held himself from speaking, and went out to the darkness and the homeward journey with his heart wrung in a passion of pity and rage.

Ten days later, in the attack on Thiepval, he saw his brother, thrusting his gasping face from the port-hole of a Tank, go by into the hell of bright fires and smashed entanglements where the Wurtembergers had died. He caught sight of Malcom, shouted something, and passed, a man in a dream.

Malcom never saw him again.

Subchapter iii
In late 1917 he lay in a field of wheat, among wheat-stalks and poppies, all one afternoon. It was a very quiet afternoon. Between the lines in the Picard country there was only an occasional rattat of snipers' fire. The Norsex had come in a week before, to take over from French troops who had previously

fallen back a distance of some three miles. The wheat field now lying midway the long, fresh scarrings of earthwork was still a recognizable field. It was a freak field and a brigade curiosity. Several times both sides had tried to burn the wheat, but it fired ill in that late, damp autumn. One shell-hole, like a geyser-burst, lay almost midway the lines; and this shell-hole became a coveted point of occupation throughout the day. From dawn one watched for the Saxon sniper who was wriggling towards it; found, one shot him. Or the German look-outs watched for the Norsex sniper, and shot *him*. It was a sport without military significance. Occasionally those two snipers stalked each other among the poppy-stalks and wheat.

Malcom had been out since dawn, and had forgotten his water-bottle. Metaxa discovered this and crawled out with it, and then perforce held Malcom company, for the German trenches had been heightened during the night and at least half a dozen rifles had attempted to pick him off, following the undulations of the wheat. He lay a little to the right of Malcom, deeper in the shell-hole than the latter was. The place was pleasant enough but for the stench from a sprawling figure in dank grey-green. He lay half out of sight, that figure, his clumsy field-boots cocked at a comical angle. There was nothing dignified or impressive about him. He was merely an unpleasant object which stank.

'Poor devil,' said Metaxa. 'I like those Saxons.'

'It's a pity he's mislaid his face,' Malcom said, indifferently. A movement on the new brown embanking of the Saxon parapet had caught his attention. Something greyish just verged the trench-edge for a moment, and in that moment, his finger gentle upon the second pressure, Malcom fired. Came the far clatter of a body falling. Malcom ejected the spent round, clicked home the bolt again, and slithered deeper into the shell-hole.

'Got him?'

'Yes. One of his eyes, I should think.'

They lay and listened to the shower of bullets pinging overhead. Their own trench took up the challenge and for a little a Saxon machine-gun bayed.

'You'd think there was a bloody war on,' murmured Metaxa.

Malcom glanced at him anxiously; he had always an absurd anxiety when Metaxa was with him under fire. The Greek knew it and caught his glance and smiled whimsically.

'I know.' He chewed a wheat-stalk and meditated. 'Though I've given up feeling that way about you. You'll be all right.' Then: 'But I think myself I'm fey.'

'Eh?'

He pulled a poppy and pressed his face against it, and for a little seemed to forget what he had been going to say.

'. . . flowers of Proserpine. A lordly Greek death for a Cairene bastard to die – among poppies and wheat. Not the kind that I'll come to, I think . . . Look here, Malcom, I know I'll go West in this show sometime. I know it just as certainly as I know that to-morrow's sun'll come up. It's like walking through a fog to the edge of a cliff. Somewhere I know I'll fall off. I'm not depressed or sick. I just know.'

Malcom had met several men with just such premonitions. Not one of them who stayed within his ken but had been killed. Perhaps some sixth sense awoke in one there, or evolved and shaped and came to being. He was to remember that he attempted then neither consolation nor contradiction. He just lay and stared at his rifle.

But Metaxa had turned on his back among the crushed corn-stalks and brown earth and lay considering the sky and inviting a stomach-wound. 'And it's not unpleasant, this death-sentence. Once I thought a man would go mad with such knowledge as mine. But I feel as sane as ever. Only, of what remains – Christ, how I want to live it!' He was silent for a moment and then whispered to himself, remotely, almost in the thought-images of the wistful Robert, dead and lost at Thiepval: 'God, the miracle of wheat . . .'

He lay quiet for a little while, then turned his head towards Malcom, restlessly. 'Wonder what's beyond the cliff, after all? Thank God I'm an atheist! . . . Did you hear that R.C. padre last week asseverating that anyone who goes West in the front line goes straight to heaven – mixed symbolism and all?'

Malcom grunted. He considered the proper study of R.C. mentality a subject for the pathologist.

'Yes – right to a de-loused immortality beyond the reach of whizz-bangs . . . What a life! What a death!' The Greek chuckled and stirred to exposition. 'Think of the collisions among the various denominations scooting skyward, all over the world at the moment, to their various vexatious heavens . . . Lord, what post-mortem retreats there have been: Paradise, Avilion, Valhalla, Nirvana, Hades, Mictlan . . . Wonder if those rival blisses ever go to war? Sure to. Must be fun to be an Aztec ghost under Huitzilopochtli and lead out a Mexican Expeditionary Force against Jehovah, captaining the defunct Israelites. Or serve under Gabriel when Jesus and Siva meet in dispute on some celestial frontier . . . Can't you imagine the trumpeting and tub-thumping and the posters pasted up all along the Christian heaven: "Why haven't you military wings up, young shade?" "Jehovah expects every saint post-dating the Reformation to do his duty." "Yahveh wants you." "*Armageddeon Courier!* Brightest News and Pictures! Virgin inspects detachment under Henry VIII. Mohammed betrayed by a Houri: Reported in Flight from Paradise."'

This was the kind of blasphemy they both found exceedingly funny. Their laughter echoed up over No Man's Land. Malcom kept his eyes on the slumberous Saxon lines the while Metaxa lay and searched the sky.

'Mictlan . . . Those Central Americans were the only logical theologians who ever lived. The Toltecs and Aztecs, I mean. Not after centuries of progress did they depart from the stern, unbending creed of their fathers. *They* never transmogrified the old agricultural cannibal sacrifice into a Communion with snippets of bread and sips of wine. All the necessary blood and none of the unnecessary squeamishness. Your Wee Frees were prinking Progressives compared with them. They sat down to table after each sacrifice, nicely dressed in scented clothes, and gossiped intellectually of art and the weather and palace-building and the latest Nezahualcoyotl ode the while they ate well-cooked cutlets sliced from the slaves dragged screaming to the altar-stone an hour before . . . Christ – logicians who weren't afraid of the price of civilization! . . . Different stock altogether from the Mayans.'

Malcom was mildly fogged, but interested. He knew nothing then of Mexican archæology, except what little he had gathered in boyhood from the flowery pages of the genteel Prescott. 'Much the same as the Aztecs, weren't they?'

'The Maya? Good Lord, no. They weren't Nahuas at all. Doubt even if they were Red Indians. Never read of them? Never heard of your namesake, the Mayan Maudslay? . . . The only interesting people of pre-history – oh, not because my father was an American and I've drunk cocktails in Greenwich Village.'

'Tell us about them.'

An aeroplane, black-crossed, droned overhead. A Fokker fighter. In the north, beyond a clump of hills, an artillery duel was creeping up to intensity against the greyness of the after-noon, like a thread of mercury creeping up a thermometer.

'. . . came south into Central America two thousand two hundred years ago, bringing with them a culture which was ancient even then. They were alien to the natives of the time. The Toltecs and Aztecs hadn't yet separated from the other Red

183

Indian nations in the north. And for seventeen hundred years, like men in a nightmare, those Maya wandered Central America, building cities and rearing stupendous monuments – I've seen photographs in the Peabody Museum and the architecture's extraordinarily good – and then abruptly deserting cities and monuments and fleeing in a night. They were old and decadent in Yucatan before the Danes came to England. They were cannibals at the time of the Norman Conquest. They left behind them, on temple lintels and stelae and a few manuscripts, a script which is still undeciphered . . . That's about all. They nearly made me an archæologist myself. I intended having a shot at Central America when the Meyrin-Beard do was over in the Mesaleekh. Think of them – cannibals with a script – a script more ancient and involved than the Chinese! If a man could read the Mayan glyphs, what story mightn't they tell?'

'Raids and rapings, wars and widowings, hates and horrors. The usual stuff.'

'Who knows? They may have been the last fugitives of drowned Atlantis. They may have evolved philosophy before Plato, discovered gravitation before Newton. They may have attempted and failed a civilization to escape the horrors of civilization – half history's a record of such attempts. They may have built the City of the Sun in some American bush – its ruins may lie there still . . . Compared with theirs our calendar is the work of a dithering infant. They may once have had keys to all the secrets of life and death and time.' He rolled over. 'Perhaps the undeciphered glyphs contain the key to even – *that*.'

He nodded to where the Saxon lines were already dark in the false twilight. Malcom lay beside him, his imagination kindling, caught as ever by the wonder of such fairy tale in the history of men.

'By God,' he said, unconscious how far in the years to

come he was to pursue that resolution, 'I'm going to learn more about your Maya.'

Subchapter iv

Early in 1918 they managed to get leave together – their first leave since their arrival in France – and went to Paris. There they spent a curiously oppressed eight days, putting up at a little hotel, 'on the wrong side of the Seine,' which catered almost exclusively for warrant officers and N.C.O.'s of the British, Colonial, and American armies. In Paris Malcom saw his first American; Paris was flooded with Americans.

'Negroes among them, too,' he observed, unnecessarily.

Metaxa, eyebrows a-tilt, remonstrated. 'Coloured men, Malcom, coloured men. No nigger alive admits he's black; he is quite passionately coloured. Spectrum worship . . . Fancy a white man speaking of himself as a member of the bleached race! Still, we wouldn't like to be called blancers . . . Another bottle?'

They were sitting in the open air, looking at Paris. Malcom shook his head.

'No thanks. Sour stuff.'

Metaxa ordered another bottle.

'I'll drink your half. Then I'm going out to get a woman. Coming?'

Slightly drunk, he leant his arms on the table and grinned at Malcom's unreproducible libel on French-women. After a solitary experiment Malcom had practised a fastidious continence in France. All his life there was something virginal in his nature which balked at such ogling, leering, pawing – and yet matter-of-factness – as characterized the practice of French lust. Unreasonably, he never ceased to detest the Latins for this matter-of-factness which he himself championed in theory . . . Metaxa finished the bottle.

'Of course it's foolishness and a waste of time – not to

mention that other waste you've so delicately deplored. But what the hell does it matter to me? Humanity might as well play itself out that way as any other. I've no children or any intention of fathering any. I've no faith in the future of those that are fathered. Me, I'm for the ants.'

'Eh?'

'The ants. When man wipes himself off the earth as a disciple of Onan or in the next outburst of international sadism, some other life-form will rise to take control. Everything points to the ants. We blasted mammals have had our show: we're probably as doomed as the dinosaurs. Way for the Insectidæ! I pin my faith to the ants . . . Christ, do you remember how I bleated about the Defile of history that afternoon at Stonehenge? How the crook-boned apes might yet reach beyond the sewers and cesspools of civilization to the Light above the Pass? What a bloody bleary anthropoid I must have been!'

He had grown strangely bitter in the past six months. Malcom watched him blankly.

'The Light – God, never! A lump of seasonable carrion in my belly and a warm hide against mine – the best I can ever hope for . . . Almost drunk again. I'm going. Go mad if I sit here and stare at the traffic and think of the Line back there.'

He rose up, staggered a little, then put on his Sam Browne and buckled it. 'How are *you* going to kill the rest of the day?'

'Going to hunt up a book about the Mayans. Those glyphs of theirs interest me.'

'The freak Azilian worrying over his grandmother's thighbone . . . I prefer such members flesh-clad.' He laughed, a little too loudly. 'Meet early to-morrow, shall we? Come to the Café Desruit at eleven?'

'Where is it?'

'Boul' Mich'.'

Next day Malcom sat in the Café Despruit from half-past

past ten till half-past twelve, very little interested in war-time Paris, but deep in the book he had purchased that morning after a notable struggle to pronounce the word 'Maya' French fashion. It was the Abbé Brasseur's translation of Landa's *Relacion de las cosas de Yucatan* which he had finally secured, and sitting reading it he forgot for a little that aching unease awaiting him and Metaxa in the east. It haunted him probably as much as it did the Greek, though with an intense foreboding oddly impersonal.

There came a rattling of chairs. Metaxa sat down opposite him, ordered an absinthe, and drank the sickly liquid with twitching lips. But he was not drunk and showed no particular effects of dissipation but for an odd look in his eyes, as though they had been sprinkled with fine sand.

'Had a good time?'

'Bong, tray bong, as they say in the French classes in Aberdeenshire . . . Oh, damned funny.'

'What?'

'Nine years ago my wife sat here with me in this café. Her bag lay where you have that book. I remember the nick in the arm of that chair.'

'Your wife? I never knew you were married—'

Their eyes met and Malcom's shivered away from the meeting. The Greek's voice droned in a thin, flat sing-song.

'Nine years ago. We'd been honeymooning in England. Three months. Then we came through Paris and later went on to Rome and so to Cairo. My architect fees in Koubbah carried us through. We sat here one afternoon and watched the Boul' Mich' go by . . . She was tired, I remember, and laid her head against the back of that chair, and we were so friendly we had no need to speak. Nine years ago. What's the book?'

'Eh? Landa's *Relacion*. About the Mayans. Read it?'

'I went to a Blue Lamp last night, Malcom, and bargained for a second-class "amie," because my money was nearly done.

The patronne had just one disengaged at the moment, and sent me up to her. I went into the room and – oh, Christ, Malcom – *it was my wife!*'

Subchapter v

He looked up and saw a patch of starlit sky, powdered blue paling to a pearly effulgence. He stared at it uncomprehendingly for a moment. And then he understood. It was moonrise.

He bit his lips and lay still, listening. The ravine was filled with the mutilated undead. The stupefying shock of wound and blow had passed, and agony with distorted mouth whimpered amid the sprawling heaps. A man somewhere to the right and below him cried for water, pitifully, reasonably. 'Water – only a mouthful. Only a mouthful, orderly. Oh, Christ, only a mouthful . . .' Further up the slope someone screamed and screamed, with a horrible rhythm in his screams.

Someone on the wire.

Presently, looking out and up, he saw against the moonlight the sprawling brakes of wire, with broken standards and torn stanchions, and beyond them, right on the crest, a zig-zag against the sky, the German trenches. He himself, tripping and twisting his ankle in the evening attack of the Norsex, lay half-way up the slope, but it was plain that not a man in 'A' or 'B' companies had gained the crest. Dark bundles of bloody rags hung here and there amidst the strands. Above him, to the right, half-hid by a little dip from the German trench, but clear to his eyes in the ghastly light, one figure hung upon the wire with drooping head and arms outflung, grotesquely crucified . . . Then the Maxim bayed again and he ducked back into cover behind the body of Sergeant Morgan, burrowing his chin in the mud and feeling the dead body drum and quiver against his steel helmet.

The Maxim choked and spluttered to silence. Somewhere,

behind, across the valley, a chloric light rose and poised and burned with a green incandescence. He turned his head and watched it and then fell to listening again. Should he attempt to crawl down the slope – or up to that party which had gained the shelter of a shell-hole just under the German wire to the left? Had they been wiped out? The bombing of the spot from the crest had ceased . . .

A great cloud blinded the moon. The machine-gun opened again, raking the ground, apparently to guard against the crawling approach of night-raiders. A bee pinged and buzzed from the steel heel of his boot. His rifle-sling, jerking free in the darkness, lashed him across the face. The screamer on the wire ceased to scream. The cries for water fell away into a drooling under-moan.

Were there any Germans left at all on the crest apart from those gunners? Retreating everywhere, Metaxa had said.

Metaxa?

It must have been near midnight before the crucified figure on the wire awoke again to the torture of its torn body and broke into screams and pleadings in a crescendoing hysteria. The moonlight sprayed and dimmed through the flapping of the ragged cloud-curtain, and Malcom lay and heard the voice in the dance and sweep of the frozen shadows. He lay and twisted and covered his ears and whimpered.

It was John Metaxa.

Subchapter vi

For hour upon hour – though they may have been only so many minutes – he seemed to lie and listen to the voiced anguish of the mutilated, mindless thing that had once lived and moved and questioned the world and loved him. And then an extraordinary calmness came on him, that slobbering agony in his ears. He rose and took his rifle and limped up the .

moonlit ravine, treading and slipping amidst the spewn lumber of the dead. He walked without concealment and without heed. Once the machine-gun rattled down the slope again. Not a bullet touched him.

With every upward step he took the screaming tore more fiercely at his ear-drums . . .

When he stumbled into the leftwards crater under the German wire he found some half-dozen men and a corporal still alive. He stumbled amongst them, and avoided a bayonet thrust, and was recognized.

'Christ, Sergeant, you! Thought you'd gone West with "A". Where've you been?'

Malcom laughed foolishly and sat down and heard his own whisper from very far away. *The Defile of the Beast! The Defile of the Beast!*

'Sorry I nearly jabbed you, but I'm jumpy as hell. There's a poor bastard on the wire there been screaming his guts out . . . Quiet now.'

'I killed him,' said Malcom.

In the Bag
(1975)

Robert Garioch

We lost our freedom on a Saturday, and spent our Sunday in a cage. An enclosure for prisoners of war is called a cage: but that in which we found ourselves vindicated the poem which we used to learn at school, by not being made of iron bars. Its bounds were defined by guards with rifles, surrounded by a great deal of desert, which kept us in, effectively enough. But freedom was not our immediate want; even the desire for freedom is a luxury: what we needed first was a drink of water, and, after that, something to eat. Saturday was a heavy day on water. The army water-bottle holds a quart, and not many bottles had been filled since early morning, because of the shelling, and principally because we had not expected to be in such trouble by Sunday evening.

The struggle for water had begun on Sunday's walk to Tobruk aerodrome, where we were herded together on the sand beneath the sun. There had been a leaky pipe-line where men fought for water; and a water-point farther on, where things were so difficult that the German in charge became excited, as even the most stolid Germans will, and began to let fly with his pistol: so we got no water. Perhaps it had not been intended that we should get any; we may have passed that water-point only by accident: we wouldn't know.

That Sunday walk had been wasteful of kit, too. We had straggled for very many miles along the desert track: it was the hottest part of the day in the hottest time of the year, and it came at the end of many exhausting days. Lack of food made us weak, also. Somewhere on the way we found some Italian army biscuits, good food, but perfectly dry and hard. Our teeth ground them into dry crumbs, which grated round in our mouths till we scooped them out with dirty fingers. We should have thrown away the boot-brushes and other things in our small-kit, and carried those biscuits with us, whatever else we lost. We should have done many sensible things. We should have held on to greatcoats, even in midsummer, in the Desert. But we had to keep up the pace of the column. We would realise that one slowly plodding man and then another had overtaken us: the horrors of the limping rearguard were getting nearer. If a man had a greatcoat, that would be the moment when he let it drop on the sand. As we walked, our feet avoided strewn objects: a greatcoat, a blanket, a complete bulging pack, a small prayer-book, lost by accident, certainly, but nobody would pick it up. But never a water-bottle, not even an empty one.

We reached the cage towards evening. It was on the Tobruk aerodrome, a great level space of sand, a receptacle into which the prisoners poured like a viscous fluid which slowly separated and clotted into distinct masses. A man would find a group of his mates and attach himself, longing for organisation. Once we got organised, we might get some water. One load of water did arrive. Thousands raced to get there first. Somewhere in the centre of the mob there was anguish and struggle. Those on the outside had no hope, but they would not move away. A few men at the centre got some water, but much of it was spilt on the sand.

We needed organisation. Without it no crowd of men can maintain decency. We must take orders from someone in authority. Normally, we are kept in order by society, and life goes on at least smoothly enough to let our minds dwell on the desire for greater liberty. When the system is good enough, we may even have leisure to discuss the advantages of anarchy. To the Germans, apparently, we were just a population in an enclosed space; they took care that we should not escape, and it appeared that they would supply our needs, more or less: but otherwise they accorded us the exercise of free will, or, to put it otherwise, neglected us. The result was misery, until we found some sort of order.

The British officers, it appeared, began to take charge. We knew nothing of the system, but what we did know was that we were formed into groups, each group having its own strip of sand to sit on. Thus we found ourselves in units small enough to comprehend: what other groups were doing did not concern us. We found a man of some rank high enough to take charge of the group, and this group leader formed small sections, each under a section-leader. How vividly factual is the detail in the story of the Feeding of the Five Thousand! Meanwhile, the officers were wrangling with the Germans for a water-supply. We had no idea what difficulties they had to overcome. All we knew was that, after many hours, some water did arrive for our group, and was distributed so that our section got its share, in an opened-up petrol tin. It didn't look very much. Our tongues were sticking to the roofs of our mouths. The sight of the water made us almost desperate. Not quite desperate, however, for we took time to dole it out properly. No-one touched his share until all had been measured out. We made the most of that water, letting it trickle slowly in our mouths, easing it round our stuck tongues. We wished there had been more. We wished we could turn it on at a main tap and let it gush into our mouths. We thought how good it would be, if ever we got home again, to turn on the tap and watch the water flowing.

The hateful sun disappeared beyond the world's rim, burning us to the very last. I had managed to carry one army blanket on the march. It was a fine big one. It covered me when I lay down on the sand, leaving plenty of margin. A man lay down next to me. He had a good-sized pack, but no blanket nor greatcoat. He looked at me, sizing me up.

'Think we could sleep two men to a blanket, mate?' he asked. I had a look at him. He was not thin, but he was a smallish man.

'We can try,' I said.

The night is cold in the Desert, but we slept, having accomplished the first full day of this strange kind of life. There were plenty of bad days to follow, but none quite so bad as this just over. But that was something we could not have known.

Two Men & a Blanket. Some more water was issued next day, early in the forenoon. There were so many of us that extraordinary methods had to be improvised. There were plenty of large oil-drums lying about, and these were collected and used to fetch water on trucks. Most of them had a thick coating of Diesel oil on the inside, but that could not be helped. We drank black oily water, and were glad of it. Perhaps Diesel oil is not injurious when taken internally; perhaps we did not get enough to do us any harm. Or that may have been partly the cause of the dysentery that broke out shortly afterwards. Anyhow, it did not take away our appetite. We began to understand what hitherto we had only known, that the body must be given food and more food. After a few hours it will want some more again. Of course, we all know this, in normal times, but without understanding it so long as we are comfortable. Perhaps that is how we can still tolerate the fact of poverty, even in the midst of plenty, in the twentieth century, and in peace-time.

We became obsessed by thoughts of food. Then the rumours began. We did not believe them with the mind, but responded to them emotionally. Somebody brought news that Rommel had fallen into a trap, deceived by the fall of Tobruk. That was why they could not organise supplies for us. We would certainly be rescued, or re-press-ganged, before evening. We didn't believe that one, but we cheered up, none the less. But we were illogically depressed by the next rumour, that we had destroyed the Tobruk food-dumps before retiring.

The monotony was broken when a fair-sized body of Highlanders marched into the cage, as light and gay as though they were about to occupy the place as a victorious force, marching in good order, clean and smart, with the pipes playing at their head. We lined their way across that patch of desert, so that it looked like a street, and cheered them as they passed.

At this stage we did not wander far from our own group's territory, where we arranged ourselves roughly in a long narrow rectangle. It was wise to keep near your group-commander in case he might get something to ration out. Sometimes I would go as far as the wrecked Italian biplane (which had an Italian maker's nameplate and R.A.F. markings) and sit near it, not immediately in the shade of its wings, which, being the only shade in the camp, was already occupied, but in the nearest vacant spot which in due course would have its turn of shade as the sun moved westwards. There I sat and thought of food, and hoped that it would come soon, and that I should be there to draw my issue.

After much patient endurance, I watched the sun withdraw beyond the aeroplane wing, and felt cooler immediately. Just then, a certain agitation could be felt among the masses of men everywhere, and a muttering that grew to a rumbling, as, though some thousands of men were saying, 'Rations'. I got back among my group in a hurry. Everyone was excited. Then I heard for the first time a stirring cry, a shout as yet devoid of association, which in years to come would stir the blood, the command:

'TWO MEN AND A BLANKET!'

Two men got hold of a blanket and set out in a smart and soldierly manner at the heels of the group leader. The rest of us waited anxiously. My mate of the previous night, a quiet man who had the knack of disappearing, now turned up just at the right time. The two men reappeared, staggering, with the blanket bulging between them, and on a chosen spot poured from it a quantity of tins of bully beef. Beautiful bully, never since have I despised thee! How carefully those tins were counted and laid in rows and subdivided, and what a time it took to do all this! We watched with the greatest concentration of attention. The sections drew their rows of tins in turn, and divided each tin between one pair of men. Now we heard another phrase that was to become, with numerical variations, a kind of magic formula:

'ONE TIN BETWEEN TWO!'

And so my mate and I got a tin between us, and quickly opened it. The heat had made it very sticky, so we could not help getting some sand on it before we finished the division into two exact halves. My mate did the cutting, by means of his clasp knife, so it was my prerogative to choose my half. I picked mine up, he picked up his.

Derna & Benghazi. Days and nights followed, all alike. The nights were cold, and in the early morning there was a dew, which collected on the tops of the oil-drums. It was possible to have a slight wash in that dew. The brutal sun would force its way into the sky and scorch us immediately. We hung blankets on barbed wire and tried to lie under them. We queued for water when the issue came up, counting the men before us and fearing that the water would give out too soon. Here and there, groups of Indians sat in a circle and played music; sometimes a couple of Scottish pipers would march up and down, playing their more familiar tunes. When an issue of food came up it was divided with care and quickly eaten. There never was enough of it. It was a relief to see the sun pass its zenith, and to know that half of the day's burning was over. So one day followed another: I have forgotten how many days. There were weary scenes of dysentery at the latrines which we dug round the edge of the camp. Nobody could do anything for the sick, except a few of the Medical Corps who had some dressings; and there were men with wounds going wrong for lack of attention. The place would be intolerable for any length of time, but there was no sign of our moving out. The rumours said there was no transport, and that we might be marched by the desert tarmac to Derna or Benghazi, but we hoped the rumours might be wrong. Indeed, we hoped we might even be rescued, having no news of how the war was going.

Some trucks arrived without warning, and carried off a good number of men. They were big Diesel trucks with trailers. They collected men from a place separated from the main part of the camp, and now everyone's problem was how to get into that enclosure as soon as possible. The trucks kept on arriving and departing all day, and we gradually moved towards them.

When our turn came, we heaved ourselves on to the trucks. We crammed ourselves in so that the sides bulged outwards, which effect was counteracted by means of a chain stretched across the truck and hooked to either side. When the truck moved over the uneven road, that chain sawed to and fro across our legs. We passed familiar scenes: the town of Tobruk, with the harbour full of wrecks; Mussolini's signpost farther on, where two roads met, and the rest was unfamiliar to most of us. We travelled all day, and in the evening we swung down the spectacular road, down the escarpment to Derna, and passed through the town, which looked beautiful to us, with gardens. But we left the town half a mile behind, and came to a terrible place. This camp at Derna was said to be 'an old Arab cemetery'. The walled side faced the road, and on the other side was a fence, and some open ground, and then the sea. We were crowded into this place. As we passed inside, another stream of men flowed outwards: for some, it happened, were being sent off on the next stage of the journey. A man in front of us slipped into the outgoing crowd and vanished with them, having sized up the situation and done the right thing. Should I do the same? I hesitated; there was much pushing from behind. I was inside, and it was too late.

This place was so crowded that there was no room to lie down so that a man's legs could be stretched out. Men were lying right next to the latrines: it was impossible for them to find a better place. They would watch the pools overflowing towards them and shout at the men who kept making the flooding more severe, but the men could not help it.

Here we lived on a biscuit a day and a tin of Italian bully. It was not a very big tin. But there was plenty of good Derna water, brought in a tanker. The Italians were running the place; we had been captured by the Germans, but were in Italian hands, and so we were to remain, as it happened, until the Germans drove us out of Italy after the capitulation, along with a lot of wretched Italian slave-labour. The Italians were very much on top at the moment, however, and came among us to gloat. They would stand on the side of the camp next the sea, and stare at us through the railings. A submarine officer in immaculate white uniform came to photograph us in our ragged tropical shirts and shorts. Each time he raised his camera, the men would give him the V-sign, and this exasperated the people outside. One of the guards began to get excited: the gestures continued. Suddenly the guard aimed his rifle straight into the mass of men and fired. A hollow space appeared in the crowd. There was a commotion, and stretchers were brought into use. That was just one incident.

Everybody wanted to get out of that place in the earliest possible batch. To do this it was necessary to pass through a gate into the next enclosure; and the gate was liable to open at any time. So the crowd in the inner camp became a kind of permanent queue, except that it did not form a line, but pressed forwards towards the gate. We lived in this queue for several days.

The next stage in the journey took us to Benghazi. We were loaded on to trucks and trailers. Rations for the day were a biscuit each and a tin of bully among three. Many men now had dysentery, and had lost control of their guts. An Arab employed by the Italians sat facing backwards on top of the driver's cabin, and would not allow a man to get off the truck all day for any reason.

In the evening we came to Benghazi and marched through the white streets to a fenced-off stretch of sand, where we found a heap of tent-sheets. We fastened them by their buttons, erected them in long lines, and crept inside. Early next morning, we looked at the town over a sand-flat and investigated our new camp. There was a medical tent, which reassured us; and in the corner stood a water-tank. In due course a tanker drove up and began to deliver a great quantity of water. The latrine ditches, moreover, had wooden tops to them. Guards were posted around the wire, and there were machine-guns at the corners. In the distance the usual Arab was seen, with the usual camel. A clump of palm-trees not far off looked interesting, and so it was, for when the Liberators came next day to bomb the harbour, A.A. guns opened up from those trees.

We divided ourselves into sections, as before, and rationed out our loaf per man, our little tin of bully between two, and a little sugar and coffee-substitute. If you could find a bit of wood, you brewed the coffee, drank it, and spread the grounds on a piece of your bread. We were permanently hungry by this time. There were tantalising rumours of a cigarette issue. It was useless to try and smoke coffee-grounds wrapped in pieces of paper. Five Italian cigarettes per man did turn up in course of time, and continued to do so every two days. Things were looking up.

We passed the hot hours in our tents, mostly, and walked up and down when it grew cooler towards evening. Somebody had brought a pack of cards, which we used continually so long as there was daylight. The usual crown-and-anchor man unrolled his mat, and people played for cigarettes and pound notes. We still had some idea of the value of money: but the value of cigarettes rose enormously. In Tobruk I had seen a pound note exchanged for a pint of water: now it could fetch a few smokes. Money, it was recognised, was an uncertain, and probably a very long-term investment. Our other daytime diversion was washing. This was an unexpected treat. An elaborate wagon came into the compound one day, with hinged sides which opened to form a spray-room, and with a pump and various other pieces of equipment, which went to make a portable bath. When we used it first, the sand poured out of our hair in yellow streams; it was the first real wash we had had for a very long time. We used to queue up, and contrive with any luck to get a spray-bath nearly every day.

A religious revival took place in this camp, quite spontaneously. In the evening a crowd would gather at one particular spot to sing hymns, and one man or another would stand up to speak or to pray. It was very moving to hear those hymns, and to join in with a few remembered words to the familiar tunes. Those meetings continued late into the night, until the crowd became a few, and the few disappeared by twos and threes. When the singing was over, we would walk slowly round our little paddock, beneath the stars; and we would experience a tremendous and gentle calm.

First Battle
(1996)

W. A. Elliott

Night had now fallen although there was bright moonlight. The thunderous roar of our own guns and distant explosions from those of the enemy, followed by the interlacing whine as the shells crossed overhead, formed a deafening accompaniment – so deafening that one soon lost all sense of sound. We seemed to be groping our way silently through the moonlight as in a dream. We kept right up under our own barrage, for I knew it was better to risk casualties from one's own shrapnel than to let the enemy have a few seconds breathing space to recover themselves after the barrage lifted. Owing to the height of the railway embankment we were able to keep to within fifty yards of our shells bursting on the far side, thereby achieving unusual covering fire. Two of my men, however, were hit by one shell falling short.

I thought we might have to fight to secure the tunnel itself carrying a small river under the railway line for it was here I had seen the Germans forming up. But there was no interference as I got Sergeant Stewart's men down into the knee-deep stream as silently as possible and formed up the remainder behind. We had timed things to a nicety, for our barrage now lifted, dying away into the distance and leaving us only with the sound of water dripping from our sodden clothes.

We clambered catlike out of the far end of the tunnel where the open fields – white in the moonlight and flanked by the even more ghostlike tobacco factory – stretched across to the Battipaglia road. We spoke in whispers and as we formed in extended line our pace was stealthy and feline. A long dark hedge which stretched across the fields to the main road seemed the only vestige of cover, while on our left the railway embankment in deep shadow stretched as far as the railway station. It was here that I had seen the Germans forming up. But now there was no sound except for the subdued chirping of crickets. Sergeant Stewart whispered that he thought there was a booby-trap on the path. I advanced, revolver in hand, to examine it and found a rifle leaning against a carrier of mortar bombs. For a second it did not dawn on me these must be German. Then suddenly, and almost subconsciously, I noticed a cluster of black figures lying sheltering along the embankment at my very elbow. I spun round, yelling 'Hands up!' in German. There was a shower of sparks as one of them fired at me. I promptly fired my revolver point-blank at the nearest two who were now sitting up; and they rolled towards me screaming. As a practised revolver shot and at that range, I could hardly miss. All hell now broke loose as the silence was shattered. Everyone started yelling. Other Germans, sitting on the embankment, fired at us. Ex-Sergeant Hutchison finished one of them off, then, thank God, the remainder stuck up their hands.

An awful savagery now seemed to take hold of us as we rushed along the embankment shouting oaths and shooting at Germans who were lying there. I felt as if some wild animal had got me by the throat and I had to keep shouting and shooting or else my normal self would return bringing fear along with it. There was even a savage pleasure in it. One German was truculent, refusing to double back down the line, and while we were arguing and threatening him, other Germans fired at us out of a trench thirty yards off. I shot him point-blank; the effect was electric and we rushed headlong at the Spandau. Oblivious to sound again, one only saw the flashes coming from the gun muzzles and the sparks from our own rifles as we closed in, firing from the hip. I fired the remaining shots from my revolver. Paterson was going berserk with rifle and bayonet.

We doubled along a hedge which led to our objective, the main road, giving tongue like a pack of wolves. I found it awkward reloading my revolver on the move; in addition my belt was failing miserably to keep up my soaking trousers. I had completely abandoned all thought of tactics and had allowed the lust of battle to take hold. We were halfway alongside of the tobacco factory when some enemy entrenched there opened fire on us, but in the dark their bullets passed over our heads. As we were now right in the middle of their positions they obviously did not know where to shoot. One German came running up shouting and we shot at him amidst much cursing. It was incredible how much we all cursed and swore.

My leading section overran another Spandau post without a shot, but on reaching the main road to Battipaglia, which was our objective, we were heavily fired on from positions guarding a bridge. This was protected by a four-foot ditch and impossible for my first section, now reduced to four men, to assault alone. As another guardsman dropped wounded, I yelled at the second section to come up. They seemed to take a long time and their sergeant was a new man who was in a daze. Some of the Germans were now standing up to shoot at us as we crouched by the hedge shooting back. I fired another drumful from my revolver to try and make them keep their heads down. When the second section came level we all assaulted together, clambering over the ditch. In the darkness one was only conscious again of the sparks coming from the enemy's gun muzzles. One German threw a grenade which landed in the ditch at my feet, while Hutchison who had been foremost in the attack got a burst of Spandau through his shoulder. After some wild shooting the rest of this German post surrendered and we clambered over a fence on to the main Battipaglia road. We were now at the back of the tobacco factory. I sent a man back with Hutchison who seemed badly wounded. He was one of the old desert sergeants who had been demoted for his part in the North African 'mutiny'.

I was now so flushed with excitement that I was finding it difficult to think clearly or to control my guardsmen who were rampaging round like foxhounds. Sergeant Stewart, still surviving but with only two left in his section, insisted on trying to attack a German platoon in a spinney to our right and kept yelling at them in broad Scots, 'Come on out and fight you f—bastards!' The Germans, however, would not oblige and did not even shoot as there was such a mix-up now of British and Germans. I yelled at Stewart to come back so that we could get organised for consolidating on our objective. One tiny little German who looked absurd in an outsized coal-scuttle helmet kept on wanting to surrender to us but leapt back into his trench whenever there was another burst of fire.

Finally he came running across the road to join us amidst roars of applause.

Guardsman Chadwick, who was now temporarily commanding my second section, was trying to locate some Spandaus firing on us from the direction of the crossroads and got a bullet through his mess tin for his pains. He was an old soldier, at one time in the Special Air Service. I thought they might be British Bren guns and not Spandaus firing, so I shouted the password 'Wellington' in their direction. But there was no reply of 'Barracks', only dead silence. As they stopped shooting, however, they must have imagined I was a German. I had thought they might have been 'G' Company who should have been level by this time. (Later I was to learn that 'G' Company managed to fight their way into the disused factory building, but later had to be withdrawn for fear of being cut off.) 'F' Company, to their left, who had already lost their company commander, fared even worse. The first wave of their attack had been shot to pieces in the bright moonlight and two of their platoon officers killed. The Germans had then counter-attacked and overrun the rest of the company. Their Company Sergeant-Major, an old Battalion man, escaped later in the night only to be killed by a shell on rejoining our lines.

My company had only reached its objective because we had been able to use the tunnel under the embankment to move right in under our barrage before the Germans had time to recover. Also because there was such a mix-up in the darkness that the Germans did not know who was who and where to shoot. Meanwhile, oblivious of the fact that we were the only company to capture its objective, we strutted about as proud as peacocks in the midst of a still intact German battalion heavily supported by tanks.

8 Platoon now crossed the road on to the fields beyond and started to try and dig in but the ground was as hard as concrete

and they only had small entrenching tools. As the moon rose I sent Chadwick's section in the direction of the crossroads, which was now a hundred yards to our left, wishing to know if the shouting and noise of tracked vehicles coming from that direction meant the arrival of 'G' Company. Suddenly Chadwick shouted to look out as there were tanks coming straight down the road at us. I didn't react at once, thinking these might be our own Shermans. There was a sinister grinding and squeaking of bogie wheels and two German tanks or half-tracks came clattering straight for us down the tarmac. The road was a death trap with high barbed wire fences on either side and our Plat (anti-tank projector) was with platoon headquarters. Cursing the moonlight, I yelled at everyone to lie face downwards at the side of the road, trusting the tank driver's lack of vision. I could feel all my muscles contracting with fear as the metal tracks passed within yards of my elbow scattering sparks in all directions. The tanks, however, passed straight on over the bridge beside 7 Platoon.

I stood up again, sobered and bewildered, not knowing of any battle drill to fit such a perilous situation and trying desperately to think what to do next. I thought that if the reserve company would now come up, we might still have taken the tobacco factory and vital crossroads; but things were now beginning to get out of hand. I told my leading section to get quickly into a house (which, unknown to me, was full of Germans) and ran back to try to find my platoon HQ with its anti-tank projector which had been lost in the mêlée. I only got as far as my second section when I saw some more tanks approaching from the other direction with the moonlight glinting on their turrets. To my horror I realised that they were not simply motoring through us again but were part of a coordinated infantry-supported counter-attack. Long lines of German infantry stretched behind them, coming in from our right side and rear. They quickly overran my platoon HQ who were now climbing on to the road, finding there was little they could do against a combination of enemy infantry and armour when they were not dug in. Company headquarters, which was also coming up, only just managed to shoot their way out.

The tables were now completely turned and the rest was a humiliating fiasco. I got caught on a barbed wire fence under the very guns of the tanks but managed to extricate myself, shouting to all my nearby men to follow me into the ditch. I arrived there with four others. We were hardly into the ditch before the converging lines of German infantry started jumping over it and some took up positions further along. The five of us started a somewhat futile discussion on how to rectify the situation as more half-tracks came coursing down the road to stop opposite with a screech of brakes and seal us off from Ian Fraser's platoon which had crossed on to the other side of the main road wondering what was happening. I heard Chadwick shouting for me and then silence which meant that he too had been put 'in the bag'. We poked a gun gingerly over the top of the bank, but firing it would have served no purpose as there were now Germans behind and in front of us and our prisoners mixed up with them. On all sides Germans were crawling out of slit trenches which we had failed to clear or perhaps even see in our initial assault.

Some Germans now came clearing down the ditch along which we had started to crawl. They must have seen us jump into it for they searched methodically and extracted two of my party at gunpoint. But they missed Coyle, Murphy and myself. We were lying full length in the muddy water under some bramble bushes so they never saw us and passed further on down the ditch. We started to crawl again. The ditch became deep and dark and completely overgrown with brambles. It was very quiet down below – apart from the droning of the mosquitoes.

I stalked what I thought to be a wounded German in our path with my revolver, but it turned out to be a piece of sacking.

Germans were passing frequently along the path overhead, talking noisily. I tried to make out what they were saying, as I knew some German – but I could only catch the word 'Englander'. I suppose they were re-occupying the ground we had captured and recovering their dead and wounded. It was an unpleasant feeling to be suddenly a fugitive instead of an attacker. The three of us crawled another fifty yards until the ditch became full of water and the brambles grew right down to the surface. We seemed to make an awful noise splashing. I returned my revolver to its holster as I did not think it would fire any more after being stuck in the mud. The mortification of the situation weighed heavily upon me, especially the knowledge that the Germans must have captured all our wounded and retaken a number of their own prisoners. I did not relish returning to the Battalion with only two of my men.

A large shell crater blocked the ditch and I could hear Germans talking on the other side where they had re-occupied a machine-gun post. It was obvious we would have to stay in this ditch till the moon sank in the early morning and the dawn mists allowed a chance to crawl across the open fields to the railway line. It was now about 10 p.m. and the moon's vertical rays glinted on the water of the ditch which submerged us up to our waists. I found difficulty in getting one leg under a bush as a party of Germans passed overhead conversing in loud voices. I thought one of them had seen me, as he appeared to stop, but he passed on again. We had not yet abandoned hope: there still seemed a chance that if the other companies had been successful, the reserve company might be sent through to regain our sector. At one moment indeed I thought I heard guttural Scots voices shouting 'Come here' – but it was only some Germans. It now became evident that the attack had been called off as a costly failure, although it may have helped to knock the Germans off balance at a time when they themselves had been preparing to counter-attack and drive us back on to the beaches.

The ensuing two hours were like a nightmare, but more unreal. So complete was my exhaustion, I was too tired to care. I did not even feel the discomfort of the water in which I lay, or of a gash on my leg. Although there was a German post within twenty yards I dozed off for half an hour. Murphy did the same, but we later had to wake him because of his snores. He then started a feverish coughing that I feared must reveal our presence. Suddenly some Verey lights went up beyond the main road on the original company objective, and there was a roar from about six machine-guns firing belt after belt, all at once. Our spirits revived at the prospect of rescue. But there followed dead silence. It was only some remnants of the company surrounded by the Germans behind their lines. This turned out to be Ian Fraser's platoon which had followed behind us through the gap we had opened up.

It was now about 11 p.m. We were getting very cold sitting in the water, but had to do so as Germans were still passing to and fro above our heads. Murphy's coughing was now becoming uncontrollable despite a handkerchief we stuffed in his mouth. It was incredible that the Germans did not hear us. I decided that we would have to start crawling away from them towards the main road again and wait there for the moon to set before making a dash for it. But our movements led to unavoidable splashing and brought on a further spasm of hysterical coughing from Murphy. The Germans really did hear us this time. They started shouting to each other and came running towards us. I now realised the game was up when they were standing right above covering us with their Schmeisser machine-pistols.

Consanguinity
(1969)

Ronald Duncan

The *Flying Scotsman* was two hours late. That used to happen frequently during the war, especially when the Heinkels had been over during the night. The train was blacked out, the lights were dim; two officers sat opposite each other in a first-class compartment. Rather appropriately, one of them was reading *The Idiot*; the other, a Major of about thirty-five, sat huddled in a corner staring intently in front of him as though examining a scene which lay behind his eyes. He smoked continuously. Neither of the men had spoken for four hours; they had been in the train for four hours five minutes. Even then their conversation had been restricted, and omitted any introductions. Captain Maclean of the Seaforth Highlanders had permitted himself to remark that 'it was a perfect bore carrying these bloody gas-masks around', and in reply Major Buckle of the Black Watch had grunted. Their reticence was, however, not due to the notices displayed above their seats to the effect that 'Idle chatter helps Hitler', but to the fact that neither had any curiosity about the other. Perhaps both had seen too much of their fellow men to want to get to know another. That was true of Captain Maclean at least, who had just endured nine weeks of a crowded troop ship. To him, understandably, silence now seemed a luxury and solitude an indulgence.

He planned to spend his leave in complete privacy. It was unlikely that his sister, who kept house for him in Edinburgh, would do anything to spoil his brief retreat. But as a precaution he had delayed informing her of his arrival, and merely sent her a wire from King's Cross. He did not wish to be met at Waverley Station by a gathering of the clan.

The train jolted suddenly to a standstill. A cloud of steam from the vacuum brakes oozed into the compartment.

'Signals, I suppose,' Maclean said, putting down his book and glancing at the blind over the window. 'This will make us later than ever.'

Major Buckle looked at his watch. Comment was unnecessary. A stop was unlikely to hasten their arrival.

But after about ten minutes the Express edged its way forward again and eventually sidled unobtrusively into a station. This moment always provided an opening gambit for conversation during the war, which even Captain Maclean could not resist.

'Where are we?' he asked, peering round the blind at the completely darkened platform.

'God knows,' Buckle replied. 'It looks like hell. Maybe it

is hell. I think I recognize it. I used to go to the St Leger occasionally. This will be Doncaster.'

They both remarked almost simultaneously that they should have been eighty miles nearer Edinburgh by this time, after which observation they felt almost old friends. Nothing joins people together so quickly as a mutual complaint.

'It's bloody rough,' Maclean muttered, 'catching a train that's half a day late when you've only got a fortnight's leave.'

'Been overseas?' Buckle asked, without the slightest interest.

'Singapore.' The reply was curt but not rude.

'Tough.' The comment was sympathetic without sentiment.

Not a word more was said. The fact that Maclean's regiment had retreated for four months through the Malayan jungle, only to be practically annihilated on the docks at Singapore, and that he was the only officer of his brigade alive to tell the tale, was no excuse for him to do so. It was not shame that kept him silent; he would have been just as reticent if he had taken part in a victory. One did not talk shop.

'Seen any good shows in London recently?' he asked.

'*The Relapse* wasn't bad.'

'But that came off months ago.'

'Did it?'

'Yes. Time passes.'

'Does it?' Buckle asked pointedly.

Maclean looked embarrassed, sensing some philosophical edge behind the question. Then suddenly he smiled with relief.

'Ah, of course, I see what you mean. Time certainly does drag in a train.'

'That's not what I meant.'

'Oh.'

Maclean picked up his book. Within five minutes, both officers were sleeping. The train tore through the night, carrying its ungainly passengers forward while they crawled back into their dreams. Dreams of a severed hand like a glove on the floor. Dreams of a negress with a necklace of breasts. But Maclean remembered neither when he awoke in the half light with a crick in his neck. Quickly he straightened his tie and combed his hair.

'What we need is a cup of char,' he said.

'We've just passed through Carlisle,' Buckle told him. 'We should be in in about an hour.'

One could not say that the two officers had slept together, but the fact that they had sprawled within the same compartment seemed to ease their relationship. The morning found them much more talkative than they had been the night before.

'Do you live in Edinburgh too?' Maclean asked.

'No, but I used to. That's why I'm going there.'

Paradoxes always annoyed Maclean. He was afraid that somebody was pulling his leg.

'You mean you live just outside the city?' he asked, hoping to clear up the apparent contradiction.

'No, I don't live anywhere now,' Buckle answered without a note of regret.

Immediately three garish pictures floated into the Captain's mind: first, he visualized the Major standing beside a bombed-out house, smouldering in ruins, where lay the bodies of his entire family. For some reason a rocking-horse and a teddy-bear were to the fore in this image. The second visual headline showed the Major driving his tank through the approaches to Benghazi. A dispatch rider hands him a cable. It is from his wife. Maclean could read it clearly over Major Buckle's shoulder. 'I am sleeping occasionally with the postman, but I am pregnant by the milkman. When you get this I shall be living with the dustman. Your loving wife.'

'War's a bloody bore, the way it uproots chaps,' he said.

Then the third picture came into his mind. He saw his

sister Angela standing waiting on the platform, her mouth as full of questions as his nanny's used to be of pins.

'If you've nowhere to stay in Edinburgh, my sister and I would be awfully pleased to put you up.'

'Thank you. I should be glad of your hospitality for a night or two.'

'And, of course, your wife, if . . .'

'No, I am alone.'

The second image flashed like a film trailer across Maclean's mind. 'I am not married.'

It faded. And the third picture, of his sister standing on the platform, came into focus. He had not the slightest doubt that she was there waiting.

Everything about Angela was a compromise, even her sex. With her cairn puppy waiting beside her and her smart, crocodile handbag tucked under her arm, she looked completely unobtrusive. Her whole appearance was a compromise, for though Angela knew that her looks were striking, and wished to be the centre of attraction, yet she dressed so tastefully and stood so demurely that you would not pause as you passed her or notice what she wore. Her rather chic hat suggested a femininity and gaiety which the severity of her tweeds contradicted. In one hand she twirled a pretty French parasol, but her stance was that of a man. Nobody had ever told her that she had beautiful legs and a pretty instep, but she knew. Perhaps that was why she wore the sheerest nylons, and the flattest and heaviest of brogues to ruin the effect. Just so nature had failed to make up its mind, giving her straight, dull hair (whereas her brother's was naturally curly), and the prettiest eyes and mouth above a rather too heavy chin. Her hips were distinctly boyish, but not even the tightest bra could hide her breasts. Though Angela was nearly thirty she was as embarrassed by her breasts as she had been when they first leaned out from their boyish tree. Alex had laughed at her then; she still feared his derision and wished her womanhood away. For it was that which confused their relationship. Ever since their mother's death she had been both mother and sister to Alex. For the last ten years she had been wife in all but shame. She was of course quite unaware of any incestuous leanings; she merely liked Alex more than any other man, and had turned away from the attentions of several admirers because any surrender to them had made her feel unfaithful to him. They were happy living together in the old house in Prince's Crescent. They could read books at table, they could sit on the edge of each other's bed.

She had counted the days, the hours till this train should bring him back to her. And as it steamed into the platform and she saw him stepping down from his compartment, she felt entire again for the first time in twelve months. First her eyes, then her feet ran to meet him, as though she would embrace him and erase the months of anxiety she had endured but dared not show. He was all the world to her – or almost. For the rest, perhaps one day she would adopt one.

'Alex!' she cried. But there was no embrace. The cairn on the lead took one hand and her parasol the other. 'Here's Boxer to see you. He's awfully patient. Your train's hours late.'

Alex was both officer and gentleman. He gave his sister a smile, but kissed and fondled the dog.

Then, turning, he introduced her to the Major. But Angela had no eyes for him; she was wholly absorbed in her brother. Like any woman, though, she was more observant than she was curious, and noticed detail even when she was not looking for it. In the cursory but polite glance she gave Major Buckle as he shook her hand, Angela formed an indelible impression. She saw him as a lonely, shy and pathetic figure, and was not in the least taken in by his strong build and hearty manner. His light blue eyes gave him a remoteness, a coldness which attracted her, while his lips, which seemed unnaturally red against the pallor of his skin, gave his mouth a sensuousness and warmth which repelled her. She also noticed that his batman had ironed the wrong side of his tie.

Buckle, on the other hand, had every opportunity to look at Angela while she chatted away so excitedly to her brother. And though his eyes grazed over her closely, he saw only her wet lower lip, her breasts and her narrow hips, and was quite unaware of the colour of her eyes and hair, or what she was wearing. By the time they had reached the ticket barrier, he knew that he wanted to sleep with her. It was a bore that he would be her brother's guest.

The next few days were the happiest in Angela's life. She did not know why. Historians maintain that wars are caused by economics. They are wrong. Economics is their excuse; the reason for war is that it destroys that which we all want destroyed: the *status quo*, with which we identify our own inhibitions. War alone releases our personal relationships. It is not a necessary evil but a necessary pleasure. If we were honest, we would admit that all the slaughter, cruelty and suffering which war entails remain for us merely a matter of regrettable statistics. What means something to us is that war provides us with that sense of insecurity which is life, when peace has seemed as respectable and as dull as death. It is true that a drunken orgy might provide a similar release, but it is quite difficult to remain completely drunk for several years and impossible to indulge in the briefest fling without some curious sense of remorse. In war, we can release ourselves without guilt; indeed, our excuses become duties and any behaviour is condoned under the blanket of the great sacrifice which we curse publicly, but enjoy privately. National disasters can be borne with comfortable fortitude: it is personal sorrow, not the grief for another but a lack in our own life, which is so unbearable. It is a burden we would put down though a million men fall with it.

Angela sang as she skipped about the kitchen in dressing-gown and mules getting the breakfast. Angela sang as she carried first one tray and then the other up to the two men's rooms. She had got up early and done all the housework and prepared a picnic. Now as she ran her bath and admired her figure in the mirror above it, she was radiant with happiness. It was nice having two men to fuss over again. She had not felt so useful since her father had died. It was nice getting up early to cut sandwiches, make a salad and iron shirts; and what doubled her pleasure was that she could now indulge her affection for her brother with a certain sense of virtue, or even sacrifice. His leave was short: it was right he should have breakfast in bed. And the presence of a guest in the house gave another excuse for any of the luxuries she planned. As she stepped into the bath she decided she would give them salmon for supper. Then she remembered she had not locked the bath-room door. She got out of the bath to do so. Still singing gaily, she stepped into the water again. The door remained ajar.

'I'll sling this sponge at you, Alex, if you rinse your razor in my bath. It's a filthy trick.'

There was a note of soft petulance in her voice, the tone women use when they complain about those masculine habits which are so endearing to them.

'Hurry up and get out of that. Buckle will want a bath too.' Alex dipped his razor beside her, and turned to lather his face.

Angela lay full length, swishing the water together with her legs so that it flopped up over her flat tummy. It was a sort of aid to meditation she had employed since childhood.

'Alex, do you like him?'

Her casual voice betrayed the fact that the question meant a great deal to her.

218

'Immensely,' he replied.

Angela sat up, relieved, and began soaping herself energetically. His answer had meant everything to her.

'We seem to get on so well together,' she said. 'I can hardly believe you only met him in a train three days ago. And yet he's so reticent. I hardly know a thing about him.'

'Do you need to?' Alex mumbled, his face contorted beneath his blade.

'Not if you like him.'

The trio passed the next few days very idly, without plan or purpose, driving out for a picnic during the day and pubcrawling of an evening. This was to please Alex, who still had literary aspirations. Edinburgh is probably the only city in the British Isles where writers still congregate at their regular tavern, and not even the war dispersed this coterie of affable but garrulous cadgers. Angela liked to hear her brother talk; after a couple of whiskies she, too, was convinced of his talent. She felt as proud as a mother, and listened as indulgently as a wife while he told the synopsis of a play he intended to write one fine day to a Scotch Nationalist poet who accepted Drambuie and beer in strict rotation. Angela knew the plot better than Alex, prompted him here and there, and remarked that a scene reminded her of a play by Bridle she had seen years ago at the Kings. After all, she was his sister. Throughout these sessions Major Buckle sat content, yet contributed little to the conversation beyond an admission that he had not read whatever book they happened to be discussing. But he seldom took his eyes off Alex, and though he himself had no literary pretensions and did nothing to express his own personality, he was plainly impressed by that of his friend. It was this shadow-like loyalty to her brother that made Angela warm to Major Buckle. He didn't attract her physically. Both his appearance and her responses were far too vague, nebulous and undefined for her to have any feeling as precise as that. On the other hand, his features were regular and inconspicuous and his personality so passive that she could not possibly find him objectionable. It was, she felt, as if she now had two brothers, and the better they got on together, the fonder she became of each.

As they walked home after the third evening spent in The Green Dragon, Angela slipped her right arm through her brother's and, since Buckle was on her left, she gave him the other. After the fifth evening, she kissed her brother goodnight, and since Buckle was sitting beside Alex, she gave him a peck too. They seemed such good friends it was only right they should share her favours. After the seventh evening spent in precisely the same fashion, and following the consumption of half a dozen whiskies, Angela and Buckle found themselves alone in the back of a car. Sometimes the suggestive environment can be mistaken for personal feeling. Major Buckle took the initiative. He smudged her lips and undid the buttons of her blouse, only withdrawing when the intricacies of her bra defeated his fumbling fingers. By the end of a fortnight, it was agreed that there was some sort of understanding between them, though neither could have told precisely what was understood. It certainly was not love; it looked dangerously like the imminence of marriage. Events moved quickly in war and nobody looked too closely. It was agreed that the three of them should go to London and see a few shows.

As her relationship with Buckle developed, Angela relaxed. She took to wandering in and out of her brother's bedroom clad in her undies, or precariously swathed in a bath-towel. Their rooms in the hotel adjoined; she used to sit for hours gossiping to Alex as he lay in bed. Buckle's room was only across the corridor. But he remained undisturbed. Nevertheless, his presence there was an indispensable catalyst. Angela felt that, now she had a man of her own as it were, there was nothing to inhibit her enjoying such harmless intimacies with her brother. Another factor, of course, was that she knew her brother's leave would soon be over. No one knew then when or whether they would see each other again. In those circumstances, when there were air raids every night to remind people how transient their moment was, despair was often mistaken for desire, but sometimes desire found its own desperation.

Buckle proposed to Angela while she lay beside him on the platform of Lancaster Gate Tube Station. It seemed the decent thing to do, though even Major Buckle, who was not sufficiently a realist to have a sense of humour, recognized something slightly inappropriate in making plans for the future in the middle of a series of air raids which had already destroyed several square miles of the city. Perhaps their horizontal position on the asphalt floor compensated for the less romantic aspects of the occasion. They had been forced to seek shelter in the tube on their way back to their hotel from the Mercury Theatre. That was four hours ago. The all-clear had not sounded. Alex lay beside them sleeping, The rest of the platform was covered with ungainly bodies slunked in sleep and covered by a single blanket. These were the regulars, timid termites who had taken to sleeping in the tubes every night. Trains did not wake them, passengers walking by did not disturb them, nothing embarrassed them. Couples, old and young lay under the slot machines and wire refuse baskets, and even on the stairs, as though in the privacy of their own bedrooms. Though the English are supposed to be prudes, once they are horizontal, in parks or on the beach, they lose all modesty and have less inhibitions in public than they have in the privacy of their homes. Many a man now walking in the sun was begotten on the steps of an escalator in the full glare of a neon light.

In such an environment, Angela could hardly have refused. Death was in the air and birth, or something extraordinarily like it, lay all about her. She snuggled up to Buckle and smiled over his shoulder at her brother. They were joined in holy wedlock two days later by special licence at Caxton Hall. Alex gave her away and Buckle received her, both slightly hilarious and a little drunk. Only Angela was serious or sober.

After the sordid civic ceremony, where the officializing bureaucrat apes a clergyman by intoning the regulations with his hands clasped together, and gives you a receipt with all the unction of handing you a sacrament, the couple drove straight to Victoria Station. Alex accompanied them on to the platform to put them in the train for Brighton. He stood by the window talking to his sister. There were tears in her eyes. Only four days of his leave remained. She could not bear to leave him.

'Couldn't Alex come too?' she pleaded, turning to her husband.

Together they dragged him into the carriage just as the train started. Alex felt rather an intruder and a little foolish, holding a bag of confetti in his pocket. He could scarcely open it now, and fling it over them before sitting beside them for the rest of the journey.

'I've only got a platform ticket,' he said.

'Let's go along to the bar and have a drink,' Buckle suggested.

The two friends immediately left the compartment. Angela smiled indulgently after them, then glared into her compact and powdered her nose. It all seemed a dream to her. She glanced at the ring on her finger. Like any virgin, she was terribly frightened. She knew she was going to lose something she had preserved but did not want. It was like going to the dentist.

But it was nice that Alex had come too. She used her lipstick with deliberation, then crossed her legs and looked out of the window, counting the telegraph posts which passed in a minute. She knew that they stood fifty-five yards apart, and from that data could compute the speed of the train. It was a trick she had learned from her father.

Angela awoke the next morning, but before she was conscious of the light she was aware of her dream. Before opening her eyes, she tried to recall it . . .

She had been out hunting, but instead of riding a horse she had dreamed she was sitting astride a giraffe. The animal had galloped, quite out of control, through a forest where every tree was on fire, each separate limb of timber blossoming with a flame. Having recalled her dream, she remembered, and raising her thighs, removed the bath-towel beneath her. She got out of bed and carried it into the bathroom. Buckle was not in the bed, neither was he in the bath. She frowned, then dimly remembered that he had said something or other about going downstairs to get an evening paper. But that, she realized, must have been last night. He must have returned since then. There was proof of that. She rang for her coffee, got back into bed and lit a cigarette. Probably her husband and Alex had gone for a dip. The hotel was by the beach. At any rate she did not feel like bathing: she felt very refreshed. She had never slept so deeply or woken so well. For an hour she lay enjoying the sensation of heaviness in her limbs. It was to her as if her youth had been a drought and now it had rained and she was the rain and she was the river. But for all that she could recall nothing of the storm, nor did she try. It was enough to lie there enjoying the sensation of being quenched. Her limbs had drunk from her own desire. Her thighs and her breasts felt heavy, and yet it was this that at the same time made her feel so light as though she might float. It was the first time that Angela had been aware of her own body as an instrument of pleasure. She had previously regarded it as a vehicle for health.

She had her breakfast and then decided for once in her life not to take a bath. She did not want to wash this feeling away. She looked carefully at her nakedness in the mirror. She looked just the same.

'Appearance can be deceptive,' she thought, and stretched like a cat.

She dressed quickly and went along the corridor to her brother's room, expecting to find her husband jawing to him. Alex was alone; he lay in bed reading, *The Turn of the Screw* of course.

'Have you and Peter been out for a bathe?' Angela asked him.

Alex shook his head.

'I wonder where he's gone?'

'Probably for a walk?'

Angela nodded.

For the next hour, neither gave Buckle a thought. But when they went downstairs Angela asked the hotel porter if he had seen Major Buckle. The man was not helpful. He had not seen anyone go out, and since he had not been on duty the previous evening when Angela and her husband had arrived, he would not have recognized him anyhow.

'If he didn't have breakfast with you upstairs he must have been into the dining-room,' Alex suggested.

But the head waiter assured them that nobody had been to Angela's table that morning.

They decided that Buckle had gone for a bathe or taken a walk, and set out to wander along the front. At first they tried to see if they could spot him amongst the bathers who already sported themselves on the beach, but after a few moments their own conversation became absorbing, they forgot their search, thinking they would find Buckle at the hotel when they got back. They walked for about three miles along the front, stopped and had coffee and then returned leisurely to their hotel.

'Have you seen my husband?' Angela asked the porter as he handed her the key to her room.

'No madam,' the man replied cheerfully, as if reassuring her.

'That fool thinks we're having an affair, and that you're frightened your husband will come and catch us red-handed,' Alex joked as they went up in the lift.

Angela said nothing. She was not amused.

Her room was empty. There was no note or message from Buckle.

For some reason, neither Angela nor her brother thought of looking in the bathroom or on the dressing-table to see whether Buckle's shaving kit or hairbrushes were still there. But when he did not appear for lunch, or turn up during the afternoon, they decided that he had probably been called up to London by the War Office on some urgent business and been delayed longer than he expected.

'That sort of thing often happens these days,' Alex told his sister, 'a chap in our regiment got called off on some Secret Mission the first day of his leave.'

'He could have phoned.'

'Maybe he did when we were out.'

'Then there'd have been a message.'

'If he's in London, he's bound to have lunched at the club. I'll ring and ask if they've seen him.'

Alex shook his head as he returned from the kiosk. They sat for a few minutes in silence.

'I'll go and pack,' Angela said.

She was now very worried. So was her brother, but with more reason. He had not told her that when he had enquired for her husband, the Secretary of the Club had blandly replied that Buckle was dead. Of course Alex realized that there must have been two members with the same name. Still, it had been a shock to him.

Early next morning, Alex accompanied his sister to the War Office. A Colonel Hutchison received them. Alex explained: if Buckle had been recalled to his unit or despatched on some mission, it was only fair that his wife should be told of his whereabouts, especially in these circumstances . . .

'What circumstances?' the Colonel asked sympathetically.

'We were on our honeymoon,' Angela said, 'we were only married yesterday afternoon.'

'You did say Major Buckle of the Black Watch?' the Colonel asked.

'Yes, sir,' Alex replied rather shortly.

'Are you sure there's not some mistake?'

'A woman's hardly likely to forget her husband's name,' Angela said.

The Colonel rang a bell on his desk.

'Bring me the army list of the Black Watch,' he told the secretary.

When this was handed to him he glanced rapidly down the list of names. Then he got up and looked out of the window.

'I thought it was unlikely. But there was just a chance that there were two officers of the same name and rank in the same regiment.'

He turned and faced the brother and sister.

'As I said, there must be some mistake. Major Buckle was blown to pieces before my eyes six months ago.'

'Impossible!' Angela blurted out.

'A mine exploded under his car. Very little was left of Buckle, but quite enough to identify him. The man whom you married yesterday must have been masquerading as Major Buckle.'

'I'm sure he was genuine,' Maclean said. 'I'd have spotted it if he wasn't.'

'I'm sorry, Captain, but I doubt it. There are plenty of these people who pass themselves off as officers these days. We must trace this Major Buckle of yours. Intelligence will want to question him. I suppose you've got a photograph of him? Did he look remotely like this?'

The Colonel produced a photograph from the drawer of his desk.

'Yes, that's Peter,' Angela said.

'That's impossible I'm afraid, madam. If you have a photograph of your husband you can compare it with this. I am sure you will see that the likeness is only enough to justify the impostor in his attempt. Have you such a photograph?'

Angela shook her head sadly, and then remembered.

'Oh yes, I took several snaps of my brother and my husband at a picnic we had outside Edinburgh a couple of weeks ago.'

'May I see them?'

'The film hasn't been developed yet,' Alex explained.

'Then go and get it immediately, Captain, and we'll have it developed here.'

Half an hour later, Alex returned with the camera and handed it to the Colonel. Then he took his sister into the canteen while the film was developed. They waited.

Colonel Hutchison looked hopelessly embarrassed as he placed the six prints on the table before them.

'Your brother looks quite a film star,' he muttered, then immediately regretted the remark.

Angela stared at the prints. There were six photos of her brother, but no trace of any figure, however dim, standing beside him.

The Rape of Lucrezia
(1946)

Eric Linklater

'Come triste la vita!' sighed Lucia, and lifted and stretched her plump brown arms, and opened her wide red mouth in a desolate yawn. The day was hot, and little yellow feathers clung to her fingers and stuck to her wrists. 'Nothing ever happens,' she said. 'Life goes by and leaves us here, alone and idle, without our men and therefore without pleasure or purpose in our existence. Oh, I am so dissatisfied, Lucreziat!'

She and Lucrezia, her younger sister, had been plucking a pair of hens in the green shade of a great vine that half-covered the wall and overhung the back door of a farmhouse. Beyond the farmyard the ground fell steeply to a narrow glen, and rose again to a round hill like a pudding-basin, but patched with trees and circled by a climbing path that here and there showed white among them. On the other side of the farmhouse was the large, squarely-built mansion of the Noble Lady of Rocca Pipirozzi.

The Noble Lady had been obliged to give hospitality, some weeks before, to a prolific niece and her seven children who had fled from their own house near Chiusi when the Germans entrenched in its grounds. As the Noble Lady lived in straitened circumstances, the Countess of Pontefiore had come to her help, and to augment her small domestic staff had sent her Lucia and Lucrezia Donati. They had come willingly enough, pleased by the offer of a change of scene, but soon had grown weary of a house duller than they had been accustomed to, and dominated now by a woman with a grievance and her numerous unattractive family. In memory, even so short a memory, Pontefiore and their own overcrowded home acquired a charm and a gaiety they had never, or never fully, appreciated till now. They longed to return, and with a desire sharpened by ennui they yearned for the company of their lovers.

'It is no life at all,' Lucrezia agreed, and holding up a naked hen she plucked from its loose skin a few remaining pin-feathers. Lucia clasped the other bird in her hands, and leaning forward, stared with mournful eyes at a daydream of her lost husband.

'It is more than a year since Enrico was taken,' she said, 'and who knows now whether he is alive or dead?'

'It is ten months since Angelo came home and went away again,' said Lucrezia, 'and I do not know whether he – he, my Angelo – is alive or dead.'

'You were not married,' said Lucia. 'It is not so bad for you.'

'It is worse for me,' said Lucrezia, 'because my nature is more affectionate than yours.'

'You have not so much self-control: that is what you mean, and we know that already.'

'I have so much self-control that often I am astonished at myself.'

'I remember one occasion when you astonished every body.'

'That is the sort of occasion you would remember. But there are other occasions, which may be very numerous indeed, to which no one pays any attention; and they are the very important occasions on which a person conducts herself with virtue and restraint. All that goes quite unnoticed, but if for a moment or two a person is ill-advised in her behaviour, then everybody stares.'

'Enrico's absence has made no difference at all in my behaviour. I have been strictly faithful to him.'

'Your nature is comparatively cold, Lucia.'

'Well, that is a new discovery! Nobody ever said that before. Enrico never said so, and if anyone should know, it was Enrico.'

'Enrico, it may be, was easily contented.'

'Enrico was a husband that any woman might be proud of. Enrico was a true man —'

'Oh, do not tell me about Enrico! Be quiet, Lucia. I want to think about my Angelo, and how can I do that while you are shouting *Enrico, Enrico, Enrico*?'

'If I thought he could hear me, I would shout till my throat split in two!'

They were silent for a little while, and then Lucia cried, 'I must talk about him to someone! You are so selfish, Lucrezia, that a conversation with you is no pleasure at all. I shall go and talk to Emilia Bigi. She will listen to me, and be glad to listen.'

'Emilia Bigi has never had the chance to learn about men for herself, but only from women who have been deserted or betrayed, and go to her to confide their troubles.'

'She is truly sympathetic!' Lucia shouted, and without waiting for an answer threw down the hen she had plucked and set off with indignant speed, her short skirt in a flurry above her bare legs and her arms swinging to and fro like a soldier's. Quickly she disappeared from sight in the narrow glen, then reappearèd a few minutes later on the path that girdled the round hill beyond it. Lucrezia watched her – intermittently in view among the farther trees – without much interest, and listened with no interest at all to the distant sounds of battle. Somewhere to the east and somewhere to the west the foreign armies were fighting each other. Field-guns were firing, but the explosion of their shells was muffled by intervening hills. Sometimes a machine-gun fired and was answered, as it seemed, by a boy rattling his stick along iron railings. Lucrezia sat in the very midst of war, but the war was not near enough to be frightening, and presently, with her hands folded in her lap and her head drooping, she fell into a light and pleasant sleep.

She began to dream about a harvest field, and herself cutting with a steady sickle the dry varnished stems of the wheat. Then, quite suddenly, panic took her, for another reaper had seized her hair in mistake for a handful of corn, and was pulling it towards him, ready to cut. She woke with a gasp of fear, and felt indeed the tug of a strong hand. Her head was jerked back, her eyes that were still half-full of the dream saw a familiar face come swiftly down, and her lips that were opening to scream were closed by an imperative warm kiss. The back of the wooden chair on which she was sitting broke with a crack, she tumbled to the pavement, and Angelo came down with her. Brown feathers that had been gathered tidily on a sheet of newspaper were scattered here and there as they lay for a minute in a commotion of mutual embraces. But then they sat up; and Lucrezia stared at Angelo, and cried, 'No, be still! I want to look at you, I want to be sure it is you. Dear Angelo, in my dream you were going to cut my head off!'

'I like it very well where it is,' said Angelo. 'Even in your dreams you should be aware of that. You must be getting morbid, darling Lucrezia, and the only cure for that is to be married. When shall we be married?'

'Oh, soon, quite soon, I think. But first of all tell me how you are, and what you have been doing, and how you came here. Listen! The guns are firing again. Oh, my dear, it must have been dangerous for you to come. Where did you sleep last night?'

'In a cave in the woods not far from Pontefiore. Some men I knew were also sleeping there, and it was from them that I learnt you were here. But if you want to know everything I have done since I last saw you, you will have to listen for a long time, because I have had many adventures.'

'Do not tell me about the adventures, tell me about yourself. Do you still love me, Angelo?'

Several minutes passed before he was allowed to explain his presence. He had come through the German lines, he said, on a perilous and important mission. No, he had not been alone. An English officer, a Captain Telfer, had come with him, and the manner in which he had first met Captain Telfer, many months before, was extremely interesting. To make his story comprehensible, he suggested, he should really begin at the very beginning –

'There will be time in plenty for that,' said Lucrezia. 'We have all our lives before us.'

'Indeed, I hope so,' said Angelo, 'though in times like these a long life is by no means certain.'

'Oh, do not be so gloomy when I am full of happiness to see you again. Was it not wonderful, Angelo, that I should be dreaming of you at the very moment when you arrived? Tell me about yourself, tell me everything!'

'That is what I am trying to do, dear Lucrezia.'

'Did you ever dream about me when you were away?'

'Yes, often.'

Lucrezia moved nearer to him, sighed, and leaned her head against his shoulder. 'Tell me more,' she whispered.

'Certainly,' said Angelo. 'As I was saying, Captain Telfer and I broke through the German lines in what was undoubtedly a very hazardous enterprise; though I do not wish to boast about it, for we' – Angelo cleared his throat – 'we of the Eighth Army do not find it either necessary or seemly to boast about ourselves.'

Lucrezia disappointingly made no comment, and Angelo continued: 'I was chosen for this duty because, of course, I know all the country here quite intimately. But I did not know the German dispositions, so we were met by a young Englishman called Corporal Trivet, who escaped from the Germans a long time ago and has been living in Pontefiore. I saw him when I went there last year.'

'Yes,' said Lucrezia.

'Did you know him?'

'Everybody knew him.'

'Was he well liked?'

'By some, yes. There are always certain people who will make much of a stranger.'

'I found him very friendly and agreeable,' said Angelo.

'By those who came to know him quite well, however, it was agreed that he was shallow and deceitful and incapable of true feeling; as all the English are.'

'Did you, then, meet a lot of Englishmen while I was away?' asked Angelo.

But Lucrezia was no longer listening. She was sitting upright and staring with dilated eyes at two figures that had appeared, in a gap among the trees, on the basin-shaped hill in front of them. They were a considerable distance away, but the light fell sharply on them and their costume was distinctive. They wore long hooded cloaks of grey wool.

'*Marocchini!*' she exclaimed.

'They are Goums,' said Angelo. They advance very quickly, and often they arrive in parts of the country where nobody expects them. But you need not be alarmed, they are on our side.'

'Not if you are a woman,' said Lucrezia; and in fierce words related the legend that these wild irregulars from the Atlas had created for themselves in their swift advance from Ausonia to the bare downs of Siena. They were devils incarnate, she said. Even the Tedeschi dreaded them, and to women they were the personification of all the terrors that walk by night. Her own cheeks grew pale as she spoke, and Angelo was infected by her fear. But he tried to reassure her, and himself as well, by calling attention to the deep shade in which they sat, that would make it difficult if not impossible for the Goums to see them. 'And look!' he said, 'they are moving now, they are going in the opposite direction.'

'Towards the house of Emilia Bigi,' exclaimed Lucrezia, 'where Lucia went an hour ago to talk about Enrico her husband.'

'That will do her no harm.'

'It will do her harm enough if she encounters two *Marocchini* on the way back. Angelo, you must go and warn her!'

'I see no necessity for that.'

'It is my own sister of whom we are talking! Lucia, my sister, is about to be raped, and you do not see the necessity to warn her!'

'You are becoming excited, Lucrezia.'

'In the circumstances that is not unnatural. Would you remain calm and unperturbed if your sister were in immediate danger of being assaulted, outraged, and assassinated?'

'I should first of all ask myself if the danger were real or imaginary.'

'And while you were arguing on this side and that, and

never reaching any conclusion, your sister would have been waylaid and maltreated, undone and destroyed!'

'The situation is unlikely to occur,' said Angelo stiffly, 'because, as you are well aware, I have no sister.'

'But I have, and already she may be in the clutches of the *Marocchini*. You must go and rescue her, Angelo!'

She rose and dragged him to his feet, and as he felt in the strength of her grasp the intensity of her emotion, Angelo's heart began to beat with uncomfortable speed. Nervously he exclaimed, 'But you do not understand! The Goums are, it is true, our allies, and they have many good qualities. But they are sensitive people, they are easily offended. If I were to interfere with two men who are merely taking a quiet walk in the country, they would of course feel insulted.'

'You are afraid of them,' said Lucrezia.

'That is not the point.'

'You who belong to the *Ottava Armata*, who boast about your Eighth Army, are afraid of two poor ignorant *Marocchini*.'

'They are very redoubtable, everybody knows that.'

'You carry a revolver at your belt, and yet you are afraid. You are no use to me, Angelo.'

'If it were possible to gather a party, a fairly large party –'

'There is no one here but old women and children. The men have all gone.'

With a pitiable expression and a stammer beyond control, Angelo said, 'You know that I have a certain weakness. I have never tried to conceal or deny it, and all my friends are well aware of it. Many people possess the *dono di coraggio* in great measure, and never pause to think how fortunate they are. But I, who was born without it, know that life can be very miserable to those who lack it.'

'I am not thinking about your misery, but about Lucia's,' cried Lucrezia. 'If you want to stay here and pity yourself while Lucia is being ravished and strangled, you can do so. But do not ask me to stay beside you, and never ask me again to listen to your adventures, which I should not have believed in any case. – I give you a last chance: will you go and rescue her?'

Angelo hung his head and whispered, 'What you said is quite true. I am afraid.'

'Then give me your revolver,' said Lucrezia, and beating down his protesting hands she seized him by the belt, unfastened the holster, and took out the pistol. 'If you will not go, I must,' she exclaimed, and ran across the farmyard and down into the narrow glen.

Angelo followed her, crying breathlessly, 'No, no, you must not! You must not, Lucrezia. Those men are dangerous, you do not realize how dangerous they are.'

Lucrezia made no reply, but roughly pushed him away when he tried to hold her, and with swift steps climbed out of the glen and strode resolutely over the rising ground beyond it. They passed through a belt of woodland, Angelo at her heels still begging her to return, and came out on the path that ran upward round the side of the basin-shaped hill.

Now Lucrezia's pace grew a little slower, and when Angelo pleaded with her yet again to think of the danger she was inviting, she answered not unkindly, 'It may be dangerous for you also. I thought you were too much afraid to come.'

'What do I matter? I am thinking about you, Lucrezia. Oh, come back! Come back before it is too late.'

'I am thinking about Lucia,' she said, but walked closer to him and took him tightly by the hand.

Slower and slower became their pace, but both were breathing as deeply as if they had been climbing a mountain at utmost speed. Nervously they peered ahead, and furtively from side to side. Where the path ran bare beneath the sun they felt as though a thousand eyes were watching them, and when they walked beneath overarching trees they dreaded instant capture. But still, with faltering steps, they went on.

The guns were no longer firing, and the silence of a summer afternoon lay heavy on the little hill. Then suddenly, as if the silence were a curtain caught in a madman's hand, it was torn again and again by frightened screams.

'Oh, Lucia!' cried Lucrezia.

'But that was a man's voice,' said Angelo.

White and trembling, they stood and stared at each other. 'Take this,' said Lucrezia, and gave him the pistol.

'It is not loaded,' said Angelo.

'Then load it, for God's sake load it!'

With nerveless fingers he fumbled at the stiff button of his cartridge-pouch, but before he could unfasten it Lucrezia uttered a shuddering cry and fell in a dead faint at his feet. Two yards away a man rose from behind a bush, a man who wore a grey woollen cloak striped thinly with bearish brown. His black eyes glittered like a hawk's, his nose had a hawkish curve. His cheeks were rather grey than brown, and the downward crescent of his narrow moustache was like a dreadful grin.

'Good afternoon,' stammered Angelo, and let his empty pistol fall. He bent to retrieve it, and with the speed of a stooping hawk the Goum leapt forward and struck him on the back of his head with a heavy cudgel.

The pain of the blow was so momentary that Angelo hardly felt it until he began to recover consciousness, and when that returned he grew aware of a further unhappiness that divided his mind evenly between it and his aching skull. The sun was now at tree-top height, and the guns were firing again. The explosions struck his sore head like little blows, and every movement he made brought a gyre of giddiness. He longed to lie still, to remain quiet and undiscovered in the cool shadow, but his fearful anxiety for Lucrezia gave him the resolution and the strength to get up.

He found her a few yards away, and the sight of her distress came near to banishing his own. Kneeling beside her, he undid the strips of her dress with which her hands had been tied and her mouth gagged, and taking her into his arms he held her for a long time until her sobbing stopped, and she lay so quietly that he thought she must be sleeping. But presently, without raising her head, she spoke to him. 'And now,' she said, 'you will never marry me.'

He held her more tightly, but did not answer, and a little while later she said again, 'You will not want to marry me now. You could not, Angelo, could you?'

'Darling Lucrezia,' he said, 'in the hope that you may find comfort in another's misfortune, I think I should tell you that I am in somewhat the same plight as yourself. For I also have been humiliated. But there is nothing to be gained by going into mourning for misfortunes that come to us through no fault of our own. True, I forgot to load my revolver, and that was negligence, but even had it been loaded in all chambers my hand was so tremulous that I could not have fired to any purpose; so I do not think my negligence mattered very much. No, Lucrezia, we are not to blame, so the best we can do is to let bygones be bygones, and thank God we are still alive.'

A House in Sicily
(1951)

Neil McCallum

The house stood on the north side of the courtyard. It was pleasantly neat and the door was closed, locked, and painted green. The shutters were folded quickly over the windows. A yellow mat of plaited grass hung on the parapet of a well. Beside the well a bucket and a coil of chain shone with a clean pewter colour. The portico, which stretched along the front of the house, was shaded by a wooden trellis on which purple bougainvillea grew thickly. Tall trees framed the entire house as a hat frames a face.

Once every morning and once every evening Fortunato

Sacco came down from his room above the stables, holding the large key of the green door. After breakfast and after supper, with Mario, his grandson, he unlocked the door and examined each room of the house. Little Mario, eleven years old, enjoyed these caretaking duties enormously. He loved the passageways, bright with light from the small unsealed windows. He loved the rooms, mysteriously dark, vast in the sombre light that seeped through the joints of the shutters.

The old man and the boy were the only two left at the house. The other workers and servants had gone when the padrone, Signor Francesco, had packed his young wife, his year-old baby, and two suitcases into the car, and vanished over the hill-crest where the road turned towards Catania.

Old Fortunato had refused to go. 'I will stay,' he had told the padrone gravely. 'I have been no further than Enna and Catania in all my years. A war cannot uproot me. I have become old here and here I will die in God's time.'

At that short speech the padrone had looked nervous. He had glanced from Fortunato to the polished car. He had wiped his large fleshy face with a silk handkerchief. 'I should like to stay,' he had said, looking now only at the car, 'but it will be nothing. Soon it will all be over and peace will be back.'

This evening, the fourth since the red car had gone, Fortunato and the boy walked through the house. It was of two storeys. The ground floor was a series of store-rooms. When the first door was opened the floor looked like heaped gold, till, in the gloom, the eyes saw a sea of grain held back against the walls by wooden boards. In the cheese-room the small round cheeses were laid on the floor like checkers. Another room was thick with the vinegar smell of maturing wine.

Mario liked the coolness and the smells of the store-rooms, but it was upstairs that he preferred to go, looking over the arm of his grandfather as the doors were held open. He was fascinated by the solemn furniture, faintly shining in the dark, the warm smell of clothes and fabrics, the quick sparkle of glasses and the gleam of plates. The odours that came from the rooms were rich and dizzying, like the scent of the signora when she used to sit in the shade of the portico.

Mario sniffed and his eyes stared. He wondered if his grandfather enjoyed it as he did.

'Everything is all right, small one. Let us hope the padrone will soon be back.'

'Yes, grandfather.'

They went downstairs and locked the green door and then climbed the outside staircase to the small room they lived in above the stables. Before it was quite dark they went to bed. From his bed Mario could see the smoke of Mount Etna become red in the evening sun and then golden, like a long flat plume.

When the sky was lightening with dawn they were awakened by the crackling of rifle and automatic fire. It was not very near. They went down to the courtyard where the cobbles were still warm from yesterday's sun. In the west there were small spurts of flame.

It grew lighter. The firing continued, moved behind the house and up to the top of a long hill where three olive trees grew in a triangle. On the hill there was an indistinct movement of men.

The answering fire was far away. They told it by the duller, quicker rattle of automatic weapons. Stray bullets whined far above their heads and twice something smacked sharply into the slates of the house.

'Are you afraid, young one?'

'No, grandfather.'

'That is good. There is nothing to fear unless they have big guns.'

It was very light. Soon the sun would rise.

The firing worked into a crescendo and six times there was a swelling burst of mortar bombs, muffled by the hill with the olives. Then silence, so sharp that when a cock crowed behind them they started.

'Boy,' said the old man. 'We have forgotten the horses. The cock doesn't forget to crow because there is a war. Let us look to the horses. They may be nervous.'

They went to the stables and found that the two horses were quiet, indifferently chewing their fodder. The old man then went upstairs to prepare breakfast. Mario watched the hill where everything was now plainly visible. There were soldiers digging. He could hear the sound of their picks biting into the hard brown earth. As he watched he saw a few people leave the hill and come towards the house. A tall man walked in front with a revolver in his hand. Two of the others had rifles and there was one with a short weapon, like a very small shotgun.

'Grandfather, the soldiers are coming.'

They both stood in the courtyard as the small party arrived. Sicilians and soldiers looked at each other, unsmiling, but without hostility.

The tall man, an officer, tried to open the green door. Fortunato hurried up to him and explained he would bring the key. The officer was impatient and did not understand. He spoke to the man with the small gun and the man fired into the lock. The officer burst open the doorway and the soldiers went in, their boots ringing on the stone passage.

The boy looked at his grandfather, expecting him to be angry. 'They are very tired,' said the old man.

The shutter of an upper window was flung back and a white handkerchief was waved as a signal. More men, nearly twenty, came down from the hill and when they arrived the officer placed them round the house where they began to dig small trenches under the trees. Then the well was discovered and all the men swarmed round it. For five minutes there was no more digging till everyone had drunk his fill and the portico was wet with water spilled from the bucket.

Mario had never seen anyone with so much energy as the officer. One minute he was in the house, peering from the windows. Then he was rushing through the garden, talking to the men. Then he would go back to the house again and place a machine-gun to point to the main road. Out in the garden again he stationed a man under a tree to watch the countryside through binoculars.

At last the officer relaxed. He came up to Fortunato and smiled.

'*Guerra. Finito,*' he said, and then he pointed to his mouth.

'*Mangiare?*' said the grandfather.

The officer nodded.

'Mario. Bread and wine and cheese for the soldiers.' Mario ran off to gather the food.

In the cheese-room the officer sat at a table. The men came in by twos and threes and were given food and drink. Outside they had finished their digging in the soft garden earth and they lay on the ground, resting. A few wandered into the house, opened the drawers of the furniture, pulled out sheets and rugs and fell asleep on the beds. They were all tired, but felt a sense of well-being now that the fighting was done and they had eaten.

The officer called the sergeant into the cheese-room.

'Let the men use the house for resting. Keep a couple of sentries on duty. I'm going to snooze for half an hour, then I'm going to see the company commander. Waken me in time.'

The officer went upstairs. On the passage walls there were prints and small pictures. He paused to examine them and yawned, then he looked into the rooms. Heavy carpets made him aware of his dirt-encrusted boots. In one room he found silk fittings, on wrought bronze rails, hanging over a silver crucifix on the wall. The shutters had been opened and the room was filled with a soft light.

Everything was in perfect taste, he noted, and for a moment the thought struck him that he himself was the cause of the occupants fleeing from this house to which they had given so much care. He felt himself a strange intruder. Then he yawned again and took off his equipment and was going to place it on a small fragile table. He paused and with a weary smile he put his kit under the bed. Without removing his boots he lay on the pink silk bed-cover. How uncivilized we are, he thought, stretching luxuriously, and then he fell asleep.

His sergeant awakened him.

'Have you seen the house, sir? Some place.'

'Pretty good, isn't it? Everything quiet?'

'Not a sign. Must have spent a pretty penny on this place. Sort of gets you, a place like this.'

'You feel that way,' said the officer, wondering at his sergeant who had been a butcher and looked like a prize-fighter. 'Gets all of us,' he told himself, 'when you haven't known what a home is for umpteen years.'

'That furniture's good stuff, sir.'

'D'you know about furniture?'

'My father-in-law was a cabinet-maker – old-fashioned man but a craftsman. Don't find the like of him nowadays. He taught me a lot about furniture. Made his own coffin, too. Wonderful heavy oak it was. And polished. It was a shame to think of the worms getting it.'

They went round the other rooms, cool inside the thick walls. A few of the men were rummaging in drawers, pulling out coloured fabrics, handling suits and dresses.

'No fountain-pens or watches?' asked the officer. The men

smiled. 'No, but we're still trying.' One of his men appeared with a woman's hat on and a frock bunched round his waist. He looked like a ploughman in ballet dress.

They need this sort of idiocy, the officer thought. It is as good as being out of the line for a spell.

In one of the bedrooms there was a cradle with a cascade of white lace falling from the high carved back.

'Jesus!' said the sergeant. 'They didn't ought to let us see things like that. Makes you think. Oh, what about the Sicilians, the old man and the boy?'

'What about them?'

'D'you think they're all right? They're hanging around watching everything.'

'They're all right, I suppose. They don't seem to worry one way or the other. If they're not all right the only thing to do is shoot them. D'you want to shoot them, sergeant?'

'Why . . . Oh no.'

'I'm going to see the company commander now . . . my god! what in hell . . .'

There was no need to ask what it was. The familiar scream was followed by the familiar explosion. Inside the building everyone ran downstairs. The officer went outside. The shell had landed in a field, fifty yards short of the garden.

'Tanks. They're hull down about a mile away.'

The next shot went over the roof. The officer lay flat behind a low wall. Out of the corner of his eye he saw the old man and the boy climb the staircase to their room. Wonder if they know what's coming, he thought. Probably they feel safe there; no one can picture the inside of his own home as a battle-ground. At the same time he wondered how long their own guns would take to range on the tanks. Maybe the guns had not yet arrived in support. What a bloody picnic, and meantime they had to lie down and be shot at.

He had counted on a quiet day and resented the unannounced tanks, as though they had deliberately fired to shatter the harmony of the house and the garden and the memories evoked by the furniture in the cool rooms.

The next shot went clean through an upper window, and just after it there came the whine of the first artillery shell in reply, high above their heads.

A tank shell screamed into the garden. Shrapnel slashed the trees and made bright cuts in the stonework of the house. A rain of clods and earth and stone pattered heavily to the ground.

'Anyone hurt?'

A muffled voice replied, 'No.'

Then the air was loud with the shriek of their own shells passing overhead and the ground around the tanks erupted in smoke. A vague hysterical cheer came from the garden. 'That'll fix the bastards. That'll fix 'em.'

In five minutes all was quiet again. A column of black smoke came from the area of the tanks.

The men came to fill their water-bottles. 'Gives you a thirst, don't it!'

The officer saw the old man and the boy come down to the courtyard. The man was dignified and quiet. The boy was smiling. He made a whooshing noise. 'Boom, boom,' he said. The soldiers looked at him and winked. 'The little bastard thinks he's been to the pictures.'

'I'm going off. Keep a look-out,' said the officer to the sergeant.

When he came back, an hour later, no one was about. He saw a few people lying in the garden, and the lookout with the binoculars was behind a tree, scratching his head.

He went into the house. The shell that had gone through the window had exploded on an inside wall upstairs, blowing a hole in the wall and filling the upper passage with plaster and bricks. An ornamental chandelier lay like a metal octopus, sprawling on the floor.

He looked for the sergeant. In the first room there was no one. An indescribable mess littered the floor. Drawers had been ransacked and the contents strewn wildly. The door of a cupboard hung awry on one hinge.

What in hell has happened, he muttered, growing angry. He scrambled through plaster and broken glass to the next room. Paper and clothes and scores of snapshots lay on the floor beside upturned drawers. The air was heavy with the smell from a broken scent bottle. Curtains had been wrenched from the rails. In one corner he saw two of his men asleep. On the bed, fat flesh lax in sleep, was the sergeant, wrapped in the lace net from the cradle. Two flies buzzed over his face.

'Sergeant, wake up. What in God's name has happened?'

'Ugh! Wassamarrer. Eh! Oh, I've been taking forty winks.'

'Yes. Yes. But the house. It looks as though a horde of lunatics have been running wild.'

'I know, sir. It's bad. I tried to stop it but I was too late. I was in the garden talking to the N.C.O.s and a lot of men came from the other companies for water. I didn't know what they were doing . . .'

'All right. They've gone through the place like savages. But it's not so important as some other things, I suppose.'

He went into the third room and his heel came down on something hard. It was a rosary. A bundle of letters lay on a chair, spilled from the ribbon that tied them. A jumble of clothing was strewn across the bed. Books were scattered in the fireplace. Picture frames were smashed.

Damned ruffians, he muttered. He felt slightly sick and he wondered why he should be so moved by this petty destructiveness in the midst of war's normal carnage.

'Sergeant, I don't like this. The men are bloody ruffians. Have the two Sicilians seen it?'

'Yes. The boy started to cry. The old man said nothing. Just walked away.'

I should like to apologize to them, he thought, but I can't. I'd like to tell the old man that these soldiers have been far away from their homes for so long that they have become barbarians, that their own homes are so far away and they have been away for so many years they have forgotten many things, that doing this was maybe a kind of revenge for their being away. But I can't explain it, nor can I explain that it is better to do this than take a man's guts out with your bayonet. I can't explain anything. The shell, yes, that would merit the usual formula, *la guerra*, or whatever their word is. But this hooliganism, even though you understand it, it makes you angry, because it is wild and berserk and outside the pattern of behaviour even in war.

'Sergeant, we're leaving in half an hour. Battalion is advancing. Get the men ready.'

Alone, he sat in a chair, surrounded by the debris of the household. He was surprised at his own anger, that out of the vast destruction of lives and places in which he took part every day he should single this one act of riot. The absurdity of it amused him and he started to laugh, rocking in his chair like a madman, as the spasm of humour gripped him and the tears rolled down his cheeks.

When he joined the men in the courtyard they were ready to leave. The sergeant shouted. They moved off, marching in files to the road.

The midday sun burned hotly on the house. The shutters lay loosely open. One was broken by a splinter of shell and the yellow wood was like a wound. Bits of branches and rubble lay in the portico.

Fortunato and Mario walked slowly into the house. When they came out some minutes later they pulled the broken door behind them. Fortunato dangled the useless key from a finger. Mario sobbed, rubbing his knuckles into his eyes. His grandfather patted his head.

'This afternoon, my boy, we must start to work. The soldiers will not come back and there will be no more fighting here. We must tidy and clean. Even the shell hole we can try to mend with bricks and mortar. Soon we will put things to rights. The war has passed. Look, Mario, away there.'

On the foothills below Mount Etna tiny puffs of smoke were born like young clouds, exploding suddenly into existence. Mario stopped sobbing as he watched.

On the roads the files of soldiers, already minute, marched steadily towards the shell-bursts.

The Wireless Set
(1969)

George Mackay Brown

The first wireless ever to come to the valley of Tronvik in
Orkney was brought by Howie Eunson, son of Hugh the
fisherman and Betsy.

Howie had been at the whaling in the Antarctic all winter,
and he arrived back in Britain in April with a stuffed wallet and
jingling pockets. Passing through Glasgow on his way home
he bought presents for everyone in Tronvik – fiddle-strings for
Sam down at the shore, a bottle of malt whisky for Mansie of
the hill, a secondhand volume of Spurgeon's sermons for Mr
Sinclair the missionary, sweeties for all the bairns, a meerschaum

pipe for his father Hugh and a portable wireless set for his mother Betsy.

There was great excitement the night Howie arrived home in Tronvik. Everyone in the valley – men, women, children, dogs, cats – crowded into the but-end of the croft, as Howie unwrapped and distributed his gifts.

'And have you been a good boy all the time you've been away?' said Betsy anxiously. 'Have you prayed every night, and not sworn?'

'This is thine, mother,' said Howie, and out of a big cardboard box he lifted the portable wireless and set it on the table.

For a full two minutes nobody said a word. They all stood staring at it, making small round noises of wonderment, like pigeons.

'And mercy,' said Betsy at last, 'what is it at all?'

'Its a wireless set,' said Howie proudly. 'Listen.'

He turned a little black knob and a posh voice came out of the box saying that it would be a fine day tomorrow over England, and over Scotland south of the Forth–Clyde valley, but that in the Highlands and in Orkney and Shetland there would be rain and moderate westerly winds.

'If it's a man that's speaking,' said old Hugh doubtfully, 'where is he standing just now?'

'In London,' said Howie.

'Well now,' said Betsy, 'if that isn't a marvel! But I'm not sure, all the same, but what it isn't against the scriptures. Maybe, Howie, we'd better not keep it.'

'Everybody in the big cities has a wireless,' said Howie. 'Even in Kirkwall and Hamnavoe every house has one. But now Tronvik has a wireless as well, and maybe we're not such clodhoppers as they think.'

They all stayed late, listening to the wireless. Howie kept twirling a second little knob, and sometimes they would hear music and sometimes they would hear a kind of loud half-witted voice urging them to use a particular brand of tooth-paste.

At half past eleven the wireless was switched off and everybody went home. Hugh and Betsy and Howie were left alone.

'Men speak,' said Betsy, 'but it's hard to know sometimes whether what they say is truth or lies.'

'This wireless speaks the truth,' said Howie.

Old Hugh shook his head. 'Indeed,' he said, 'it doesn't do that. For the man said there would be rain here and a westerly wind. But I assure you it'll be a fine day, and a southerly wind, and if the Lord spares me I'll get to the lobsters.'

Old Hugh was right. Next day was fine, and he and Howie took twenty lobsters from the creels he had under the Gray Head.

It was in the spring of the year 1939 that the first wireless set came to Tronvik. In September that same year war broke out, and Howie and three other lads from the valley joined the minesweepers.

That winter the wireless standing on Betsy's table became the centre of Tronvik. Every evening folk came from the crofts to listen to the nine o'clock news. Hitherto the wireless had been a plaything which discoursed Scottish reels and constipation advertisements and unreliable weather forecasts. But now the whole world was embattled and Tronvik listened appreciatively to enthusiastic commentators telling them that General Gamelin was the greatest soldier of the century, and he had only to say the word for the German Siegfried Line to crumble like sand. In the summer of 1940 the western front flared into life, and then suddenly no more was heard of General Gamelin. First it was General Weygand who was called the heir of Napoleon, and then a few days later Marshal Petain.

France fell all the same, and old Hugh turned to the others and said, 'What did I tell you? You can't believe a word it says.'

One morning they saw a huge gray shape looming along the horizon, making for Scapa Flow. 'Do you ken the name of that warship?' said Mansie of the hill. 'She's the *Ark Royal*, an aircraft carrier.'

That same evening Betsy twiddled the knob of the wireless and suddenly an impudent voice came drawling out. The voice was saying that German dive bombers hand sunk the *Ark Royal* in the Mediterranean. 'Where is the *Ark Royal?*' went the voice in an evil refrain. 'Where is the *Ark Royal?* Where is the *Ark Royal?*'

'That man,' said Betsy 'must be the Father of Lies.'

Wasn't the *Ark Royal* safely anchored in calm water on the other side of the hill?

Thereafter the voice of Lord Haw-Haw cast a spell on the inhabitants of Tronvik. The people would rather listen to him than to anyone, he was such a great liar. He had a kind of bestial joviality about him that at once repelled and fascinated them; just as, for opposite reasons, they had been repelled and fascinated to begin with by the rapturous ferocity of Mr Sinclair's Sunday afternoon sermons, but had grown quite pleased with them in time.

They never grew pleased with William Joyce, Lord Haw-Haw. Yet every evening found them clustered round the portable radio, like awed children round a hectoring schoolmaster.

'Do you know,' said Sam of the shore one night, 'I think that man will come to a bad end?'

Betsy was frying bloody-puddings over a primus stove, and the evil voice went on and on against a background of hissing, sputtering, roaring and a medley of rich succulent smells.

Everyone in the valley was there that night. Betsy had made some new ale and the first bottles were being opened. It was good stuff, right enough, everybody agreed about that.

Now the disembodied voice paused, and turned casually to

a new theme, the growing starvation of the people of Britain. The food ships were being sunk one after the other by the heroic U-boats. Nothing was getting through, nothing, nor a cornstalk from Saskatchewan nor a tin of pork from Chicago. Britain was starving. The war would soon be over. Then there would be certain pressing accounts to meet. The ships were going down. Last week the Merchant Navy was poorer by a half million gross registered tons. Britain was starving –

At this point Betsy, who enjoyed her own ale more than anyone else, thrust the hissing frying pan under the nose – so to speak – of the wireless, so that its gleam was dimmed for a moment or two by a rich blue tangle of bloody-pudding fumes.

'Smell that, you brute,' cried Betsy fiercely, 'smell that!'

The voice went on, calm and vindictive.

'Do you ken,' said Hugh, 'he canna hear a word you're saying.'

'Can he not?' said Sandy Omand, turning his taurine head from one to the other. 'He canna hear?'

Sandy was a bit simple.

'No,' said Hugh, 'nor smell either.'

After that they switched off the wireless, and ate the bloody-puddings along with buttered bannocks, and drank more ale, and told stories that had nothing to do with war, till two o'clock in the morning.

One afternoon in the late summer of that year the island postman cycled over the hill road to Tronvik with a yellow corner of telegram sticking out of his pocket.

He passed the shop and the manse and the schoolhouse, and went in a wavering line up the track to Hugh's croft. The wireless was playing music inside, Joe Loss and his orchestra.

Betsy had seen him coming and was standing in the door.

'Is there anybody with you?' said the postman.

'What way would there be?' said Betsy. 'Hugh's at the lobsters.'

'There should be somebody with you,' said the postman.

'Give me the telegram,' said Betsy, and held out her hand. He gave it to her as if he was a miser parting with a twenty-pound note.

She went inside, put on her spectacles, and ripped open the envelope with brisk fingers. Her lips moved a little, silently reading the words.

Then she turned to the dog and said, 'Howie's dead.' She went to the door. The postman was disappearing on his bike round the corner of the shop and the missionary was hurrying towards her up the path.

She said to him, 'It's time the peats were carted.'

'This is a great affliction, you poor soul,' said Mr Sinclair the missionary. 'This is bad news indeed. Yet he died for his country. He made the great sacrifice. So that we could all live in peace, you understand.'

Betsy shook her head. 'That isn't it at all,' she said. 'Howie's sunk with torpedoes. That's all I know.'

They saw old Hugh walking up from the shore with a pile of creels on his back and a lobster in each hand. When he came to the croft he looked at Betsy and the missionary standing together in the door. He went into the outhouse and set down the creels and picked up an axe he kept for chopping wood.

Betsy said to him, 'How many lobsters did you get?'

He moved past her and the missionary without speaking into the house. Then from inside he said, 'I got two lobsters.'

'I'll break the news to him,' said Mr Sinclair.

From inside came the noise of shattering wood and metal.

'He knows already,' said Betsy to the missionary.

'Hugh knows the truth of a thing generally before a word is uttered.'

Hugh moved past them with the axe in his hand.

'I got six crabs forby,' he said to Betsy, 'but I left them in the boat.'

He set the axe down carefully inside the door of the out-house. Then he leaned against the wall and looked out to sea for a long while.

'I got thirteen eggs,' said Betsy. 'One more than yesterday. That old Rhode Islander's laying like mad.'

The missionary was slowly shaking his head in the doorway. He touched Hugh on the shoulder and said, 'My poor man –'.

Hugh turned and said to him, 'It's time the last peats were down from the hill. I'll go in the morning first thing. You'll be needing a cart-load for the Manse.'

The missionary, awed by such callousness, walked down the path between the cabbages and potatoes. Betsy went into the house. The wireless stood, a tangled wreck, on the dresser. She brought from the cupboard a bottle of whisky and glasses. She set the kettle on the hook over the fire and broke the peats into red and yellow flame with a poker. Through the window she could see people moving towards the croft from all over the valley. The news had got round. The mourners were gathering.

Old Hugh stood in the door and looked up at the drift of clouds above the cliff. 'Yes,' he said, 'I'm glad I set the creels where I did, off Yesnaby. They'll be sheltered there once the wind gets up.'

'That white hen,' said Betsy, 'has stopped laying. It's time she was in the pot, if you ask me.'

The Tattie Dressers (1946)

Fred Urquhart

They were going to dress Gladstones at the pit near the old sandstone quarry. It was just after seven o'clock on a bleak, cold April morning. While the men were taking the Potato Sorter off the lorry, the women and the loon started to tirr the pit which stretched uphill over the brow of the field like a furrow thrown over by a giant plough. Maggie Jane straddled on the top and shovelled down the earth, uncovering the straw. She was wearing a crimson waterproof pixie-cap which was almost the same colour as her pretty, round face. It was so cold that even she was silent for once. But as she got warmer she began to speak about how much syrup she had got from the

Co-Operative van the day before. 'A pund, Mrs Strachan! Hoo long dae they think that's goin' to last me and the loon?' she cried, her dark eyes flashing vivaciously. 'The vanman said I widna get ony mair till the fourth o' May.'

Mrs Strachan said, 'Ay, ay,' every now and then and went on unhapping the pit. She was a thin, wiry woman with a brown face and grey hair pulled tightly under an old black felt hat. She shovelled the dirt briskly; always three jumps ahead of Maggie Jane. The loon worked steadily, not listening to his mother's chatter. He was a sturdy boy of fourteen with fine eyes like his mother's.

After the men had got the Potato Dresser into place, they set to tirring the pit, too. In no time they had done more than the women and the loon. When they had taken off the first half dozen yards of earth, old Ake said they had better begin to take off the straw. Young Dod and Chae were forking it off at one side when they heard Maggie Jane exclaim from the other: 'My Christ, look at this! Come on awa' hame!'

'What's adae wi' ye, wifie?' Chae called.

She was standing with her graip in one hand, staring down at the potatoes she had uncovered. 'Goad Almichty!' she said slowly.

The two young men grinned at each other. Dod pushed back his cap and scratched his short curly fair hair. 'Dinna stand lookin' at them, wife!' he said. 'Bend yer back! Or can ye nae bend for yer stays?'

'She hasna got stays on by the look o'her,' Chae grinned.

'But I have sut,' Maggie Jane said with a perky toss of her pixie-cap.

'Ye have nut!' Chae imitated her high-pitched voice.

'I have sut,' she said. 'Would ye like to see?'

'No, we'll leave that to Ake!' Chae winked at Dod and spat on his hands before forking off another bunch of straw.

Mrs Strachan and Maggie Jane stood and shook their heads. The potatoes were so badly frosted that they were welded together in a black pulp, smooth and mottled as a snake's skin. They were like prunes that had been dipped in syrup. Many of them had white and yellow fungus-spots on them. The stench was appalling. Maggie Jane held her nose as she bent down and began to pick gingerly at them. 'Ye'd need yer gas-mask on for this job, Mrs Strachan!'

'Ay, they're gey lads, thae,' old Ake said, bending down and digging his hands into the black morass. 'They need a blitz!'

'Oh, we'll gi'e them that a' richt,' said Maggie Jane.

'Ay, we'll just ha'e to dae oor best to get rid o' them. They're only fit for swine to work amongst. But farm servants are just swine, onywye,' Ake added, grinning maliciously. 'They're awfa fine fowk the now, but just wait till the war's ower!'

'That'll dae ye noo!' Maggie Jane laughed.

'Ay, ay,' Mrs Strachan said. 'Ye've been a farm servant long enough yersel'.'

'Forty years.' Ake shook his head mournfully. 'I was nae as auld as the loon here when I started.'

When they had picked off the worst of the frosted potatoes they wiped their mucky hands on the straw and sacks. 'Eh, but it's richt cauld on the fingers,' Maggie Jane said.

'Ay, ay,' Mrs Strachan said, stepping on the flat box beside the elevator of the Potato Sorter. Maggie Jane stood beside her and they stamped their feet on the box, waiting for young Dod to start scooping the potatoes into the machine. Ake put on sacks for the Seed, and Chae threaded a long needle with binder's twine. The loon put down wicker sculls for the Brock and got the bags ready for the Ware.

'Are ye ready, Dod?' Ake started the engine, and when it was going steadily Mrs Strachan pushed over the handle. There was a rattle as Dod scooped in the first lot of potatoes.

Ake leaned on the end of the machine and watched the potatoes sliding up the elevator towards him. 'Ay, they're gey lads, thae,' he said, watching the women's hands dart out and in, picking out the frosted ones and throwing them away. 'Dae ye ken fut they mind me on?' He deftly unhooked the first sack to be filled and dumped it on the weighing-machine. 'It minds me on yon movin' staircase in London. Eh, ye never saw such a thing! Ye just need to stand ontil't and it moves up, takin' ye along wi' it. Thae tatties are gey like the fowk ye see standin' on the staircase. They're a gey mixed breed.'

'Ay, ay,' Mrs Strachan said, without looking up from the potatoes. They were all used to Ake's reminiscences about London which he had visited once for a Cup Final years before.

'Here, here, wifie, dae ye see that!' Chae took a frosted potato out of the bag he was sewing and held it up in front of Maggie Jane's nose.

'Ay, I see it,' she said. 'I thocht I'd let ye ha'e it.'

Ake frowned as he saw what was coming up the elevator. 'Here's a lot o' gey bubbly-nosed lads!'

'Ay, put it off, put it off!' Maggie Jane cried frantically, her blue-fingered mittened hands lost amongst the rotten tatties piling up in front of her.

Mrs Strachan pushed back the handle and the elevator stopped. And for two or three minutes the women picked out the rotten potatoes, making exclamations of disgust as they squashed to pulp in their fingers.

'A' richt noo?' Ake said, and Mrs Strachan said 'Ay, ay,' and started the elevator again. 'Nae sae fast, Dod!' she called.

'They're gettin' better,' she said after a while. 'They're nae sae weet noo.'

'It's nae afore time,' Maggie Jane said. 'Ma bloody hands are freezin'.'

Occasionally the men swung their arms, slapping their

thighs and shoulders to get some heat into their cold fingers. But the women contented themselves with stamping their feet on the box.

'I wish the sun would come oot,' Maggie Jane said.

'It would just bring ower the Jerries,' Ake said. 'It's better to stay cloudy.'

'I wonder where they were last night?' Mrs Strachan said.

'Ye dinna need to worry yersel',' Ake said. 'I dinna think they'll bother themsels payin' a veesit to the Howe o' the Mearns.'

'Begod they'd better nae!' Maggie Jane said.

'Fut would ye dae noo, wifie, if they did?' Ake asked, throwing away a frosted potato that the women had let past them.

'Christ, I'd just dive right under the dresser,' Maggie Jane grinned. 'I'd even dive under the frosted tatties!'

After Dod had been scooping for half-an-hour there was such a big space between the dresser and the pit that he cried: 'We'll ha'e to shift the cuddy!' So Chae scooped out the dirt and potatoes that had accumulated under it, and then they all pushed. The machine moved slowly up the slope. It would not sit evenly, so they had to put sacks under the wheels. 'Are ye ready, you wifies?' Ake shouted to the women who were kneeling beside the two back wheels with folded sacks in their hands. 'Noo, lift!' And the men strained, waiting for the women to put in the cleek-brakes in the holes in the wheels. 'Come on, wifie!' Chae called to Maggie Jane. 'Can ye nae find the hole?' And he muttered something to Ake that made the old man guffaw ribaldly.

'Fut was that?' Maggie Jane cried, dusting the earth from her knees.

But Chae merely grinned and said to Dod: 'It's ma turn for the scoop.'

'What aboot gi'en us a shottie?' Maggie Jane asked. 'We're that cauld standin' here.'

'Ay, ay,' Mrs Strachan said. But Chae grinned and flung a scoopful of potatoes into the dresser. And the women, after running to fling their scullfulls of Brock on the Brock pile, went back to their box.

'Hoo are ye gettin' on wi' the Ware, loon?' Ake asked, threading the needle. 'Are ye managin' to get them into the wagon?'

'Nae bad,' the loon said.

'There was a whilie there when I thocht ye looked real trauchled,' Ake said. 'The wagon's gey heich for ye. Maybe Dod would take a shottie o' it for a while and ye can shoo the bags.'

Another half-hour passed. It still remained dull and the wind blew the dust off the potatoes into their faces. About half-past eight it began to rain. The wind drove it into the women's backs, and they huddled their heads into their collars. 'It winna last long,' Mrs Strachan said. 'It's just an April shower.'

But the rain fell heavier and heavier. Their clothes began to stick to their shoulders and arms. 'The joys o' bein' a farm servant!' Ake said, brushing the raindrops off his lean brown face.

'April showers bring forth May flowers!' Maggie Jane laughed.

'Ay, we'll get flowers quick enough if this rain lasts,' Dod said. 'On our graves!'

They all laughed and repeated this, and Chae stopped scooping to ask what they were laughing at. He came up beside the elevator and looked down at the potatoes. 'Dae ye see that, Mrs wifie!' He held a potato that Maggie Jane had missed in front of her nose. 'Dae ye see that? Fut dae ye think the mannie would say if he'd gotten that among his Seed?'

'Go to hell!' Maggie Jane said in exasperation.

'Go to hell yersel'!'

'I'll gang soon enough,' she said, laughing. And she leaned on the edge of the elevator and said; 'Did ye hear the bar aboot Hitler?'

They all listened, but the machine was making so much noise and she laughed and giggled so much, running her words together, that they couldn't make out what she was saying. 'Put it off, Mrs Strachan,' Ake said.

'Well, it was like this,' said Maggie Jane. 'Hitler and Churchill and Mussolini a' died and went to Hell. The Devil asked them hoo many lies they had tellt, so Churchill tellt him and the Devil said he was to run aince roond Hell. Then Mussolini tellt him and the Devil said he was to run three times roond Hell. Then he turned to ask Hitler hoo mony lies he had tellt. But Hitler was awa' for his bicycle!'

When they had stopped laughing and repeating the joke, Chae began to chaff Maggie Jane about how often she would need to run round Hell. 'Ye'll need new tyres for yer bike afore ye're half feenished,' he said.

'I will nut,' she said.

'Ye will sut!' he said, leaning forward and grinning mischievously in her face. 'Ye're a gey lass!'

'Ye're a gey lad yersel',' she said. 'I doot a bike'll be nae guid for ye.'

'No, I'll need a motor-car!'

'I'll sell ye mine!'

'It's a car I want,' he said. 'Nae a bloody go-car!'

And he laughed and went back to scooping. Ake looked round to see how the loon was getting on with the sewing of the sacks of Seed. 'Eh, John, but I doot we'll ha'e to gi'e somebody else that job,' he said. 'Ye're nae managin' weel ana. Can ony o' you wifies shoo bags?'

'Ay, I'll take a shottie,' Maggie Jane said.

'Dinna let her dae it,' Chae roared. 'She tried it the other day and she sewed hersel' to the bag!'

'I did nut,' Maggie Jane said with dignity, stepping off the box and taking the needle from the loon.

'Ye did sut!' Chae called.

She sewed industriously, frowning as she pushed the long thick needle through the sacking. 'Hurry up, wifie!' Ake said with a laugh as he put another sackful on the machine. 'Ye're fa'in' ahint!'

And when he dumped the next sackful on the weighing-machine he grinned when he saw that Maggie Jane was still frowning over the first bag. 'It's a guid job that this is nae piece-work,' he said. 'Or ye widna ha'e much in yer envelope at the end o' the week.'

He leaned on the end of the dresser and watched Mrs Strachan picking the potatoes. Occasionally he put out his hand and picked one that she had missed. But it was seldom that he needed to do this; she was an expert, her arms flying out and in like pistons, throwing the potatoes on the ground on the other side of the dresser or into the sculls. Dod picked the Ware opposite her and whenever his sacks were full he unhooked them and carried them on his back, emptying them into the wagon. The loon emptied the sculls of Brock and attended to the Chats which came out of a hole at the side of the potato sorter.

'Is it nae near piece time?' Mrs Strachan asked without looking up from the potatoes rolling upward in front of her.

Ake took a metal watch with a dingy yellowish glass out of his trousers-pocket and scanned it. 'It wants five meenits to nine,' he said.

'Well, we'll ha'e oor piece when we've feenished this bit,' Mrs Strachan said. 'While you lads are shiftin' the dresser.'

'Ah, but that'll nae dae,' Dod said. 'Ye'll ha'e to shove wi' the rest o' us.'

'I ken somebody that's fairly shovin' the noo.' Ake looked round and grinned at Maggie Jane who was struggling to keep in time with him. Three bags were standing beside the weighing-

machine waiting to be sewed. 'It's nae the bags she's shooin'
– it's the arse o' ma breeks!'

'Well, ye should keep yer big dock oot o' the way!' Maggie
Jane retorted. 'And, onywye, ma hands are that cauld they can
hardly haud the needle.'

'Never mind, Maggie Jane,' said Mrs Strachan. 'Here's the
sun comin' oot.'

The women huddled in the lee of the Ware wagon and ate
their piece while the men shifted the dresser. By the time they
had finished, the sun was shining quite brightly. Maggie Jane
lifted her skirts and gave a few skips as she came back to her
place on the box. 'Oh, the nightingale sang in Berkeley Square!'
she skirled.

'It's nae a nightingale that's singin' at the Barns o' Dallow,
onywye,' Chae grinned. 'It's a gey auld hen.'

'And here's a worm for ye!' he cried, throwing it at her.

Maggie Jane wriggled her shoulders with disgust. 'Eh,
Chae, ye dirty devil!' And she aimed a kick at him with her
wellington boot. He jouked round her and skelped her
playfully on the bottom. She chased him round the dresser,
but she turned and ran in the opposite direction when he
picked up the worm again and held it in front of her. He
smacked his lips and said: 'This would gang fine wi' thae
frosted tattles!'

'Feech!' Maggie Jane made her eyes cross with disgust.

'We'll may be ha'e to eat waur yet,' Ake said. 'Ye never
ken. They had to eat dogs in Germany in the last war.'

'Well, I nivir!' Maggie Jane exclaimed.

'There's some fowk eatin' dogs the now,' Chae said. They
tell me that the Polish sodgers at Auchencairn ha'e eaten a
wifie's dog.'

Maggie Jane and Mrs Strachan would not believe this, but
Chae swore that it was true. 'The doggie's disappeared,'

he said. 'Ay,' and he grinned and winked to Ake, 'and it's nae only doggies the Poles are eatin'! Ane o' them bit a woman doon by Stonehaven!'

'Well, I nivir!' cried Maggie Jane. Then she looked at Chae and said. 'Ach, he did nut.'

'He did sut!'

'Ye're a richt leear, Chae,' Mrs Strachan said, without looking up. 'It's richt, isn't it, Ake?'

'Ay, it's richt,' Ake said, leaning on the edge of the sorter and spitting into a bag. The Pole took a richt lump oot o' her. He was walkin' her oot and they had a row, so he ups and bites her. There's to be a coort case ower the head o' it.'

'Well, a' I can say is that it serves the bitch bloody well right,' Maggie Jane said decisively. 'She's got nae mair than she deserved for goin' oot wi' ane o' thae bloody foreigners.'

'Ye'll ha'e to watch yersel' the next time ye gang to the pictures,' Chae said. 'See and nae sit doon aside a Pole. Ye never ken fut he might dae in the dark.'

'No, for he'd ha'e a lot o' territory to work on!' Ake said.

'There's nae danger,' Maggie Jane tossed her head. 'I'm havin' nothin' to dae wi' ony bloody Pole.'

They were almost ready to shift the dresser again when they heard a sound above the rattle of the engine. Three aeroplanes were zooming across the sky towards the coast. 'Spitfires!' said Ake.

'They're nae,' Chae said. 'They're Blenheims.'

'Nae, they're Hurricanes,' said Dod.

Mrs Strachan was the only one who did not look up. She went on picking. Maggie Jane craned her neck until the planes were out of sight. 'It's a guid job they're nae Jerries, onywye,' she said, turning her attention to the potatoes.

'They micht be for a' ye ken,' Ake said.

'No, they're Hurricanes,' Dod said.

'Listen!' Mrs Strachan stopped picking. 'Listen!' she cried again.

There it was unmistakably: the wail of the siren in Auchencairn. 'Goad Almichty!' Maggie Jane said. 'That's surely somebody wi' an awfa sair guts after their breakfast!'

They worked on steadily. One or two aeroplanes flew high overhead, but they knew by the sounds that they were British machines. Suddenly there was a rattle like machine-gun fire. 'Maircy on us!' cried Maggie Jane. 'Fut was that?'

'A stane's got caught in the elevator,' Ake said. 'Put it off, Mrs Strachan.'

They all peered under the rollers, looking for the stone. Mrs Strachan seized the opportunity to get down on her knees and pick up some of the Brock that hadn't gone into the sculls.

'There it is,' Maggie Jane cried. 'See, doon there!'

'Ay, she kent where it was a' the time,' Chae grinned. 'For it was her that did it! She's been workin' for that a' mornin'. Sabotage!'

'I did nut,' Maggie Jane cried indignantly.

'But ye did sut!' he grinned and slapped her on the bottom.

Maggie Jane picked up a frosted potato and threw it at him. But he ducked and the potato went into the Ware wagon. 'Bullseye!' he cried.

Mrs Strachan laughed and began to sing: 'He gets the bullseye! Oh, what a clever young man! He gets the highest score out of a possible eighty-four! Because I love him!'

'He simply is divine!' Ake joined in, driving the needle through the sack in time. 'And I'm going to marry the man who gets a bullseye every time!'

'Ay, I doot that dates us, Mrs Strachan,' he said. 'They hinna got sangs like that nooadays!'

'No, there's a lot o' blethers o' sangs nooadays,' she said.

'Such daft-like words they've got and a' this shakin' their shoothers and a'.'

'Ach away!' Chae said. 'There was nae guid sangs when you were young.'

'That's right, Charles,' said Maggie Jane in a very polite accent. 'Maircy on us! Fut was that?' she cried suddenly, lapsing again into broad Mearns speech.

They all stood and listened to the echo of the crash. A flock of crows flew upwards, startled, from a clump of fir-trees. The whirring of their wings continued the sound for a few seconds, then there was silence. Mrs Strachan had put off the machine to listen.

'That's either a bomb,' Ake said. 'Or a plane down.'

'I thocht for a meenit it was Maggie Jane fa'in' intil a bag,' Mrs Strachan said. 'I looked up expectin' to see her heels stickin' oot o' the bag.'

'I wonder what it could be?' Maggie Jane said.

'Ach, we'll soon find oot,' Ake said. 'Put it on again, Mrs Strachan. We maun get thae Seed dressed, war or nae war.'

In the afternoon they heard that it was a German plane that had been brought down three miles on the other side of Auchencairn. The pilot, a loon of nineteen, had been killed instantly.

'Puir bastard!' old Ake said, throwing aside a frosted potato. 'He was somebody's bairn.'

The First Year of My Life
(1968)

Muriel Spark

I was born on the first day of the second month of the last year of the First World War, a Friday. Testimony abounds that during the first year of my life I never smiled. I was known as the baby whom nothing and no one could make smile. Everyone who knew me then has told me so. They tried very hard, singing and bouncing me up and down, jumping around, pulling faces. Many times I was told this later by my family and their friends; but, anyway, I knew it at the time.

You will shortly be hearing of that new school of psychology, or maybe you have heard of it already, which after long and far-adventuring research and experiment has established that all of the young of the human species are born omniscient. Babies, in their waking hours, know everything that is going on everywhere in the world; they can tune in to any conversation they choose, switch on to any scene. We have all experienced this power. It is only after the first year that it was brainwashed out of us; for it is demanded of us by our immediate environment that we grow to be of use to it in a practical way. Gradually, our know-all brain-cells are blacked out, although traces remain in some individuals in the form of E.S.P., and in the adults of some primitive tribes.

It is not a new theory. Poets and philosophers, as usual, have been there first. But scientific proof is now ready and to hand. Perhaps the final touches are being put to the new manifesto in some cell at Harvard University. Any day now it will be given to the world, and the world will be convinced.

Let me therefore get my word in first, because I feel pretty sure, now, about the authenticity of my remembrance of things past. My autobiography, as I very well perceived at the time, started in the very worst year that the world had ever seen so far. Apart from being born bedridden and toothless, unable to raise myself on the pillow or utter anything but farmyard squawks or police-siren wails, my bladder and my bowels totally out of control, I was further depressed by the curious behaviour of the two-legged mammals around me. There were those black-dressed people, females of the species to which I appeared to belong, saying they had lost their sons. I slept a great deal. Let them go and find their sons. It was like the special pin for my nappies which my mother or some other hoverer dedicated to my care was always losing. These careless women in black lost their husbands and their brothers. Then they came to visit my mother and clucked and crowed over my cradle. I was not amused.

'Babies never really smile till they're three months old,' said my mother. 'They're not *supposed* to smile till they're three months old.'

My brother, aged six, marched up and down with a toy rifle over his shoulder:

The grand old Duke of York
He had ten thousand men,
He marched them up to the top of the hill
And he marched them down again.

And when they were up, they were up.
And when they were down, they were down.
And when they were neither down nor up
They were neither up nor down.

'Just listen to him!'

'Look at him with his rifle!'

I was about ten days old when Russia stopped fighting. I tuned in to the Czar, a prisoner, with the rest of his family, since evidently the country had put him off his throne and there had been a revolution not long before I was born. Everyone was talking about it. I tuned in to the Czar. 'Nothing would ever induce me to sign the treaty of Brest-Litovsk,' he said to his wife. Anyway, nobody had asked him to.

At this point I was sleeping twenty hours a day to get my strength up. And from what I discerned in the other four hours of the day I knew I was going to need it. The Western Front on my frequency was sheer blood, mud, dismembered bodies, blistered crashes, hectic flashes of light in the night skies, explosions, total terror. Since it was plain I had been born into a bad moment in the history of the world, the future bothered me, unable as I was to raise my head from the pillow and as yet only twenty inches long. 'I truly wish I were a fox or a bird,' D.H. Lawrence was writing to somebody. Dreary old creeping Jesus. I fell asleep.

Red sheets of flame shot across the sky. It was 21st March, the fiftieth day of my life, and the German Spring Offensive had started before my morning feed. Infinite slaughter. I scowled at the scene, and made an effort to kick out. But the attempt was feeble. Furious, and impatient for some strength, I wailed for my feed. After which I stopped wailing but continued to scowl.

The grand old Duke of York
He had ten thousand men . . .

They rocked the cradle. I never heard a sillier song. Over in Berlin and Vienna the people were starving, freezing, striking, rioting and yelling in the streets. In London everyone was bustling to work and muttering that it was time the whole damn business was over.

The big people around me bared their teeth; that meant a smile, it meant they were pleased or amused. They spoke of ration cards for meat and sugar and butter.

'Where will it all end?'

I went to sleep. I woke and tuned in to Bernard Shaw who was telling someone to shut up. I switched over to Joseph Conrad who, strangely enough, was saying precisely the same thing. I still didn't think it worth a smile, although it was expected of me any day now. I got on to Turkey. Women draped in black huddled and chattered in their harems; yak-yak-yak. This was boring, so I came back to home base.

In and out came and went the women in British black. My mother's brother, dressed in his uniform, came coughing. He had been poison-gassed in the trenches. *'Tout le monde à la bataille!'* declaimed Marshal Foch the old swine. He was now

Commander-in-Chief of the Allied Forces. My uncle coughed from deep within his lungs, never to recover but destined to return to the Front. His brass buttons gleamed in the firelight. I weighed twelve pounds by now, I stretched and kicked for exercise, seeing that I had a lifetime before me, coping with this crowd. I took six feeds a day and kept most of them down by the time the *Vindictive* was sunk in Ostend harbour, on which day I kicked with special vigour in my bath.

In France the conscripted soldiers leapfrogged over the dead on the advance and littered the fields with limbs and hands, or drowned in the mud. The strongest men on all fronts were dead before I was born. Now the sentries used bodies for barricades and the fighting men were unhealthy from the start. I checked my toes and fingers, knowing I was going to need them. *The Playboy of the Western World* was playing at the Court Theatre in London, but occasionally I beamed over to the House of Commons which made me drop off gently to sleep. Generally, I preferred the Western Front where one got the true state of affairs. It was essential to know the worst, blood and explosions and all, for one had to be prepared, as the boy scouts said. Virginia Woolf yawned and reached for her diary. Really, I preferred the Western Front.

In the fifth month of my life I could raise my head from my pillow and hold it up. I could grasp the objects that were held out to me. Some of these things rattled and squawked. I gnawed on them to get my teeth started. 'She hasn't smiled yet?' said the dreary old aunties. My mother, on the defensive, said I was probably one of those late smilers. On my wavelength Pablo Picasso was getting married and early in that month of July the Silver Wedding of King George V and Queen Mary was celebrated in joyous pomp at St. Paul's Cathedral. They drove through the streets of London with their children. Twenty-five years of domestic happiness. A lot of fuss and ceremonial handing over of swords went on at the Guildhall where the King and Queen received a cheque for £53,000 to dispose of for charity as they thought fit. *Tout le monde à la bataille!* Income tax in England had reached six shillings in the pound. Everyone was talking about the Silver Wedding; yak-yak-yak, and ten days later the Czar and his family, now in Siberia, were invited to descend to a little room in the basement. Crack, crack, went the guns; screams and blood all over the place, and that was the end of the Romanoffs. I flexed my muscles. 'A fine healthy baby,' said the doctor; which gave me much satisfaction.

Tout le monde à la bataille! That included my gassed uncle. My health had improved to the point where I was able to crawl in my playpen. Bertrand Russell was still cheerily in prison for writing something seditious about pacifism. Tuning in as usual to the Front Lines it looked as if the Germans were winning all the battles yet losing the war. And so it was. The upper-income people were upset about the income tax at six shillings to the pound. But all women over thirty got the vote. 'It seems a long time to wait,' said one of my drab old aunts, aged twenty-two. The speeches in the House of Commons always sent me to sleep which was why I missed, at the actual time, a certain oration by Mr. Asquith following the armistice on 11th November. Mr. Asquith was a greatly esteemed former prime minister later to be an Earl, and had been ousted by Mr. Lloyd George. I clearly heard Asquith, in private, refer to Lloyd George as 'that damned Welsh goat'.

The armistice was signed and I was awake for that. I pulled myself on to my feet with the aid of the bars of my cot. My teeth were coming through very nicely in my opinion, and well worth all the trouble I was put to in bringing them forth. I weighed twenty pounds. On all the world's fighting fronts the men killed in action or dead of wounds numbered 8,538,315 and the warriors wounded and maimed were 21,219,452.

With these figures in mind I sat up in my high chair and banged my spoon on the table. One of my mother's black-draped friends recited:

I have a rendezvous with Death
At some disputed barricade,
When spring comes back with rustling shade
And apple blossoms fill the air –
I have a rendezvous with Death.

Most of the poets, they said, had been killed. The poetry made them dab their eyes with clean white handkerchiefs.

Next February on my first birthday, there was a birthday-cake with one candle. Lots of children and their elders. The war had been over two months and twenty-one days. 'Why doesn't she smile?' My brother was to blow out the candle. The elders were talking about the war and the political situation. Lloyd George and Asquith, Asquith and Lloyd George. I remembered recently having switched on to Mr. Asquith at a private party where he had been drinking a lot. He was playing cards and when he came to cut the cards he tried to cut a large box of matches by mistake. On another occasion I had seen him putting his arm around a lady's shoulder in a Daimler motor car, and generally behaving towards her in a very friendly fashion. Strangely enough she said, 'If you don't stop this nonsense immediately I'll order the chauffeur to stop and I'll get out.' Mr. Asquith replied, 'And pray, what reason will you give?' Well anyway it was my feeding time.

The guests arrived for my birthday. It was so sad, said one of the black widows, so sad about Wilfred Owen who was killed so late in the war, and she quoted from a poem of his:

What passing-bells for these who die as cattle?
Only the monstrous anger of the guns.

The children were squealing and toddling around. One was sick and another wet the floor and stood with his legs apart gaping at the puddle. All was mopped up. I banged my spoon on the table of my high chair.

But I've a rendezvous with Death
At midnight in some flaming town,
When spring trips north again this year,
And I to my pledged word am true,
I shall not fail that rendezvous.

More parents and children arrived. One stout man who was warming his behind at the fire, said, 'I always think those words of Asquith's after the armistice were so apt . . .'

They brought the cake close to my high chair for me to see, with the candle shining and flickering above the pink icing. 'A pity she never smiles.'

'She'll smile in time,' my mother said, obviously upset.

'What Asquith told the House of Commons just after the war,' said that stout gentleman with his backside to the fire, '– so apt, what Asquith said. He said that the war has cleansed and purged the world, by God! I recall his actual words: "All things have become new. In this great cleansing and purging it has been the privilege of our country to play her part . . ."'

That did it. I broke into a decided smile and everyone noticed it, convinced that it was provoked by the fact that my brother had blown out the candle on the cake. 'She smiled!' my mother exclaimed. And everyone was clucking away about how I was smiling. For good measure I crowed like a demented raven. 'My baby's smiling!' said my mother.

'It was the candle on her cake,' they said.

The cake be damned. Since that time I have grown to smile quite naturally, like any other healthy and house-trained person, but when I really mean a smile, deeply felt from the core, then to all intents and purposes it comes in response to the words uttered in the House of Commons after the First World War by the distinguished, the immaculately dressed and the late Mr. Asquith.

Captain Errol
(1988)

George Macdonald Fraser

Whenever I see television newsreels of police or troops facing mobs of rioting demonstrators, standing fast under a hail of rocks, bottles, and petrol bombs, my mind goes back forty years to India, when I was understudying John Gielgud and first heard the pregnant phrase 'Aid to the civil power'. And from that my thoughts inevitably travel on to Captain Errol, and the Brigadier's pet hawks, and the great rabble of chanting Arab rioters advancing down the Kantara causeway towards the thin khaki line of 12 Platoon, and my own voice sounding unnaturally loud and hoarse: 'Right, Sarn't Telfer – fix bayonets.'

Aid to the civil power, you see, is what the British Army used to give when called on to deal with disorder, tumult, and breach of the peace which the police could no longer control. The native constabulary of our former Italian colony being what they were – prone to panic if a drunken *bazaar-wallah* broke a window – aid to the civil power often amounted to no more than sending Wee Wullie out with a pick handle to shout 'Imshi!'; on the other hand, when real political mayhem broke loose, and a raging horde of fellaheen several thousand strong appeared bent on setting the town ablaze and massacring the European population, sterner measures were called for, and unhappy subalterns found themselves faced with the kind of decision which Home Secretaries and Cabinets agonise over for hours, the difference being that the subaltern had thirty seconds, with luck, in which to consider the safety of his men, the defenceless town at his back, and the likelihood that if he gave the order to fire and some agitator caught a bullet, he, the subaltern, would go down in history as the Butcher of Puggle Bazaar, or wherever it happened to be.

That, as I say, was in the imperial twilight of forty years ago, long before the days of walkie-talkies, C.S. gas, riot shields, water cannon, and similar modern defences of the public weal – not that they seem to make riot control any easier nowadays, especially when the cameras are present. We didn't have to worry about television, and our options for dealing with infuriated rioters were limited: do nothing and get murdered, fire over their heads, or let fly in earnest. There are easier decisions, believe me, for a youth not old enough to vote.

The Army recognised this, and was at pains to instruct its fledgling officers in the techniques of containing civil commotion, so far as it knew how, which wasn't far, even in India, with three centuries of experience to draw on. Those were the post-war months before independence, when demonstrators were chanting: 'Jai Hind!' and 'Pakistan zindabad!', and the Indian police were laying about them with *lathis* (you really don't know what police brutality is until you've seen a *lathi* charge going in), while the troops stood by and their officers hoped to God they wouldn't have to intervene. Quetta and Amritsar were ugly memories of what happened when someone opened fire at the wrong time.

Bangalore, where I was completing my officers' training course, was one of the quiet spots, which may have been why the authorities took the eccentric view that instruction in riot control could be imparted through the medium of the theatre. If that sounds unlikely, well, that's the Army for you. Some genius (and it wasn't Richard Brinsley Sheridan) had written a play about aid to the civil power, showing the right and wrong ways of coping with unrest, it was to be enacted at the garrison theatre, and I found myself dragooned into taking part.

That's what comes of understudying Gielgud, which is what I like to think I had been doing, although he didn't know it. In the last relaxed weeks of our officers' training, a few of us cadets had been taking part in a production of *The Harbour Called Mulberry* for India Radio, with Cadet MacNeill as the Prussian general riveting the audience with his impersonation of Conrad Veidt; it was natural that when Gielgud's touring company arrived in town with a double bill of *Hamlet* and *Blithe Spirit*, and some of his cast went down with Bangalore Belly, our amateur group should be asked to provide replacements in case they needed a couple of extra spear-carriers. I was fool enough to volunteer, and while we were never required even to change into costume, let alone go on stage, we convinced ourselves that we were, technically, understudying the lead players – I mean to say, Bangalore Belly can go through unacclimatised systems like wildfire, and in our backstage dreams we could imagine being out there tearing the Soliloquy to shreds while Gielgud was carted off to the sick-bay. He wasn't, as it happened, but no doubt he would have been reassured if he'd known that we were ready to step in.

That by the way; the upshot was that, having drawn attention to ourselves, my associates and I were prime targets when it came to choosing the cast for the aid-to-the-civil-power play, a knavish piece of work entitled *Nowall and Chancit.* I played Colonel Nowall, an elderly and incompetent garrison commander, which meant that I had to wear a white wig and whiskers and make like a doddering Aubrey Smith in front of a military audience whose behaviour would have disgraced the Circus Maximus. The script was abysmal, my moustache kept coming loose, the prop telephone didn't ring on cue, one of the cast who took acting seriously dried up and fainted, and in the last act I had to order my troops to open fire on a rioting crowd played by a platoon of Indian sepoys in loin-cloths who giggled throughout and went right over the top when shot with blank cartridges. The entire theatre was dense with cordite smoke, there seemed to be about seven hundred people on stage, and when I stood knee-deep in hysterical corpses and spoke my deathless closing line: 'Well, that's that!' it stopped the show. I have not trod the boards since, and it can stay that way.

My excuse for that reminiscence is that it describes the only instruction we ever got in dealing with civil disorder. Considering that we were destined, as young second-lieutenants, to lead troops in various parts of the Far and Middle East when empires were breaking up and independence movements were in full spate, with accompanying bloodshed, it was barely adequate. Not that any amount of training, including my months as an infantry section leader in Burma, could have prepared me for the Palestine troubles of '46, when Arab and Jew were at each other's throats with the British caught in the middle, as usual; the Irgun and Stern Gang were waging their campaign of terror (or freedom-fighting, depending on your point of view), raid, ambush, murder, and explosion were commonplace, the Argyll and Sutherlands had barbed wire strung across the inside corridors of their Jerusalem barracks, and you took your revolver into the shower. It was a nerve-racked, bloody business which you learned as you went along; commanding the Cairo–Jerusalem night train and conducting a security stake-out at the Armistice Day service on the Mount of Olives added years to my education in a matter of days, and by the time I was posted back to my Highland battalion far away along the North African coast I felt I knew something about lending aid to the civil power. Of course, I didn't know the half of it – but then, I hadn't met Captain Errol.

That wasn't his real name, but it was what the Jocks called him because of his resemblance to Flynn, the well-known actor and bon viveur. And it wasn't just that he was six feet two, lightly moustached, and strikingly handsome, he had the same casual, self-assured swagger of the man who is well content with himself and doesn't give a damn whether anyone knows it or not; when you have two strings of ribbons, starting with the M.C. and M.M. and including the Croix de Guerre and a couple of exotic Balkan gongs at the end, you don't need to put on side. Which was just as well, for Errol had evidently been born with a double helping of self-esteem, advertised in the amused half-smile and lifted eyebrow with which he surveyed the world in general – and me in particular on the day he joined the battalion.

I was bringing my platoon in from a ten-mile route march, which they had done in the cracking time of two and a half hours, and was calling them to march to attention for the last fifty yards to the main gate, exhorting McAuslan for the umpteenth time to get his pack off his backside and up to his shoulders, and pretending not to hear Private Fletcher's sotto voce explanation that McAuslan couldn't march upright because he was expecting, and might, indeed, go into labour shortly. Sergeant Telfer barked them to silence and quickened the step, and I turned aside to watch them swing past – it was a moment I took care never to miss, for the pride of it warms me still: my platoon going by, forty hard young Jocks in battle order, rifles sloped and bonnets pulled down, slightly dusty but hardly even breaking sweat as Telfer wheeled them under the archway with its faded golden standard. Eat your heart out, Bonaparte.

It was as I was turning to follow that I became aware of an elegant figure seated in a horse-ghari which had just drawn up at the gate. He was a Highlander, but his red tartan and white cockade were not of our regiment; then I noticed the three pips and threw him a salute, which he acknowledged with a nonchalant forefinger and a remarkable request spoken in the airy affected drawl which in Glasgow is called 'Kelvinsaid'.

'Hullo, laddie,' said he. 'Your platoon? You might get a couple of them to give me a hand with my kit, will you?'

It was said so affably that the effrontery of it didn't dawn for a second – you don't ask a perfect stranger to detach two of his marching men to be your porters, not without preamble or introduction. I stared at the man, taking in the splendid bearing, the medal ribbons, and the pleasant expectant smile while he put a fresh cigarette in his holder.

'Eh? I beg your pardon,' I said stiffly, 'but they're on parade at the moment.' For some reason I didn't add 'sir'.

It didn't faze him a bit. 'Oh, that's a shame. Still, not to panic. We ought to be able to manage between us. All right, Abdul,' he addressed the Arab coachman, 'let's get the cargo on the dock.'

He swung lightly down from the ghari – not the easiest thing to do, with decorum, in a kilt – and it was typical of the man that I found myself with a valise in one hand and a set of golf-clubs in the other before I realised that he was evidently expecting me to tote his damned dunnage for him. My platoon had vanished from sight, fortunately, but Sergeant Telfer had stopped and was staring back, goggle-eyed. Before I could speak the newcomer was addressing me again:

'Got fifty lire, old man? 'Fraid all I have is Egyptian ackers, and the Fairy Coachman won't look at them. See him right, will you, and we'll settle up anon. Okay?'

That, as they say, did it. 'Laddie' I could just about absorb (since he must have been all of twenty-seven and therefore practically senile), and even his outrageous assumption that my private and personal platoon were his to flunkify, and that I would caddy for him and pay his blasted transport bills – but not that careless 'Okay?' and the easy, patronising air which was all the worse for being so infernally amiable. Captain or no captain, I put his clubs and valise carefully back in the ghari and spoke, with masterly restraint:

'I'm afraid I haven't fifty lire on me, sir, but if you care to climb back in, the ghari can take you to the Paymaster's Office in HQ Company; they'll change your ackers and see to your kit.' And just to round off the civilities I added: 'My name's MacNeill, by the way, and I'm a platoon commander, not a bloody dragoman.'

Which was insubordination, but if you'd seen that sardonic eyebrow and God-like profile you'd have said it too. Again, it didn't faze him; he actually chuckled.

'I stand rebuked. MacNeill, eh?' He glanced at my campaign ribbon. 'What were you in Burma?'

'Other rank.'

'Well, obviously, since you're only a second-lieutenant now. What kind of other rank?'

'Well . . . sniper-scout, Black Cat Division. Later on I was a section leader. Why . . . sir?'

'Black Cats, eh? God Almighty's Own. Were you at Imphal?'

'Not in the Boxes. Irrawaddy Crossing, Meiktila, Sittang Bend—'

'And you haven't got a measly fifty lire for a poor broken-down old soldier? Well, the hell with you, young MacNeill,' said this astonishing fellow, and seated himself in the ghari again. 'I'd heap coals of fire on you by offering you a lift, but your platoon are probably waiting for you to stop their motor. Bash on, MacNeill, before they seize up! Officers' mess, Abdul!' And he drove off with an airy wave.

'Hadn't you better report to H.Q.?' I called after him, but he was through the gate by then, leaving me nonplussed but not a little relieved; giving lip to captains wasn't my usual line, but he hadn't turned regimental, fortunately.

'Whit the hell was yon?' demanded Sergeant Telfer, who had been an entranced spectator.

'You tell me,' I said. 'Ballater Bertie, by the look of him.' For he had, indeed, the air of those who command the guard at Ballater Station, conducting Royalty with drawn broadsword and white spats. And yet he'd been wearing an M.M. ribbon, which signified service in the ranks. I remarked on this to Telfer, who sniffed as only a Glaswegian can, and observed that whoever the newcomer might be, he was a heid-case – which means an eccentric.

That was the battalion's opinion, formed before Captain Errol had been with us twenty-four hours. He had driven straight to the mess, which was empty of customers at that time of day, smooth-talked the mess sergeant into paying the ghari out of bar receipts, made free with the Talisker unofficially reserved for the Medical Officer, parked himself unerringly in the second-in-command's favourite chair, and whiled away the golden afternoon with the *Scottish Field*. Discovered and gently rebuked by the Adjutant for not reporting his arrival in the proper form, he had laughed apologetically and asked what time dinner was, and before the Adjutant, an earnest young Englishman, could wax properly indignant he had found himself, by some inexplicable process, buying Errol a gin and tonic.

'I can't fathom it,' he told me, with the pained expression he usually reserved for descriptions of his putting. 'One minute I was tearing small strips off the chap, and the next you know I was saying "What's yours?" and filling him in on the social scene. Extraordinary.'

Having found myself within an ace of bell-hopping for Captain Errol by the same mysterious magic, I sympathised. Who was he, anyway, I asked, and the Adjutant frowned.

'Dunno, exactly. Nor why we've got him. He's been up in Palestine lately, and just from something the Colonel said I have the impression he's been in some sort of turmoil – Errol, I mean. That type always is,' said the Adjutant, like a dowager discussing a fallen woman. 'Wouldn't be surprised if he was an I-man!'

'I' is Intelligence, and the general feeling in line regiments is that you can keep it; I-men are disturbing influences best confined to the higher echelons, where they can pursue their clandestine careers and leave honest soldiers in peace. Attached to a battalion, they can be unsettling.

And Captain Errol was all of that. As he had begun, with the Adjutant and me, so he went on, causing ripples on our placid regimental surface which eventually turned into larger waves. One of the former, for example, occurred on his first night in the mess when, within half an hour of their first acquaintance, he addressed the Colonel as 'skipper'. It caused a brief silence which Errol himself didn't seem to notice; officially, you see, there are no ranks in the mess, but junior officers (of whom captains are only the most senior) normally call the head man 'sir', especially when he is such a redoubtable bald eagle as our Colonel was. 'Skipper' was close to the edge of impertinence – but it was said so easily and naturally that he got away with it. In fact, I think the Colonel rather liked it.

That, it soon became plain, was Errol's secret. Like his notorious namesake, he had great charm and immense style; partly it was his appearance, which was commanding, and his war record – the family of Highland regiments is a tight little news network, and many of the older men had heard of him as a fighting soldier – but most of it was just personality. He was casual, cocky, even insolent, but with a gift of disarmament, and even those who found his conceit and familiarity irritating (as the older men did) seemed almost flattered when he gave them his attention – I've seen the Senior Major, a grizzled veteran with the disposition of a liverish rhino, grinning sourly as Errol teased him. When he was snubbed, he didn't seem to notice; the eyebrow would give an amused flicker, no more.

The youngest subalterns thought him a hell of a fellow, of course, not least because he had no side with them; rank meant nothing to Errol, up or down. The Jocks, being canny judges, were rather wary of him, while taking advantage of his informality so far as they thought it safe; their word for him was 'gallus', that curious Scots adjective which means a mixture of reckless, extrovert, and indifferent. On balance, he was not over-popular with Jocks or officers, especially among the elders, but even they held him in a certain grudging respect. None of which seemed to matter to Errol in the least.

I heard various verdicts on him in the first couple of weeks.

'I think he's a Bad News Type,' said the Adjutant judicially, 'but there's no doubt he's a character.'

'Insufferable young pup,' was the Senior Major's verdict. 'Why the devil must he use that blasted cigarette holder, like a damned actor?' When it was pointed out that most of us used them, to keep the sweat off our cigarettes, the Major remarked unreasonably: 'Not the way he does. Damned affectation.'

'I like him,' said plump and genial Major Bakie. 'He can be dashed funny when he wants. Breath of fresh air. My wife likes him, too.'

'Captain Errol,' observed the Padre, who was the most charitable of men, 'is a very interesting chentleman. What d'ye say, Lachlan?'

'Like enough,' said the M.O. 'I wouldnae let him near my malt, my money, or my maidservant.'

'See him, he's sand-happy. No' a' there,' I heard Private McAuslan informing his comrades. 'See when he wis Captain o' the Week, an' had tae inspect ma rifle on guard? He looks doon the barrel, and says: "I seem to see through a glass darkly." Whit kind o' patter's that, Fletcher? Mind you, he didnae pit me on a charge, an' me wi' a live round up the spout. Darkie woulda nailed me tae the wall.' (So I would, McAuslan.)

'Errol? A chanty-wrastler,' said Fletcher – which, from that crafty young soldier, was interesting. A chanty-wrastler is a poseur, and unreliable.

'Too dam' sure of himself by half,' was the judgment of the second-in-command. 'We can do without his sort.'

The Colonel rubbed tobacco between his palms in his thoughtful way, and said nothing.

Personally, I'd met plenty I liked better, but it seemed to me there was a deeper prejudice against Errol than he deserved, bouncy tigger though he was. Some of it might be explained by his service record which, it emerged, was sensational, and not all on the credit side. According to the Adjutant's researches, he had been commissioned in the Territorials in '39, and had escaped mysteriously from St Valéry, where the rest of his unit had gone into the P.O.W. bag ('there were a few heads wagged about that, apparently'). Later he had fought with distinction in the Far East, acquiring a Military Cross ('a real one, not one of your up-with-the-rations jobs') with the Chindits.

'And then,' said the Adjutant impressively, 'he got himself cashiered. Yes, busted – all the way down. It seems he was in charge of a train-load of wounded, somewhere in Bengal, and there was some foul-up and they were shunted into a siding. Some of the chaps were in a bad way, and Errol raised hell with the local R.T.O., who got stroppy with him, and Errol hauled out his revolver and shot the inkpot off the R.T.O.'s desk, and threatened to put the next one between his eyes. Well, you can't do that, can you? So it was a court-martial, and march out Private Errol.'

'But he's a captain now,' I said. 'How on earth—?'

'*Chubbarao*, and listen to this,' said the Adjutant. 'He finished up late in the war with those special service johnnies who were turned loose in the Balkans – you know, helping the partisans, blowing-up bridges and things and slaughtering Huns with cheese-wire by night. Big cloak-and-dagger stuff, and he did hell of a well at it, and Tito kissed him on both cheeks and said he'd never seen the like—'

'So that's where he got the M.M.'

'And the Balkan gongs, and the upshot of it was that he was re-commissioned. It happens, now and then. And of late he's been undercover in Palestine.' The Adjutant scratched his fair head. 'Something odd there – rumours about terrorist suspects being knocked about pretty badly, and one hanging himself in his cell. Nasty business. Anyway, friend Errol was shipped out, p.d.q., and now we're landed with him. Oh, and another thing – he's to be Intelligence Officer, as if we needed one. Didn't I say he was the type?' The Adjutant sniffed. 'Well, at least it should keep him out of everyone's hair.'

The disclosures of Errol's irregular past were not altogether surprising, and they helped to explain his *alakeefik* attitude and brass neck. Plainly he was capable of anything, and having hit both the heights and the depths was not to be judged as ordinary mortals are.

His duties as I-man were vague, and kept him out of the main stream of battalion life, which may have been as well, for as a soldier he was a contradictory mixture. In some things he was expert: a splendid shot, superb athlete, and organised to the hilt in the field. On parade, saving his immaculate turn-out, he was a disaster: when he was Captain of the Week and had to mount the guard, I suffered agonies at his elbow in my capacity as orderly officer, whispering commands and telling him what to do next while he turned the ceremony into a shambles. Admittedly, since McAuslan was in the guard, we were handicapped from the start, but I believe Errol could have reduced the Household Cavalry to chaos – and been utterly indifferent about it. Doing well or doing badly, it was all one to him; he walked off that guard-mounting humming and swinging his walking-stick, debonair as be-damned, and advising the outraged Regimental Sergeant-Major that the drill needed tightening up a bit. (He actually addressed him as 'Major', which is one of the things that are never done. An R.S.M. is 'Mr So-and-so'.)

Being casual in all things, he was naturally accident-prone, but even that did nothing to deflate him, since the victim was invariably someone else. He wrecked the Hudson Terraplane belonging to Lieutenant Grant, and walked away without a scratch; Grant escaped with a broken wrist, but there was no restoring the car which had been its owner's pride.

He was equally lethal on blue water. Our garrison town boasted a magnificent Mediterranean bay, strewn with wrecks from the war, and sailing small boats was a popular pastime among the local smart set; Errol took to it in a big way, and from all accounts it was like having a demented Blackbeard loose about the waterfront. I gather there is a sailing etiquette about giving way and not getting athwart other people's hawses, of which he was entirely oblivious; the result was a series of bumps, scrapes, collisions, and furious protests from outraged voyagers, culminating in a regatta event in which he dismasted one competitor, caused another to capsize, and added insult to injury by winning handsomely. That he was promptly disqualified did not lower the angle of his jaunty cigarette-holder by a degree when he turned up at the prize-giving, bronzed and dashing, to applaud the garrison beauty, Ellen Ramsay, when she received the Ladies' Cup. She it was who christened him the Sea Hog – and was his dinner companion for many nights thereafter, to the chagrin of Lieutenant MacKenzie who, until Errol's arrival, had been the fair Ellen's favoured beau.

None of which did much for Errol's popularity. Nor, strangely enough, did an odd episode which I thought was rather to his credit. The command boxing tournament took place, and as sports officer I had to organise our regimental gladiators – which meant calling for volunteers, telling them to knock off booze and smoking, letting them attend to their own sparring and training in the M.T. shed, and seeing that they were sober and (initially) upright on opening night. If that seems perfunctory, I was not a boxer myself, and had no illusions about being Yussel Jacobs when it came to management. Let them get into the ring and lay about them, while I crouched behind their corner, crying encouragement and restraining the seconds from joining in.

The tournament lasted three nights, and in winning his semifinal our heavyweight star, Private McGuigan, the Gorbals Goliath, broke a finger. Personally I think he did it on purpose to avoid meeting the other finalist, one Captain Stock, a terrible creature of blood and iron who had flattened all his opponents with unimagined ferocity; he was a relic of the Stone Age who had found his way into the Army Physical Training Corps, this Stock, and I wouldn't have gone near him with a whip, a gun, and a chair. Primitive wasn't the word; he made McAuslan and Wee Wullie look like Romantic poets.

Left to find a substitute willing to offer himself for sacrifice at the hands of this Behemoth, I got no takers at all, and then someone said he had heard that Errol used to box a bit, and must be about the right weight. There was enthusiastic support for this suggestion, especially from the older officers, so I sought the man out in his room, where he was reclining with a cool drink at his elbow, shooting moths with an air pistol – and hitting them, too.

'What makes you think I could take Stock, if you'll pardon the expression?' he wondered, when I put it to him. 'Or doesn't that matter, as long as we're represented?'

'Someone in the mess said you used to be pretty useful . . .'

'Did they now? That's handsome of them.' He grinned at me sardonically. 'Who proposed me – Cattenach?' This was the second-in-command, Errol's principal critic. 'Never mind. It's not on, Dand, thanks all the same. I haven't boxed for ages. Too much like work.'

'There's no one else in the battalion,' I said subtly.

'Stop waving the regimental colours at me.' He picked off a large moth on the wing, bringing down a shower of plaster. 'Anyway, I'm an interloper. Let Cattenach take him on if he's so damned keen; God knows he's big enough. No, you'll just have to tell 'em I've retired.'

So I reported failure, and there was disappointment, although no one was daft enough to suggest that Errol was scared. The Adjutant, who was a romantic, speculated that he had probably killed a man in the ring – his fiancée's brother, for choice – and vowed never to box again; he would have joined the Foreign Legion, insisted the Adjutant, if it hadn't been for the war. Others joined in these fine flights, and no one noticed the Colonel sauntering out of the mess, but later that evening he told me casually that I could pencil in Errol for the final; he had been persuaded, said the Colonel, filling his pipe in a contented way. Knowing his fanaticism where the battalion's credit was concerned, I wondered what pressure he had applied, and concluded that he probably hadn't needed any, just his gentle, fatherly insistence which I knew of old. He could have talked a salmon out of its pool, the same Colonel – and of course the possibility that his man might get half-killed wouldn't even cross his mind.

It crossed mine when I saw Errol and Stock face to muzzle in the ring; so might Adonis have looked in the presence of a silverback gorilla. Stock stood half a head taller, two stone heavier, and about a foot thicker, especially round the brow. He came out at the bell like a Panzer tank – and Errol moved round him as though on rollers, weaving and feinting until he'd sized him up, and then began systematically left-handing him to death. It was Carpentier to the town drunk; Stock clubbed and rushed and never got near him until the second round, when he had the ill-judgment to land a kidney-punch. Errol came out of the clinch looking white and wicked, and thereafter took Stock apart with clinical savagery. The referee stopped it in the third, with Stock bloodied and out on his feet; Errol hadn't a hair out of place, and I doubt if he'd been touched more than half a dozen times.

But as I said, he got no credit from that fight. It had been so one-sided that all the sympathy was for the battered Stock, and there was even a feeling that Errol had been over-brutal to a man who wasn't in his class as a boxer. Which was unfair, since he had been reluctant to fight in the first place – my guess is that he knew exactly how good he was, and that Stock would be no contest. But if he compared the polite clapping as he left the ring with the thunder of applause for his groggy but gamely smiling opponent, it didn't seem to worry him; he strolled back to the changing-room cool and unruffled as ever.

It was immediately after this that he finally fell from grace altogether, and the mixed feelings of the mess hardened into positive dislike. Two things happened to show him at his worst; neither was earth-shattering in itself, but in each case he displayed such a cynical indifference that even his friends could find no excuses.

In the first instance, he stole another man's girl – and it wasn't a case of cutting out someone like MacKenzie, the battalion Lothario, with Ellen Ramsay, whose admirers were legion (including even the unlikely Private McAuslan, whose wooing I have described elsewhere). Boy met, dated, and parted from girl with bewildering speed in post-war garrisons, and no harm done, Errol himself must have been involved with half the nurses, A.T.S., Wrens, and civilian females, and no one thought twice, except to note jealously that while the rest of us had to pursue, he seemed to draw them like a magnet.

But the case of Sister Jean was different. She was a flashing-eyed Irish redhead, decorative even by the high standard of the hospital staff, and her attachment to a U.S. pilot at the bomber base was the real thing, what the Adjutant called Poignant Passion, engagement ring, wedding date fixed, and all – until Errol moved in on the lady. I was on detachment at Fort Yarhuna during the crisis, but according to MacKenzie it had started with casual cheek-to-cheek stuff on the dance-floor at the Uaddan Club, progressing to dates, picnics, and sailing-trips on Errol's dinghy while the American was absent on his country's service, dropping sandbags on the desert (I quote MacKenzie). In brief, Jean had been beglamoured, her fiancé had objected, a lovers' quarrel had ensued with high words flying in Irish and American, the ring had been returned, the pilot had got himself posted to Italy in dudgeon, and the hapless patients in Sister Jean's ward were learning what life was like under the Empress Theodora.

'Talk about hell hath no fury,' said MacKenzie. 'She's lobbing out enemas like a mad thing. You see, not only is her romance with Tex kaput, *bus*, washed up; on top of that, the unspeakable Errol has given her the gate and is pushing around the new Ensa bint – who is a piece of all right, I have to admit. What women see in him,' he added irritably, 'I'm shot if I know. The man's a tick, a suede-shoe artist, a Semiramis Hotel creeper of the lowest type.'

'Didn't anyone try to steer him away from Jean?' I asked, thinking of the Colonel, who when it came to intervening in his junior officers' love lives could have given Lady Bracknell a head start. 'Why didn't you tackle him yourself?'

'Come off it. Remember what happened to Stock? Actually, Ellen Ramsay did get stuck into him at one stage . . . gosh, she's a honey, that girl,' said MacKenzie, smiling dreamily. 'I think I'll take her grouse-shooting when we go home. You know, dazzle her with Perthshire . . . Eh? Oh, well, she tore strips off Errol, and he just laughed and said: "Why, darling, I didn't know you cared," and swanned off, cool as be-damned, to take Jean swimming. And now, having wrecked her future, and Tex's, he goes around blithe as a bird, as though nothing had happened. Yes – a total tick, slice him where you will.'

A fair assessment, on the face of it, and the temperature dropped noticeably in the mess when Errol was present, not that he seemed aware of it. Otherwise the incident was closed; for one thing, there were far more urgent matters to think about just then. Political trouble was beginning to brew in our former Italian colony, with noisy nationalist demonstrations, stoning of police posts by Arab gangs, and the prospect that we would be called out to support the civil administration. If there's going to be active service, the last thing you need is discord in the mess.

Even so, Errol's next gaffe came close to blowing the lid off
with his bête noire, Cattenach, the second-in-command; it was
the nearest thing I ever saw to a brawl between brother-officers,
and all because of Errol's bloody-minded disregard for other
people's feelings. He had set off early one morning to shoot on
the salt flats outside the town, and came breezing in just as we
were finishing breakfast, calling for black coffee and telling Bennet-
Bruce that his shotgun (which Errol had borrowed, typically)
was throwing left. Bennet-Bruce asked if he'd had any luck.

'Nothing to write to the *Field* about,' said Errol, buttering
toast. 'In fact, sweet dam'-all, except for a couple of kites near
the Armoury. Weird-looking things.'

Cattenach lowered his paper. 'Did you say near the
Armoury? Where are these birds?'

'Where I left them, of course; somewhere around the
Armoury wall. They weren't worth keeping.'

Cattenach looked thoughtful, but went back to his paper,
and it wasn't until lunchtime that he returned to the subject.
He brought his drink across from the bar and stopped in front
of Errol's chair, waiting until he had finished telling his latest
story and had become aware that Cattenach was regarding him
stonily. The second-in-command was a lean, craggy, normally
taciturn man with a rat-trap mouth that made him look like
one of the less amiable Norman barons.

'You may be interested to know,' he said curtly, 'that the
"kites" you shot this morning were the Brigadier's pet hawks.'

There was a startled silence, in which the Padre said: 'Oh,
cracky good gracious!', and Errol cocked an incredulous
eyebrow. 'What are you talking about – hawks? Since when
do hawks stooge around loose, like crows!'

'They were tame hawks – something unique, I believe,' said
Cattenach, enjoying himself in his own grim fashion. 'A gift
to the Brigadier from King Idris, after the desert campaign.

Quite irreplaceable, of course, as well as being priceless. And you shot them. Congratulations.'

Well, you and I or any normal person would at this point have lowered the head in the hands, giving little whimpering cries punctuated by stricken oaths and appeals for advice. Not Errol, though; he just downed his drink and observed lightly:

'Well, why didn't he keep them on a leash? I thought it was usual to put hoods over their heads.'

We stared at the man, and someone protested: 'Oh, come off it, Errol!', while Cattenach went crimson and began to inflate.

'Is that all you've got to say?' he demanded, and Errol regarded him with maddening calm.

'What d'you expect me to say? I'm sorry, of course.' If he was he certainly didn't sound it. 'I'll send the old boy a note of apology.' He gave Cattenach a nod that was almost dismissive. 'Okay?'

'Just . . . that?' growled Cattenach, ready to burst.

'I can't very well do anything else,' said Errol, and picked up a magazine. 'Unless you expect me to rend my garments.' To do him justice, I believe that if anyone else had brought him the glad news, he'd have shown more concern, but he wasn't giving Cattenach that satisfaction – just his cool half-smile, and the second-in-command had to struggle to keep a grip on himself in the face of that dumb insolence. He took a breath, and then said with deliberation:

'The trouble with you, and what makes you such an unpleasant regimental liability, is that while most of us couldn't care more, you just couldn't care less.'

No one had ever heard Cattenach, who was normally a quiet soul, talk with such controlled contempt – and in the mess, of all places. A little flush appeared on Errol's cheek, and he rose from his chair, but only to look Cattenach in the eye and say:

'You know, that's extremely well put. I think I'll enter it in the mess book.'

That was when I thought Cattenach was going to hit him – or try to, because Errol, for all his composure, was balanced like a cat. Suddenly it was very ugly, the Padre was making anxious noises, and the Adjutant was starting forward, and then Cattenach turned abruptly on his heel and stalked out. There was a toe-curling silence – and of course I had to open my big mouth, heaven knows why, unless I thought it was time to raise the conversation to a higher plane.

'Why can't you bloody well wrap up, just for once?' I demanded, and was told by the Adjutant to shut up. 'I think you've said enough, too,' he told Errol. 'Right – who's for lunch?'

'I am, for one,' said Errol, unabashed. 'Drama always gives me an appetite,' and he sauntered off to the dining-room, leaving us looking at each other, the Padre muttering about the pride of Lucifer, and the M.O., after a final inhalation of the Talisker, voicing the general thought.

'Yon's a bad man,' he said. 'Mercy is not in him.'

That was a fact, I thought. Not only had he shown a callous disregard for the feelings of the Brigadier, bereaved of his precious pets, he had strained the egalitarian conventions of the mess to the limit in his behaviour to Cattenach – who, mind you, had been making a meal of his own dislike for Errol. It was all enough to make one say Tach!', as my grandmother used to exclaim in irritation, and lunch was taken in general ill-temper – except for Errol, who ate a tranquil salad and lingered over his coffee.

And then such trivia ceased to matter, for at 2.15 came the sudden alarm call from the Police Commissioner to say that the unrest which had been simmering in the native quarter had suddenly burst into violence: a mob of Arab malcontents and bazaar-wallahs were rioting in the Suk, pillaging shops and fire-raising; one of the leading nationalist agitators, Marbruk es-Salah, was haranguing a huge gathering near the Yassid Market, and it looked only a matter of time before they would be spilling out of the Old City and rampaging towards the European suburbs. Aid to the civil power was a matter of urgency – which meant that at 2.45 the two three-ton trucks bearing the armed might of 12 Platoon pulled up on the great dusty square east of the Kantara Bridge, and I reviewed the force with which I was expected to plug that particular outlet from the native quarter.

In theory, the plan for containing unrest was simple. The Old City, an impossible warren of tall crumbling buildings and hundreds of crooked streets and narrow alleys, spread out like a huge fan from the waterfront; beyond the semi-circular edge of the fan lay the European suburbs of the Italian colonial era, girdling the squalid Old City from sea to sea in a luxurious crescent of apartment buildings, bungalows, shops, restaurants, and broad streets – a looter's paradise for the teeming thousands of the Old City's inhabitants, if they ever invaded in force. To make sure they didn't, the 24 infantry platoons of our battalion and the Fusiliers were supposed to block every outlet from the Old City to the New Town, and since these were innumerable, careful disposition of forces was vital.

Kantara was an easy one, since here there was an enormous ditch hemming the native town like a moat, and the only way across was the ancient bridge (which is what Kantara means) which we were guarding. It was a structure of massive stones which had been there before the Caesars, twenty feet broad between low parapets, and perhaps twice as long. From where I stood on the open ground at its eastern end, I could look across the bridge at a peaceful enough scene: a wide market-place in which interesting Orientals were going about their business of loafing, wailing, squatting in the dust, or snoozing in the shadows of the great rickety tenements and ruined walls of the Old City. Behind me were the broad, palm-lined boulevards of the modern resort area, with dazzling white apartments and pleasant gardens, a couple of hotels and restaurants, and beyond them the hospital and the beach club. It looked like something out of a travel brochure, with a faint drift of Glenn Miller on the afternoon air – and then you turned back to face the ancient stronghold of the Barbary Corsairs, a huge festering slum crouched like a malignant genie above the peaceful European suburb, and felt thankful for the separating moat-ditch with only that single dusty causeway across it.

'Nae bother,' said Sergeant Telfer. Like me, he was thinking that thirty Jocks with fifty rounds apiece could have held that bridge against ten times the native population – provided they were empowered to shoot, that is. Which, if it came to the point, would be up to me. But we both knew that was highly unlikely, by all accounts the trouble was at the western end of the Old City, where most of our troops were concentrated. Kantara was very much the soft option, which was presumably why one platoon had been deemed enough. They hadn't thought it worth while giving us a radio, even.

Since it was all quiet, I didn't form the platoon up, but showed them where, in the event of trouble, they would take up extended line, facing the bridge and about fifty yards from it, out of range of any possible missiles from beyond the ditch. Then they sat in the shade of the trucks, smoking and gossiping, while I prowled about, watching the market for any signs of disturbance, vaguely aware of the discussion on current affairs taking place behind me.

'Hi, Corporal Mackie, whit are the wogs gettin' het up aboot, then?'

'Independence.' Mackie had been a civil servant, and was the platoon intellectual. 'Self-government by their own political leaders. They don't like being under Allied occupation.'

'Fair enough, me neither. Whit's stoppin' them?'

'You are, McAuslan. You're the heir to the pre-war Italian government. So do your shirt up and try to look like it.'

'Me? Fat chance! The wogs can hiv it for me, sure'n they can, Fletcher? It's no' my parish. Hi, corporal, whit wey does the government no' let the wogs have it?'

'Because they'd make a bluidy mess o' it, dozy.' This was Fletcher, who was a sort of Churchillian Communist. 'They're no' fit tae run a mennodge. Look behind ye – that's civilisation. Then look ower there at that midden o' a toon: that's whit the wogs would make o' it. See?'

So much for Ibn Khaldun and the architects of the Alhambra. Some similar thought must have stirred McAuslan's strange mental processes, for he came out with a nugget which, frankly, I wouldn't have thought he knew.

'Haud on a minnit. Fletcher – it was wogs built the Pyramids, wisn't it? That's whit the Padre says. Aye, weel, there ye are. They cannae be that dumb.'

'Those werenae wogs, ya mug! Those were Ancient Egyptians.'

'An Egyptian's a wog! Sure'n he is. So don't gi' me the acid, Fletcher. Anyway, if Ah wis a wog, Ah wid dam' soon get things sortit oot aboot indamapendence. If Ah wis a wog—'

'That's a helluva insult tae wogs, right enough. Ah can just see ye! Hey, fellas, meet Abu ben McAuslan, the Red Shadow. Ye fancy havin' a harem. McAuslan? Aboot twenty belly-dancers like Big Aggie frae the Blue Heaven?' And Fletcher began to hum snake-charmer music, while his comrades speculated coarsely on McAuslan, Caliph of the Faithful, and I looked through the heat haze at the Old City, and thought about cool pints in the dim quiet of the mess ante-room.

It came, as it so often does, with daunting speed. There was a distant muttering from the direction of the Old City, like a wind getting up, and the market-place beyond the bridge was suddenly empty and still in the late afternoon sun. Then the muttering changed to a rising rumble of hurrying feet and harsh voices growing louder. I shouted to Telfer to fall in, and from the mouth of a street beyond the market-place a native police jeep came racing over the bridge. It didn't stop; I had a glimpse of a brown face, scared and staring, under a peaked cap, and then the jeep was gone in a cloud of dust, heading up into the New Town. So much for the civil power. The platoon were fanning out in open order, each man with his rifle and a canvas bandolier at his waist; they stood easy, and Telfer turned to me for orders. I was gazing across the bridge, watching Crisis arrive in a frightsome form, and realising with sudden dread that there was no one on God's green earth to deal with it, except me.

It's quite a moment. You're taking it easy, on a sunny afternoon, listening to the Jocks chaffing – and then out of the alleys two hundred yards away figures are hurrying, hundreds of them, converging into a great milling mob, yelling in unison, waving their fists, starting to move towards you. A menace beats off them that you can feel, dark glaring faces, sticks brandished, robes waving and feet churning up the dust in clouds before them, the rhythmic chanting sounding like a barbaric war-song – and you fight down the panic and turn to look at the khaki line strung out either side of you, the young faces set under the slanted bonnets, the rifles at their sides, standing at ease – waiting for you. If you say the word, they'll shoot that advancing mob flat, and go on shooting, because that's what they're trained to do, for thirty bob a week – and if that doesn't stop the opposition, they'll stand and fight it out on the spot as long as they can, because that's part of the conscript's bargain, too. But it's entirely up to you – and there's no colonel or company commander to instruct or advise. And it doesn't matter if you've led a section in warfare, where there is no rule save survival; this is different, for these are not the enemy – by

God, I thought, you could have fooled me; I may know it, but I'll bet they don't – they are civilians, and you must not shoot unless you have to, and only you can decide that, so make up your mind, Dand, and don't dawdle: you're getting nine quid a week, after all, so the least you can do is show some initiative.

'Charge magazines, Sar'nt Telfer! Corporals, watch those cut-offs! Mackie – if McAuslan gets one up the spout I'll blitz you! Here – I'll do it!' I grabbed McAuslan's rifle, jammed down the top round, closed the cut-off, rammed home the bolt, clicked the trigger, and thumbed on the safety-catch while he squawked indignantly that he could dae it, he wisnae stupid, him. I shoved his rifle into his hand and looked across the bridge again.

The rattle of the charging magazines had checked them for barely an instant; now they were coming on again, a solid mass of humanity choking the square, half-hidden by the dust they were raising. Out front there was a big thug in a white burnous and red tarboosh who turned to face the mob, chanting some slogan, before turning to lead them on, punching his arms into the air. There were banners waving in the front rank – and I knew this was no random gang of looters, but an organised horde bent on striking where they knew the forces of order were weakest – I had thirty Jocks between them and that peaceful suburb with its hotels and pleasant homes and hospital. Over their heads I could see smoke on the far side of the market . . .

'Fix bayonets. Sarn't Telfer!' I shouted, and on his command the long sword-blades zeeped out of the scabbards, the locking-rings clicked, and the hands cut away to the sides. 'Present!' and the thirty rifles with their glittering points went forward.

That stopped them, dead. The big thug threw up his arms, and they halted, yelling louder than ever and shaking fists and clubs, but they were still fifty yards from the bridge. They eddied to and fro, milling about, while the big burnous exhorted them, waving his arms – and I moved along the line, forcing myself to talk as quietly as the book says you must, saying the proper things in the proper order.

'Easy does it, children. Wait for it. If they start to come on, you stand fast, understand? Nobody moves – except Fletcher, Macrae, Duncan, and Souness. You four, when I say 'Load!', will put one round up the spout – but don't fire! Not till I tell you.' They had rehearsed it all before, the quartet of marksmen had been designated, but it all had to be repeated. 'If I say "Over their heads, fire!", you all take aim, but only those four will fire on the word. Got it? Right, wait for it . . . easy does it . . . take Blackie's name, Sarn't Telfer, his bayonet's filthy . . . wait for it . . .'

It's amazing how you can reassure yourself, by reassuring other people. I felt suddenly elated, and fought down the evil hope that we might have to fire in earnest – oh, that's an emotion that comes all too easily – and walked along the front of the line, looking at the faces – young and tight-lipped, all staring past me at the crowd, one or two sweating, a few Adam's apples moving, but not much. The chanting suddenly rose to a great yell, and the crowd was advancing again, but slowly this time, a few feet at a time, stopping, then coming on, the big burnous gesticulating to his followers, and then turning to stare in my direction. You bastard, I thought – you know what it's all about! We can fire over your head till we're blue in the face, but it won't stop you – you'll keep coming, calling our bluff, daring us to let fly. Right, son, if anyone gets it, you will . . .

They were coming steadily now, but still slowly; I judged their distance from the bridge and shouted: 'Four men – load! Remainder, stand fast! Wait for it . . .'

A stone came flying from the crowd, falling well short, but followed by a shower of missiles kicking up the dust ahead of us. I walked five slow paces out in front of the platoon – believe it or not, that can make a mob hesitate – and waited; when the first stone reached me, I would give the order to fire over their heads. If they still kept coming, I would take a rifle and shoot the big burnous, personally, wounding if possible – and if that didn't do it, I would order the four marksmen to take out four rioters. Then, if they charged us, I would order rapid fire into the crowd . . .

By today's standards, you may think that atrocious. Well, think away. My job was to save that helpless suburb from the certain death and destruction that mob would wreak if they broke through. So retreat was impossible on that head, never mind that soldiers cannot run from a riot and if I ordered them to retire I'd never be able to look in a mirror again. But above all these good reasons was the fact that if I let that horde of yelling maniacs reach us, some of my Jocks would die – knifed or clubbed or trampled lifeless, and I hadn't been entrusted with thirty young Scottish lives in order to throw them away. That was the real clincher, and why I would loose up to three hundred rounds rapid into our attackers if I had to. It gets terribly simple when you're looking it in the face.

The shouting rose to a mad crescendo, they were a bare thirty yards from the bridge, the burnous was leaping like a dervish, you could sense the rush coming, and without looking round I shouted:

'Four men – over their heads . . . fire!'

It crashed out like one report. One of the flag-poles jerked crazily – Fletcher playing Davy Crockett – and the crowd reared back like a horse at a hedge. For a splendid moment I thought they were going to scatter, but they didn't: the big burnous was playing a stormer, grabbing those nearest, rallying them, urging them forward with voice and gesture. My heart sank as I took Telfer's rifle, for I was going to have to nail that one, unarmed civilian that he was, and I found myself remembering my awful closing line: 'Well, that's that' from that ghastly play in Bangalore . . .

'Having fun, Dand,' said a voice at my elbow, and there was Errol beside me, cupping his hands as he lit a cigarette. Thank God, reinforcements at the last minute – and then I saw the solitary jeep parked by the trucks. Nobody else. He drew on his cigarette, surveying the crowd.

'What'll you do?' he asked conversationally – no suggestion of assuming command, you notice; what would *I* do.

'Shoot that big beggar in the leg!'

'You might miss,' he said, 'and sure as fate we'd find a dead nun on the ground afterwards. Or a four-year-old orphan.' He gave me his lazy grin. 'I think we can do better than that.'

'What the hell are you on, Errol?' I demanded, in some agitation. 'Look, they're going to—'

'Not to panic. I'd say we've got about thirty seconds.' He swung round. 'You, you, and you – run to my jeep! Get the drum of signal wire, the cutters, the mortar box, and double back here – now! Move!'

'Are you taking command?'

'God, you're regimental. I'll bet you were a pig of a lance-jack. Here, have a fag – go on, you clot, the wogs are watching, wondering what the hell we're up to.'

The lean brown face with its trim Colman moustache was smiling calmly under the cocked bonnet; his hand was rock-steady as he held out the cigarette-case – it was one of those hammered silver jobs you got in Indian bazaars, engraved with a map and erratic spelling. And he was right: the yelling had died down, and they were watching us and wondering . . .

Three Jocks came running, two with the heavy drum of wire between them on its axle, the third (McAuslan, who else?) labouring with the big metal mortar box, roaring to them tae haud on, he couldnae manage the bluidy thing, damn it tae hell . . .

'Listen, Dand,' said Errol. 'Run like hell to the bridge, unrolling the wire. When you get there, cut it. Open the mortar box – it's empty – stick the end of the wire inside, close the lid. Got it? Then scatter like billy-be-damned. Move!'

Frankly, I didn't get it. He must be doolaly. But if the Army teaches you anything, it's to act on the word, no questions asked – which is how great victories are won (and great disasters caused).

'Come on!' I yelled, and went for the bridge like a stung whippet, followed by the burdened trio, McAuslan galloping in the rear demanding to know whit the hell was gaun on. Well, I didn't know, for one – all I had room for was the appalling knowledge that I was running straight towards several hundred angry *bazaar-wallahs* who were bent on pillage and slaughter. Fortunately, there isn't time to think in fifty yards, or to notice anything except that the ragged ranks ahead seemed to be stricken immobile, if not silent: the big burnous, out in front, was stock-still and staring, while his followers raged behind him, presumably echoing McAuslan's plea for enlightenment. I had a picture of yelling, hostile black faces as I skidded to a standstill at the mouth of the bridge; the two Jocks with the wire were about ten yards behind, closing fast as they unreeled the long shining thread behind them; staggering with them, his contorted face mouthing horribly over the mortar box clasped in his arms, was Old Insanitary himself. He won by a short head, sprawling headlong and depositing the box at my feet.

'The cutters!' I snapped, as he grovelled, blaspheming, in the dust. 'The cutters, McAuslan!'

'Whit cutters?' he cried, crouching like Quasimodo in the pillory, and then his eyes fell on the menacing but still irresolute mob a scant thirty yards away. 'Mither o' Goad! Wull ye look at yon? The cutters – Ah've goat them! Here th'are, sur – Ah've goat them!' He pawed at his waist – and the big wire cutters, which he had thrust into the top of his shorts for convenient carriage, slid out of view. And it is stark truth: one handle emerged from one leg of his shorts, the second handle from the other.

I'm not sure what I said, but I'll bet only dogs could hear it. Fortunately MacLeod, one of the wire-carriers, was a lad of resource and rare self-sacrifice; he hurled himself at McAuslan, thrust his hand down the back of his shorts, and yanked viciously. There was an anguished wail and a fearsome rending of khaki, the cutters were dragged free, and as I grabbed them in one hand and the wire in the other. McAuslan's recriminations seemed to fill the afternoon. He was, it appeared, near ruined, an' see his bluidy troosersi there wis nae need for it. MacLood, an' ye'll pey for them an' chance it, handless teuchter that ye are . . .

For some reason that I'll never understand, it steadied me. I clipped the wire, and as I unsnapped the mortar box catches it dawned on me what Errol was up to, the lunatic – and it seemed only sensible to lift the lid slowly, push in the wire, fumble artistically in the interior before closing the lid as though it were made of porcelain, and spare two seconds for a calculating look at the bewildered mob beyond the bridge. To my horror, they were advancing – I looked back at the platoon, fifty yards off, and sure enough Errol was kneeling at the other end of the wire, which was attached to a metal container – a petrol jerry-can, as it turned out. He had one hand poised as though to work a plunger; with the other he waved an urgent signal.

'Get out of it!' I yelled, and as MacLeod and his mate scattered and ran I seized McAuslan by the nape of his unwashed neck, running him protesting from the bridge before throwing him and myself head-long.

It worked. You had only to put yourself in the shoes of

Burnous and Co. to see that it was bound to. We weren't wiring things up for the good of their health, they must have reasoned: that sinister mortar box lying on the bridge must be packed with death and destruction. When I had rolled over and got the sand out of my eyes they were in full retreat across the market square, a great disordered rabble intent on getting as far as possible from that unknown menace. In a few seconds an army of rioters had been turned into a rout – and the man responsible was sitting at his ease on the jerry-can, giving me an airy wave of his cigarette-holder as I trudged back to the platoon.

'You mad son-of-a-bitch!' I said, with deep respect, and he touched his bonnet in acknowledgement.

'Psychology, laddie. Not nearly as messy as shooting poor wee wogs, you bloodthirsty subaltern, you. That would never have done – not on top of the Brigadier's hawks. Not all in one day. Cattenach would have had kittenachs.' He chuckled and stood up, smoothing his immaculate khaki drill, and shaded his eyes to look at the distant remnant of the riot milling disconsolately on the far side of the market-place.

'Aye, weel, they'll no' be back the day,' he said, imitating a Glasgow wifey. 'So. Where will they go next, eh? Tell me that, MacNeill of Barra – or of Great Western Road, W.2. Where . . . will . . . they . . . go?'

'Home?' I suggested.

'Don't you believe it, cock. Marbmk wasn't with 'em – he'll still be holding forth to the main body down at Yassid. Oh, if we'd lost the bridge he'd have been over sharp enough, with about twenty thousand angry wogs at his back. But now . . . I wonder.'

I was still digesting the outrageous bluff he'd pulled. I indicated the jerry-can and the string of wire running to the bridge. 'Do you usually carry that kind of junk in your jeep?' I asked, and he patted me on the shoulder, as with a half-wit.

'I'm the Intelligence Officer, remember? All-wise, all-knowing, all full of bull. Oh, look – soldiers!' Half a dozen Fusilier trucks were speeding down the New Town boulevard towards us, and Errol shook his head in admiration as he climbed into his jeep.

'Locking the stable door,' said he, and winked at me. 'I'd better go and see which one they've left open. Buy you a drink at Renucci's, nine o'clock, okay?' He waved and revved off with a horrific grinding of metal, changing gears with his foot, which takes lots of practice.

When I showed the Fusilier Company Commander the mortar box with its fake wire he didn't believe it at first, and then congratulated me warmly; when I told him it had been Errol's idea he grunted and said, 'Oh, him', which I thought both ungrammatical and ungrateful, and told me I was to withdraw my platoon to the hospital. So I passed the remainder of that fateful day chatting up the nursing staff, drinking tea, and listening with interest to Private McAuslan telling Fletcher that it was a bluidy good job that bomb hadnae gone off on the bridge, because me an' Darkie an' MacLood an' Dysart would hiv' got blew up, sure'n we would.

'It wisnae a bomb, ye bap-heid! He wis kiddin' the wogs. There wis nothin' tae it.'

'Are you tellin' me, Fletcher? Ah wis there! Ah cairrit the bluidy thing! Help ma Goad, if Ah'd known! That man Errol's a menace, so he is; he coulda goat us a' killed, me an' Darkie an' MacLood an' Dysart . . .' You can fool some of the people all of the time.

It was only when the alert was over, and I had sent the platoon back to barracks with Telfer and foregathered at Renucci's for the promised drink with Errol, that I learned what had been happening elsewhere. It had been high drama, and the clientele of Renucci's bar and grill were full of it.

After our episode at the bridge, things had fallen out as Errol had foreseen: Marbruk es-Salah, after whipping up his followers at Yassid Market, had launched them at dusk through the old Suk slave-market in an attempt to invade the business area of the New Town, two miles away from Kantara. Part of the Suk had been burned and the rest pillaged, and the enormous crowd would undoubtedly have broken out with a vengeance if they had not suddenly lost their leader.

'Nobody seems to know exactly what happened,' a stout civilian was telling the bar, 'except that Marbruk was obviously making for the weakest point in the security cordon – you won't credit it, but there wasn't even a constable guarding the Suk Gate. God knows what would have happened if they'd got beyond it; sheer devastation and half the New Town up in smoke, I expect. Anyway, that's when Marbruk got shot—'

'But you said there were no troops there,' someone protested.

'Nor were there. It seems he was shot *inside* the Suk. What with the uproar and the fact that it was dark, even his immediate henchmen didn't realise it at first, and when they did – sheer pandemonium. But they'd lost all sense of direction, thank God – otherwise we wouldn't be standing here, I daresay!'

'Who on earth did it? Did the police get him?'

'You're joking, old boy! In the Suk, during a riot, at night? I should think our gallant native constabulary are too busy drinking the assassin's health.'

'I heard they got Marbruk's body out . . .'

I lost the rest of it in the noise, and at that moment Errol slipped on to the stool next to me and asked what I was drinking.

'Antiquary – hang on, I want to hear this.'

'Evening, Carlo.' Errol rapped the bar. 'Antiquary and Glenfiddich and two waters, at your good pleasure.' He seemed in fine fettle, glancing bright-eyed over the crowd. 'What's to do?'

'Marbruk's dead.'

'You don't say? That's a turn-up.' He whistled softly, fitting a cigarette into his holder. 'How'd it happen?'

I indicated the stout civilian, who was continuing.

'. . . probably one of his political rivals. You know what they're like – pack of jackals. With Marbruk gone, there'll be a fine scramble among his lieutenants.'

'It wasn't one of the gang with him,' said a police captain. 'Burgess saw the body and talked to informers. Shot twice, head and heart, almost certainly with a rifle, from a roof-top.'

'Good God! A sniper? Doesn't sound like a *bazaar-wallah*!'

'Whoever it was, here's to him,' said the stout civilian. 'He probably saved the town in the nick of time.'

Our whisky arrived and Errol studied the pale liquid with satisfaction. 'First today. *Slainte mhath*.' He sipped contentedly. 'Yes, that's the good material. Had dinner?'

'Too late for me, thanks. I'll have a sandwich in the mess. I've got a report to write.'

'How Horatius kept the bridge?' He grinned sardonically. 'You can leave me out of it.'

'Don't be soft! It was your idea that did it!'

'They won't like it any better for that. Oh, well, please yourself.'

'Look, if it wasn't a rival wog, who was it?' someone was exclaiming. 'It can't have been police or military, without authority – I mean to say, it's simple murder.'

'And just Marbruk – the king-pin. A political rival would have tried to knock out that right-hand man of his, Gamal Whatsit, wouldn't he?'

'Well, perhaps . . . or it may just have been a personal feud . . .'

Errol was lounging back on his stool, studying the menu on the bar, but I had the impression he was listening, not reading. I noticed that like me he was still in K.D., belt, and revolver, and less spruce than usual: there was a smudge of oil on his shirt and one sleeve was dirty. He looked tired but otherwise at peace with the world.

'When you've finished inspecting me, MacNeill,' he said, still scanning the menu, 'how about getting them in again?'

'Sorry. Two more, Carlo.'

'Anyway, it was a damned fine shot,' said the police captain. 'Two damned fine shots – and as you say, just in time, from our point of view.'

'You won't break a leg looking for the murderer, eh?'

'Oh, there'll have to be an inquiry, of course . . .'

'I'll bet there will,' Errol murmured, and laughed softly – and something in the sound chilled my spine as I put my glass to my lips. Sometimes a sudden, impossible thought hits you, and in the moment it takes to swallow a sip of whisky you know, beyond doubt, that it's not only possible, but true. It fitted all too well . . . 'killing Huns with cheese-wire by night' . . . the expertise with small arms . . . the rumours of anti-terrorist brutalities in Palestine . . . the scientific destruction of a boxing opponent . . . the cold-blooded nerve of his bluff at Kantara Bridge . . . all that I knew of the man's character . . .

'Steak, I think,' said Errol, closing the menu. 'About a ton of Chateaubriand garni – that's parsley on top, to you – preceded by delicious tomato soup. Sure I can't tempt you? What's up laddie, you look ruptured?' The whimsical glance, the raised eyebrow, and just for an instant the smile froze on the handsome face. He glanced past me at the debating group, and then the smile was back, the half-mocking regard that was almost a challenge. 'The cop's right, don't you agree? A damned good shot. You used to be a sniper – what d'you think?'

'Someone knew his business.'

He studied me, and nodded. 'Just as well, wasn't it? So . . . as our stout friend would say – here's to him.' He raised his glass. 'Okay?'

'*Slàinte*,' I said, automatically. There was no point in saying anything else.

We drank, and Errol turned on his stool to the dining-room arch immediately behind him. A little Italian head-waiter, full of consequence, was bowing to a couple in evening dress and checking his booking-board.

'Table for one, please,' said Errol, and the little man bared his teeth in a professional smile.

'Certainly, sir, this way—' His face suddenly fell, and he straightened up. 'I regret, sir – for dinner we have to insist on the neck-tie.'

'You don't mean it? What, after a day like this? Oh, come off it!'

'I am sorry, sir.' The head-waiter was taking in Errol's informal, not to say untidy, appearance. 'It is our rule.'

'All right, lend me a, tie, then,' said Errol cheerfully.

'I am sorry, sir.' The waiter was on his dignity. 'We have no ties.'

Errol sat slowly upright on his stool, giving him a long, thoughtful look, and then to my horror laid a hand on his revolver-butt. The head-waiter squeaked and jumped, I had a vision of inkpots being shot off desks – and then Errol's hand moved from the butt up the thin pistol lanyard looped round his neck, and smoothly tightened its slip-knot into a tie.

'Table for one?' he asked sweetly, and the head-waiter hesitated, swallowed, muttered: 'This way, sir,' and scurried into the dining-room. Errol slid off his stool, glass in hand, and gave me a wink.

'Blind 'em with flannel, laddie. It works every time.'

He finished his drink without haste, and set his glass on the bar. 'Well . . . almost every time.' He gave his casual nod and sauntered into the dining-room.

The investigation of Marbruk es-Salah's murder came to nothing. There was no more nationalist unrest until long after our departure, when a republic was established which turned into a troublesome dictatorship – so troublesome that forty years later the American air force raided it in reprisal for terrorist attacks, bombing our old barracks. This saddened me, because I had been happy there, and it seemed wasteful, somehow, after all the trouble we'd had just preserving that pleasant city from riot and arson and pillage. I'm not blaming the Americans; they were doing what they thought best – just as we had done. Just as Errol had done.

I lost sight of him when I was demobilised; he was still with the battalion then, going his careless way, raising hackles and causing trouble. Many years later, a wire-photo landed on my newspaper desk, and there he was among a group of Congo mercenaries; the moustache had gone and the hairline had receded, but there was no mistaking the cigarette-holder and the relaxed, confident carriage; even with middle-aged spread beneath his flak-jacket, he still had style. Yes, I thought, that's where you would end up. You see, there's no place for people like Errol in a normal, peace-time world; they just don't belong. Their time lay between the years 1939 and 1945 – and even then they sometimes didn't fit in too comfortably. But I wonder if we'd have won the war without them.

The Mourners from 19D
(1978)

James Allan Ford

After the funeral we went for a drink. Davie's widow told us
that we would be welcome at the house, but Alec said that we
would have to be getting back to work, and the rest of us just
shook hands with her. Although we had all known Davie well
enough, none of us except Alec had ever visited him at home,
and I suppose that even Alec would have felt like a stranger if
we had accepted her invitation and gone back to the house
with the folk who had gathered together, like relations, close to
the grave. He had stood with the rest of us during the ceremony,
on the gravel path, where I could hardly hear the minister and

could not see the coffin being lowered. We stood in a row, the five of us, as if we were drawn up for roll-call at Camp 19D.

The day was blustery, with a north-east wind blowing up from the Firth of Forth and scattering thin showers of snow over Edinburgh. My stomach was grumbling with the cold, and I was glad when we were on the move again, following the other mourners out of the cemetery. Just as we had formed up in line for the ceremony without Alec or anybody else suggesting it, so we brought up the rear of the procession out of the cemetery without anybody deciding out loud when we should leave, and I am not sure whether we were showing respect to Davie's kin or just thinking of Fergus, who lost a leg at 19D and has never since been able to walk far or fast.

For longer than was comfortable we were gripped by a silence which, I suppose, came from memories of Davie and the thought of death and the stiffness that slows down even fitter men than Fergus after they have been standing for a time in the cold. At 19D, which was in the north of Japan, you could become so stiff standing outside the hut for morning and evening roll-call in the winter that you had to clench your fists, to bunch up your will-power, before you could move away after Alec shouted out the order to dismiss. There was a kind of reluctance in you as well as a stiffness, and I believe that freezing may be one of the easiest ways to death. One winter night at 19D an American called Chuck Stormer was tied to a stake as punishment for stealing a pack of Japanese tobacco from the camp office, and in the morning he was as stiff as the stake and as dead, and his face was peaceful.

We started talking before we reached the cemetery gates but, although we had not seen each other for a long time, we did not at first say much about ourselves. Our minds were still on Davie.

'How old a man was he?' asked MacAndrew, ex-sergeant and work-party leader at 19D. We had called him Big Mac until

317

we were moved to 19D, where we nicknamed him 'Hancho',
which seemed to mean 'ganger'. He was one of the few big
men who had survived. The bigger you were, the less chance
you had of keeping yourself alive on a daily diet of two bowls
of millet and rat shit and two cups of salted water with a few
shreds of vegetable floating in it. He was still a big man, tall
and straight, but there was not enough of him to fill his skin,
which hung from his jaws and was rucked around his neck.

'About fifty-six,' said Alec. 'About the same age as myself.'

'Only fifty-six?' Fergus stopped for a rest. 'And what sort of
disability pension was he getting?'

I could have answered that, for Davie and I sometimes met
at the Ministry office when our pensions were being reviewed.
But I let Alec answer.

And I had a fair idea of what Fergus would say next, for he
had always been a grumbler. Even in a place like 19D where
everybody had grumbled, his bitching and binding had stood
out enough to make him a byword. If you ever had a stroke of
luck, like getting a cigarette from one of the Japanese civilians
who laboured alongside us in the foundry, someone was sure to
take you down a peg by saying: 'Only one? That's not enough
for Fergus.' And 'Enough for Fergus' came to mean twenty-
three meals a day (allowing time for sleeping) or a whole hutful
of Betty Grables (each with four breasts and four thighs) or, as
Alec put it, something else within the dreams of avarice.

'Only twenty per cent?' Fergus said. 'A man in his condition?'

Alec caught my eye but did not share my smile. 'Davie was
reasonably fit for most of his life,' he told Fergus.

'But it wasn't what you'd call a very long life,' said Fergus
sarcastically. 'And I don't see how anybody could deny that it
was 19D that wore him out early.'

Even if Fergus lives long enough to get a telegram from
the Palace, he will still be inclined to think that his time has been

cut short by 19D. But you cannot turn him aside now with a laugh and 'Not enough for Fergus.' We have not ridden him about his grumbling since his leg started to blacken in 19D.

'Well, it's all over,' said Hancho MacAndrew. 'The world's a different place. Most of the Japanese we knew will be dead themselves. It's maybe time we forgot some things.'

'Forgot?' Fergus seemed more astonished than angry. 'How can we forget things like that? How can we ever forget what those bastards did to us?'

Batty Dodds, who had a smell of whisky on his breath, spoke up. 'Slant-eyed yellow bastards,' he said, spitting the words out. Then he looked around us, grinning.

Another shower of snow came swirling up, and Alec opened his umbrella. 'Come on and have a drink,' he said in his officer's voice.

As we walked to the pub, I began to feel that I was not myself. It may just have been the break in my usual daily routine that made me slip out of my ordinary way of thinking and start seeing myself in much the same way as I saw the four other men from 19D. But I have broken my routine at other times without feeling this momentary freedom from my own skin. And I believe not only that I was experiencing something different from the distraction which often comes when you are left outside your habits but also that I was sharing the experience with the others. I believe that Batty's words had taken us all outside ourselves, that he had made us all feel our nearness to each other. We walked up the road in a silence that was no longer uncomfortable, the kind of silence that does not separate. We had suddenly fallen back into an old awareness of each other and did not have to keep talking like strangers.

I have never been a man to live in the past, to tell old soldier's stories in the regimental club, to attend reunions of prisoners-of-war. Alec himself once said in 19D, 'If we ever get out of this, I hope we'll find better things to do than remember it.' And I have always tried to find better things to do. After we came home, I did not even help Alec in his welfare work for other survivors who were in poorer health than we were, or out of work or still nearly out of their minds. When I left 19D, I left it all and kept walking away from it and tried never to stop walking away. Davie's funeral was the first thing that made me stop. There have been other funerals, plenty of them, but Davie's was the first I have attended. I went to it, I suppose, partly because of the kind of man he had been and partly because of the kind of man I had become, old enough and closely enough wrapped in my own affairs to look back without losing myself. But my memories had started running as soon as I met the four other at the cemetery gates and began to mark how little they had changed over the years. Then Batty, speaking up for the first time, speaking straight from 19D, made us feel for a few moments that nothing had changed.

The different camps I was in had different ways of life, different ways of reaching for survival. And, if anything could sum up 19D's ways, it was Batty's words, 'Slant-eyed yellow bastards.' There, the last camp I was in, it was hatred that kept us going, nothing but hatred for the Japanese. 19D was the worst of all the camps any of us had been in, not just because we were near the end of our tether but also because the Japanese were near the end of theirs. And the harder they tried to beat us into the ground, the harder we had to make our hatred. 'S E Y B,' we would say to their faces, and even the interpreter was foxed. 'Slant-eyed yellow bastards,' we would say among ourselves, until I could feel the hissing hatred of the words hurting me inside. Hating does hurt, and that was why, after we left 19D, I tried to stop hating, to stop hurting myself.

The pub was crowded with lunchtime drinkers, and we

could not find a corner for ourselves, a place where we could talk in private. We had to squeeze into an alcove that had already been taken over by a group of young men, youths really, who were none too keen to make room for us. A bunch of the kind who are all hair and prickles. It was a poor start to the occasion for men of our age, but the drink helped to loosen our tongues and we started asking about each other.

Fergus had a part-time job in an office on a building site. Hancho MacAndrew was no longer a commissionaire but had hopes of being taken on by a Government department as a temporary clerk; he is quite an educated man, Hancho. Alec, we all knew, was still a lawyer, and from the look of his clothes he was a good bit more prosperous than he had been as a lieutenant.

'And what about you, Batty?' asked Hancho.

Batty Dodds grinned and nodded. He has never minded being called 'Batty'. He has never much minded anything, except the Japanese. 'The Corporation,' he said.

Alec explained, 'Batty's working at one of the cleansing depots.'

'Heavy work?' asked Fergus.

'Heaviest in the whole place,' Batty boasted. 'I'm not one o' them long-haired boyos that can't get off their arses.'

He looked as strong as ever, although he was carrying a lot more fat. He had always, even in 19D, had the kind of strength that frightened me, that made him seem as if he would burst out of his skin one day. And he still knew the power that his strength gave him, for he grinned straight at the long-haired lads beside us when he spoke. He had taken more punishment from the Japanese than any other man in camp, and he had asked for a lot of it. He had lived his hatred in a way that was beyond the rest of us, and we had relieved some of the hurt of our hatred through him, watching how he provoked the guards, how he stood up to them when they screamed at him and slapped him and kicked him, when they beat him with sticks and rifle butts.

Then Alec, with an eye on the bully boys scowling at Batty, asked me what I was doing. He knew well enough the work I had come back to, and he knew that I was never one for chopping and changing. He was trying to ease Batty into the background rather than to find out anything about me, and I did not give him much of an answer.

'You had other ideas once,' he said, smiling,

'We all had great ideas then.'

There had been a time, before 19D, when we had helped to keep ourselves going by making plans, great plans, for what we were going to do after the war. But nothing came of my plans or, so far as I know, anybody else's.

'I was going to raise chickens,' Hancho recalled.

We used to be puzzled and tickled by that. None of us could see any connection between Big Mac and chickens.

Fergus butted in. 'If I'd kept both my legs—'

'See if you can get a chair for Fergus,' said Alec.

He was speaking to me, for I was nearest the tables and chairs at the other end of the pub. But Batty moved first, elbowing me and one of the lads aside as he went.

'Watch it, dad,' the lad warned him.

'Get stuffed,' said Batty cheerfully.

He brought a chair back for Fergus, who was still talking. 'I might have surprised you all. I knew where I was going.'

He was always going in circles. He would never be left out of the planning but could never settle on a plan of his own. He kept changing his mind about the future, as he kept foreseeing the snags of every way of life he could imagine.

'You think we haven't made enough of ourselves?' Hancho asked him.

'Well, have we?'

Hancho took no offence. 'I've sometimes wondered myself.' He emptied his glass. 'Maybe the wrong ones survived, eh? Think of young Williamson, the wee fellow from Gorebridge who could count three columns of figures at the same time. He'd have made something of himself if he'd lived.'

'We've done well enough ourselves,' said Alec. 'We've kept going.' He too drained his glass. 'And it's time I did just that – kept going. I'll have to get back to my work.'

But nobody else was quite ready to leave. We had come a long way – thirty years – to this meeting. And our minds were now quick with memory.

'We'll have a pint of beer,' Hancho suggested.

'Ach,' grumbled Fergus, 'you can't get the good old Edinburgh beer I used to dream about in 19D.'

While Alec and Hancho fetched the drinks, Fergus and Batty spoke of 19D. I was still thinking of Alec's words: 'We've done well enough. We've kept going.' With a whisky in my stomach and the sound of old familiar voices in my ears, I stood there comfortably aware of myself, a free man, thirty years and half a world away from 19D. I could feel the space I took up, the warmth I contained. The feeling of survival. And it took my mind back to the times in 19D when I would lie down on my mat and shut my eyes and put my hands over my ears and listen to the pulsing of my blood, the sound of my living.

'Aye, aye,' said Fergus, at the end of some story, 'how can we ever forget?'

Batty's face was bright with good humour and sweat. He had always sweated after drinking more than a mouthful of anything, and it was plain that he had been at the bottle before the funeral. I could understand that. I could remember how he had avoided looking at corpses. Only death itself had ever really frightened him.

'I don't forget,' he said. 'If I could lay my hands on some of them bastards—'

It struck me that, although they had survived, Fergus and Batty had never freed themselves. Nothing else in their experience had been bigger than the wooden fence with the barbed wire on top, and they still lived inside it, angry about what had happened to them but ready to boast about it, as survivors often do if they have nothing much else to boast about.

'I'll never forget the day,' said Fergus, 'when Takahashi and the guard with the celluloid teeth tried to batter you cold.'

'I showed them.'

'They had you down four or five times—'

'Six times.'

'And you kept coming back for more.'

I could remember that day and the lump of shared suffering and pride in my throat as Batty kept staggering to his feet and facing up to Takahashi and the guard. Anybody else would have had the sense to lie still the first time he was clubbed to the ground, but nobody else would have given us the kind of legend that helped to keep us going. I did not grudge Batty his moment of remembered glory. 'It was a great day,' I told him.

'I showed them.' Batty bulged inside his skin. 'And I'm still ready to show anybody else.' He was boasting now to the lads beside us.

They were a hard-faced bunch, although they were all rounder in the shoulders and shallower in the chest than Batty, the old soldier. It was understandable that they were angered by him. When we looked at him we could still see the young Batty whose slow mind and dour courage had helped to save us from the kind of humiliation that kills. But when they looked at him they would see nothing but a red-faced man in his fifties who was taking up too much room with his beef and his boasting.

'Look, dad,' said the one who had spoken to him before, 'why don't you go back to the old folks' home and sleep it off, like?'

Batty was still surprisingly quick on his feet. Before I could even think of diverting him, he had side-stepped me and whipped his arm around the lad's head and was squeezing it against his chest. 'Piss and wind,' he said savagely, 'there's nothing but piss and wind in your kind.'

The lad wriggled like a parcel of eels, lashing out blindly with arms and legs, trying to knock holes in Batty with fists and feet. His mates started to twitch, shuffling and hunching and jerking glances at each other, none of them ready to move in until all were ready. And I was trying to find something to say or do myself, when Alec was suddenly among us, snapping at Batty in a way that broke off the action. 'Give over,' was all that he said, but he said it as if he had a squad of regimental police at his back.

'Outside!' shouted the younger of the two men behind the bar. 'Outside, the lot of you!'

But it was Alec that Batty was listening to. He let the lad go. 'No harm done,' he mumbled, his anger used up. 'Just a bit of fun.'

'Outside!' shouted the barman again.

Alec stood there, facing Batty and the furious lad, his mouth tight, the reflection on his spectacles hiding his eyes from me. At his back there was only Hancho, holding a tray of beers and muttering, 'We've paid for them and we'll drink them.'

The young barman pushed in among us. 'Did you hear me? Or do I have to get the police to you?'

'We'll drink up and go,' answered Alec very coldly.

'Right. Just do that, as quick as you like.' The barman was nervous, and all the bossier for it. He turned on the gang of lads. 'I want you outside in two minutes flat. You get me?'

'Look, mac, we didn't start nothing.'

'Am I asking you who started something?' He was sweating, the young barman. He must have felt terribly tired afterwards. 'I'm telling you to get the hell out of here or I'll have the law on you.'

Then the other barman, the older one, called across in an easier tone of voice: 'Drink up and go, lads. I've my licence to think of.'

'And leave your glasses,' added the young one, to show that he could handle a thing like this without help.

They had less left to drink than we had, and they were moved out first, with the young barman at their heels like a terrier. But they took their time in walking to the door, swaggering a bit and lifting their heads in a way that I could understand, that anyone who had suffered humiliation could understand.

After the door had closed behind the lads, the barmen left us – the five short-haired, well-dressed, middle-aged customers – in peace.

'Some pub, this,' muttered Batty, with his head down.

'No harm done,' Hancho assured him. 'It was about time for us to be making tracks anyway.'

Nobody else was ready to say anything. We gulped our beer, and I took another look at them all. It struck me that I would never know anyone better than I had once known them and Davie and a few others in 19D. I had never had closer friends and was never likely to have. And yet we had seen very little of each other since the war. We had gone our own ways as soon as we had found ourselves free to choose our ways, and this was the first time in thirty years that the five of us had come together. It seemed to me that we should have more to say to each other, that we should not be standing apart.

Then Alec turned to me and, as he had often done in 19D, gave me the uneasy feeling that he could hear me thinking. 'You haven't had much to say for yourself.'

Before I could say anything for myself Hancho chipped in. 'He was always the quiet one, always a bit of a loner.'

Alec was watching me, and it began to irk me that he was still playing the officer, still trying to keep an eye on everybody.

He used to worry about my silences, because in a prison camp you can never be sure whether the quiet ones are holding their own. There is a kind of silence in which courage fails. 'Not really a loner, were you?' he said. 'You couldn't have done solitary any more than I could.'

I agreed. In 19D you needed somebody to pity besides yourself.

Batty lifted his head again. 'I done more time in that dog-house than anybody else,' he boasted.

When you were punished with solitary confinement you had to go down on your hands and knees in the yard and crawl through a hatch in one side of the wooden guardhouse and twist yourself into a space just big enough to hold you crouching with your legs bent tight against your trunk, and your head bowed over your knees.

But Alec was not ready to forgive Batty. 'Drink up,' he replied abruptly, and Batty raised his glass in submission.

Fergus grumbled that he needed more time to enjoy a pint.

'You're not the only one,' said Alec. 'Drink up and I'll see you all outside. I'd better make our apologies to the landlord before I go.'

Still playing the officer, still trying to take our responsibilities away from us. I think we were all beginning to feel the weight of his manner. We took our time about moving. We needed the time, not to empty our glasses, but to show him where we stood.

Batty, his face shining like a lamp, said, 'It was just a bit of fun.'

Hancho nodded to Alec. 'Best forgotten.'

Batty's eyes looked pitifully naked. 'I'll tell the man at the bar myself, if you like.'

But Alec, although he has always made much of Batty, has never really understood him. It's only the mind of a man that

Alec seems to understand, and Batty's mind explains very little, even to himself. He clapped Batty's arm and said to him, in a kinder voice, 'I'll see you outside.'

As he turned towards the bar, Batty and Fergus made for the door, but Hancho and I went to the toilet. It is easier to say some things in a toilet than in other places, but Hancho and I did not find much to say. I was wishing that I had not attended the funeral and muddled myself with memories, and he must have been thinking the same.

'It was all a long time ago,' he said.

I agreed.

'That's all that's worth remembering,' he muttered. 'That and the funny bits.'

I found a smile. 'There were a lot of funny bits.'

My mind was suddenly loud with remembered laughter. Through all the years of our imprisonment, even in 19D, we never forgot how to laugh. Sometimes we may have laughed at things that were more pitiful than funny, but prisons are places outside the ordinary world and you cannot expect prisoners to behave in ordinary ways.

'We should just have laughed at Batty today,' I suggested.

Hancho grinned. 'I can remember laughing once at the sight of his backside twisting and turning when he squeezed himself into that doghouse. That big backside of his looked more worried than his face did.'

We turned to each other, ready to laugh again. There were plenty of things to talk about now, true things, things that were worth remembering and would not hurt us.

'Come on,' said Hancho, 'We'll away out and raise a smile on their solemn faces.'

Alec was already on his way to the door, and he was outside before we caught up with him, standing by himself in a blinding swirl of snow that brought us up short and took the breath from me. Then we heard Fergus calling excitedly on Alec and, turning, we saw him hirpling towards us from the corner of the street.

'They got Batty!' he shouted.

We ran, all three of us. Round the corner we found Batty lying face down on the pavement.

'It was that bunch of young hooligans!' Fergus was grey-skinned and trembling. 'They were waiting for him, they all went for him.'

'The police,' said Alec, 'we'll have to get the police.'

Hancho knelt down on the pavement. 'Anything broken?'

'I'm all right,' muttered Batty, but his voice was thick with pain.

'We'll need an ambulance,' Hancho decided.

'We can phone from the pub,' said Alec. He was looking at me, but I was not looking at him. He swayed uncertainly on his feet, then hurried back to the pub himself.

'I'm all right,' Batty insisted. 'I could show them yet.' He tried to raise himself, and I saw that his face had gone as grey as Fergus's and that blood was dribbling from his nose and mouth.

'Lie still, man,' said Hancho. 'They've run away.'

'I could show them,' boasted Batty. He made another effort to rise, and Hancho and Fergus must have been remembering, as I was, how he had struggled to his feet time after time to face up to Takahashi and the guard. But that was a long time ago, and Batty could not raise himself from the pavement. He sank down, his broken breathing sounding like sobbing. And he too must have been thinking not of the young lads who had knocked him down but of Takahashi and the guard with the celluloid teeth, for he gasped out, with all the hatred left in him, 'Bastards – slant-eyed yellow bastards!'

We waited with him, and Hancho brushed the snow from his head.

Greater Love
(1984)

Iain Crichton Smith

He wore a ghostly white moustache and looked like a major in the First World War which is exactly what he had been. On our way to school – he being close to retiring age – he would tell me stories about the First World War and the Second World War, for he had been in both. As we were passing the chemist's shop he would be describing Passchendaele, walking along, stiff and erect, his eyes glittering behind his glasses.

'And there I was crouched in this trench, with my water bottle empty. I had somehow or another survived. All my good boys were dead, some of them up to their chests in mud.

The Jerries had got hold of our plans of attack, you see. What was I to do? I had to wait till night, that was clear. When the sun was just going down I crawled along the trench and then across No Man's Land. I met a Jerry and the struggle was fast and furious. I am afraid I had to use the bayonet. But the worst was not over yet, for one of my sentries fired on me. But I eventually managed to give him the password. After that I was all right.'

He would pause and then as we passed the ironmonger's he would start on another story. He taught Chemistry in the school and instead of telling his pupils about solutions or whatever they do in Chemistry, he would spend his time talking about the Marne or the Somme. He spoke more about the First World War than about the Second.

Once at a school party there was a quarrel between him and the Head of the English Department, who also had been in the First World War and believed that he had won it. He questioned a statement which Morrison had made. It was, I think, a question of a date, and they grew more and more angry, and wouldn't speak to each other after that for a year or more. As I quite liked both of them, it was difficult to know whose side to take.

The headmaster didn't know what to do with him, for parents came to the school continually to complain about his lessons, which as I have said consisted mostly of accounts of his adventures in France and Flanders. The extraordinary thing was that he never repeated a story: all his tales were realistic and detailed and one could almost believe that they had happened. Either these things had been experienced by him or they formed part of a huge mythology of legends which he had memorized, but that had happened to others. I was then Deputy Head of the school and it was my duty to see the parents and listen to their complaints.

'He will soon be retiring,' I would tell them soothingly, 'and he has been a good teacher in his time.' And they would answer,

'That's all very well but our children's education is being ruined. When are you going to speak to him?' I did in fact try to speak to him a few times but before I could start he was telling me another of his stories and I found, somehow or another, that there was no way in which I could introduce my complaint to him.

'There was an angel, you know, at Mons and I saw it. It was early morning and we were going over the top and we saw this figure with white wings bending over us from the sky. I thought it must have been an effect of the sun but it wasn't that. It was as if it was blessing us. We had our bayonets out and the light was flashing from them. I was in charge of a company at the time, the Colonel – Colonel Wilson – having been killed.'

This time I was so interested that I said to him, 'Are you quite sure that it was an angel? After all the rays of the sun streaming down, and you I presume being in an excited frame of mind . . . ?'

'No,' he said, 'it wasn't that. It was definitely an angel. I am quite sure of that. I could actually see its eyes.' And he turned to me. 'They were so compassionate, you have no idea what they looked like. You could never forget them.'

In those days we had lines and the pupils would assemble in the quadrangle in front of the main door, and Morrison loved the little military drill so much that we gave him the duty most of the time. He would make them dress, keeping two paces between the files, and they would march into the school in an orderly manner.

A young bearded teacher called Cummings, who was always bringing educational books into the staff-room, didn't like this militarism at all. One day he said to me, 'He's teaching them to be soldiers. He should be stopped.'

'How old are you?' I asked him.

'Twenty-two. What's that to do with it?'

'Twenty-two.' I said. 'Run along and teach your pupils French.'

He didn't like it but I didn't want to explain to him why his age was so important. Still, I couldn't find a way of speaking to Morrison without offending him.

'You'll just have to come straight out with it,' my wife said.

'No,' I said.

'What else can you do?'

'I don't know,' I said.

I was very conscious of the fact that I was fifteen years younger than Morrison.

One day I said to him, 'How do you see your pupils?'

'What do you mean?' he asked.

'How do you see them?' I repeated.

'See them?' he said. And then, 'They are too young to fight, yet, but I see them as ready for it. Soon they will be taken.'

'Taken?'

'Yes,' he said. 'Just as we were taken.'

After a silence he said, 'One or two of them would make good officers. It's the gas that's the worst.'

'Have you told them about the gas?' I said, seizing on a tenuous connection between the First World War and Chemistry.

'No,' he said, 'it was horrifying.'

'Well,' I said, 'explain to them about the gas. Why don't you do that?'

'We never used it,' he said. 'The jerries tried to use it but the wind was against them.' However he promised that he would explain about the gas. I was happy that I had found a method of getting him to teach something of his subject and tried to think of other connections. But I couldn't think of any more.

One day he came to see me and said, 'A parent called on me today.'

'Called on you?' I said angrily. 'He should have come through me.'

'I know,' he said. 'He came directly to me. He complained that I was an inefficient teacher. Do you think I'm an inefficient teacher?'

'No,' I said.

'I have to warn them, you see,' he said earnestly. 'But I suppose I had better teach them Chemistry after all.'

From that time onwards, he became more and more melancholy and lost-looking. He drifted through the corridors with his white ghostly moustache, as if he was looking for a battle to take part in. Then he stopped coming to the staff-room and stayed in his classroom all the time. There were another three months to go to his retirement and if he carried on this way I knew that he would fade away and die. Parents ceased to come and see me about him, but I was worried.

One day I called the best Chemistry student in the school – Harrison – to my room and I said, 'How is Mr Morrison these days?'

Harrison paused a moment.

'He's very absent minded, sir,' he said at last. We looked at each other meaningfully, he tall and handsome in his blue uniform with the gold braid at the cuffs of his jacket. I fancied for a terrible moment that I saw a ghostly white moustache flowering at his lips.

'I see,' I said, fiddling with a pen which was lying on top of the red blotting paper which in turn was stained with drops of ink, like flak.

'How are you managing, the members of the class, I mean?' I said.

'We'll be all right, sir,' said Harrison. Though nothing had been said between us he knew what I was talking about.

'I'll leave you to deal with it, then,' I said.

The following day Morrison came gleefully to see me.

'An extraordinary thing happened to me,' he said. 'Do you

know that boy Harrison? He is very brilliant of course and will certainly go to University. He asked me about the First World War. He was very interested. I think he will make a good officer.'

'Oh,' I said.

'He has a very fine mind. His questions were very searching.'

'I see,' I said, doodling furiously.

'I cannot disguise the fact that I was unhappy there for a while. I was thinking, "Here they are and I am not able to warn them of what is going to happen to them." You see, no one told us then there would be two World Wars. I was in Sixth year when the First World War broke out and I was studying Chemistry just like Harrison. They told us that we would be home for Christmas. Then after I came back from the war I did Chemistry in University. I forgot about the war, and then the Second one came along. By that time I was teaching here, as you know.'

'Yes,' I said.

'In the First World War everyone was so young. We were so ignorant. No one told us anything. We were very enthusiastic, you see. You recollect of course that there hadn't been a really big war since the Napoleonic War. Of course there had been the Boer War and Crimean War but these were side issues.'

'Of course,' I said.

'You were in the Second World War yourself,' he said, 'so you will know.'

But as I had been in the Air Force that didn't in his opinion count. And yet I too had seen scarves of flame like those of students streaming from planes as they exploded in the sky. I felt the responsibility of my job intensely. Though I was so much younger I felt as if I was the older of the two. I felt protective towards him as if it was I who was the officer and he the young starry-eyed recruit.

After Harrison had asked him his questions Morrison was quite happy again and could return to the First World War with a clear conscience. Then one day a parent came to see me. It was in fact Major Beith, a red-faced man with a fierce moustache who had been an officer in the Second World War.

'What the bloody hell is going on?' he asked me. 'My son isn't learning any Chemistry. Have you seen his report card? It's bloody awful.'

'He doesn't work,' I said firmly.

'I'm not saying that he's the best worker in the world. The bugger watches TV all the time but that's not the whole explanation. He's not being taught. He got fifteen per cent for his Chemistry.'

I was silent for a while and then I said, 'Education is a very strange thing.'

'What?' And he glared at me from below his bushy eyebrows.

I leaned towards him and said, 'What do you think education consists of?'

'Consists of? I send my son to this school to be taught. That's what education consists of. But the little bugger tells me that all he learns about is the Battle of the Marne.'

'Yes,' I said, 'I appreciate that. But on the other hand I sometimes think that . . .' I paused. 'He sees them, I don't know how he sees them. He sees them as the Flowers of Flanders. Can you believe that?'

His bulbous eyes raked me as if with machine-gun fire.

'I don't know what you're talking about.'

I sighed. 'Perhaps not. He sees them as potential officers and NCO's and privates. He is trying to warn them. He is trying to tell them what it was like. He loves them, you see.'

'Loves them?'

'That's right. He is their commanding officer. He is preparing them.' And then I said, daringly, 'What's Chemistry in comparison with that?'

He looked at me in amazement. 'Do you know,' he said, 'that I am on the education committee?'

'Yes,' I said, staring him full in the eye.

'And you're supposed to be in charge of discipline here.'

'I am,' I said. 'I have to think of everything. Teachers have rights too.'

'What do you mean teachers have rights?'

'Exactly what I said. If pupils have rights so have teachers. And one cannot legislate for love. He loves them more than you or I are capable of loving. He sees the horror awaiting them. To him Chemistry is irrelevant.'

For the first time I saw a gleam of understanding passing across the cloudless sky of his eyes. About to get up, he sat down again, smoothing his kilt.

'It's an unusual situation,' I said. 'And by the nature of things it will not last long. The fact is that we don't know the horrors in that man's mind. Every day he is in there he sees his class being charged with bayonets. He sees Germans in grey helmets. He smells the gas seeping into the room. He is protecting them. All he has is his stories to save them.'

'You think?' he said looking at me shrewdly.

'I do,' I said.

'I see,' he said, in his crisp military manner.

'He is not like us,' I said. 'He is being destroyed by his imagination.' As a matter of fact I knew that his son was lazy and difficult and that part of the reason for that was the affair the major was carrying on with a married woman from the same village.

He thought for a while and then he said, 'He has only two or three months to go, I suppose. We can last it out.'

'I knew you would understand,' I said.

He shook his head in a puzzled manner and then left the room.

The day before he was due to retire Morrison came to see me.

'They are as prepared as I can make them,' he said. 'There is nothing more I can do for them.'

'You've done very well,' I said.

'I have tried my best,' he said.

'Question and answer,' he said. 'I should have done it in that way, but they didn't know enough. One should start from the known and work out towards the unknown. But they didn't know enough so I had to start with the unknown.'

'There was no other way,' I said.

'Thank you,' he said courteously. And he leaned across the desk and shook me by the hand.

I said that I hoped he would enjoy his retirement but he didn't answer.

'Goodbye for the present,' I said. 'I'm afraid I shall have to be away tomorrow. A meeting, you understand.'

His eyes clouded over for a moment and then he said, 'Well, goodbye then.'

'Goodbye,' I said. I thought for one terrible moment that he would salute but he didn't.

As a matter of fact I didn't see him often after his retirement. It was time that Chemistry was taught properly. Later however I heard that he had lost his memory and couldn't tell his stories of the World War any more.

I felt this as an icy bouquet on my tongue. But the slate had to be cleaned, education had to begin again.

Acknowledgements

The stories appeared previously in the following publications. The publisher gratefully acknowledges permission of the copyright holders to reprint copyright material. Every effort has been made to trace the copyright holders of the works included in this volume. If any error or oversight has occurred, the publisher will correct at the earliest opportunity.

Brown, George Mackay, *A Time to Keep*, The Hogarth Press, 1969. By permission of Hachette UK.

Buchan, John, *The Complete Short Stories*, Vol. III, Thistle Publishing, 1997.

Doyle, Arthur Conan, *The Exploits of Brigadier Gerard*, George Newnes, 1896.

Duncan, Ronald, *The Perfect Mistress*, Rupert Hart-Davis, 1969. By permission of Eric Glass Ltd.

Elliott, W. A., *Esprit de Corps: A Scots Guards Officer on Active Service 1943–1945*, Michael Russell, 1996.

Ford, James Allan, *Modern Scottish Short Stories*, ed. Fred Urquhart and Giles Gordon, Faber, 1978.

Fraser, George Macdonald, *The Sheikh and the Dustbin*, Collins Harvill, 1988. By permission of Curtis Brown.

Garioch, Robert, *Two Men and a Blanket*, Southside, 1975.

Gibbon, Lewis Grassic, *Sunset Song*, Jarrolds, 1932 (original 'Harvest', renamed 'Shot at Dawn').

Gleig, G. R., *The Subaltern*, William Blackwood, 1829.

Grant, James, *Legends of the Black Watch*, Routledge, 1859.

Hay, Ian, *The Last Hundred Thousand*, William Blackwood, 1915.

Linklater, Eric, *Private Angelo*, Jonathan Cape, 1946 (original chapter 14, renamed 'The Rape of Lucrezia'). By permission of the Peters Fraser and Dunlop Group Ltd.

McCallum, Neil, *My Enemies Have Sweet Voices*, Cassell, 1951.

Macnicol, Eona, *The Hallowe'n Hero and Other Stories*, William Blackwood, 1969.

Mitchell, James Leslie, *The Thirteenth Disciple*, Jarrolds, 1931.

Munro, Neil, *The Pipes of War*, ed. Sir Bruce Seton, Maclehose, Jackson and Co, 1920.

Scott, Michael, *Tom Cringle's Log*, William Blackwood, 1833.

Scott, Walter, *Waverley*, Archibald Constable, 1814 (original title 'The Eve of Battle', renamed 'The Battle of Prestonpans').

Smith, Iain Crichton, *Mr Trill in Hades and Other Stories*, Victor Gollancz, 1984.

Smollett, Tobias, *The Adventures of Roderick Random*, Hayman, 1748 (original chapters XXXII and XXXIII, renamed 'The Siege of Cartagena').

Spark, Muriel, 'The First Year of My Life', *The Complete Short Stories*, published by Canongate Books, reproduced by permission of David Higham Associates.

Urquhart, Fred, *Selected Stories*, Methuen, 1946. By permission of Dr Colin Affleck.

Whyte, A. F., *Blackwood's Magazine*, October 1916.